Dedication

I dedicate this book to my niece, Marilyn Christian, without whose help this book would never have reached the public. It is her patience, her perseverance and her knowledge that brought my dream to fruition and this book to publication.

Disclaimer

This is a work of fiction. Names, characters, businesses, places, events and incidents are either the products of the author's imagination or used in a fictitious manner. Any resemblance to actual persons, living or dead, or actual events is purely coincidental.

ISBN: 978-1-300-33039-4

Cover illustration by Gloria Swoboda

THE SECRET IN HER HEART

A Novel by

Cassie Merko

Chapter 1

Shy and self-conscious about being at the center of so much attention, young Alvin squirmed to get away but his father held on tightly to his hand. Alvin's scorched face was crucial to Michael's "show and tell" project and Michael was not about to relinquish his captive audience. The parishioners of St. Benedict's Church always stayed for some local chit chat after the service and today, Michael could show everyone what a clever boy his son was. He spoke loudly as he informed Reverend Paul Padaman about his son's latest adventure.

"Imagine, at four-and-a-half, he figured out how to take a three-oh-three shell apart. He's always been a curious kid, Reverend Paul, but to use an awl to pry the lead out of the shell? What was he thinking? And then he strikes the gunpowder with the hammer! I tell you Reverend, this boy of mine is going to be an important scientist someday."

"That was indeed very curious, Michael. It was lucky for you his eyes were not hurt by the blast, just his hair and skin," Reverend Paul observed.

"Oh, he probably had his eyes closed... to protect them, you know," Michael explained proudly.

"Still, you have to admit it was a miracle he only ended up with just burns to his face." Reverend Paul shook his head in amazement. Michael's fixation on his son's curiosity, rather than on the hazards of following up on it, was incredible. Reverend Paul didn't mention that though.

"Oh, I understand, Reverend Paul, but my boy is destined for big things. This is the nineteen seventies. The big universities are begging for smart kids. He'll be a shoo-in!"

Kaydee walked off toward the car with Jaynee. Mother was right behind with baby Dayna in her arms. They were not a vital part of Father's audience. They never were. They always were somewhere on the distant and obscure periphery of Father's presence. No one ever really noticed or paid attention to them.

"So that was what had happened to Alvin," Kaydee thought in

astonishment. There had been no gun. It was not a shot that she had heard but a blast of gunpowder being hit with a hammer! What had possessed Alvin to do something so unbelievable? Alvin was smart as a whip, perhaps too smart for his four-and-a-half years. As Father had said, he was always a curious kid, but this seemed too far-fetched even for Alvin. Still, he had the singed hair and eyebrows and scorched face to prove it. Also, the evidence had been all there: the anvil, the hammer, and the empty shell. Kaydee had seen it herself. Maybe Father was right. Maybe Alvin was destined to be a scientist. Where else could such an inquisitive kid be heading?

Kaydee's mind retraced the events of the day before. It had all started normally enough.

"The weeds are bigger than the lilies over there. Get on your hands and knees and clean that out. Why do I have to remind you all the time? Can't you see that for yourself?" Father had snapped at her as he headed out to the shed. "And keep an eye on Alvin!"

Ever since her little brother was born, Alvin's welfare and safety had been Kaydee's responsibility. She was always expected to do double-duty and watch over curious Alvin no matter what else she was doing. She knew that and she accepted it; even liked it for that matter. Alvin had been an adorable baby. He was still adorable as far as Kaydee was concerned. But he was a handful to keep up with.

It was a beautiful and warm June day and the sun was doing its best to uphold the "Sunny Manitoba" reputation. As she busily extracted the weeds from their hiding places among the lilies, Kaydee kept a watchful eye on Alvin who was designing a rock city out of the pebbles he had collected. Then Ruby, their dappled grey mother cat, had arrived home from a mouse hunt and Kaydee's concentration was diverted. She never could resist watching the happy reunion of the furry family.

"Oh Ruby," Kaydee breathed excitedly as Ruby greeted her brood of five calico babies with licks and kisses and loud blissful purring. "See how your family missed you?"

Distracted, Kaydee turned her attention to Ruby as the mother cat positioned herself on the grass to allow her famished babies to sate their hunger. Alvin, being a typical little boy, had lost interest in his pebble city project. He took off in search of more engaging pursuits, leaving Kaydee still in her trance beside the feeding brood. Mesmerized by the purring of the squirming kittens eagerly feeding at their mother's belly, Kaydee's tranquility had been shattered by a very loud "CRACK" that sounded much like a gunshot to Kaydee. This was followed immediately by Alvin's piercing scream which cut through the air like lightning in a fierce storm.

For one fleeting moment, Kaydee had been paralyzed into immobility. Then her sanity kicked in and she tore off towards the source of that terrified scream. Panic suffocated the beating of Kaydee's twelve-year-old heart and a sickening sensation coiled like a snake in her gut, threatening to devour her from the inside.

As she rounded the corner of the shed, her lungs straining for air, she rammed into her father who was holding the frightened Alvin in his arms, soothing him and inspecting his wounds. With unmasked fury, he glared at Kaydee from behind Alvin's neck.

"Where the hell were you and why weren't you watching him?!" he roared.

Alvin was sobbing in Father's arms. Alarmed by his father's angry bellow, Alvin's sobbing ceased as he turned to look at Kaydee. With utter shock, Kaydee stared at Alvin's face, blood-red and smeared black with dirt and soot, his eyebrows scorched and the thick reddish-brown hair at his forehead singed to a brownish gray. Kaydee was too traumatized to process Father's words. Her eyes darted from Alvin's face and she stared past Father to take in the strange menagerie on the ground behind him. She was scanning the scene for a gun but she saw no gun.

"I asked you a question, you dimwit! Where the hell **were** you when this happened?!"

Too stunned to think or reason, Kaydee's mind vacillated between relief at seeing Alvin all right and horror at his appearance. Her throat constricted, as she stared, transfixed, in openmouthed incredulity.

Kaydee's continued silence infuriated Father. How dare she ignore him!

"I asked you a question! Didn't you hear me?! What the hell is the matter with you?! Answer me!" He reached for Kaydee's hair with his free left hand but Kaydee instinctively backed out of his reach. Alvin whimpered and Father pulled his hand back to enfold him.

"This kid could have killed himself! Where were you and what the hell were you doing that he was alone?! Answer me!" Father shouted furiously.

Kaydee cringed in the face of Father's obvious fury. Used to his venomous outbursts, she knew that trying to defend herself would be futile. But this time she had no defence! She had been negligent. There was no other way to explain it.

"I – auh – I was just – I just went to watch Ruby for a minute," Kaydee's voice squeaked with trepidation.

"The cat!!! You have GOT to be kidding! You went to watch the cat?!" Father ground out in disbelief, his eyes blazing, his face contorted.

"Yes, Father," Kaydee answered slowly, not daring to look away.

"You telling me you were watching a cat while this kid was off, heaven knows where, by himself?! He almost blew his head off, for God sake! You were supposed to be watching him! What the hell is the matter with you?!" Father was incredulous as well as infuriated. The ferocity on his face registered both.

Kaydee opened her mouth but no words came out. Father sputtered.

"I cannot believe such stupidity, even from you! You're supposed to be watching your brother, not that gawd-damned cat! Don't you understand?! What the **hell** is the matter with you?!"

"I'm sorry, Father," Kaydee offered but she knew it was far too little too late.

Father's voice had ground to a fierce growl by now. "When the hell are you going to grow up? So help me I'm going to..." His voice trailed off as Alvin wailed louder in the face of Father's ominous tone. Kaydee stood in stunned silence as Father turned his attention back to comfort Alvin.

"It's okay, Alvin, everything is going to be fine now. Daddy's got you. It's all right, son." Alvin quieted down as Father dusted off his clothes and held him closer.

Alvin was the only one allowed to use the word "Daddy." Kaydee was expected to use the word "Father." She had learned that quite clearly the time almost three years ago when she had trespassed on that forbidden territory. It was after she had heard Alvin say it. Father had been so pleased about it. She thought she might please him too.

"What did you say? What was that you just called me? Listen, you stupid snivelling brat. I am 'Father' to you. Do you understand? 'FATHER.' That is what you are to call me. Understand? I am not 'Daddy' or 'Dad' or any other sappy name you might feel like calling me. I am 'Father' to you! Understand?" Kaydee had been stunned into silence.

"DID YOU HEAR ME?" Father's voice thundered.

"Yes," Kaydee replied, chastised; her head bowed.

"Yes, what?!" His bellow was murderous.

"Yes, Father."

Father grabbed her by the hair and yanked her head back to face him. "Look at me when you talk to me."

"Yes, Father," Kaydee repeated, cowering under his angry glare.

With a revolted grunt, Father let her go with a shove that sent her flying across the room.

"See that you remember that," he spat as he stomped out the door. Kaydee had had no problem remembering that lesson.

Now Kaydee watched Father consoling Alvin, being so careful not to hurt him. For that, at least, she felt grateful.

"Get the hell outta here! I'll deal with you later. Right now, I can't stand the sight of you!" Father hissed through clenched teeth but Kaydee's feet refused to obey her.

"Get outta here! Now! Before I...!" he roared, cradling the upset Alvin again against his chest. "JUST... GET... THE... HELL... OUTTA... MY... SIGHT!" he hissed ominously.

Petrified, Kaydee turned and bolted out of his way, running for the house. She heard Mother in the laundry room. Trembling, she sat down by the kitchen table to wait for her.

Father's temper tantrums were not uncommon. They occurred often. They were unexpected, often over something small and insignificant: a spilled glass of milk; tripping over a toy on the floor; interrupting when he was speaking; or even just talking at the table! Almost anything could set him off. Father's tantrums were a common occurrence, but Kaydee still found them frightening.

This time, however, Kaydee felt she had earned Father's wrath. Alvin could have been seriously hurt. The sight of Alvin's singed lashes, eyebrows, hair, his whole face all attested to a near catastrophe. Father had every right to be furious with her and she had no valid defence, not even to herself.

Kaydee thought she had taken her eyes off Alvin for just a moment. But in the time that Kaydee had crouched, in fascination, beside Ruby and her litter, Alvin had wandered off and got into some kind of trouble with bullets, and gunpowder, and some kind of fire that left his face seared and his hair singed.

As Kaydee sat there in that kitchen, waiting for her mother, her mind was in a whirl. How did Alvin manage to get so hurt in such a short time? She was sure it could not have been long. Yet he had wandered away and she had failed to notice when. Perplexed, Kaydee tried to envision that interval in what she was certain could have been no more than just a few short minutes. She tried to put the puzzle together as she reviewed the scene in her mind. She had seen no gun! She remembered an anvil on some gravel. Nearby, she remembered seeing a hammer, a shell of a large two or three inch bullet with a long heavy needle thing beside it, a mangled piece of something gray next to it, but she had seen NO gun! There had been no gun anywhere in sight! Kaydee was certain of that. Nothing made any sense! So where had that shot come from and why did Alvin's face look like it just escaped a raging inferno?

Father had not followed her into the house. She was relieved. At least he didn't shove her into the "sinhole" this time. Not yet anyway. Kaydee wasn't sure if it was still coming or not but for the first time in her life, she felt she deserved to be sent there. This time she had earned it! If anything had happened to Alvin because of her carelessness, that black sinhole could never even begin to assuage her sense of guilt. She would willingly kneel there for days on end if that would help Alvin.

Yet how she dreaded that dark corner under that stairwell behind the big green chair! How often had she knelt there, cowering and trembling, while her father bellowed his poisonous hatred from behind!

"You get in that corner and get down on your knees, right now. And don't you come out until you change that damned attitude of yours. You'll learn respect if it kills you and I won't care if it does, so you had better learn it soon! I don't want to see your face or hear a peep out of you until you do. Do you hear me?"

A long, long time ago, Kaydee had learned that trying to apologize or explain was pointless. It only brought on another barrage of curses and admonitions, as did sitting back on her hunches.

"Straighten up there. I said KNEEL, not sit!" and Kaydee would straighten up, her back and knees screaming for mercy but she learned to take it in silence. Her mother never dared to interfere when Father was angry.

Too often Kaydee had knelt there cringing for what seemed like hours until her father had left the house and Kaydee dared to come out. He never told her to come out; he simply walked out and let her get up in his absence. Then she would get up gingerly, her wooden knees buckling under her. She would see her mother's ashen face, her eyes hollow and her countenance so fear-stricken, it made her own pain seem insignificant. And so Kaydee's life had been as far back as she could remember.

Kaydee knew Father's rage was murderous. She remembered vividly that terrible spring morning more than three years ago when Father's temper had cost them the life of their gentle German Shepherd dog. She could still see their beloved Auggie convulsing spasmodically under Father's beating. Auggie had become restless watching the young chicks in the little temporary coop that was always kept near the house for new fledglings. Agitated by their eager chirping, Auggie had taken to running around the small pen and barking excitedly. Father had just finished his last sip of coffee when he heard the commotion outside. With an irritated

"Damn dog!" he shoved his chair back from the breakfast table and swiped at his mouth with the napkin before heading for the door. Mother sat stone-faced, staring after him with that helpless, hopeless look that was her trademark when Father was angry. Kaydee felt alarm bells peel through her body as she raced outside in time to see Father grab Auggie by the scruff of his neck. Holding the dog with his left hand, he picked up the broken handle of a shovel with his right and struck Auggie hard across the back. Auggie fell limply to the ground. "Shut up, shut up, you damn dog!" he yelled. "Can't a man have peace around this place?! I'll teach you to make a racket!" He kept on yelling and beating the dog long after Auggie had drawn his last breath. Kaydee had witnessed the whole thing before she ducked back into the house, aggrieved and terrified. She could still picture the scene clearly in her mind to this day.

Was that going to be her fate today? Outside of yanking her by the hair or by the arm and shoving her around, Father had never physically struck her before but he could be brutal when angry. His rampages were explosive and unpredictable. Kaydee had no idea what he would do this time. Resigned to accept whatever was waiting for her, Kaydee waited despairingly for what was to befall her next.

Mother finished folding the clothes and returned to the kitchen. She had the washer and dryer going and she hadn't heard the blast and was unaware of any trouble. Trembling with apprehension and nerves, Kaydee sat at the table, her head bowed, wondering if she should tell Mother what had happened.

"Where is Alvin?" her mother asked.

"He is with Father," Kaydee answered simply, without adding any further explanation.

"Go check on Jaynee and Dayna. Change Jaynee's tee-shirt. She got it soiled and I didn't get a chance to change it. I can still put it in the wash with my next load."

Kaydee went to the other room, saw five-month-old Dayna sleeping peacefully in her crib and then pulled a clean shirt from the bureau for Jaynee. She took it to the front yard where Jaynee was busily putting plastic blocks into a big red cardboard box.

At two-and-a-half years, Jaynee was a quiet, peaceful child. She entertained herself, never seemed to need much care or attention, and seldom got into any trouble. Her serenity was her most endearing quality. Father paid no attention to her. Jaynee was simply there. She seldom got in his way and was almost never whiney. Alvin was his SON, his pride and joy. Jaynee and Dayna were of no consequence, but Kaydee always seemed to irritate her father, simply just by being!

"Hi Jaynee," Kaydee sat cross-legged on the cool thick grass beside her little sister. "What are you doing?"

"Blue block in red box. It dirty," Jaynee held out a blue block for Kaydee to inspect.

Their conversation was interrupted by the clang of the metal gate of the mesh fence separating the lawn and house from the farmyard. Still carrying Alvin in his arms, Father strode purposefully towards the house. Ruby and her kittens were still enjoying some play time together. Spotting them, Father detoured off the walkway, heaved a kick with his big boot against the unsuspecting group, and sent them flying into the air yowling in shock and pain. Satisfied he had dealt them some justified punishment, Father returned to the walkway, not even looking at the two girls sitting on the grass on the other side. Kaydee breathed a sigh of relief for her own personal reprieve as he passed them and entered the house.

"Get this boy cleaned up, pronto," he yelled at his startled wife. "Look at him! He could have killed himself. That stupid moron of yours went to watch the cat instead of watching him. The cat! I tell you. Empty head and absolutely no sense of responsibility at all. She's dumber than a doornail! No matter what you tell her, it just doesn't sink in through that thick skull of hers! That retard belongs in a looney bin!"

The few minutes of silence that followed meant that Mother must have taken Alvin into the bathroom to clean him up. When Father's tirade resumed, Kaydee supposed that Mother must have re-entered the room to give him an audience again.

Kaydee heard the rumble of Father's derogatory rant as he told Mother what had happened to Alvin.

"Do you believe that stupid half-wit of yours? Instead of looking after her brother, she's watching the damned cat! I don't ask much of her. I know enough not to expect it from that dimwit but even that seems to be too much. She'll never amount to a pile of shit! Just a bloomin' idiot is what she is, that's all. I said all along she was a half-wit. Not an ounce of brain in that bonehead. Nothing ever sinks in through that thick skull!" His ranting and raving continued, repeating the same theme he was always so stuck on.

From force of habit, Kaydee tuned out the words. She did not wish to hear them. She knew that theme by heart. He would be reminding Mother about how much he was sacrificing to keep this family together. He had served as "luftenant" in the army in Korea so he was smart, but now he was stuck here among a bunch of dimwits. Kaydee had heard the story a thousand times.

"I should have run like hell when I saw you coming, is what I should have done. I could have made something of my life, been somebody. But NO, I had to get mixed up with a bunch of half-wits. That pregnancy trap got me good. I should have used my brains then and run for the hills. Now I'm stuck with the lot of you. You stuck me good!"

As Father ranted, Kaydee could picture her mother's sullen face, taking the rant without protest or rebuke. She always just let him rave on, until he had spent his anger, left the room and left her in peace. It was as if she had developed immunity to the abuse and his insults no longer registered.

Of course, Kaydee was the result of the pregnancy trap, thus accounting for Mother's lack of intelligence with what Michael adamantly claimed was "Helen's mistake." Alvin, on the other hand, was Father's trophy offspring, his "clever" son and Father never missed an opportunity to tell everyone about how brilliant his boy was. He bragged about him to anyone who would listen, emphasizing and exaggerating all his feats, big or small. Most of the time, that bragging was done right there on the church steps. They never socialized with people otherwise.

Kaydee didn't begrudge Alvin their father's love. She loved this smart little brother of hers and she would never willingly let any harm come to him. He was always so full of questions.

No matter where they were or what they were doing, Alvin always noticed something that peaked his interest.

"Look, Kaydee, see these yellow flowers," Alvin pointed to the marsh marigolds as they ambled along the path by the creek. "They are pointing up toward the sun, as if they are trying to reach for it and bring it right into their middle. Yet, look at this blue one," closely inspecting a sprig of blue bells nearby. "See, they all hang down, looking like they are trying to hide. How come, Kaydee? Are they just shy or are they afraid?"

"Why do we only see these yellow flowers in these wet spots? How come they only grow in the spring when it's wet? How come they don't grow in summer when it's nice and dry here? Are they always thirsty or do you think they like to have the frogs sing to them? Do the flowers only grow when the frogs sing to them? Why do the frogs always croak so loud in the spring? How come we didn't hear the frogs in winter? Kaydee? Where were they in winter?"

Kaydee had never thought of some of the things that Alvin noticed so readily. Next time Granny came to visit, she posed Alvin's questions to her and, as often was the case, Alvin's curiosity was a source of education for them both.

Kaydee never questioned the "why" or the "how come" of things as Alvin did. Those questions never even entered her mind. To Alvin, however, everything mattered.

"How come chickens have feathers and horses have short hair, and sheep have wool, and pigs have only bristles and yet none of them freeze in the winter cold? How come, Kaydee?"

"I don't know, Alvin. We'll have to ask Granny when she comes down next time," Kaydee would stall him.

"But why?" was an incessant question on his lips. Every situation was a source of unending questions to Alvin and Kaydee was at a loss to answer many of them herself. Granny was her encyclopaedia. Father was unapproachable, and Mother was too preoccupied to listen.

Alvin was a wonderful little boy, and Kaydee loved him dearly. But even though Father always claimed that Alvin was "smart like his daddy," Kaydee felt sure that Alvin had not received his smarts from Father because Father's actions did not indicate any great source of intelligence. Father lived by yelling and terrorizing everybody. He never actually demonstrated his smarts; he just declared their existence, usually loudly and often repeatedly.

And Alvin sure could not have acquired his smarts from Mother either. Mother seemed to think very little and had few answers. As far back as Kaydee could remember, Mother had been this way, talking very little, performing tasks that had to be done but never appearing as if she enjoyed them, or for that matter, if she hated them. She never smiled, never laughed or cried, she never got excited or angry. It was as if her spirit had vanished, leaving behind a listless shell; a large square-shouldered body, with hair and complexion a ghostly gray; and emotions a forgotten memory. Mother's actions demonstrated limited intelligence as well. When Father was angry and yelling, Mother countered with dead silence and just shrank into oblivion.

Kaydee sat there playing with a blade of grass and thinking. It was difficult to imagine Mother as Granny's daughter. Granny was lively, self-confident and full of purpose. Mother displayed none of those attributes. Kaydee did not want to be her mother's daughter but she wanted to be her father's daughter even less.

"Kaydee," Jaynee's voice brought Kaydee back out of her reverie, "may I have my blue block?"

Kaydee had been holding the block in her hand as she brooded over her dilemma. Snapping to attention, she handed the block to Jaynee. Fearing that Father would be coming out from the house soon, Kaydee started collecting Jaynee's toys into the box. She wanted to be out of sight when Father came outside.

"Let's go get us some fresh strawberries from the garden. I bet there are some really sweet and juicy ones."

"Yeah, tweet and juioosey," Jaynee repeated excitedly as she scrambled to her feet. Taking Jaynee's hand, Kaydee led her to the strawberry patch in the garden. A few minutes later, Kaydee saw her father depart with Alvin still on his shoulder. He didn't appear angry anymore. With a sigh of surprise and relief, Kaydee took Jaynee's shirt into the house for Mother to wash.

Michael left the house, carrying his son on his shoulder. His anger spent, he now saw the incident from a different perspective.

"What a clever boy Alvin is!" Michael marvelled. "Who would have thought of removing gunpowder from a bullet? Surely this was a sign of superior curiosity and enhanced intelligence! And at just four-and-a-half! This boy was going to go places in this world!" Michael was sure of it. He felt immensely pleased by this insight and his heart swelled with pride and self-validation. In the wake of this epiphany, Kaydee's role in the accident was banished to obscurity.

Father took Alvin to the shop where they puttered around till mother called them in for supper.

Supper was a silent affair for a change, much to Kaydee's relief. As soon as she cleared the dishes and cleaned the kitchen, she made herself scarce by hiding out in her room with Jaynee. Father had taken Alvin and they sat on the recliner. Kaydee did not see either of them till the next morning when they were getting ready for church but Father resolutely ignored Kaydee throughout the whole morning. Although thankful for her peace, Kaydee nonetheless felt uneasy. She felt as if she was on the verge of some sort of explosion but she did not know where or when it would occur.

The ride to church was ominously silent and Kaydee felt tense and nervous. She would have preferred Father's wrath, his usual ranting and raving, even the sinhole! But his silence was unnerving. She wondered what was going on in his head. She needed to know where and when the axe was going to fall. Father never forgot to punish her. Why had he not done so this time? What was he thinking? What was he planning? It was as if he had forgotten she was there. Father never forgot she was there. She was always in his line of vision. Being ignored should be a blessing, so why did it set her alarm bells ringing? Kaydee just could not relax!

Chapter 2

They had almost reached the metallic green Dodge sedan when a tall and stately woman dressed in a casual gray suit appeared on the other side of the car. A pink ruffled collar of a blouse set off Katreena Banaduk's smooth features as an eager broad smile spread across her face.

"Granny!" Kaydee squealed with delight as she ran around the back of the car and hurled herself into her grandmother's arms. "You're back! I didn't see you in church. Where were you sitting? I'm so happy to see you. Please say you'll stay for a while, Granny. I've missed you so much."

Granny wrapped her arms around Kaydee, kissed her lovingly on her forehead and squeezed her tight. Jaynee, following closely at her sister's heels, was doing a little jig, clamouring to get in on the hugs. She was echoing Kaydee's beseeching pleas with her own "Yes, Gwanny, pweez." With one arm still around Kaydee, Katreena swooped Jaynee up with the other.

"Well, I must confess I wasn't in church, sweetheart. I came straight from Lanavale. I got here too late for church because I had to stop for breakfast. I'm afraid my cupboard is very bare at this point as I only came back last night so I haven't had time to shop for groceries," Katreena replied, as she looked over the car at her daughter Helen, who stood waiting at the other side of the car near the passenger door. Then, because Jaynee and Kaydee were still awaiting her answer, Katreena focused back on them.

"I've missed you too! And yes, I'm coming to visit but just for a short while. Not for long. I have a million things to catch up with at home."

Jaynee looked awed. She peered at Granny's face. "A million? Is that a lot?"

Granny and Kaydee laughed aloud. Even mother's face registered something that under a good stretch might just barely qualify as a smile. Jaynee appeared even more perplexed.

"It's okay, Jaynee, I will come back again very soon, I promise."

Granny gave Jaynee an impulsive squeeze. "Let me look at you. My gracious, you're growing faster than my sweet peas. You're going to be as big as Granny in no time." Jaynee giggled with pleasure and entwined her little arms tightly around Granny's neck. Kaydee kept her left arm around Granny's waist as the trio walked around the car and approached Mother who, holding baby Dayna in her arms, was still waiting quietly by the passenger door.

Helen's face seemed to register something akin to regret as she watched her mother and her daughters exchanging enthusiastic embraces. Alone and isolated, she appeared trapped by her own barrier of desolation. She waited patiently as her mother approached.

"Hello, Helen, how are you?" Katreena gave her daughter a quick hug and a peck on the cheek then took baby Dayna from her acquiescent arms.

"Hello Mother," Helen said by way of greeting. "How was your European holiday? Welcome home. When did you get back?"

"Last night, around seven o'clock, as a matter of fact. I haven't even unpacked yet, but I was so tired I just crawled into bed and zonked right out. We didn't get much sleep that last night in Athens because we had to be up at five to get to the airport on time. Then we waited in Frankfurt airport for five hours and another plane, then a refueling stop in the Azores and another airport change in Montreal. The trip was exhausting. We got into Winnipeg late in the afternoon. The drive home finished me off. I was happy to get to my own bed and sleep. Today, I had to see my wonderful family, so the unpacking is just going to have to wait. It feels so great to be home and see you all again." She smiled and tweaked Jaynee's nose playfully.

Looking around, she asked, "Where is that little brother of yours?"

"He wanted to come with us," Kaydee said rather hesitantly, "but Father wanted him to stay. Alvin had himself a little adventure and Father was explaining it to Reverend Paul."

Katreena looked at her daughter but Helen merely shrugged her shoulders, "You'll hear about it soon enough," fashion.

Katreena groaned. She knew what that meant. Michael would be giving her the "Michael Alvin Boyer, the Magnificent" version and she was not at all in the mood to hear it via that railroad! She had always just barely tolerated the arrogant, overbearing fellow that Helen had insisted on marrying because she became pregnant with his child after they had been seeing each other for just a few months. That tolerance had changed to disdain when, after the marriage, she saw how he demeaned her daughter.

"Don't bother explaining anything to her, Katreena," Michael had cut her off when Katreena was telling them about a project she was involved in. "She hasn't the foggiest idea what you are talking about and she couldn't care less. See what I mean?" He tossed his head with a smirk as Helen walked out of the room, obviously hurt by his remark.

Katreena's anger had flared like a gasoline torch near a spark.

"She walked out because of what you said, not because she didn't understand," Katreena yelled over her shoulder as she ran after Helen. But Helen had already busied herself with folding some laundry into neat piles and would not listen to anything Katreena had to say.

"Leave it alone, Mom. Just let it be. No, go back to the kitchen, Mom. I'll finish this myself." Helen shooed her mother away.

Back in the kitchen, Michael mumbled. "You're just babying her. Why don't you face facts lady? She's just not very bright." Katreena went livid as she bristled with an angry retort but Michael walked out the door and left her standing there with her mouth open. Katreena was fuming. The gall of the man! She had tried time and time again to talk to her daughter about standing up to Michael, but Helen wouldn't listen, remaining loyal and obedient to him above and beyond all reason.

"He doesn't mean it, Mom. You just don't understand him."

"I'm not advocating leaving him or walking out on the marriage, Helen," Katreena tried to elucidate. "Just stand up for yourself when he starts to criticize you or berate you. Tell him to stop! MAKE him stop, for heaven's sake! Tell him that's enough of that and you won't take it. I'm sure if you stood up for yourself, he would stop being such an insensitive bully."

"He knows more about the world than I do. He's been around. He likes to feel superior."

"At your expense? Honey you're not stupid, but he's making it sound like you are. For heaven's sake, Helen. Why do you let him do that to you?"

"You don't understand, Mom. Daddy never got angry with you so you don't have any idea what it's like. Michael was brought up differently. His father was the ruler in his house and Michael's mother always obeyed him. That is how Michael sees his own house. He does not like to have his authority challenged. It makes him feel threatened and that makes him angry and that is when he yells."

"But that does not give him the right to be mean, Helen. Listen to me. Your father was a gentle man and I understand why you are frightened when Michael rants and raves but nobody has a right to be mean!"

"I think some of that comes from his army days," Helen explained. "You know they train you to be loud, and rough and authoritative. He was a Lieutenant in Korea you know. He's used to being obeyed, not questioned."

"He should have left the war in Korea, not brought it here to Zelena," Katreena retorted angrily. Then quietly to herself, she added, "better still, HE should have stayed in Korea." She did not dare say that to Helen. Helen would not talk back to Michael, but she might have no problem standing up to her mother. What irony!

"What he did during the war in Korea does not have to carry on for the rest of his life! He shouldn't be continuing his war on you!"

"It's okay, Mom. He cannot help it and I understand that. If I don't cross him, he's okay. Just don't make trouble, Mom. Please try to understand. For my sake, Mom. Please?"

And so Katreena had been coerced into dropping the subject yet again.

Kaydee was fourteen months old when Helen's second pregnancy ended in miscarriage. Leaving the baby with a neighbour, Helen had gone to help Michael hauling bales. She picked the bales from the field onto the rack while Michael drove the tractor. When she went into premature labour and lost the baby, Michael attributed the miscarriage to Helen's "lack of stamina." Katreena tried to talk sense to them but Michael was adamant that this was just an unfortunate incident.

"It just happened for heaven's sake. What's the big deal? Don't make a major issue out of it. So she dropped a kid. So there'll be another one. What's the problem? She's not tough enough. Maybe she'll finish the job next time."

Katreena was furious. She could not believe anyone could be so callous.

"She shouldn't be pitching bales when she's pregnant for heaven's sake. That's no job for a pregnant woman!"

"Why don't you just mind your own damned business for a change, lady? She'd just toughen up and be okay if you didn't mollycoddle her so much. Just butt out of our lives!"

Helen was almost inconsolable about the miscarriage but again she begged her mother not to "make trouble."

"It probably had nothing to do with the pitching bales in the first place," Helen rationalized. "Sometimes God cleans up things that are not quite perfect. Maybe it was meant to be this way. Let it go, Mom. I'll be all right."

Katreena let the matter drop because she did not want to add to her daughter's distress.

Busy with her teaching career, she spent too little time on the farm to notice the damage until it was already done. By then, Helen's spirit had been broken and her will to fight back no longer existed. Michael's personal arrogant nature, his autocratic upbringing, his innate lack of compassion and whatever poison Korea had tainted him with, had all combined to do a totally corrosive number on Helen's self-esteem.

"This shirt has a button missing. How come you don't check these things before you put them in the closet? Doesn't that brain of yours ever click in? How do you expect me to go out to town with my shirt gaping like this? Grow up for heaven's sake, already." With an angry snort, he ripped the shirt off his back and threw it at Helen.

Katreena offered to sew on the button, but Michael roared, "Why don't you mind your own business and let her do her own damned work? When is she going to learn to do anything if you're constantly running interference for her? Let her develop a brain of her own, damn it. Is that too much to ask? She's a wife and mother now. Face it. She's not your little girl anymore."

Katreena temper was like a volcanic eruption. She could not hold it back. It was all she could do not to fly at him and scratch his eyes out.

"Now, that's enough, Michael. We're not..." Katreena was yelling too, and Helen's eyes went wild with fear. In the other room, Kaydee, then just seventeen months old, alarmed by the loud voices, set up a howl.

"And shut that brat up, before I lose my temper." Michael swept past Katreena. "There better be a decent shirt in that closet or you're gonna regret eating your breakfast," Michael snapped and headed for the bedroom for another shirt. The baby's crib was in his path and Helen sprang to get it out of his way. Katreena, too shocked for words, stood staring aghast as Michael marched past the crib and barked at Kaydee, "Shut the hell up, ya stupid brat!"

He grabbed another shirt from the hanger. Throwing it over his back, he was still shoving his left arm into the sleeve as his right hand turned the door handle. Slamming the door hard, he stomped out of the house.

Katreena looked at Helen's petrified face and almost lost it herself.

"That does it! You and Kaydee are coming home with me! I am not leaving you here with that madman another minute! He's a raving lunatic! We'll pack some things now and come back for the rest later."

"No, Mom, no," Helen was pleading, her tears like rapids on her cheeks. "No Mother, he is angry now, but he's not like that all the time. You must never talk back to him. I told you it makes him angry. We'll be all right Mother. Please don't make trouble. He's just angry because you talked back to him. Please, Mother, you must understand. This was just a simple fight. I can't walk out on my marriage because he yelled. I promised for better or worse. We'll get past it. Please, for the sake of God, Mom, let it go! Please. We'll be okay. Just let it be."

Finally, to appease Helen's pleading, Katreena had relented and had left Helen to deal with the situation herself. However she deeply regretted her acquiescence later, after having witnessed more of Michael's ranting and violent tirades, especially when she realized just how completely he had crushed that tender, loving soul that had been her daughter. She hated Michael for desolating Helen's once vibrant personality and even more so for making her, Helen's own mother, his inadvertent accomplice. It was more than she could bear to listen to him at all now, though Michael never even seemed to notice. His insensitivity and arrogance galled Katreena beyond limits but if she tried to voice her negative opinions, Michael just took it out on Helen and made her life more miserable. In the end, to alleviate Helen's suffering, Katreena just bit her tongue and kept her feelings to herself because Helen always reassured her that things were not as bad as they seemed.

Michael was ruthless in his denigration of Helen, however. Convinced as he was of his own intellectual superiority, Michael voiced it so often and so strongly that Helen began to believe him. Of course, she never dared contradict him. So the more Michael ordered, the more Helen obeyed, the more he yelled, the more she cowered, and the more he criticized, the more she shrank into the shadows. Now, Helen was unrecognizable to the girl she used to be and the man who made her so just strutted around oblivious and indifferent.

Helen's third pregnancy ended in a miscarriage again when she shovelled grain to level it out in the bin. After that second miscarriage, Helen seemed to lose her will to go on and just went into perpetual mourning. Seeing her diffidence and despondency now, she was still in a state of mourning, though she had carried three healthy children to term since then.

Driving home after leaving Helen in the hospital after that second miscarriage, Katreena again broached the subject of sparing Helen the hard work during pregnancy.

"You just can't make her work like that when she's pregnant," Katreena had scolded. In the car, Michael was a trapped audience and Katreena had to make him listen. He was not going to walk out on her in the middle of a sentence this time. "No woman should be shovelling grain or pitching bales when she's pregnant."

"There's nothing wrong with honest work for anyone with a normal healthy body," Michael countered. "You want to farm, you gotta work!"

"Then work it yourself. You are the farmer. Where the hell is your healthy body? What kind of man are you anyway?"

Michael was incensed. "Why don't you just mind your own business and stop butting into mine!?" It wasn't enough that he had to put up with Helen and Kaydee's insipidness but his mother-in-law was questioning his authority! He would not put up with that!

"Helen and Kaydee are my business, damn it!" Katreena yelled back. "Helen lost two babies on account of you. She should be taking it easy when she's pregnant. She's not a horse for heaven's sake."

"Wives are supposed to help their husbands. Even the Bible says that. Farming is a partnership. Women help their men in the field. She'd be just fine if you'd quit pampering her." Michael's jaw clenched on his words.

But Katreena was mad too. "Of course women help their men. But the women drive the tractor! They don't pitch the bales! Do you see Joe Drapanik sending Ellen to pitch the hay or shovel grain? Or Fred Archer sending Josie? And those women are not pregnant! Where is your pride, man?"

"That daughter of yours wouldn't know how to operate the loader or the tractor. I'd have to show her which rows to hit first. I HAVE to man the tractor."

"That's bullshit and you know it, Michael Boyer. There is nothing wrong with Helen's mind. You're just too damned lazy to pitch the bales yourself. That's your problem. You want to ask Joe, or Tom, or Fred, what they think of Helen pitching bales or shovelling grain while you sit like a king driving the tractor? I wonder what they'll say when they find out that Helen lost her babies that way. And they will find out, Michael Boyer. Make no mistake about that!" Katreena was so angry she was shaking. She just could not, would not, back down on this issue.

"Screw you," Michael yelled but his face flushed almost purple.

Katreena knew she had hit a nerve, and she knew she was going to win. She could sense her victory in the tone of Michael's voice and the flush on his face. Michael was arrogant and conceited. He liked to rate himself with the Ladducks, the Drapaniks, and the Archers even though he and Helen never associated with any of the neighbours on any personal level since the marriage. Helen's untimely pregnancy was embarrassing for both Michael and Helen, but for vastly different reasons. Brought up with a religious background, Helen had confessed her sin of premarital sex not just to the priest, but to Katreena. She was sure she had incurred God's wrath by allowing it to happen and now He was punishing her for her disobedience against her parents' teachings and for her premarital sex. No amount of reassurance on Katreena's part could erase her guilt but she swore her repentance and vowed to take her penance for her sin without complaint.

"I can't change the past but I can make up for it," she had declared. "I will be a good wife and mother."

And she did try. But she failed to take into account Michael's character. The pregnancy was a declaration of his misdemeanour too. Michael was embarrassed about it but having the neighbours tease him about it at the wedding irritated him more than he let on. The teasing was good-natured but his wounded pride could not accept the jibes and he lashed out at Helen, blaming her for the neighbours' lack of respect for him. Helen remained loyal to him and tried to appease him but it simply annoyed him more. He viewed her pleas as a sign of weakness and intellectual inferiority. Eventually his constant denigration and his volatile temper weakened her self-confidence and undermined her vitality. The two miscarriages in succession just destroyed what little stamina she had left.

Katreena knew that Michael was still vying for the respect of those affluent, well-established farmers in the area. He had feigned indifference to the lack of a relationship with any neighbours but Katreena knew he was still trying to bolster his ego by impressing them. Today, Katreena thought, Michael's vanity and conceit were finally going to work to her advantage. She would use Michael's own pride to win this one. Her daughter's health might be depending on it.

"Screw you, too," Katreena retorted in disgust, "but just you wait. The neighbours will hear about this. I dare you to check it out for yourself."

Whether it was to appease his mother-in-law or to protect his image with his neighbours, Katreena didn't know, but Michael had grudgingly spared Helen the heavy labour during her next pregnancy and it paid off in a successful birth. Of course, when Alvin was born, Michael's validation was complete and his inflated ego knew no bounds. He strutted around like a peacock fanning his feathers and crowing about his wonderful son at every opportunity. The embarrassment of Helen's untimely first pregnancy and that unwanted baby girl faded into the background as Michael felt his manhood vindicated by the birth of a son.

Katreena reeled herself back to the present. She gritted her teeth as she visualized Michael bragging all through dinner. It was going to be a gruelling afternoon if she had to listen to Michael for a whole hour. Kaydee was prodding her. "Tell us about your holiday, Granny." She loved to hear Granny relate her experiences of the trips she took, the places she saw, and the wonderful things she did. To Kaydee, it was the magic fairytale of real life.

"Oh, honey, it was a wonderful holiday. Spring is such a lovely time of the year in Europe. Everything is so lush and the blossoms are so fragrant and colourful. There are huge trees that are just full of great big flowers. They call them horse chestnuts. Isn't that a funny name for a flower?"

Kaydee giggled. "Horse chestnuts? Really and truly, Granny?"

"Really and truly, honey. They are beautiful. There are gorgeous azaleas that grow three feet tall and bloom in the ditches, like weeds. And roses, as big as your head. And fuchsias grow like miniature trees, also in the ditches. All of Europe is in bloom at this time. I really loved it. Someday, maybe you'll be able to come with me on one of my trips and see Europe for yourself."

"Oh, Granny, can I, really?" Kaydee burst out breathlessly, her eyes like saucers. "Can I truly come with you on one of your trips? Oh Granny, I would SO love to go someday."

"Me too, me too," Jaynee piped up. She always wanted to do the exciting things that her big sister did. "Me too, me too," was her constant refrain. She was an easygoing child but she openly adored her big sister and was always trying to emulate her. They laughed at Jaynee's enthusiasm. Jaynee was not always sure what she wanted, but if Kaydee wanted it, it had to be good, and if it was good, Jaynee knew she wanted it too.

Both Kaydee and Granny thought Jaynee was so cute and comical. Often, they would be talking about something while Jaynee played nearby. It would seem like she wasn't paying any attention, but if something was said about Kaydee doing something or going somewhere, Jaynee's head would jerk up with that enthusiastic "Me too! Me too!" It always cut all other conversation short.

"Well hello, Katreena. And how is the world traveller?" Michael came bounding up towards them, Alvin trotting by his side, being towed along by his father's powerful grip on his little hand. Evidently, Michael had lost his audience on the church steps, because he was not one to walk away while people were still willing to stand and listen to him.

"Hello, Michael," Katreena offered her hand perfunctorily to this man whom she despised so much, but for the sake of her daughter and her grandchildren, she could not show it. "I'm fine, thank you. Still pretty tired, mind you, but nothing a couple nights' sleep and a couple of days of relaxation won't cure."

Alvin was tugging at his father's hand, trying to get to Katreena, but, ignoring him, Michael held tight. Defeated, Alvin looked up at Katreena and offered a subdued, "Hi, Granny."

Katreena smiled at him brightly, noting his seared face and scorched hair but aware that Michael was holding him firmly at bay. "Hi Alvin," then with a wink she added "See you later." Alvin's eyes brightened immediately but he stood obediently at his father's side.

"Okay, gang, let's pile into the old heap and head for home," Michael announced, ignoring Katreena as he unlocked the car doors and lifted Alvin into the front seat, setting him in the middle. "Let's head for that chicken dinner Mother has waiting for us back at the farm."

Helen always made certain that there was dinner ready to go on the table within half an hour of their arrival from church on Sundays. Michael put great store in taking his family to church each Sunday. It was part of that high profile he, and his father before him, had insisted on maintaining. An autocratic man, old Daniel Boyer had ruled his family with an iron hand. Many of his edicts were drilled so deeply into Michael's childhood psyche, that the passing of time, and then of his parents, did nothing to eradicate, or even dim, them from his mind. Michael didn't like to have to wait for a meal so Helen had learned long ago that the best way to keep the peace was to prepare ahead. She had become very proficient at it.

Emboldened by Granny's presence at her side, Kaydee seized the opportunity and asked quickly, "May I please ride with Granny, Father?"

"Me too, me too," Jaynee piped up immediately.

Father stopped for a moment, looked first at the two girls, then at Katreena whose eyes were boring into his, fairly daring him to refuse. He hesitated, then, shrugging his shoulders, "Okay."

He got in the car, turned the key, and started the motor. He obviously was in a good mood today. Katreena groaned inwardly as she realized that he was vying for a receptive audience for his narrative. She'd be listening to his baloney all through dinner!

Helen took Dayna from Katreena's arms and got into the passenger side next to Alvin. As the Dodge pulled away from the curb, Granny picked up Jaynee and walked toward her own white Pontiac Catalina with Kaydee at her side.

The bright red seats of Katreena's car were plush covered and soft. Kaydee got into the passenger side while Jaynee waited patiently for her turn. Teasingly, Katreena opened the back door and Jaynee's face fell. Granny laughed, and gave Jaynee a tight squeeze.

"Don't you worry sweetheart. Granny wouldn't make you sit in the back seat by yourself." She put Jaynee into Kaydee's lap, and strapped them in. Seatbelts were not mandatory but Granny always used them. She let Jaynee sit on Kaydee's lap for the six-and-a-half mile trip to KD Acres because she just couldn't bring herself to separate those two.

Katreena got behind the wheel and tweaked Jaynee's nose. "Comfortable now?" Jaynee giggled impishly and snuggled her face under Kaydee's arm.

Kaydee smiled at Granny gratefully. "Thank you, Granny," she mouthed, as she wrapped Jaynee even tighter in her arms. "Thank you so much."

It warmed Katreena's heart to see that closeness of the two sisters. In fact, in all the times Katreena had visited KD Acres, she had never witnessed the usual bickering or whining among the kids. It was almost abnormal, because typically, almost all kids whine and bicker. But then this family was not normal. With a father a live volcano about to blow at any given moment, and a mother cringing in fear all the time, perhaps the children had to turn to each other for support. Katreena's eyes misted. These girls expected so little and were so grateful for even the tiniest of favours. At least, they were able to glean comfort from each other.

Chapter 3

Katreena was both anticipating the visit and dreading it at the same time. She knew that Michael would monopolize all conversation. Helen and Kaydee would sit there with downcast eyes not daring to interrupt. No matter what question Katreena would ask, she would get her answers via the longwinded and biased Michael Boyer approach. She would have to listen his bragging; his inane attempts at humour; and his superficial pretences at being the genial host. But the thing that Katreena dreaded most was hearing Michael order Kaydee around. Kaydee was his Cinderella girl, and Michael played the wicked stepmother to the umpteenth degree. It took all of Katreena's resources to maintain silence during those times.

"Kaydee, get those dishes on the table. What are you waiting for?"

"Wipe that drool off that kid's face. Do I have to tell you everything? What the hell do you think that napkin is for?"

"You got goop on your clothes. When are you going to learn to eat properly? You stopped being a baby years ago. Stop acting like one!"

"Get up and start clearing the table, stupid. How many times do you have to be told to do that? Can't you see everyone is finished eating?"

It was bark, bark, bark, all the time. Never a pleasant word at the table, just criticism and harsh orders. No wonder Kaydee was insecure!

Katreena was not sure of when she had become aware of Michael's austere treatment of Kaydee, but it seemed that since Alvin was born, Kaydee always seemed to be in the line of fire for one reason or another. At first it had been subtle, but eventually Michael had grown bolder and Katreena had noted almost a brutality in Michael's demeanour towards the girl. When she had questioned Helen about it, she had only received vague answers and veiled excuses for Michael's merciless behaviour.

"Michael is just being Michael." Helen explained. "He doesn't mean anything by it. Kaydee knows that. He wouldn't hurt her. She's used to his yelling. Please let it go, Mom."

Katreena had wanted to believe her. She had NEEDED to believe her. Against her better judgment, she had suppressed her misgivings and just resolved to give Kaydee more concentrated attention to compensate for Michael's callousness.

As they drove onto the highway, Katreena asked, "So tell me Kaydee, what was this adventure that Alvin had?" Perhaps if she could get the full story from Kaydee, she wouldn't have to listen to Michael's version and could intercept him before he got too far into it. That could save her at least some of the aggravation of listening to him.

"I really didn't see what happened myself, and I should have been watching him. I'm sorry, Granny. Ruby had come home to feed her babies and I stopped to watch. Then Alvin went off and suddenly, I heard a gunshot. I heard Alvin crying so I ran to him. But it wasn't a gunshot, Granny. Alvin took out the inside of a big bullet and then he hit the gunpowder on the anvil with a hammer, and it sounded like a shot. I heard Father telling Reverend Paul about it so that is how I found out."

"I see," Katreena tried to visualize the scene, recalling Alvin's scorched face. "What happened next?"

"Well, I was so scared because I thought somebody got shot, and I was afraid for Alvin. Father was very angry with me because Alvin's hair and eyebrows got burned and his face got very red because of the fire. Alvin got his face burned. I'm really very sorry, Granny. I didn't mean for Alvin to get hurt." Kaydee looked so distressed, so burdened by her guilt.

"I promise to be more careful next time, Granny."

"I know you will sweetheart. I know you didn't do it on purpose. We all know Alvin is a curious little boy and he needs watching very closely. Don't worry about it. Alvin is fine. He has to learn not to do such dangerous things. Did your father punish you?"

"He did a lot of yelling, at me and at Mother, and he was really angry. I thought he would send me to the sinhole for sure, or something worse, but he didn't. Maybe he forgot and he will still punish me," Kaydee finished worriedly. Katreena grimaced at the mention of the sinhole. Kaydee had told her about it but Katreena had never witnessed that punishment. Michael made sure of that. He knew that Katreena would not stand for it.

"I don't think he will," Katreena tried to sound confident. "He's probably thinking of other things now. By the way, how did you do at school?" Katreena deliberately changed the subject to prevent any further torment for Kaydee. She had enough information on the subject. Now she needed to distract Kaydee, so she could stop feeling that overwhelming guilt.

Poor Kaydee. Michael had her carrying the weight of full responsibility on her young shoulders. She was just a child, but he was expecting her to think, and act, like an adult. It was so unfair. Deliberately setting unrealistic goals for Kaydee, he labelled her as retarded when she failed to measure up to those standards. But Katreena felt that Kaydee's dysfunction, both at home and at school, was the result of so much fear of Michael. He yelled at her, criticizing her constantly! No wonder the girl was distracted and apprehensive all the time.

Kaydee's enthusiastic response superimposed itself on Katreena's thoughts and cheered her heart. "Oh Granny, I love it at school now. Mr. Norchak is very nice. He is always so kind to me and to the other kids. We have fun at school. On the last day of school, we went on a field trip to the Broban River and we saw so many things. Mrs. Norchak came with us. They were so much fun. Mrs. Norchak walked right into the river and Mr. Norchak ran to get her out. They both fell down and got their clothes wet but she said she had to show us something, so she ran back into the water. She brought us some frog eggs. Mr. Norchak made a face and said, "Oh, Yuk," because they were so slimy. Everybody laughed so hard at them."

Kaydee had started school as a normal child, but quickly fell behind the other children until, in the middle of her third year, Mr. Koolidge had suggested that Kaydee would be better off in Special Education classes because she required more focused attention.

"Didn't I tell you all along that kid was retarded? Didn't I?" Michael had exploded when they got the letter announcing the change. Katreena had been visiting at KD Acres when Kaydee brought Mr. Koolidge's letter home that day. Katreena had witnessed the whole scene.

"She doesn't even belong in that school at all. She should be in a looney bin. I should just send her there and let her rot there for the rest of her life, so I wouldn't have to be reminded of her stupidity every day. She's never going to amount to a pile of shit anyway."

Katreena had hoped for a reproach from Helen at that point, but the silence that followed made Katreena lose all control and she thundered at Michael.

"You will do no such thing! Kaydee is part of this family and if anyone is going to leave here, it is going to be you, Michael Boyer. I will see to that myself, even if I have to get all the neighbours, the police, and the law involved. Make no mistake about it. I will fight you to the bitter end on this. Kaydee will go to this Special Ed class and that is that! There are other kids in that class. Their parents live right here in the community. If that is where they wish to put Kaydee, then that is where Kaydee goes, and I will hear no more about it or the whole community is going to hear about your damned attitude. Do you really want that, Michael?"

Katreena knew first-hand about Michael's weakness regarding community status, and she counted on it. Even though the Special Ed class was the ultimate source of bitter embarrassment for Michael, she knew that exposition of his attitude towards the situation would be a risk he would not dare ignore.

"Okay, okay, okay. So she goes to those retard classes. She belongs there anyway," Michael recanted his words as he stomped out of the house. So Kaydee was moved to the Special Ed class but Michael began calling her a "retard" incessantly after that. He picked on Kaydee relentlessly in private, and refused to acknowledge her in public, because he was ashamed to admit that he had a "retard" in the family.

Katreena was drawn back to the present as Kaydee happily recounted the events of that last day at the river. The girl had totally forgotten about her guilt for Alvin's accident.

"Did you ever see frog eggs, Granny? They look like the tapioca pudding that Mother makes for dessert, only more slimy. Mr. Norchak said the eggs would hatch into tadpoles and then he went into the water and caught some tadpoles for us. He said the tadpoles would become frogs one day. They would just grow so fat, that the tails would disappear and legs would grow out the sides."

Kaydee was so animated, she was tripping over her words.

"Did you know that some insects can actually walk on water? I knew they don't weigh much, but I never knew that anything can walk on water. Mr. and Mrs. Norchak showed us all kinds of things and then we had a picnic. They showed us how to find sticks to build a fire, and then Mr. Norchak made a fire while Mrs. Norchak showed us how to spear the wieners on a stick so they don't fall into the fire. Mr. Norchak took a tree branch and swished it at Mrs. Norchak to keep the mosquitoes away, and Mrs. Norchak said he was a bigger mosquito and she chased him away." Kaydee giggled at the memory. "They were so funny."

Kaydee prattled on and on, excited and lively, and Katreena's heart swelled with pride and relief. She was glad that Kaydee's Special Ed teacher was a man. Kaydee needed a normal male figure in her life. She needed to see that men, and marriages, were different from what she saw at home. The Norchaks were obviously a pleasant young couple who seemed to be genuinely interested in the progress of those kids. It appeared to Katreena that they offered Kaydee a positive and healthy perspective on life.

Katreena kept watching the girls out of the corner of her eye. They both seemed happy in spite of their chaotic home life. Jaynee didn't even try to talk. She just sat there, looking blissful. She had her grandmother and her sister close by! She was engrossed in Kaydee's spellbinding account of the wonderful day she had had. Both girls were enjoying this temporary reprieve from the realities of their otherwise love-starved life.

Katreena felt a sudden rage sweep over her as she thought of Helen before she married Michael. How completely she had changed. She used to be such a happy girl, quiet and a bit of a loner perhaps, with a passion for books. Katreena could still visualize her bouncing through the door, a radiant smile on her face as she called out a cheery, "Hi, Mom."

Then Michael came into town, good-looking, and sounding worldly and self-confident. Poor Helen was beside herself when he asked her out. She was nineteen at the time, and, although she had dated before, she had been inept at dealing with the likes of Michael Boyer. Michael was seven years older than Helen, and both Katreena and Daniel had opposed the relationship, but Helen was so enthralled with the man, she challenged her parents and saw Michael anyway. At first it was in secret, then openly, in defiance of their wishes. Eventually, to allay Helen's pleading and to prevent further disobedience, they had acquiesced and relaxed their objections. Katreena was aware of Michael's propensity to brag, but she attributed it to his eagerness to impress his girlfriend's parents. For his part, Michael had seemed sincere, ignoring other girls even though a number of them openly flirted with him and tried to lure him away from Helen. His resistance to their advances had been a point in his favour.

Looking back now, Michael had been smooth, — and calculating perhaps? The Banaduks were financially comfortable. Marrying their only child would assure Michael a share of that comfort. Perhaps if Daniel had lived, things may have been different, but that fall, Daniel was driving to town and a wheel came loose off an oncoming tractor trailer, crossed the meridian and smashed into Daniel's windshield, killing him instantly.

During the weeks that followed, Katreena could scarcely function herself, let alone watch what was happening to her daughter. When Helen and Michael approached her about marriage in January of 1958, Katreena had resisted, saying Helen was too young, that they should wait.

It was then that Helen announced, "Mom, there is something I have to tell you. I am pregnant. I'm so sorry Mom."

Katreena was stunned speechless.

"I'm so sorry, Mom." Helen repeated, her voice hoarse with guilt and remorse.

Michael stood by, saying nothing, waiting for Katreena's answer.

Katreena was too distraught to think straight. After more apologies from Helen and many promises that all would be fine, Katreena finally consented because she felt she had no other choice. Michael had remained unnaturally silent throughout the whole session.

Looking back now, Katreena realized she should have tried to stop the marriage anyway, even if it had meant having Helen, an unwed mother, raising Kaydee on her own.

By the time Katreena realized just how rough Michael was with her gentle and quiet daughter, Helen had lost two babies and was pregnant with her fourth child. It was true that losing two babies in a row was devastating, but after Alvin was born, Katreena realized that Helen's depression went far beyond simple grief over her miscarriages. She had abandoned all pretext of a love in bioom and descended into a vortex of pervading despair that rendered her virtually impassive to everything, particularly when Michael threw one of his temper tantrums.

Michael kept the children coming now that he had learned how to bring them to term, and Katreena could see no way to rescue her daughter since Helen seemed so emotionally bound to Michael. The permeating influence of love deprivation hung like a cloud over the family and Michael's condemnations suffocated all chances for a normal home life. Katreena was convinced that Kaydee could do well at school if she had a stable home life.

Katreena sighed. It was all water under the bridge now. There were now four children involved but without Helen's help, Katreena could do little except try to provide some of that love herself, especially to Kaydee. So far as she knew, Michael's rages had never resulted in physical beatings. Helen said little and never spoke ill of him, and Kaydee just seemed too obedient or too scared to complain.

Now, watching their carefree expressions, Katreena marvelled at how easily the girls' moods could be transformed from bleak to one of peace, serenity and something almost resembling rapture. It was so unfair. These children needed to feel loved and cared for, but in her present melancholy state of mind, Helen was too troubled to expose the ravaged chasm that sorrow and guilt and anguish had carved across her soul. Michael, well, Michael cared about no one other than himself and perhaps about Alvin to some degree. But Michael's love for Alvin was a selfish one. Alvin was an accomplishment that Michael could show off. He had produced a son! In Michael's macho mind, Alvin was the "supreme fete-de-compli," the certification of his manhood. As far as Katreena could see, Michael was incapable of true love for anyone.

Michael certainly did not demonstrate any feelings of love for Helen. Katreena was certain that Helen's prospects to the family fortune had been a contributing factor to Michael's interest in Helen. Especially since his parents had both passed on and left him nothing more than bad memories. "Who knows," thought Katreena, ruefully, "Perhaps he had even planned the early pregnancy as a kind of insurance policy in case we opposed the marriage."

As Katreena rounded the corner and drove along the last quarter of a mile to KD Acres, she noted with appreciation the vast fields of lush green crops undulating in the summer breeze. It made her heart skip a beat with longing. How she had enjoyed living in this serene central Manitoba countryside. Daniel had inherited this quarter from his father who had acquired it as a homestead stake for ten dollars when he came to Canada from Ukraine back in nineteen hundred. After the end of the First World War, old Mr. Banaduk had purchased the other three quarters of the section. When he fell ill and died in 1936, Daniel, at twenty-five, had inherited all the land because his other two brothers had died in the diphtheria epidemic. In 1938, Katreena came to teach school in the district and she and Daniel fell in love and married. By working and pooling their resources, they had acquired the rest of the acreage together, legally registering it as "KD Acres" (K for Katreena and D for Daniel.) Life was good for the young couple and their daughter until that summer when Michael came into their life. Helen's determination to see him in spite of her parents' opposition unsettled the harmony of their life but it was Daniel's untimely death that altered the course of it.

Helen's marriage to Michael, necessitated by her unexpected pregnancy, put Michael in a solid position to fill Katreena's dire need of a manager for the farm. By virtue of his farm background, he filled the gap naturally because Katreena was still under contract to teach. Katreena sold KD Acres to him, knowing it would remain in the family. Michael never referred to it as "KD Acres," however. He simply called it "the farm."

When Kaydee was born, Helen insisted on calling her by her mother and her father's names, Katherine Danielle. Michael acquiesced because his own father's name was Daniel so he felt he was being represented. Eventually, baby Katherine came to be called simply as "Kaydee" and it stuck. Later, Michael made the connection between Kaydee and KD Acres and tried protesting that too much reference was being made to Helen's parents but by then the name had been so engrained in everyone's mind (Michael's included) that change was impossible.

As she turned into the maple-lined driveway, Katreena was pleased to see that Helen had kept the flower garden neatly groomed around the deck at the west and south sides of the house. Katreena and Daniel had always enjoyed that deck. She could almost feel the summer breeze on her face as she recalled sitting there with Daniel on warm summer evenings sharing a cup of tea or a glass of sherry. The smell of newly-mown grass permeated the air of her memory and a profound sense of nostalgia overwhelmed Katreena as she stepped out of the car and walked towards the deck to admire the flowers.

Before Katreena had left for her trip abroad, the grounds had been bleak and only crocuses and tulips had been in bloom. It had been too early to do much with the rest of the flower garden, even though many of the plants there were perennials. Still it required care and right now, the results of that care were evident. Helen and Kaydee must have put in long hours to achieve that park-like appearance of the yard. The delicate bleeding hearts and bush roses were ablaze with pink and yellow blossoms. Brilliant red geraniums, orange tiger lilies and black-eyed-susans alternated between white daisies and baby's breath that were just breaking into bloom. The green foliage of late flowering mums were awaiting their turn behind them. Impatiens and dusty millers bordered the beds from the neatly clipped lawn. The hollyhocks were reaching three feet now and Katreena could visualize the tall spires of pink blossoms against the deck wall in a month or so.

Alvin came racing towards her and hurled himself into her arms the minute she got out.

"Granny, you're back, you're back. Are you going to stay with us now, Granny? Are you?" He was wiggling and squirming in her arms like a corkscrew, hugging her tightly and pulling back and gazing at her face, beseeching her affirmation. His hair and eyebrows were singed but outside of the red blotches on his face, he was none the worse for wear.

"Yes, Granny will stay for a while, but she has to go home and do some work there too so I will come back again soon. Is that all right?" Katreena laughed.

Alvin seemed to think it over and then with a triumphant smile, he nodded, his head bowing forward and up so fast, Katreena thought he'd hurt himself. Jaynee and Kaydee were holding on to her like a lifeline.

Katreena felt the burden of the children's needs draining her. Judging by the reception she had received, her daughter was obviously still struggling in that vortex of depression which left the children starved for love and attention. Torn between duty and guilt, Katreena was overcome with hopelessness. On her trip, she had met someone with whom she could foresee a future together. Yet how could she provide these poor children with the time and affection they craved so guilelessly and still maintain some semblance of a personal life for herself?

Worst yet, even if she were to try helping Helen and her children, how could she do it with Michael in the picture? He had legal title to KD Acres, not only through marriage, but Veteran's Land Act helped him purchase the adjoining section from Katreena. Never suspecting that his good nature and jovial attitude were but a façade for an egocentric and conniving character, she had sold it to him for less than market value. Above that was Helen's irrational loyalty to her husband. Helen was completely and blindly obedient to the man, no matter how despicably he treated her or the children. Regretfully, Katreena had to confess, the reason for this could lie in that deep Christian belief in the sanctity of marriage that Katreena and Daniel had themselves proudly instilled in her. Regardless of the shortfalls of Michael's character, Katreena knew she would score no points by trying to come between them.

"All right everyone," Michael's voice was no longer jovial. It was authoritative, but not yet harsh. Kaydee, anticipating the worst, immediately left Granny's side and ran to the house before he was able to say another word. Michael, seeing that, finished lamely, "Let's get to that dinner on the table."

Chapter 4

Dinner was Michael's forum as Katreena had expected. He went on and on about Alvin's feat, spewing off accolades of praise for Alvin's cleverness at retrieving the gunpowder.

"You know, most kids would never even know or care what a bullet consists of. This one, he's not satisfied to let it be. He wants to KNOW! And he does something about it. That's how great scientists are made. They question everything. The big universities are the answer for these guys. There, they have to have a place to grow. Great brains need that, you know. We'll have to make sure this little man has the preparation for whatever he wants to do in the future."

Alvin ate in silence, oblivious to, or perhaps not quite fully understanding, the praise his father was heaping on him. Silence at the table was not unusual in this family. Indeed it was welcome because the alternative was Michael's angry orders or criticisms. Today, Michael was painting a colourful future for his boy and nobody was questioning him or contradicting him.

"But Alvin could have really been hurt had he not protected himself. That was what that dimwit was supposed to be doing, taking care of him. One of these days that retard is going to do something so stupid there will be no going back. She's lucky I didn't rip her head off. It's a good thing Alvin has brains enough for both of them. If she had half the brains in her head that he has in his little finger she'd be almost normal! Looks like Alvin just has to learn to do things on his own 'cause that retard will never be of any help to him, that's for sure!"

Helen cast a warning look in her mother's direction but Katreena knew that Kaydee had not been punished for her misdemeanour yet so she bit her tongue and was careful not to contradict Michael even though her stomach lurched at Michael's every derogatory remark. So far, due to his vanity about his son's inquisitive adventure, thoughts of punishing Kaydee seemed to have faded into the background but now that his anger had resurfaced, he may still decide to dole it out. To keep from antagonizing Michael by objecting, Katreena just tuned him out and kept on eating. If this was what it took to keep the peace, so be it. She could hardly wait to get up from the table and start the dishes. She hoped that would make Michael take off for the outdoors and then she could have the girls to herself, on their own turf.

Seeing that Katreena was not the ardent audience he had hoped for, Michael was ready to hit for more neutral ground the second the last mouthful had been swallowed. "Come on Alvin," Michael turned to his son, "let's let the women do their work. We men will find something much more interesting to do."

The moment the door closed behind Michael, Katreena turned to Kaydee and suggested, "Why don't you take Jaynee and Dayna for their nap and later you and I will go for a nice long walk? Your mother and I will do the dishes today."

"Oh, I'd love that, Granny," Kaydee gave Katreena a quick hug and taking a wet washcloth, quickly washed up Dayna's face and hands and checked Jaynee for spills.

"Come on Jaynee, let's go," Kaydee called as she picked up Dayna and headed for the bedroom. She was eager for that walk. It had been two months since they had done that and she missed their talks. Granny was her only real confidant and Kaydee counted on her empathy.

Knowing she had Helen to herself, Katreena felt this was the best way to really find out how her daughter was functioning, mentally and physically. As they worked side-by-side clearing the food and the dishes, Katreena broke in gently, "You've done a wonderful job with the flower garden, Helen."

"We finished with the seeding early and it was still too soon to spray or summerfallow, so Michael said to do the yard work."

"How is the garden? Did you get a chance to get that in on time or did you have to wait for the field work to be done first?"

"I had Annie stay with the children during the week, while we worked on the fields. Then Michael just asked her to stay an extra day while I planted the garden. I finished it all in one day but the hoeing and cleanup, I just do in bits and pieces whenever I have a spare moment." Helen seemed at ease and not at all resentful that her mother had not been there to help when she was needed.

Katreena was relieved. She had agonized about going away in the spring. Since her retirement from teaching two years ago, Michael expected Katreena to babysit the children while Helen pitched in with the farm and field work. She had missed an opportunity last year to go on a vacation with some retired teachers because she opted to help out on the farm. This year, however, those same friends decided to take a couple of four-week, back-to-back tours of Europe and the British Isles and they again asked her to come along. At first, she had declined, stating that she was needed on the farm.

"But spring is the perfect time to see Europe," Evie Gowyn had urged. "You must start living for yourself sometime. How long are you going to stay tied down to that farm? You've retired, Katreena. Come on! Live a little!"

"But two months!" Katreena protested in shocked disbelief.

"So what?" Len, Evie's husband countered. "You're retired. You've put in your time. It's time you started reaping some of the benefits of your labours. You've always put your family, your work, your farm and all your responsibilities first. How about you? Isn't it about time to give Katreena a chance? You've been so busy making a living, you haven't had time to live. You won't feel like travelling when you're old and feeble. Now is the time, Katreena!"

It all made perfect sense and Katreena knew it. In the end, they finally convinced her. She had announced her intentions to Michael and Helen one day in March. Michael had been aghast but Helen had taken it with her usual lack of concern or protest.

"You would think that, as a grandmother to the children of your only child, you would want to spend the time with them rather than going gallivanting all over creation." Michael had complained, but Katreena had stuck to her guns and not allowed Michael to spoil this opportunity. She had to start putting herself first or Michael would bring her down to the same level as Helen. That very idea evoked a sense of defiance in Katreena. Who was Michael to be telling her how to live? It was bad enough he had harnessed Helen into a life of drudgery and despair.

Katreena was determined not to succumb to Michael's dictatorship!

So on May fourth, she had packed her bags and left Michael and Helen to fend for themselves. Guilt plagued her for the first couple of weeks of the trip, but then she relaxed and reasoned that she had earned this vacation, and she owed it to herself to enjoy it. To her amazement, the holiday had been a wonderful experience. It had released within her a sensation of freedom such as she had not known since before Daniel's accident. Obviously, Helen held no grudges, and even Michael seemed to have forgotten his earlier objections. They had again engaged the services of their cordial neighbour, Annie, and managed quite well without Katreena.

Annie Dorozeck was a sixty-eight-year-old, plumpish, good-natured widow who lived on the farm on the next quarter. With her ruddy complexion and ape-like features, she was no beauty queen. Her bucktoothed jaws fused into a non-existent chin that somehow just disappeared in her neck. But what Annie lacked in appearance, she made up in personality! She had the patience of Job, and the compassion of a saint. Her perpetual smile was contagious and her infectious laugh seemed to erupt from somewhere deep inside her very soul. Her constantly positive attitude made her an asset to every gathering.

Annie rented out her land to Michael but retained the use of her yard. This opportunity to be useful fell right in with her needs. She was no stranger to the kids having helped the family out before Katreena retired from teaching. Katreena felt relieved that the situation had resolved itself so naturally. Now, she could try to move on with her own life much more freely. The thought was exhilarating, especially because it could make it possible for her to spend more time with the handsome Dusty Duganyk, whom she had met on the tour.

"How did school pan out for Kaydee? Did that Mr. Norchak have anything to report at the end of the term?" Katreena was anxious to hear about Kaydee's progress in school. For some reason, she felt that Special Education classes for Kaydee held the key to some kind of mystery about Kaydee. Katreena had always felt that Kaydee was special, yet it was puzzling that she could not make it in a class of regular students. She was definitely not retarded.

Helen stopped her scraping motion on the pot, her whole body arrested in mid-motion. She looked thoughtful, almost wistful for a moment. For just a second, Katreena caught a flash of the "before Michael" Helen. "Is there hope of real feeling and concern? Is my real daughter still lurking behind that expressionless puppet?" Katreena wondered.

"You know, Mother, that Mr. Norchak is something else. For the Parent and Teacher meeting, I had to see him myself, of course, because Michael did not want to go. Mr. Norchak spent over an hour with me. His wife even came in to talk to me for a while. They asked me all sorts of questions, about Kaydee, about us, about our life, about Michael, especially about Michael, about everything. Then they told me something funny. They said Kaydee was specially gifted, that she did not belong in that class. Mrs. Norchak then had to leave but Mr. Norchak kept on talking to me. He said Kaydee would be better off at Lawn Haven Academy in Portmont, but, if that were impossible, he would keep her in his class for another year, if I agreed to let his wife work with her a few hours every week. I told this to Michael, but he said we didn't have that kind of money to waste on Portmont and that we needed Kaydee to look after the kids. I haven't given Mr. Norchak an answer yet."

Katreena's heart lurched. She didn't even know why, but she felt elated, vindicated somehow. "I knew it, I knew it. My instincts had been right," her mind asseverated triumphantly. Then Helen's words re-echoed in her brain and their impact came as an icy shower on her elation.

"Helen, you wouldn't deny Kaydee a chance at education just because Michael wants a babysitter, would you?" Katreena's voice was unintentionally sharp, admonishing. "Surely if Kaydee could benefit from this special tutorship, you wouldn't let Michael deprive her of it. If money is the problem, I'll absorb the cost for Portmont. As for babysitting, the children are not Kaydee's responsibility!"

Helen fairly shrivelled up. Too late, Katreena realized her mistake. Her daughter had opened up to her, had actually shown some initiative in voicing a concern and her mother had reprimanded her just as Michael always did. Instead of commending her budding concern, Katreena had scolded her for daring to venture out of her self-imposed protective cocoon.

Feeling chastised, Katreena sought to repair the damage her instinctive rebuke had provoked. Helen's show of interest or concern was rare and precious and needed to be nurtured above everything else. Katreena so wanted Helen to come back to the loving, caring, sociable person she had been before the ill-fated pregnancy that had penalized her so drastically. Marriage to Michael had not only cost Helen her freedom; it had destroyed her spirit and her will to fight back, and to genuinely care, not just for her herself, but for her children. Her only remaining self-defence was this barrier of lethargy and indifference that shut everyone and everything out. In desperation, Katreena tried to reopen the subject in a gentler tone.

"I'm sorry. I didn't mean it the way it sounded. I know you'll do the best for Kaydee. Does Mrs. Norchak often work with special children? Does she have credentials for it?"

"I don't know," Helen spoke listlessly but with finality. She had already crawled back into her apathetic, detached shell. Katreena was shattered. She had had a fleeting opportunity to persuade Helen to do something decent and constructive and she, her own mother, had crushed it. How she wished she had thought before blurting out her disbelief and her objection. She had been no better than Michael, riding roughshod over Helen's feelings, belittling them, giving her no credit for having a valid opinion. She had spoken without thinking, selfishly assuming that Helen would not have considered doing the right thing. Helen had not said she was not considering it. She only said she had not given Mr. Norchak an answer yet. Why had she assumed that the answer would be Michael's "no" instead of Helen's "yes"? Silently, bitterly, Katreena reproached herself as she put the last of the dishes away.

She'd have to pursue the subject on her own if she wanted to find out any more about this special tutoring. And she definitely did want to know more. Here was a possibility that she had dreamed about, but had barely dared hope for. Now it was beckoning to her with a furtive wave from behind the perceptive eyc of a Special Ed teacher who worked with mentally challenged students. It was the realization of a lasting daydream, the vindication of Katreena's unfailing and profound conviction that Kaydee was not retarded but had some inner source of acumen that had remained untapped or undiscovered, a recess of the mind unreachable by conventional methods.

Kaydee appeared in the archway leading from the living room. She was dressed in blue-jean shorts and a white tee-shirt. Her long golden hair was pulled back off her face and tied in a ponytail that hung down almost to her shoulders. Kaydee had beautiful hair, thick and with just a hint of a wave that lent a flattering fullness around her face. Her hazel eyes peered out from under heavy lashes in puppy dog fashion. When she was happy, those eyes glowed like pools in the sunshine and her mouth widened across her face curving up at the sides, a dramatic change from her usual downcast, apprehensive expression. She was smiling now, watching in anticipation for her grandmother to say the word that she was ready to go for the walk she had promised.

"So, are we ready to take off?" Katreena hung the tea towel on the rack and came to put her arm around Kaydee's shoulders. Kaydee beamed up at her. Kaydee was tall for her age and because she was so slim, her five-foot-three-inch frame seemed to take on an even more linear appearance. Still, her grandmother was five-foot-seven and she towered over her, especially when she wore the heels which were such a trademark of her garb. To Kaydee's impressionable mind, Katreena was the epitome of sophistication, beauty and grace. She was the idol of her dreams and the model she strived to emulate in appearance, in mannerisms, and lifestyle. Kaydee adored her grandmother.

"Perhaps after supper, we'll take the girls with us and all go together for a short walk," Katreena told Helen. "Right now I'd like to go down towards that west meadow. The path along the creek must smell like heaven with the wild roses all in bloom. It's much too nice a day to spend indoors." Katreena watched Helen as she centered the vase of fresh flowers on the table and straightened the crocheted doily underneath it.

"Yes, I know. You two go ahead. Enjoy yourselves." Helen dismissed them casually but with no notable sadness. Katreena was relieved. Quickly she changed into the loafers that she kept in the hall closet for such occasions, threw her jacket over her shoulders, and she and Kaydee left the house.

Crossing the spacious yard to the back field and the creek beyond, Katreena noted with satisfaction how neat everything was. The large shed, newly-painted last year, looked good and all the equipment was neatly parked under its roof. There was no trace of the usual oily stains on the white trim around the door of the tool shed, although Katreena was aware that Michael did a lot of machine maintenance work there. In the last two years, Michael had purchased three more graineries and by moving the three original ones, he now had them situated at the northwest corner of the yard, creating an efficient semicircle accessible to one single move of the grain auger. The cattle shelter at the far north end of the yard was clean and a small stack of straw bales, neatly piled, stood in one corner. There was no debris visible anywhere. Everything was in its proper place.

The grass was neatly cut around every inch of the yard, and even the four rows of maples encircling the yard were neatly trimmed, with no root brush visible. Katreena knew that it was Helen or Kaydee that actually ran the lawn mower, and probably did the brush cutting as well. It would have been done under Michael's strict orders, though. Not that Katreena minded that well-manicured look on the yard. She actually felt gratified to see her old home so well maintained. Michael may be an arrogant, self-centered bully but his determination to present an organized and prosperous farmyard to the community made him a scrupulous manager. He knew how to run the farm efficiently – even if it was by the toil of someone else's brawn! Whatever his other faults, Michael was well organized and meticulous.

Katreena sighed wistfully. Life was good but it certainly had its downside even at its high peaks. With Kaydee beaming happily beside her, Katreena wished fervently that Michael had been a more decent man. It felt good to have the farm in the family. Having her daughter and grandchildren within an hour from her house could be the perfect situation for Katreena in her retirement years. And if Michael were not such a cruel dictator, Katreena knew that Helen could have been very happy here also. If only she could somehow change Michael into a loving husband and father, life could be so perfect for her family!

Michael and Alvin were by the shed inspecting Alvin's brand new two-wheeled bicycle. As Katreena approached, Alvin ran to meet her and took her hand.

"Did you see my new bike Granny? Daddy bought it for me. It's a two-wheeler." Alvin emphasized the last two words with awe and obvious pride.

Kaydee and Katreena approached and Kaydee reached out to touch the bright blue metal frame. Michael yanked it instantly out of her reach.

"Get your dirty hands off that bike," he snapped. "You'll get smudge marks all over it."

"But I washed them," Kaydee started timidly.

"None of your lip now, girl. You watch that attitude of yours and no mouthing off. I'll not have you talking back to your father!"

"Michael!" Katreena began, but Michael cut her off.

"That girl has got to learn to mind her manners and show some respect. She's too gawd-damned lippy!"

Kaydee bowed her head and stepped back without a word. Alvin glanced at Kaydee, then at his father with a somewhat puzzled look on his face. Then, uncertain if he, too, should not be touching the bike, stepped back as well. Michael picked up on it immediately.

"C'mon, Son, it's your bike. Let's show the women how fast you can ride it."

But Katreena had lost interest in the cursed bike. She was fuming. "Come on, Kaydee, let's go for that walk." She squeezed Kaydee's hand and without even looking at Michael, she purposefully led the young girl away from the shed.

Katreena was shaking. How could Michael treat Kaydee that way? How could he be so cruel? The absolute gall of the man was appalling. She had often seen him snap at Kaydee, but this had been totally uncalled for. Katreena had barely kept her tongue at the table when he had been so nasty to Kaydee at dinner.

"Stop your slurping and slopping! You eat like a pig. It's disgusting! You make me wanna puke! And wipe that look off your face. Don't you give me no attitude now! Sit up straight for heaven's sake, quit slouching. You look like an old hag!"

This was so typical of Michael. Any situation had the potential for a confrontation for him.

Katreena recalled a drive she had once been on with the family. Kaydee had tried to stretch her arms into a new position and Michael had exploded. "Can't you sit quiet, out there? How am I supposed to concentrate on driving with you waving your damned arms around like a crazy gorilla? Why can't you be like a normal kid?"

Katreena flared. "Were they to sit motionless no matter how long the trip was?"

Michael blew up, "The kid's got to learn manners and discipline! It would help if you stopped interfering!"

Katreena had stifled further protests to avoid escalating an all-out shouting match but she vowed never to ride with Michael and the kids again though she worried about what the kids were putting up with, in her absence. No wonder Kaydee was unable to function at full potential. With the threat of such scorn hanging over her head, it was a wonder she could function at all. No matter what she did or when she did it, her father's verbal abuse was brutal and unrelenting.

Kaydee walked along quietly at Katreena's side, her manner subdued and pensive. Katreena felt an overpowering urge to protect this child from the influence of this callous man who had the potential to destroy her. But how could she do that? Engrossed in her own thoughts, she was surprised when Kaydee, obviously feeling forgotten, squeezed her hand. Drawn out of her preoccupation, Katreena looked into the sad, questioning eyes and realized that her silence was contributing to Kaydee's pain.

"Don't you worry, sweetheart, we'll have much more fun than they will." She winked at Kaydee and immediately that beguiling smile spread across the young face. They had just reached the belt of maples that encircled the yard. Above them, the lush green leaves, still young and fresh from spring's emergence, rustled softly in the warm breeze. Birds warbled and chirped in the trees, and occasionally, the flashing brown of a sparrow, the blue streak of a jay, or a robin's orange breast appeared and disappeared among the dancing leaves.

"Look," Katreena pulled Kaydee to a sudden stop. Silently, they stood watching as a robin, oblivious to their presence, scratched in the moist soil, hopping with both feet, searching for grubs. Kaydee was spellbound.

"Oh, Granny, she must have babies somewhere and she's getting their dinner," she whispered. They watched, fascinated, as the robin located its quarry, pulled hard at it until she fell back on her tail, then recovering, pecked the long worm with her beak, and flew off with her prize. Kaydee giggled with amusement at the opportunity to witness the comical scene.

The afternoon sun bathed them in warm rays and Katreena wished she had left her jacket back at the house. She considered taking it back but, reluctant to encounter Michael again, decided against it. Resolutely, she draped it over her arm and took refuge in the welcoming shade of the green canopy of the maples. A gray squirrel scampered in front of them, raced up a tree, then, its bushy tail twitching, turned around to scold them for trespassing on its territory.

"Okay, okay, we're going. We were only passing through, honest." Katreena chided defensively, looking up at him. Kaydee laughed, a merry, light titter and Katreena knew that the memory of Michael's berating was already forgotten. She was glad Kaydee forgot so readily. Katreena wished she could. How resilient children are, she marvelled!

As they emerged from the cool shade of the shelter belt, the sun's intensity once more beat down on them with unrelenting fervour. Katreena wished they had brought their sunglasses as they squinted out across the meadow towards the luxuriant vegetation along the creek. Native grasses mingled with the wild daisies, clovers, alfalfa blossoms and various other spring blossoms and plants, and the air smelled fresh and sweet. The meadow hummed with the sound of bees, birds and the soft hiss of the zephyr through the grasses. An air of contentment and tranquility permeated the atmosphere and in this peaceful haven,

Katreena felt her troubles fade into obscurity. It was good to be alive!

"So tell me about what you have been doing these last two months while I have been away," Katreena prompted.

"Well, mostly I have just been going to school and taking care of Alvin and Jaynee. I helped Mother with the flowers and the garden and I mow the lawn at least twice a week, so things are good except when Father gets angry with me. He gets very angry a lot, but I don't know how not to get him angry. The worst time was when that rooster was around. He used to chase Alvin and me, and I just couldn't protect Alvin. Honest Granny, I couldn't stop him. That bad rooster would chase us, and peck, and scratch, and beat us with his wings. Both Alvin and I had a lot of bruises all over our bodies. Father was very angry with me for not protecting Alvin. He pulled my hair and made me kneel in that sinhole for hours, and he made me promise to take better care of Alvin. But I tried Granny, honest I tried. This happened many times, until finally Mother went and killed that rooster. Only then, Father got angry at Mother. He told her that she should let me grow up. But Granny, I was really glad Mother killed that terrible rooster."

"I'm glad your mother killed that rooster too. She should have killed him right after the first time he started chasing you kids. And you're doing a wonderful job with Alvin so don't you let your father tell you otherwise." Katreena finished vehemently. It burned her no end to think that Michael could be so callous and for the thousandth time she wished there was some way she could get Helen and the kids away from him.

They continued their stroll along the creek, Kaydee's hand damp in Katreena's. They admired the flowers, the birds, the fragrance in the air and the earthy smell of the damp ground beneath their feet as they made their way amid silky grasses and thorny briers of the wild roses whose perfume wafted softly up to tantalize their senses. The goldfinches swayed on the thistles here and there, and Kaydee chuckled as they scolded and chattered noisily in protest as the pair interrupted their feeding frenzy.

It was peaceful here and yet Katreena's emotions were churning. Michael's attitude toward Kaydee seemed to have deteriorated to the point of open hatred and Katreena felt an almost acute urgency to get the child away from there. A sense of foreboding hung like a cloud over the girl when Michael was around. It was as if the very essence of the girl provoked some demonic beast within him.

Kaydee took the abuse as a matter of course although she visibly shrank away from Michael's anger. She had never known his love, had no idea what a father's love was, so she didn't miss it. Still it galled Katreena to think that Michael could be so heartless and mean to her and yet act so righteous about it. If only there were some way Katreena could change those circumstances...

The breeze picked up and the leaves danced a jig above them. Katreena looked at her watch. Twenty-five to four. Where had the time gone? They had arrived at the far end of the farm, and they crossed the fence to get on the road. Over in the west, some cottony clouds drifted lazily across the blue sky and several sea gulls arced their way beneath them. The warm early summer breeze softly caressed their cheeks, bringing with it a heady aura of nature's own perfumery. Katreena inhaled the ambience of beauty and tranquility. Humble gratitude enveloped her as she acknowledged how beautiful, peaceful, happy even, life could be! All avenues pointed to nature's abundance and God's infinite munificence. So why did she have this ponderous oppression interrupting her flashes of serenity?

She considered all the pros and cons of the different facets of her life. She was retired; therefore presumably free to do as she wished, when she wished. She was financially stable; and her family was nearby. She had even met an interesting man lately who seemed to be interested in her. Life should be hers to live. "So live it," she scolded herself. "Stop moping!"

"*Lead; follow; or get the heck out of the way.*" She could still hear Art Jesop, her school supervisor, during his motivational speech, when she retired. If only it were that easy. Katreena felt despair ballooning in her chest as she looked at her granddaughter. Determined not to succumb to melancholy, she rallied.

"Let's go get your mother and your sisters." she playfully slapped

Kaydee's bottom as they scampered out of the ditch and onto the road. "This day is too beautiful for them to sit inside."

"Let's go get them!" Kaydee echoed. Eyes dancing merrily, she clasped Granny's outstretched hand.

Chapter 5

As they neared the yard, Katreena felt a cold shudder engulf her. She had no idea why but she felt an urgency to get home. Not wishing to frighten Kaydee unnecessarily, she let go of her hand, because her palms suddenly felt clammy and cold. Instinctively she picked up her pace, her heart hammering in her chest.

Michael's raspy voice cut through the air as he emerged running from behind the machine shed carrying the lifeless body of Alvin in his arms. He was charging toward the cars, holding his son tightly against his chest. Alvin's head hung to the side like he was a rag doll. Katreena forgot about Kaydee at her side, but the girl was way ahead of her, flying towards Michael and Alvin. Katreena felt like she was in a dream as she raced towards the two figures, her feet like heavy weights of lead beneath her. She could not move fast enough.

Kaydee reached them first. "What happened?" Katreena heard her gasp.

"Don't touch him. The tractor, Katreena, I have to take him to the doctor. Get away from him," he barked at Kaydee who was trying to touch Alvin's drooping arm.

Michael was barely coherent but snapped at Kaydee automatically, even in his anguish. Kaydee, in complete shock, stood rooted to the spot, staring after them as Michael ran toward the white Pontiac, Katreena in hot pursuit.

"To the hospital, fast!" Michael panted. Katreena jumped into the driver's seat, fishing keys out of the jacket still draped over her arm. Michael yanked the passenger door open with one hand and positioned himself inside holding Alvin tightly with the other. In a shower of gravel, Katreena rammed the gear in reverse, tore out of the driveway, then shifting into drive, floored the accelerator.

With a furtive glance at her traumatized passengers, Katreena rasped. "What in God's Holy Name happened out there?"

Michael was sitting quietly, his terror-stricken face ashen, eyes bloodshot as he gently rocked his listless son. Alvin looked barely alive as rasping breaths sporadically hiccupped through his otherwise inert body.

"I was backing up the tractor from the fuel tank. He was behind. I didn't know he was there until I saw the front wheel roll over him. I didn't see him, Katreena. Oh, God, I didn't see him until it was too late."

"You drove over him with the tractor?" Katreena gasped, horrified.

"Only with the front wheel. I didn't know he was there. I had no idea. I didn't see him. I swear. I didn't see him until it was too late." Michael kept repeating the words as if in a trance, desperately trying to justify himself to Katreena, but, possibly, even more to himself. Katreena tried to envision the scene, but the picture would not formulate. Michael's pallor spoke volumes of his grave concern as he held his son's limp body.

Katreena pushed hard on the accelerator. The speedometer needle was reading ninety-five miles per hour, too fast for a gravelled road. She could spin out. "Be careful," she admonished herself. But this was the longest three-and-a-half miles Katreena had ever driven. She drove Helen at this speed when she was ill but this was different. This was worse, much, much, worse.

"Please God, let him be all right," she prayed. It was no use talking to Michael. He was in too much of a shock to think straight. If she could only get him to the hospital in time. The highway! Thank goodness! Stop, Katreena. Make sure it's safe. Now turn! Go! Go! Hurry!

Three more miles! As her hands clutched the wheel, her mind raced in several directions at once. It suddenly struck her how quiet Michael was. The depth of his concern was evident in this unnatural silence. Michael, who seldom lacked words except when deliberately ignoring someone, now had no words! All he did was stare at the road ahead as if willing it to advance by the sheer force of his will. Alvin's harsh breathing was irregular but the raspy sound came more frequently and somewhat stronger. Or was this wishful thinking? Every now and then he coughed weakly and Michael watched his face with great concern. Katreena felt as if her whole life had gone into slow motion. She desperately wanted to snap out of it; needed to snap out of it. She needed to think, needed to feel normal again.

Finally, Katreena turned and accelerated up the ramp to the emergency entrance. She had hardly shifted into park before Michael leapt from the car and ran for the emergency door. Leaving the Pontiac in the driveway, Katreena raced after him.

Inside the door they startled the nurse beside the counter. "Help him" Michael gasped. "The tractor rolled over him. He can't breathe." The nurse sprang into action. "Get Dr. Walley, stat!" she called to receptionist as she took the boy's limp form from Michael and rushed away. Michael was right at her heels and Katreena followed.

"We'll give him oxygen to help him breathe and the doctor will check him when he gets here. It won't be long. He's in the building. Can you tell me what happened?"

"I was on the tractor fuelling up. He must have been behind me, but I didn't know he was there. When I finished, I started backing the tractor up and that's when I saw him lying on the ground. I jumped down and picked him up but he wasn't breathing, so I shook him and he started gasping, but he hasn't been breathing properly at all, just now and then, those awful rasping noises. You gotta make him better. Please!" Michael voice broke. He was wringing his hands, stepping from one foot to the other as if he wanted to go somewhere but didn't know where to go; do something but didn't know what to do.

Katreena stood by helplessly, wishing the doctor would arrive. The nurse put Alvin on a stretcher and started to prepare the oxygen. Deftly, she slipped the tubes over Alvin's ears and inserted the cannula into his nose. As she adjusted the valves on the oxygen tank, she watched Alvin's reaction intently. An audible hiss told them the life-giving air was on its way to the ravaged lungs.

A commotion in the hallway told them that the doctor had arrived and they looked up as a tall, heavy-set, slightly-balding man, possibly in his mid-forties, entered the room. Clad in a long white hospital coat, he looked the model of efficiency. His demeanour was authoritative but pleasant and comforting.

"What have we here?" he asked, inspecting the eyes of the patient by gently opening them with his fingers. Softly, the nurse at his side filled him in on the scant details. Michael and Katreena stood by silently. Alvin's breathing had become more even and somewhat quieter now with that pure oxygen entering his battered lungs.

"Tell you what, folks. You go out there to the office and tell the nurse what happened and how, then fill in all the admission papers and I will check this little fellow for broken bones and other injuries. I will talk to you in a little while. Now, you go do your thing and I will do mine." With a dismissive wave of his hand, he shooed them out and Michael and Katreena found themselves in the hallway as the door closed firmly behind them.

"You go to the office," Katreena told Michael. "I'll go and move the car before they tow it away. I'll be back shortly. Go ahead, it's just around the corner to the right."

Outside, Katreena suddenly realized that Helen had no idea what was happening and heaven only knew what Kaydee may have said in her distressed state. They must be frantic. Heart pounding, Katreena pulled the Pontiac out of the Emergency Entrance and drove to the parking lot at the back of the hospital. Checking to see that the doors were locked, she quickly walked through the back door, went straight to the pay phone, and dialled KD Acres.

Helen answered before it completed the first ring. She must have been sitting there waiting for word.

"Look honey, we're at the hospital. The doctor is checking Alvin as we speak. They gave him oxygen and he is breathing fine. We don't know more than that at this point but I'll let you know as soon as I find out anything. How is Kaydee?"

"Kaydee has been crying ever since she came into the house. I can't make any sense out of anything she says. Mom, what in God's name happened?"

"I'm not even sure myself yet, honey. Michael is in a state of shock and can barely speak coherently but he did give me the basics. Apparently he was backing up the tractor and Alvin somehow got pushed underneath and the front wheel rolled over him. That's all I know. Don't worry. Alvin seems to be all right. The doctor is with him now. I'll let you know as soon as I find out anything, I promise. Bye for now, I'll talk to you soon."

Katreena hated to leave Helen hanging like that but she really had no choice. She didn't know anymore at the moment, and she was wasting precious time if the doctor had any news for them. As she hurried along the long corridor to the emergency station, Alvin's face flashed through her memory and she remembered the bruises on his cheek and forehead. Funny, she hadn't thought about them before. Was that where the tire had rolled over him? His face hadn't healed from the gunpowder incident yet, but Katreena recalled the fresh bloody scrapes. They were different. They were new. Did he have head injuries then? A cold chill rippled through her body from her toes all the way to the ends of the hair on her head.

"Oh please, Lord, let him be all right," she prayed.

Outside the office, Katreena heard Michael answering the questions the nurse was asking. His voice was subdued and his manner contrite. All that bravado had gone out of him like starch out of a shirt in the rain. Gone was his self-confidence, his arrogance, his harshness, and his nastiness. He was just a normal father worried about his wounded son. He was almost likeable, Katreena thought, in amazement. It's not like him at all but then he is worried sick about Alvin. Katreena felt truly sorry for him as she stood outside the door of the admissions office listening to his anxious voice and his submissive answers.

Not wishing to disturb them, she turned toward the Emergency Treatment room in search of the doctor and hopefully some good news. The door was still closed and she stood there, uncertain and apprehensive, wondering how long she would have to wait before somebody came out with some information. A nurse passed by, obviously in a hurry carrying a treatment tray but she went into another room. Katreena wondered if they may have moved Alvin and the equipment was really to be used on him but then a very distraught young man came out of the room and Katreena's taut nerves relaxed. A little Phillipino nurse was with the man and she was obviously trying to reassure him in gentle low tones with words that Katreena could not make out. She felt deep pity for the man who speechlessly followed the pretty young nurse toward the admissions office.

Katreena stood staring after them. Her heart went out to the man and she wondered what tragedy had brought him here and who the person in that room was. Was it his wife, his child or his parent? Dr. Walley's light tap on her shoulder broke her reverie and she jumped.

"Mrs. Banaduk, I'm sorry I startled you. I just wanted you to know your little boy is fine. So far as I can determine, there are no broken bones but I have scheduled some X-rays just to be sure. He has some extensive bruising on his head, his chest, his hip and his left leg, but I think he will be all right. He is breathing normally now. Hopefully he has no broken ribs but I feel quite confident that he is only badly bruised. Children's bones are soft and they give a great deal. That wheel must have run over the full length of his body, judging by the bruising. The shaking may have been more harmful, but we will know more after the results of the tests come in. I think the weight of the tractor was on the back wheels since it was backing up so that the front wheel probably just squeezed the air out of his lungs. I will keep him in the hospital for a day or so for observation, but if all goes as I think it will, he may be ready to go home tomorrow. Don't worry. Children are very resilient. He's breathing on his own now, but his chest will be sore for a while. He won't be jumping rope for a few days but I believe he'll be fine. I better go find Mr. Boyer. They should be just about finished with the report by now. You coming?" He turned and started toward the office.

Katreena stared after him wordlessly. She hadn't realized how much stress her body had been under. Now, relief flooded over her like a tranquilizing drug. Her legs suddenly felt like they were about to buckle and her body turned to mush. She felt weak and dizzy as she struggled to maintain her balance. She looked around for someplace to sit, spied a chair further down the hallway and stumbled toward it. Dr. Walley glanced back, noticed her stumbling, and quickly came to her assistance.

"Are you all right? Do you want me to give you something? I can get the nurse to get you a sedative." Dr. Walley's concern was obvious as he eased her into the chair.

"No, thank you. I'll be all right. Just give me a moment. I don't want anything. You go ahead. I'll be there shortly. Thank you."

After he left, she suddenly realized she hadn't even asked Dr. Walley if she could see Alvin. She'd been so intent on the news she had forgotten completely. Abruptly, she sat bolt upright. Helen! And Kaydee! She must let them know. They'd be worried sick. Armed with a purpose, she willed herself to get up and go to the nearest phone.

"Helen? He's fine, Helen. He's bruised and sore, and Dr. Walley has scheduled X-rays to rule out any broken bones, but he says that children's bones are soft and they 'give,' so he is confident that he'll be fine. He wants to keep Alvin in the hospital at least for the night, just for observation but he was very reassuring. He said Alvin will probably be able to go home tomorrow or the day after so that really sounds good. How is Kaydee?"

"She's been crying all the time and I can't even talk to her, but maybe now she'll be better. She can't understand what happened and she's so afraid for Alvin." Helen's voice muffled as she obviously turned to give Kaydee the good news. Katreena waited while they exchanged some words, then Helen came back on the line.

"Kaydee and I would like to come and see him, but I'm not sure I can drive right now. I feel so shaky."

"Don't worry, honey, I'll come and pick you all up, then I can sit with Jaynee and Dayna while you go see him. I haven't even seen him myself, neither has Michael, since we left him. Michael has been in the office filing the report and filling out the admission papers but Dr. Walley is giving him the news now. I am certain he'll want to stay and see Alvin so he won't even know I'm gone. I'll see you shortly. Bye now."

As Katreena manoeuvred her car out of the crowded parking lot, she thought back over the day's events. Was it just a few of hours ago that Michael had been bragging about how smart Alvin was? He had been so proud of Alvin's "smarts" that he had totally ignored the possibility that those smarts could have resulted in a tragedy, too. Later, at the shop, he had made such an issue of the fact that the new bike was for Alvin only, and Kaydee had no right to even touch it. He had yanked it out of Kaydee's reach so roughly like she might contaminate it with her touch.

He had been so intent on spending the time with Alvin himself. Whatever had possessed him to fuel the tractor up on a Sunday anyway? He never worked on Sundays, that Katreena knew, so why was he refuelling the tractor today? What an ironic twist of fate!

Well at least this is one time Michael could not blame Kaydee. He had sounded so meek while filing the report in the office. Would he finally acknowledge his own shortcomings now? Michael was an egotist and did not accept the blame for his own mistakes, but he could hardly blame anyone but himself today. Certainly Kaydee could not be a candidate for blame this time.

Katreena pulled into the driveway at KD Acres and Kaydee came flying out of the house before she even stopped the motor. Her face was tear-stained, her eyes bloodshot and swollen. Behind her, Jaynee came running also, her short legs making her waddle as she hurried towards them. She hadn't been told what was happening but Kaydee's sobbing had her frightened and confused. Helen came out last, with Dayna in her arms. Katreena hugged each one in turn, holding Kaydee particularly close, knowing that her concern was most acute because from the day Alvin was born, Kaydee had been programmed to feel responsible for his safety and welfare.

"How is he? Did you see him yet? Do you know how it happened?" The questions tumbled out one on top of another.

"I haven't seen him since we dropped him off but I saw them give him oxygen and the doctor told me later that Alvin was breathing on his own so it must have helped him a lot. They were taking him down to X-ray for broken bones, but Dr. Walley said it was just a precaution. We'll know more after he sees the X-ray. Come on, I'll tell you the rest in the car."

One more time Katreena went through the explanation of what had happened as far as she knew. That was not a great deal of course, she realized. Michael had not given her that much information. Perhaps he never would. After all, he was hardly one to point the finger of irresponsibility at himself at the best of times. "Anyway," she thought to herself, "who cares? As long as Alvin comes out of this all right. And Kaydee."

As they drove the six-and-a-half miles to Zelena, Katreena marvelled how much shorter the distance seemed this time than it had been an hour ago. It had taken forever to get to that hospital with Alvin gasping sporadically at, what had seemed at that time, his dying breath. "But we're not out of the woods yet," Katreena reminded herself as she hurried back to the hospital room to where she had left Alvin less than an hour ago. With Dayna in her arms, Helen hastened after Katreena. Kaydee was right behind with the bewildered Jaynee hanging on tightly to Kaydee's neck.

Outside of the emergency room door, they encountered Michael, still subdued, his face drawn and his eyes bloodshot.

"Have you heard anything?" Katreena asked in alarm, seeing his tormented look.

"No, they just took him to X-ray. We should know soon. I saw him for a few seconds when they took him out. He looks better." Totally ignoring Kaydee, he nodded absentmindedly to Helen but made no move to touch her. Kaydee stood apart, dejected and concerned, waiting to be included in the circle. The little Philippino nurse walked by and seeing them all standing there in the hallway, suggested that they come and wait in the lounge where they could be more comfortable.

"The doctor will see you there as soon as he has any news," she added compassionately.

Kaydee was anxious and antsy. She desperately tried to control her fidgeting as she watched her father's stone-faced stare which, for once, did not seem to be focusing on her. Still, she was cautious and apprehensive. Father's temper was unpredictable and explosive. Kaydee's stomach was a mess of knots and she felt sick, but she fought to maintain control of her emotions. She couldn't let herself get sick or appear fidgety. She had to find out more about Alvin. He just had to be all right. She could not stand it if something bad happened to him. She loved that little boy.

Finally, after what seemed like an eternity, especially to Kaydee, a man in white came to talk to them. He was smiling as he held out his hand to Mother. Father's face looked like it was about to crumble.

Kaydee had never seen Father look so helpless or subdued.

"I have good news for you," the doctor looked from Mother to Father to Granny and then to Kaydee. "Alvin will be all right. He has no broken bones. He is badly bruised but much like we expected, no sign of any fractures or breaks. Children's bones are soft and pliable. They will give a long way before they break."

Mother and Father both started to cry and laugh at the same time and for the first time in her life, Kaydee saw them hug each other. It gave her a funny feeling.

The doctor continued. "Alvin will feel pretty rotten for a few days, but he will be good as new within a couple of weeks when the bruises heal. I will keep him here for a day or so for observation but don't worry, he'll be just fine. You may see him, but only for a short while. I have ordered a painkiller for him and it may make him groggy so don't worry if his responses are lethargic. He needs to rest now. He's been through a rough ordeal. No more than two visitors at once though and no more than five minutes at a time, all right?"

Granny came and put her free hand around Kaydee's shoulder as she took Dayna from Mother's arms. Totally bewildered, Jaynee stood wide-eyed, watching this unfamiliar display of family unity with a realization that something very important had just happened. She had never seen her parents in a hug. As Mother and Father walked out together to see Alvin, she clung to Granny and Kaydee, the only sources of stability she knew.

When it came Granny and Kaydee's turn to go see Alvin, they walked into the small hospital room where he lay as in a cage, protective chrome bars raised on either side of him, his small frame dwarfed by the big bed. He looked vulnerable and pathetic. His face was bruised and scratched where the gravel had left indelible raw grooves in his tender skin. The pale blue pyjamas with the puppy print, failed to diminish the pallor of his undamaged skin. He smiled weakly at them when they walked in to the room.

Kaydee approached the bed slowly, holding tight to her grandmother's hand. "Does it hurt bad?" she whispered.

Alvin shook his head. "Not too much now," he said but his eyelids were heavy and his speech somewhat slurred.

"The doctor says you can come home soon," Kaydee tried to sound cheery and brave. "He said you need a lot of rest."

Alvin was fighting to stay awake. Katreena could see him struggling against the effect of the drug Dr. Walley had told them about. "We are going to go home and let you sleep now. We'll come back and pick you up when you're ready to come home."

Gently, Kaydee touched Alvin's bruised face. "I can hardly wait. I'll take good care of you, Alvin. I promise." Then, seeing that Alvin had already drifted off to sleep, she stopped talking and glanced up at her grandmother.

"It's okay, honey. The medicine they gave him is making him sleep. The medicine makes the pain go away. He's all right. Let's let him sleep now." Katreena whispered reassuringly and then, quietly, they tiptoed out the door.

Alvin was scheduled to come home the following afternoon. Katreena had stayed over, foregoing her plans to go home, unpack and re-establish herself in her own home after a two-month absence. She was concerned for Alvin, but she was also curious about Michael's behaviour in the aftermath of this accident. Michael always needed a scapegoat but he had none this time. Kaydee's predisposition to accepting responsibility for her little brother's safety may make her vulnerable to Michael's unreasonable demands for his care at this time.

Michael said nothing all the way home, apparently absorbed in his own world. No one dared question him for fear of releasing a torrent of emotions that might get out of hand for everybody. Both Helen and Katreena were fearful that he might mistake their questions for accusations and get angry. Since he was obviously not going to volunteer any information about the accident they drove home in silence, compelled to be content with the scant information Katreena had provided. At home, Michael went straight to the shop and stayed there till evening, not even coming in for supper when Katreena called him, stating he was not hungry. When he did come in late in the evening, he went straight to the bathroom, cleaned up, ate the supper Helen put out for him then, ignoring everyone, he went to bed without a word to anyone.

The next morning they called the hospital and were assured Alvin was doing fine and would be released at two o'clock. Hearing the news, Michael again withdrew to the safety of the shop leaving the women to their own speculation about his conduct. His silence was unnerving but, given his unpredictable and volatile nature, they felt a sense of relief that, perhaps, this was better than any alternative behaviour. They spoke in hushed tones of the events that had transpired in the last twenty-four hours and wondered what the coming days would bring in light of those events.

Michael insisted Helen stay home with the kids while Katreena drove him to the hospital to pick up Alvin. Kaydee, he ignored completely. They drove in silence until they got to town, then Michael asked Katreena to stop at K-Mart, where he picked up a large brown teddy bear with embroidered eyes and nose.

"Those beaded eyes are dangerous for kids. Alvin knows enough not to take stuff like that into his mouth but with the smaller girls in the house, why take chances?"

"Yes, why?" Katreena agreed, adding to herself silently. "Like you will let the girls even touch that bear." But she said no more, mutely noting that it was remarkable for Michael to even consider the girls in the first place. Could it be that Michael had somehow undergone a character transformation? "Yea, right. Dream on," She told herself grimly.

At the hospital, Michael greeted Alvin with a cheerful but cautious hug.

"How is my little man today? Did you get a good sleep? Does anything hurt? Are you ready to come home?" When Alvin nodded wordlessly, Michael became more subdued but maintained his upbeat tone.

"Where are your clothes? Let me help you dress up and we'll be on our way. I bought you a surprise. Here, open this package. I hope you like it."

When Alvin saw the bear, his eyes registered approval but not the excitement Michael seemed to have hoped for. He became more solicitous as he helped Alvin dress. As they walked past the office, the nurse asked him to come in. He went in, deliberately closing the door behind him so Katreena could not follow him. After a few moments, he emerged and without a word picked up Alvin in his arms and walked off toward the door. Katreena followed.

He could not do enough for Alvin. He carefully opened the car door and bent down to slide the seat as far back as it would go. Then, careful not to cause Alvin any discomfort, he positioned himself into the seat with Alvin on his lap. As Katreena manoeuvred the car out of the parking lot, she could see Michael bracing himself against the side to protect Alvin from the sway and she eased up on the accelerator. "Careful," she told herself. "Take your time. No need to hurry now."

"You'll have to take it easy for a few days, son, but when the fair comes to town in a couple of weeks, you and me are gonna take it in. You can go on any ride you want. We are going to have a wonderful time. You just wait and see. You just get good and strong and healthy. We're gonna do lots of things together. Maybe one day we may even go fishing. Just you and me, son. Would you like that, huh son?"

Alvin turned a languid countenance to Michael and replied listlessly, "I don't know. I never been out fishing before. I don't know how."

"I'll teach you son. You'll like it, you'll see. Maybe we will even buy a boat."

Michael kept talking to Alvin all the way home, holding him close, rocking him ever so gently. Alvin sat quietly, obviously still in some discomfort, though he had received a pain killer right after lunch. Katreena said nothing, concentrating on her driving, fascinated by this tender side of Michael that she had been unaware of. She had almost come to the conclusion that Michael, in his zeal to impress and brag and exaggerate every situation for the purpose of emphasizing his own importance, was incapable of genuine love. But this was no put-on. This was the real thing. Katreena was pleasantly surprised. She could actually like this Michael!

They pulled into the driveway and as they started to get out of the car, Kaydee came running to greet them, obviously excited to see her little brother.

"Don't you touch him!" Michael barked and sharply turned to keep Alvin out of her reach. Kaydee's face fell and she froze in her tracks. Michael, still holding Alvin in his arms deliberately walked around her and went into the house. Katreena tensed. So much for Michael's tender side. She should have known it was too good to be true. Winking nonchalantly at Kaydee, she gently took her hand and led her to the house.

"Get some pillows on that couch and put a clean sheet on it. What's the matter with you people? Kaydee, what are you waiting for, stupid? Get a move on and stop that snivelling." Kaydee took off running to get the linens.

"But we prepared the bed for him in case he wanted to lie down," Helen interjected. "I thought..."

"You thought? You thought! You mean, you didn't think! You expect him to lie there in bed by himself while everyone else is here?" Michael spat in disgust. "How would you like to be banished out of sight? Kaydee!! What the hell is keeping that dimwit?"

Katreena clenched her teeth. She looked at Helen who was cowering in the corner. Alvin and Jaynee remained quiet, eyes wide, lips tightly closed. But even Alvin, supposedly safe in his father's arms, looked uneasy. Things were back to normal. This was it. The routine rampages, the yelling, the belittling, the name-calling. Katreena couldn't take it anymore.

"Alright Michael, that's enough. That was uncalled for and you know it." Michael glared at her.

"Well, there you go mollycoddling them again. This should have been ready for him when he got home. They had the time to do it, but I guess without being told what to do, they wouldn't know, would they?" Michael gave Katreena a look that clearly said "Point made."

Alvin, sensing that he was the cause of the problem, promptly interjected, "It's okay Dad, I can wait. I don't mind, really."

"You're gotta get proper care, Alvin. You need to get better soon. The fair, you know."

Kaydee arrived with a sheet, a pillow, and a blanket. Katreena helped her unfold it and together they made up a bed for Alvin on the couch. Helen held back dejectedly, standing quietly in the corner, her pale face and gray hair contrasting sharply against the lush green pothos vine that wound its way on the trellis behind her. She said nothing and Kaydee, sensing this to be the best strategy for the moment went to stand beside her. Katreena was fuming. She would have liked to have given Michael a piece of her mind but did not wish to create a scene in front of the children. It was bad enough to have him ranting and roaring. She was not going to stoop to his level.

Michael propped Alvin up comfortably, tucked the new teddy bear into his arms and ordered Helen to get him some hot chocolate and cookies.

"We're going to have your special pizza for supper tonight, son. How is that gonna be?"

For the first time since they had walked into the house, Alvin's face registered a response to the circumstances around him but, though he nodded his agreement unenthusiastically, he was still uneasy about the tension that hung in the room like smoke from a smouldering log, threatening to explode into roaring flames at any moment.

Michael turned to Helen. "I've got to get that sprayer ready for tomorrow. That north field is starting to show mustard and those seventy acres across the creek need tillage. The hay will be ready for cutting and the fences will have to be checked so you better arrange your schedules accordingly." This was directed at Helen but obviously meant for Katreena, so she would be prepared to stay with the kids because Helen was needed in the fields.

Then, kneeling down beside Alvin, he kissed him on the forehead. "Take care of those bruises, son, and heal up fast. We have a fair to go to in a couple of weeks, remember. I'll see you later."

Once up, he glared at Kaydee. "You stay close by in case he needs anything. And none of your shenanigans like goofing off or chasing out to some God forsaken place. If he wants something, you get it for him, you hear me?" He shook his finger menacingly in her direction. "And don't you touch him. I don't want you doing anything to hurt him, understand?" Ignoring Katreena's accusing stare completely, he stalked out of the room.

From the doorway, he called to Helen. "You get going at that pizza. Supper better be on time. That boy needs nourishment! Put that retard to work. It should keep her out of trouble."

As soon as the door closed behind Michael, the atmosphere in the room changed. The tension lifted from the stone faces. Helen's face did not actually show a smile like those of her children but her relief was evident.

Kaydee was on her knees beside Alvin immediately, her eyes full of concern. Helen and Jaynee were right beside her. Katreena noticed the tears running silently down Helen's cheek, as she begged softly, "Alvin, can you tell us what happened and how?"

Four sets of eyes and four sets of ears were intently tuned in on him and for the first time since the accident, Alvin retraced the events of the previous day. Till now, he had not bothered to think about it.

"Well, Daddy was fuelling up the tractor and I wanted to climb up to him but Daddy did not see me and he started backing up so the tractor pushed me down and I couldn't get up and the wheel rolled over me. And the next thing I knew I was in the hospital and I hurt all over." Alvin stopped and glanced from one astonished face to the other. "Honest, that's all I remember!"

A dead silence engulfed the room as the incredible picture formulated in the minds of Helen, Kaydee, and Katreena.

Kaydee was the first to break the spell. "Does it still hurt badly, Alvin?"

Alvin smiled, first at Kaydee and then looking up at his mother, his grandmother and even poor little Jaynee who stood by, in awe, not quite sure what was going on.

"Naw, it's all right, really. It hurts a little but that nice doctor and those nurses were so kind to me. They said it's going to get better. Look, they gave me this little toy tractor. They said it's safe to play with this one."

Proudly, unclenching his fist, he produced a tiny little red toy so small that they had not noticed it before. He waved it up at them letting them inspect it.

"Here Kaydee, you can look at it. It's alright, honest. And I'm already better. It hurt a lot yesterday, but today I'm better already. Honest, I am. Really!" He gazed up at them with that beguiling smile, willing them to believe him. He certainly was not one for self-pity or self-indulgence. He didn't want any pampering.

"What a kid!" Katreena marvelled to Helen who nodded proudly in agreement because she was too choked up to talk.

"You must promise me that you will never go near the tractor when it's running. Stay far away, understand?" Helen choked.

"Yes, mother, I promise. I know Daddy didn't see me. I should have been more careful. I'm sorry, honest. I won't do it again. I'm sorry." His repeated simple apology to his distraught mother and his doting older sister touched Katreena's heart. Even at his young age, he was more concerned about them than about himself. He certainly didn't take after his father!

Kaydee was chopping the onions for the pizza while Helen kneaded the dough and Katreena prepared the meats and other ingredients. Jaynee was peacefully playing on the living room floor with some game and Dayna wiggled contentedly in the jolly jumper. Their easy laughter mixed with Alvin's weak chuckles now and then. Katreena felt a kind of comfortable camaraderie working with her daughter and granddaughter. In a low, gentle voice, so the kids wouldn't hear, she tried to broach the decade-old subject for the hundredth time.

"You really shouldn't let Michael talk to you and the kids that way, Helen. It is very degrading. He is..."

"Mother, he doesn't mean any harm. That is just the way he is. He is my husband. I married him. I promised to love, honour, and obey. Please don't make trouble."

"I'm not making trouble, honey, but look at what he has done to you. Can't you see? Please sweetheart, it hurts me to see him treat you and the kids that way."

"Mother, it hurts me when you talk like this. I married him. I did that and I have to live with it! That is the way he is. Please don't make trouble. Please, Mother." The urgency of her appeal tugged at the very core of Katreena's heart.

"Alright, sweetheart, alright." Katreena finished in exasperation. "I won't say another word. I'll do whatever you want. I will support you no matter what you do. But promise that you won't hesitate to come to me if you need help – with anything. I love you and the kids, honey. Please remember that, sweetheart." Instinctively, she came around the table and put her arms around her daughter. Helen leaned her head onto Katreena's shoulder.

"I promise, Mother. But we'll be all right." Then, almost inaudibly to herself she added, "Somehow..."

Kaydee had listened to this discourse in silence. She had heard it before, both sides of it, but she never got involved. She was just Kaydee, the retard. What could she have to contribute? This was the way it had to be. Adults knew best.

After supper, Katreena left for Lanavale.

"I'll be back on Thursday to stay with the kids," she promised.

Chapter 6

Katreena's own house needed attention after her two-month absence. Her suitcases were still in the bedroom, waiting to be unpacked. She had tons of laundry to do and although Janine and Vance had been especially great at maintaining the lawn and flower beds, she could hardly expect them to continue now that she was home. Michael will just have to wait a couple of days.

Janine and Vance were her good friends and neighbours that took care of her place when she was away. She hadn't even talked much to them yet, except to drop in briefly to let them know she was home and deliver the matching hand-made wool sweaters she had brought for them from the old woman who lived in the quaint little thatched cottage on the moor of the windblown Arran Islands, off the Irish coast.

The ride home was pleasant, peaceful. Deliberately she forced all thoughts of the farm, and the family out of her mind. Worrying about them was a waste of time if there was no prospect of a solution. Besides, she had Dusty Duganyk to think about now. The thought gave her a soft warm feeling and she felt a tingle of excitement spread through her body as his broad, engaging, smile flashed across her memory.

She remembered them standing in the tower above the majestic cliffs of Mohair in Ireland, Dusty's arm casually around her shoulders, listening to the thundering waves of the ocean below them. Neither one of them had traveled abroad before and every new sight and sound had enthralled them. A quiver ran up her spine, as she recalled him holding her while she kissed the Blarney Stone at Blarney Castle in Ireland. She smiled at the memory of the supper at the Cardiff Castle in Wales when Dusty's waitress had become so fascinated by his story about catching lake trout, that she had overfilled his pewter mug with mead, the Welsh traditional beverage. The hard-working waitresses, who carried the huge cast iron pots full of soup on one arm and ladled it onto their plates with the other, later entertained them with their singing after the supper and joked with them as if they were intimate friends.

Dusty had made everything on the trip so unforgettable: the gondola ride down the canals of Venice with guys serenading them as they floated along under the Bridge of Sighs; getting lost in the crushing crowd in the Sistine Chapel in Rome because they were so fascinated by the ceiling paintings they failed to watch where their group went; climbing the Tower of Pisa and waving to their tour mates far down below; standing in the rain at the Coliseum in Rome. She recalled how he had taken her sun visor hat off when they went on the Rhine cruise in Germany because he said he didn't want her to miss the castles along the banks of the river. His engaging company made the trip for her. Katreena wished she could go back to those carefree days.

Janine was working by her roses and waved to Katreena as she pulled into the driveway.

"Welcome back, Katty. How is your family?" she called from across the lane.

Katreena really did not wish to get into it at this time but she knew that she would feel even less like it later so she went over to explain to her why she had not come right back on Sunday like she had promised she would.

Janine was aware of the tension between Katreena and Michael. She had been a close confidante for Katreena through grief, frustration, and triumph. Janine shared Katreena's agony over Helen's troubled marriage; her grief about the miscarriages; her pain about the missed vacation last year; and Janine had cheered triumphantly as she helped her pack for that vacation this year. Katreena also knew that Janine would be there with enthusiastic support when she heard about Dusty. But it was Michael's behaviour, and not Dusty's that dominated Katreena's emotions now, much to her own anguish, and Katreena spilled her guts to her faithful friend.

"He's worse than ever, Janine," Katreena confided. "Honest, sometimes he acts like a spoiled brat throwing tantrums all the time. I'd like to throttle him but Helen just keeps saying, 'Don't make any trouble.' He's so mean to Kaydee, it's all I can do to grit my teeth and not speak out. I don't want to cause a war in front of the children and it's really not my place to tell them how to raise a family but there are times when I'd like to sic Family Services on him for vicious verbal abuse. Ugh!" Katreena shuddered as she concluded her account of the events that had kept her at the farm the last couple of days.

Janine let her vent. This was not the first time and obviously would not be the last. The situation on the farm was beyond what Janine could comprehend. She had met Michael, Helen, Kaydee and the other kids. She had witnessed enough scenes with Michael's arrogant and abhorrent behaviour to know that Katreena was not exaggerating. She would not have believed it otherwise; very few people would have. Michael was an enigma, one of a kind, and thank God for that. The world could not handle too many Michael Boyers. It would self-destruct. The other part that was so unbelievable was that Helen was allowing him to get away with it. Helen was an enigma too. No wonder Katreena felt so frustrated!

"You do what you have to do and stay as long as you have to. Don't worry about your place. We'll take care of things here. I can only imagine what you must be going through. Phew, what a homecoming!" Janine shook her head. "I hope Alvin will be all right."

"I think he will be. He's a little trooper and he's being so brave about it. He says it doesn't hurt much but you can see him wince. It will slow him down for a while but I'm sure that he'll be all right in a week or two. The doctor said it is just severe bruising but no permanent damage because he is so young. Honestly, he is positively unbelievable!"

"That's great, Katty. Just put it out of your mind for now. Go home, unpack, go to bed and have a good night's sleep. Forget about Michael. You cannot change him and obviously you cannot change the situation at this point so until you can, forget about it."

"You're right Janine. Thanks for letting me vent. What would I do without you?"

"I'm here for you and if you ever want to shoot that son-in-law of yours in the you-know-where, I'll be there to help you point the gun. The pleasure will be all mine too so just never hesitate to ask for help, you hear?"

"Thanks, pal. You never know when I may take you up on your offer, you know. Goodnight. I'll see you tomorrow."

The phone was ringing when she got home. "Well, you're a tough lady to track. I've been calling since ten this morning. I had to come to town for the day and I thought we'd get together for a cup of coffee. I thought you had work to catch up with at home and could not find any time for me! Were you out gallivanting somewhere, shifting both your work, and me, to the back burner?" Dusty teased, his voice tenderly familiar.

Katreena's heart skipped a beat. Dusty Duganyk had been her source of strength throughout the trip and had brought much laughter to her days. Her attraction for him was undeniable. She missed him and she knew she wanted to keep seeing this man who so unabashedly adored her. His obvious shyness was appealing but he continued to pursue her, his interest unwavering. Here was an opportunity to find out whether this man was a keeper. He was easy to talk to, and gave her every reason to believe he was sincere.

"Actually, Dusty, there have been some problems out at KD Acres since I got back but it's too long a story for the phone. Why don't you come by the house? I don't feel like going out right now but if you give me a few minutes..."

"I'll be right there," Dusty said eagerly. "Thank you for seeing me, Katreena."

Katreena flew to the bathroom. No time for a shower, but she brushed her hair, did a quick adjustment to her makeup, then raced to the closet and snatched the blue floral cotton shift with the wide white belt that flattered her tall frame so well. She flushed with the realization that she was preening for Dusty and was surprised at her eagerness to please him. Finally she eyed herself in the mirror. "Ahh. Simple, yet elegant enough for a late evening coffee call!"

Hurriedly, she stashed her still-unopened suitcases neatly behind the chiffonier in the bedroom and had just put the coffee on when the doorbell rang. At the door Dusty stood smiling broadly, a huge bouquet of pink lilies and white baby's breath in his hand. He was wearing the white tee-shirt with the small blue Eiffel Tower embroidered just below his left shoulder. Katreena remembered the day he bought the shirt. They had just come down from the Tower on that hot afternoon in Paris and the souvenir shops were right in the tower's shadow. He had rummaged through piles of tee-shirts to find just the right one. He wanted a keepsake but a somewhat inconspicuous one. Now, standing here in her doorway, his blue slacks accentuating his tall lean frame, his sandy hair somewhat tousled, Katreena clearly understood why she was so eager for this relationship to develop.

Handing her the flowers, he grinned, "Nice to see you again. You're looking good."

Katreena blushed. Perhaps she had fussed too much. Suddenly she felt self-conscious. They had had such a casual and fun relationship on the tour, yet now, here on her own turf, where she should have been more at ease, calmness eluded her.

"They're beautiful, but you shouldn't have." She took the flowers as he stepped inside.

"Actually I should have, but I didn't. I cheated." Dusty confessed. "Truth is, these are from my own garden. I told you that gardening is one of my passions. The sin I must confess to is presuming that you would see me. You know that 'ships that pass in the night' thing. I took a chance, hoping that I could drop them off this morning. In fact, these poor guys have been sitting in a hot car all day so they aren't as fresh as I'd have liked them to be. I'm sorry."

"Oh, don't be sorry. They're gorgeous and they'll perk up in no time with a drink of fresh cool water. Have a seat," Katreena indicated towards the living room. "I'll get us some coffee as soon as I make these beauties comfortable."

She arranged the flowers in a large crystal vase, filled it with water and placed it on the cherrywood dining room table. She stood back and admired them appreciatively.

"Oh Dusty, aren't they just lovely? Thank you so very much. Your garden must be a fascinating dream place."

"Yes, I admit I love it. Ever since I retired, I spend a great deal of time there. I am lucky to have enough room to experiment with the different varieties of plants and I love lilies. They are easy to grow and adapt to almost any conditions. They don't require much pampering, either so I can enjoy their beauty without devoting all my time to them. You'll have to come see my garden one of these days. I think you'd enjoy it."

"I'm sure I would. I love flowers, but my space is so finite on this lot, that I must budget carefully to accommodate all my gardening passions. I will not give up my salad garden, so my sunny back yard must be devoted to vegetables. Most flowers require sunlight, and the tall trees in my front yard do not allow it to penetrate, so I am limited to the few plants that do well in a shaded area. I also cannot dedicate too many hours to my garden, because I spend so much time helping my daughter and her family at KD Acres."

Katreena had not told him anything about Helen and Michael or about the farm before now. She had not wanted anything unpleasant to intrude on their carefree time but now the time had come to lay the cards on the table. If they were going to see each other at all, he would have to be prepared to make allowances for the other half of her life. If he could not do that, then their relationship was doomed and it would be best to find that out now rather than later.

"Tell me about that, Katreena." Dusty sounded genuinely interested, not at all guarded. "You never talked about your family before. I'd like to hear about them."

Katreena put the two mugs of coffee, cream, and sugar on a tray and brought them to the coffee table. Handing Dusty his coffee, she offered him the sugar and cream which she knew he took, then, sitting down on the couch facing him, she sighed.

"It's a long story but I'll try to condense it as best I can. I must warn you, though, it may not be the most pleasant one you've heard."

"Look, it can't be that bad and I assure you I don't have anyone waiting for me anywhere so take your time." Then, to put her at ease he added, "Who knows, I may even be able to help. I wouldn't mind. No, actually, I really would like to try," he clarified.

Slowly, methodically, Katreena unfolded the patchwork of her life. She told him about Daniel, their life together, his tragic accident and subsequent death. She explained how devastated she had been and how her teaching career had offered her a haven in her grief. She recounted how Michael had filled the gap with the farm work when she was so overwhelmed by it and how she, in her grief, had failed to foresee the impending danger of his invasion into their vulnerable lives until it was too late and Helen was already married.

"I should never have allowed that marriage to take place, even though Helen was pregnant. She was only nineteen," Katreena recalled, incensed with frustration. "Pregnancy was not a good enough reason for her to marry him though Helen insisted that she was in love with him. I should have hired someone to do the farming or rented the land out, and we certainly could have raised the baby ourselves and saved Helen all that suffering. I blame myself for it all. I just wasn't functioning at full capacity at that time, and now we're all paying for it, most especially, Helen and the kids. Every mistake I've made seems to have multiplied a thousand-fold. Instead of things getting better, they keep getting worse."

Katreena told Dusty about Michael's arrogance, his demeaning dictatorial tactics, his demoralizing verbal abuse, and his overbearing attitude. "I cannot do any more than help them in a physical sense, like babysit or take some of the physical load off Helen and Kaydee but I cannot protect them from Michael's verbal abuse nor can I alleviate their emotional suffering. Helen is so blindly loyal to him that she refuses to even listen to reason. And that, too, may be my fault. Daniel and I always taught her that marriage was sacred and that a promise made to God was something to be honoured above all else. I could never have imagined a scenario in which I would personally advocate breaking a promise to God. Yet, I doubt that even God would ask her to honour her promise under those conditions." Katreena sighed. "Sometimes I get so outraged, I could explode. Instead I have to keep quiet. It hurts!"

Dusty sat silent and still as he listened to Katreena's story. When she finished, he got up from the chair he was sitting in and came to sit beside her on the couch. His hazel eyes full of concern, he took her hands in his.

"That was what you were carrying on your shoulders those first few weeks of the tour, wasn't it? I knew there was something major troubling you, but then you seemed to snap out of it and I thought the problem had gone away. But it didn't go away, did it?"

"No, it didn't." She then recounted the events of the last couple of days at the farm. "And he is more nasty to Kaydee now than he ever was," she finished in exasperation.

He squeezed her hand. "Don't worry, we'll lick this somehow. Together, we'll do it together. Because I'd like to be there with you if you will allow me."

Katreena felt her onerous spirit lift a little as she unburdened herself to him.

"Thank you," she said emotionally, choking over the lump in her throat.

Seeing her so close to tears, Dusty put his arm around her shoulders and gave a gentle squeeze.

"When do you have to go back there?"

"Well, I want to finish unpacking and run some laundry and then catch up with a few things around here, but I promised I'd be back there on Thursday. Michael has some fieldwork for Helen to do, so I'll be staying with the children. They had a neighbour doing that while I was away, and it seems to have been working out quite well, but now that I'm back, he's going to give Helen a hard time if he has to ask the neighbour to babysit."

Dusty nodded understandingly. "I'd like to help. Would you mind if I drove out to KD Acres to meet the family?"

Katreena thought about it. She had not considered getting Dusty involved but she certainly could use an outside opinion, especially one from a man's perspective. Maybe even Michael could respect an opinion offered by an outsider, a male outsider, at that. Michael was always trying to impress Fred Archer, Joe Drapanik, and Tom Ladduck. Maybe... She thought it over.

"Perhaps not at this time. I'll try to broach the subject with Helen and see if I can ascertain her possible reaction. I should be home for the weekend and we'll decide then. Would you mind?"

"Of course not, Katreena. You do what you think is best. Just remember I'm here for you. I'd like to help any way I can. Please call me as soon as you get back to town, okay?" He handed her a slip of paper with his phone number and address on it.

They finished their coffee and Dusty left, assuring her that all would be well.

Thursday morning arrived too soon. Katreena had barely had time to finish her laundry, restock the kitchen, pay her bills, enjoy some fresh salads from the garden and mow her lawn. Thank heavens, Vance and Janine had kept the weeds down in the flowers and garden. She hardly had had time to think, as she hurried from one task to another, driven by determination to leave no job unfinished for the weekend. She kept in touch with the family by phone, and Helen and Kaydee assured her that all was well with Alvin and that he was recuperating comfortably.

With a heavy heart, Katreena covered the forty miles back to KD Acres. "It shouldn't be this way," she told herself. "Life should be pleasant. Oh why couldn't Helen have married some decent fellow who loved her, respected her, and who adored all his children equally, male or female?" It could have been so nice to be going back to the farm to spend a day with a happy, normal family that enjoyed everyday things together.

Michael was out in the shed when Katreena pulled in to the yard and she was glad she didn't have to see him. She wanted to start the day on a pleasant note. She hurried into the house where Helen was already dressed in her work jeans and ready for the field. Kaydee was washing up Jaynee after her breakfast but Alvin and Dayna were still asleep.

Katreena kissed Helen, Kaydee and Jaynee, took the tea towel from Helen, and said gently, "You go help Michael hook up. Kaydee and I will take care of things around here now. Anything special I should know about? Was there anything specific you wanted for lunch?"

"No, not really. You know where everything is. We'll be fine with whatever you make." Katreena had done this many times before and Helen knew she required no direction.

"We'll see you at noon then. Have a good day."

A pang of regret and reproach enveloped Katreena at the relief she experienced to see Helen leave the house, yet the sooner the machinery was hooked up and ready to go, the less likely it was that Michael would come back to the house to create a scene. "It is a legitimate relief," she assured herself, nonetheless her sense of shame and guilt continued to gnaw at her.

It wasn't long before they heard the roar of the tractors and soon, Helen drove out of the yard with the cultivator behind her and Michael followed with the haybine. "Phew," Katreena breathed. "Guaranteed peace for four-and-a-half hours."

Kaydee picked up Jaynee and kissed her, bouncing her up and down as the child giggled. "It's so good to have you back, Granny. Annie is very nice and she's very kind but I like having you stay with us."

"I like having me stay with you too, sweetheart," Katreena gave Kaydee and Jaynee an impulsive hug and a kiss. "I am one very lucky grandma!"

"We love you, Granny," Kaydee declared solemnly, her voice thick with emotion, a pensive, faraway look in her wistful eyes. Jaynee immediately echoed, "Vuv you, Gwanny."

Katreena noted Kaydee's wistfulness. "What the matter, honey? Is anything wrong? Did something happen?" Katreena tensed with apprehension.

"No, not really. It's just that I like having you here. I miss you when you go away."

From the back bedroom, they heard Dayna whimpering and Kaydee immediately put Jaynee down, handed her a small box of miniature toys, and headed for the bedroom. Nonchalantly, Jaynee started taking the toys out of the box and placing them in a row on the floor. Katreena marvelled at the serenity of the child. Cast in this unpredictable and often explosive household, Jaynee seemed blissfully detached from it. The turmoil did not concern her and therefore she just tuned it out, harshness, abuse and negativity, all of it. Her own little world was peaceful, and she was content to keep it that way. "If only we could all follow your example," Katreena sighed.

Kaydee entered with the sleepy-eyed Dayna in her arms and Alvin walking beside her, his hand tightly in Kaydee's.

"Granny!" he called as soon as he saw Katreena. He quickened his step to reach her but Katreena noticed him wince as he reached up to put his arms around her neck.

"Good morning sunshine. How are you feeling today?" Katreena stooped down to him, being careful not to hug him tightly. He was obviously still having considerable discomfort.

Still Alvin put on a brave face and smiled brightly up at her. "I'm getting much better, Granny. Kaydee takes very good care of me."

"Now isn't that nice. All right, let's get you two washed and fed. You must be starved." Katreena was glad for the diversion of purpose. Between her and Kaydee, the second breakfast shift was underway.

Kaydee continued to work with the children, cleaning them up, grooming them, then dressing them. It was a well-rehearsed routine for her. Even at twelve, she was used to taking charge of this schedule of duties. Katreena decided not to interfere when Kaydee put Dayna into the playpen, then brought a blanket, folded it and put it on the floor in the adjoining room, adding a pillow and a couple of picture books nearby for Alvin.

Noting Kaydee's efficiency with approval, Katreena turned her own efforts to the preparation of lunch.

"I'll chop up the vegetables for the soup now and get everything prepared early so we have as little work as possible at the last minute. That will give us time to take the children out into the yard for some games before we have to put the lunch on."

Glancing toward the next room where Alvin, propped up against the pillow, was quietly turning the pages in his children's book, she asked softly, "How has Alvin really been doing?"

"He's alright, Granny. I think Rusko is worse than Alvin is because he misses him so much. Alvin has been sleeping a lot and last night he and Father watched television till late so he slept in this morning. He's not running around much like before, so it must still hurt a lot but I really think he's doing fine. He has some really bad blue marks on his body, but he says they don't hurt very much. Some of them are starting to look green and Father called him "his little Martian." Father has not mentioned that thing with the gunpowder any more. I thought he would have sent me to the sinhole for that but he hasn't mentioned it since that Sunday at the dinner table when you were here." Kaydee ended, speaking in low tones so Alvin would not hear. She sounded relieved but wary, still uncertain that her reprieve would last.

Helen was not protecting Kaydee from Michael and Katreena knew that she herself wasn't there enough to shield her from his abuse. Still there had to be something she could do to provide the poor girl with a buffer against Michael's denigration. But what? How? Why, oh why, oh why did Michael have to be so mean?

By ten o'clock, they had Dayna's playpen out on the deck and had spread the blanket onto the hammock where they had carefully helped Alvin make himself comfortable. With her favourite miniature dolls and accessories beside her, Jaynee was methodically rearranging them according to her personal blueprint, and, as she did so, she kept up a running conversation with them that only she could understand. Alvin and Dayna were dosing while Katreena sat with Kaydee listening to sparrows arguing over territorial rights with robins at the bird bath, while finches and pinesiskins fought for the tiny Niger seeds in the birdfeeder that hung from the maple nearby. They talked in low tones about school and teachers as they watched the humming birds darting among the few remaining old caragana blossoms near the fence and the fresh flowers near the deck. The sun shone warmly from above but the temperatures had not yet reached the range of discomfort. This was a perfect early July day.

The drone of a jet hummed in the sky above them and when they looked for it, they had difficulty locating the tiny silver speck in the vast blue of the southwest heavens. The heady perfume of the roses wafted softly in the almost undetectable breeze and then blended with the fragrances of the other flowers as the zephyr shifted direction. Katreena was overcome with the tranquility of the moment and nostalgia overwhelmed her. Suddenly she missed Daniel, missed him so badly it hurt. Tears welled up in her eyes as she recalled their hopes for their future that day when Helen was twelve. They had just finished the deck the week before and it had been a day very much like today that they had sat on this deck and basked in the glow of their dreams.

Helen had loved books all her life and that spring, she had started keeping a journal. It wasn't quite a diary. She used to read her entries to Katreena and Daniel many times. At times it was in the form of poetry, other times it was in the form of a short story about some specific event. Many times those readings were done right here on this deck where the three of them sat enjoying an hour or two of peace and harmony. Whatever had happened to that journal of Helen's? Did she still have it? Katreena wondered. An idea sprang into her head and a surge of hope pulsed through her brain. That could be the key to their dilemma with Kaydee now. If she could convince Kaydee to start a journal, it may just help her to ease the turmoil in her life. Hummm, maybeee...

"Did your mother ever tell you about the journal she used to keep when she was your age?" Katreena suddenly wanted to know.

"A journal?"

"Yes, a journal. You know, a sort of diary about things that happened. Only it wasn't a secret because she used to read parts of it to your grandfather and me many times while we sat right here on this deck. Sometimes she wrote poems, sometimes stories. Most of the time she just wrote about things she felt, or thought, or wished."

Kaydee looked like she had had the wind knocked out of her.

"Mother...? wrote... a... journal?" Kaydee's astonishment was beyond words as she stared incredulously at her grandmother. "You can't be serious." She gaped at Granny and flatly dismissed the idea as ludicrous.

"No, honest. I am serious. She wrote! A lot! She had tons of poems and quite a few stories. If I'm not mistaken she had the book almost full. Why is that so hard to believe?"

"Well... because Mother is... well, Mother is... well she... she never says much!" Kaydee stared openmouthed at Katreena, completely at a loss for words.

"I'm not making it up, sweetheart. Ask her yourself. She did good writing too. She was co-editor of the school newspaper called *The Social Standard,* and she belonged to the drama club, and the school choir. That was before she married your father, of course. But she used to be good at all of those things. She was a very busy girl at school and she was popular. Everybody liked her. She had lots of friends." Katreena concluded, looking directly into Kaydee's bewildered eyes.

Finally, after a stunned silence, Kaydee, still awed, blurted out, "I'm sorry, Granny, I didn't mean to be rude. I just never knew that Mother could do those things, be those things."

"Well she can, baby, it's just that she doesn't do them at this time. Ask her." And then, as an alarming thought dawned on her, she added, "Just don't say anything when your father is around. Wait until she is alone, okay?"

Kaydee thought that over, then nodded. "Yes, I understand. I promise, Granny." Then, as the significance of this information overcame her, she looked at her grandmother almost accusingly. "Why have you never told me this before?"

"You know, honey, now that you mention it, I wonder why myself. You really know so little about your mother and that is because nobody ever talks about the good times in this house. But that is going to change, sweetheart. I promise. It is time you got to know what your mother was really like."

"What did Mother write? Was it good? Where did she keep it?"

"She wrote many stories and lots and lots of poems and some of them were published in the school paper. As for where she kept it, I don't know. She used to bring it out and read it to us often, right here on this deck."

"Tell me more about Mother," Kaydee begged, now fascinated beyond words.

"We'll have to do that later. Right now it's time to get that lunch ready, or your father will have reason to yell. After lunch." Katreena promised and stood up resolutely. She had a goal now, a ray of hope in this bleak hopelessness and she was determined to pursue it.

"Perhaps you better stay here with the children, just in case they need anything. I can handle things inside the kitchen." With that, she left Kaydee still sitting on the settee, deep in thought, staring into space with a look of wonder in her eyes.

"Mother, a writer," Kaydee said to herself, over and over again. "A writer!" For some reason, knowledge of that secret generated within her a reaction so profound it sent her emotions into a tailspin. The very magnitude of this revelation seemed to empower her. It also provided her with a new-found unmistakable respect for her mother such as she had never experienced before. Still, to Kaydee's regret, they never did get to discuss the journal that afternoon.

Chapter 7

"Mother, Granny said you used to keep a journal when you were my age. Do you still have it?"

The question caught Helen completely off guard. It seemed like it had come so casually out of the blue, but Helen had no idea how long Kaydee had rehearsed this scenario in her mind. She had no idea how patiently she had waited for just this perfect moment when she knew that she would not be interrupted because Father was out in the field, and Alvin, Jaynee, and Dayna were down for their afternoon naps. Alvin, the curious one, had started taking afternoon naps after that terrible Sunday afternoon when the tractor wheel had flattened him to the ground. Kaydee was glad because it gave her private time with Mother; time in which to explore this fascinating aspect of Mother's past life that Kaydee never knew existed.

Last night, just before Granny left for Lanavale, she had warned Kaydee again with a whispered, "Remember, don't let Father hear you asking about the journal," and Kaydee had whispered a fervent, "I promise, Granny," as she kissed her goodbye.

"Do you still have that journal?" Kaydee repeated.

Helen fairly shrivelled under her daughter's scrutiny. She shuddered involuntarily.

Kaydee pushed on. "I'd like to read it."

Turning slowly to face her daughter, Helen's face crumbled.

"I'm sorry, honey. I don't have it anymore."

"Where is it?" Kaydee was like a bulldog. She wasn't going to give up.

Mother's head bowed as tears spilled from her eyes. Kaydee realized how painful this was for her. Kaydee had not seen tears in Mother's eyes except when they heard that Alvin was going to be all right. That was an intense moment. Did this moment carry the same weight? Mother didn't cry often. She was sad all the time, but she didn't cry. But she was crying now!

"What happened to the journal, Mother?" Kaydee had to know.

"Well, you see, your father, well, he doesn't like those kinds of things." Mother's voice trembled and cracked under the strain. She hesitated, weighing each syllable as she continued.

"He thought it was stupid. Especially the poems. He especially hated the poems. He said that they were childish and I shouldn't be wasting time with such foolish things so one day, when he was very angry, he threw it in the fire and it burned. You were a very little girl then. I haven't written anything since. That is why I cannot give it to you to read. It's gone!" She finished with a choking sob.

Kaydee was horrified. She had witnessed so many of Father's rages so often that it was not something of note in her life. But to think that one of them had actually cost her mother the loss of something as precious as her personal memoirs! That was awful. For the first time in her life, Kaydee felt anger and something akin to hatred for her father. All her life he had ridiculed her; had belittled her; had tormented her; her and her mother, and all that time, Kaydee had felt only fear of him. She had never dared to doubt him; never considered the possibility that he was anything less than right, because he was Father. But this was not right! Suddenly she wanted to read her mother's writings. She wanted to know that person that Granny had described; that person who was co-editor of a school paper; who performed in drama clubs; who was popular with the kids in school; who wrote poems and stories and read them to her parents as they sat on the deck. Somehow Mother had taken on a new persona, other than the weak and lifeless coward that Kaydee had assumed her to be.

Kaydee walked over and put her arm around Mother's shoulder. It was a time of enlightenment. Mother was not unfeeling, unthinking, mindless. She needed help, and she, Kaydee, was going to try to help her. But first she had to get all the facts and get them right.

"You let Father burn all your writings?"

"Well you know what he's like when he's angry. It was a Sunday afternoon and I was sitting on the deck writing in the journal. Your father was sleeping on the hammock. You were playing with some blocks when Auggie – you remember Auggie, the dog, was trying to distract you to play with him. As Auggie ran by, he hit the table and knocked over a glass of water. It fell to the floor and broke. Father heard the glass break and woke up. He was very angry and started yelling that I should have been watching you two and not writing in a 'stupid' journal. He just grabbed it from my hand, went into the house and threw it in the woodstove, like a block of wood. It was the only copy I had."

Helen finished and then, seeing Kaydee's face fall, she added quickly. "You were just a baby and Auggie was just playing, but you know how very angry your Father gets."

Kaydee's heart plummeted with overwhelming anguish. It wasn't just the loss of the journal, though she saw that as an irreplaceable loss. But it was much more than that. She felt a sense of intense sorrow for her mother for all the torment she had endured over the years at the hands of someone who could be that cruel. She and Mother, and, perhaps even Granny as well, had let him get away with it. That was not right. That realization infuriated her, but at the same time it filled her with passion and an indomitable resolve to change things.

"I know, Mother, it's okay," Kaydee soothed. "We will find a way to get through this." The sight of her mother sobbing so brokenly tore at Kaydee's heart. Suddenly, Kaydee felt fiercely protective towards her mother. Mother was not a spineless half-wit nor was she an imbecile as Father often called her. Was she weak, or had she been weakened by Father's constant criticism and yelling? Now Kaydee knew that Father was not always right. He was not someone to be respected! This epiphany incensed Kaydee as she reviewed the years of their anguished lives. It was one thing to be obedient, but another thing to let him criticize you all the time. Mother needed help to get back on her feet and once again become the person that Granny had described. And Granny was right. Mother should not let Father treat her that way.

Kaydee needed Granny. Her head was full of questions, accusations and recriminations and she had no avenue on which to vent them. She felt angry and guilty, anxious and terrified all at the same time because she knew that things would never, ever, be the same for her again.

Kaydee put her arm around Mother's waist and leaned her head on her shoulder. "Mother, I'm going to start my own journal. I will write in it every day. I will read it to you sometimes, just like you did for Granny, but I will never let Father see it or know about it." Kaydee wanted to wipe that dejected look off Mother's face. Now that she knew Mother could be a person with such depth, she wanted to draw on it. Somehow, she would make their world into a better place! She had heard Granny speak to Mother many times about "standing up to Michael," but Mother had always told her not to "make trouble." Well, maybe they had to make trouble to fix the trouble in their lives, and, if that was what it took...

It was eleven o'clock when Katreena arrived home late that Thursday night but she felt the need to hear Dusty's voice. She dialled his number nervously, hoping he was not sleeping yet.

"Hope you weren't in bed yet. I took a chance calling this late," she apologized.

"Oh no, I was sitting here reading. I was hoping you'd call. How did everything go?"

"Well, there were no major uproars. Michael and Helen were in the field most of the time so everything was quite peaceful. I think I hit a milestone with Kaydee though, but I don't want to get into it over the phone."

"I'd like to hear about it. Are you free for dinner on Saturday? We'll go to the Olive Garden and then we can step in at the Jade Palace for a few dances. I'm dying for a nice waltz. Put on that long blue crepe that you wore to Pigalli's in Paris. It looks so good on you."

Katreena laughed. "You still want to do that dip, don't you? At least the Jade Palace should have more room for dancing than we had at that club."

Dusty laughed too. He had wanted to dip when they were dancing at that club in Paris but the postage stamp dance floor had been so crowded that the best they could manage was to remain upright. They had waltzed to the music of a three-piece band that had entertained them through dinner and for an hour after. Dusty had held her tight, and she had wondered if the overcrowding had merely afforded him the legitimate excuse for it.

They chatted for a few more minutes, then hung up with plans for Saturday afternoon for five o'clock.

On Saturday, Katreena took extra pains to look her best. She phoned Pheobee's Fashion Emporium and made an appointment to get her hair done at half past three then rushed through her chores, finishing with the vacuuming by noon. After a quick lunch of pasta with a couple of devilled eggs and fresh salad from the garden, she cleaned up the kitchen and checked her blue crepe to make sure it was perfect. Setting it out on the hanger in the spare room, she assembled her undergarments, pantyhose, the fringed white shawl with the lurex thread running through it and the pearl and rhinestone necklace and earrings set she had purchased in Florence. Then running herself a hot bath, she poured a generous amount of the aromatic bath oil into the tub and lay back in the water to soak.

Excitement mounted within her, sending a hot flush to her cheeks that had nothing to do with the hot bath. She reflected on her situation. There was no law that said she should never consider another relationship. She wasn't two-timing Daniel. He was gone. He would want her to go on living. Up until now, she had not done anything about her life because there was no one that interested her but things were different now. She had served her time and now she could start living again. Dusty made the prospect appealing. He was a professional, enjoyed the same things she did and shared her beliefs and her faith. He was a retired stationary engineer, working in northern regions most of the time and moving often, he had not had the opportunity to form lasting relationships, so had never married. That was all she knew about him but then she had known no more about Daniel when she had married him. Katreena's instincts about Dusty's integrity were good, and strong. He seemed genuinely interested in her and sincerely concerned about her family. This may be her one chance for real happiness again. She was ready to take the chance and see where it would lead.

When Dusty arrived, she was coifed, dressed, perfumed, and ready for a night out.

"Wow!" he breathed as he stood there in her doorway, staring openmouthed in admiration. He appeared flustered and shy, like a young teenager who found himself at a loss for words on his first date. Katreena could not help but note his consternation and she found it strangely appealing. It dawned on her that Dusty was not a macho Don Juan who expected her to fall at his feet. He was simply shy and eager to please. Sensing his sincerity, she realized how much she wanted this unpretentious man in her life.

"Wow yourself," she laughed self-consciously, trying to make light of his reaction and the happiness it invoked. This handsome, tall broad-shouldered fellow with the ready smile was nothing to scoff at. His sandy hair brushed back with just enough of a wave to render it full body, his laughing eyes aglow with anticipation; and his lean figure were casting their own spell on her responses. She opened the door wider and bid him come in.

Without taking his eyes off her, he stepped inside.

"I had Nancy, at the Enchanted Garden, make you up a wrist corsage. I knew we could not put one on that dress. The roses are from my garden, of course. I just wanted us to be connected somehow," he admitted shyly, as he opened a small box he was carrying.

"Oh, thank you. That was very sweet of you." She held out her hand and he slipped the elasticized band over her wrist. Two small pink bud roses, surrounded by fine baby's breath and green fern dazzled her with their beauty. "They're lovely, Dusty," she breathed. "Come on in and relax. What time do we have to be there? Do we have a few minutes?"

Dusty was still struggling with his composure. "Perhaps we had better head for the restaurant. I made the reservations for half past five, but there was a snarl in the traffic and I got held up getting here. If parking becomes a problem, well, we don't want to be late."

Katreena picked up her shawl and, taking his arm, they went out to his Buick. As he held the door open for her, Katreena saw Janine working among her rosebushes and waved to her. Janine waved back and stood watching as Dusty came around to the driver's side, got in and they drove off. Tomorrow, Janine would be full of questions, but Katreena knew that she would be congratulating her and encouraging her, too. Janine and

Vance wanted to see her happy. They had been encouraging her to "start living" for years now. She and Daniel had first met them at a Teachers' Christmas Party more than twenty-six years ago and they had been close friends ever since.

"Friend, or just a neighbour?" Dusty had noticed the friendly wave and Janine's scrutiny as they had driven away.

"Janine and Vance have been close friends for twenty-six years, ever since they moved to Lanavale. They're the salt of the earth. You'll have to meet them someday."

"I'd like that." Dusty glanced at her with a grateful smile.

"They've been my anchor for many years. Whenever something happens, good or bad, they're always there for me to laugh or cry with. Sometimes I don't know what I'd have done without them."

"Everyone needs friends like that. You're lucky you have them. I'm glad for you."

They had arrived at the Olive Garden Restaurant, and Dusty manoeuvred the car into the only available spot at the far corner. "This is perfect. It will be easy to get out of when we're ready to go," he said. "We don't want to waste any dancing time. I want to show my beautiful girl off tonight." His smile was shy but appreciative.

Their table was at the far end of the room, enclosed by walls that were topped with stained glass dividers and they entered this alcove through a small ivy covered archway. Katreena had been here only once before, about six years ago, with a Teachers' Retirement Luncheon but she had never seen this part of the restaurant before. Perhaps it had been added since then. She liked the cozy feeling and the ambience the alcove provided. It made her feel like a queen. Outside of the few times when they had gone to some elegant restaurants on the European tour, she hadn't experienced such luxury since Daniel's death. It felt good to be pampered, to be treated like someone special. And it felt good to know that someone like Dusty Duganyk thought her worthy of this kind of treatment.

The prompt and gracious waiter took their order and brought their wine immediately. Waiting for Dusty to sample it, he smiled as Dusty bowed and motioned for Katreena to taste. The fruity flavour was mellow with just a hint of sweetness that tickled her tongue as it warmed its way down her throat. She nodded her approval to the waiter who disappeared discreetly, leaving them alone in their own private little hideaway.

"Now tell me about your trip to the farm, Katreena," Dusty said when they were alone.

Katreena sighed, remembering how relieved she had felt when Helen had left the house. "You know, Dusty, sometimes I feel like such a bitch. I have such a hard time controlling my resentment for Michael that I really despise myself for the things I do because of it." She told him about sending Helen out of the house quickly so she would not have to see Michael and the shame and regret she felt about it. "Talk about the typically critical, bitchy mother-in-law! I know I fit the bill. I hate it and I hate myself, but I honestly don't think I even want to change! Isn't that awful?"

"Oh come on, Katreena. You are not a bitch. From what you describe, I think that son-in-law of yours is some kind of psychopathic control freak. There are people like that, and it's tragic that your daughter got mixed up with one, but stop beating yourself up for wanting something better for her. You wouldn't be normal if you didn't. Now tell me what happened."

Katreena told him about Kaydee. "The teachers have placed her in a Special Education class because she cannot function in the regular classes. Michael is convinced she is retarded, but I do not believe it, though for a while he almost had us convinced she might be. She was so withdrawn and apathetic. But there is a teacher in that Special Ed class, Ed Norchak, who seems to have gotten through that wall somehow. His wife Sandy works with special children and she's been helping him with Kaydee. They told Helen that Kaydee is gifted, and she should be going to the Lawn Haven Academy in Portmont. The wife has even offered to work with Kaydee for a while if Kaydee cannot leave home."

Dusty gave a low whistle. "Pheew! Lawn Haven Academy! That's a pretty prestigious school. These people must really see something in your Kaydee!"

"That's what I thought. Anyway it's just a pipe dream. Michael won't let Kaydee go."

"Have you talked to these people yourself?" Dusty's interest was now keenly peaked.

"No, not yet. Helen only told me about this last Sunday, and I really don't know too much about it at this point. I haven't had a chance to get in touch with the Norchaks so far. But I want to call them and set up an appointment, hopefully next week."

"Yes, do that as soon as you can." Dusty prompted. "I would like to meet the family. Especially Kaydee. Did you get a chance to talk to Helen about me? Honest, Katreena, I might be able to help. I don't know how, but I would like to try."

"Thank you, Dusty. I know you mean well, but I'm really not sure what you can do. However, I do want you to meet the family. I'll talk to them next week. This week was just too hectic to get any communication underway. I promise you, I will arrange it. You will like Kaydee. She is a sweet girl."

Katreena then told Dusty about Helen's journal and how surprised Kaydee had been when she heard about it.

"It's really my fault, to be honest about it. I have always treated Kaydee like she was a child, like she could not understand anything. I must confess that, perhaps, although I hate to admit it, I probably bought into Michael's assessment that Kaydee was somehow deficient. I have never given her the benefit of a doubt. I never discussed Helen with Kaydee. Basically, I was so preoccupied with my aggravation at Helen's plight that I failed to see that Kaydee might be just as affected by that plight, only from a very different perspective. She sees her mother as mentally deficient, and it's my fault for not setting her straight before this."

"Don't fret about it. It's not too late and it appears like you have already set the wheels in motion towards that goal. Do you think Kaydee will question Helen now?"

"Oh, I know she will. But what I am hoping is that Kaydee will take up journaling herself. Purging may give her a buffer against Michael's raving. She needs something to help her tune him out. Like Jaynee. You should see that little kid. Nothing fazes her. It's like she doesn't even hear Michael when he starts to roar. She just gets out of his way and goes on with whatever she was doing, usually humming peacefully to herself, even as Michael rants and raves. I so wish we could all tune him out like that."

"Does Michael ever get angry at her?"

"Only if she does something to irritate him, like spilling something at the table, but that seldom happens. She has pretty well learned to avoid the pitfalls. She's a very quiet and serene child, so you never even know she's there. Mostly Michael just ignores her. It's Alvin who is his pride and joy. The girls don't count. He hates Kaydee because he feels that she was a disgrace to him due to the premature pregnancy and having her put into Special Ed classes just exacerbated the situation. He calls her a retard all the time, often to her face."

They finished their meal and Dusty sat back against the padded back of the seat. "You know, I don't know when I have enjoyed a meal this much. Thank you, Katreena, for accepting my invitation."

"You're welcome, but somehow, I find it hard to believe that the subject of our conversation could have contributed to your pleasant evening. Now be honest, if I didn't bore you to tears, I must have at least depressed you to no end," she laughed.

Dusty took her hand between his two and declared seriously, "Katreena, you will never bore me or depress me. I meant it when I said I'd like to help. I feel your burden. I'd like to take that burden off your shoulders or at least help you carry it. Please let me be there for you."

Moved by the candor in his voice, Katreena studied him for a minute, then, her voice husky, she told him, "You may be getting in way over your head, you know."

"Try me." He challenged solemnly.

"Now how can I refuse a request like that? But when you meet this pernicious family of mine, you can tell me if you still feel the same," she teased with a smile.

"Deal!" Dusty laughed, then, putting some bills on the waiter's tray, he got up, bowed low before her and held out his arm. "Now we have some fancy stepping to do, milady. Let's hit the Jade Palace and trip the light fantastic!"

It was raining Sunday morning but Katreena got up early for the first Mass at St. Joseph's. She preferred the nine o'clock Mass because it did not break up her day. She could go to church and still have the rest of the day for herself. Last night had been wonderful and Dusty had brought her home at twelve forty-five. By mutual agreement, they had decided to call it a night, since they both planned to attend church the next morning. For the afternoon, Dusty said he had to go see his brother's family as they always had Sunday supper together.

"Della is a creature of habit. It's her religion. I'd have to do penance for a year if I messed up her routine without a valid reason," he explained.

At the door, he had held her tight and kissed her tenderly, then, promising to call her the next day, had taken his leave. Katreena had been glad that he had not insisted on coming in. She wanted to take it slow. In fact, they had talked about it briefly while they danced. She didn't want any mistakes. But she had to admit, she missed him already.

After church, she met Janine and Vance for brunch at Chemille's, and, as she had expected, Janine could not contain her curiosity.

"Who was that handsome hunk that took you out last night? Come on. You've been holding out on us. Out with it," Janine commanded as Vance laughed tolerantly at his wife's impudence.

Katreena apologized for not telling them about Dusty before. "It's just that life's been so hectic since I got back," she explained. She told them who Dusty was, how she had met him and his determined pursuit of her. "He's very understanding and patient. He never pushes, but he is persistent. In fact, he just kind of pleads for attention. His shyness is endearing."

"Okay, okay, okay," Janine teased. "I get the picture. He's Mr. Wonderful and I do declare, are those stars I see in them beautiful brown eyes of yours?"

Katreena blushed and hit Janine with her fork. Janine ducked and all three laughed.

It was Vance who went serious on them first. "I'm happy for you, Katreena. He sounds like a nice guy. It's about time you picked up the pieces of your life and put them together with something more worthy than that family of yours. Not that you shouldn't be involved with them, mind you," he added quickly, "but you deserve a life with a bit of real happiness thrown in."

"Amen to that," Janine asserted, her eyes shining with the genuine affection.

Katreena reached for their hands and squeezed them tightly. "Thanks, guys, you're the best. You will get to meet him soon. He's already asked. He saw you last night when you waved to me," Katreena added, answering the unspoken question in Janine's raised eyebrows.

When they arrived home at half past eleven, Katreena sat to work on her mail. She had several letters to answer and now had a few new ones to write to people who had befriended her on the tour. These folks had been so pleasant, she did not want to lose touch with them. Then there were the old friends she needed to phone now that she was back. She had always maintained a close liaison with her fellow teachers, even after she retired and she wanted to preserve these relationships. These were good friends she did not wish to lose.

Chapter 8

Katreena worked well into the afternoon. At three o'clock Dusty called.

"So, did you get enough sleep? Or are you ready for more dancing? You certainly outdid yourself in the energy department last night. You looked like you could keep on going all night and never play out."

"Hello Dusty. Yes, I had plenty of sleep and yes, I probably could have danced longer if the band had kept the music up. But you were pretty good yourself. Seems to me I didn't hear you complaining," she laughed. Then on a serious note, "Thanks for a wonderful evening, Dusty. I love dancing and good music makes me just want to keep on going."

"I'm glad you enjoyed our evening together, Katreena. It was the best time I have had in years and that is not a line! I hope we can do a lot more of that in the future." His voice was husky and serious, but he was pleading again and Katreena smiled. He was so sweet but he was shy and somewhat insecure.

"Well," she told herself, "It sure beats arrogant and egotistical."

"I hope we can do a lot more of that in the future too," she repeated his words and they both laughed. "In fact, mister, I'm already looking forward to it, so you better not keep me waiting too long. I've got to keep in shape, you know." She teased deliberately, wanting to put him at ease, wanting to erase that sound of pleading from his voice. He didn't have to work so hard, she was already under his spell.

"Don't know what you've been doing, lady, but you're in perfect shape any way I look at it."

"Flatterer!" she scolded.

"I was not. I meant every word!" he defended himself fervently. "Anyway, did you get to church this morning or did you sleep in?"

"No way! I was up at eight. After church, I went for breakfast with Janine and Vance, and, like I expected, I got the third degree about 'the handsome hunk' who took me out last night." Katreena envisioned his flushed face and laughed. Few men would blush at a compliment but she was sure that Dusty did. Then, because Dusty remained silent, she added, "Don't worry, those two are in your corner all the way. If you try to get away, they will probably physically drag you back, by the hair on your head if necessary."

"Well, it's nice to know I have some allies I can count on. I'd like to meet them."

"You will," she assured him.

They bantered around a few more minutes then, Dusty got serious.

"I better get over to Wayne's. Della will have my hide if she has to hold dinner on my account. One of these days you'll have to meet them. You going out to the farm this week?"

"I want to call the Norchaks to set up an appointment with them, but I don't want Helen and Michael to know about it, yet. So if the Norchaks give me a time, I will drive out whenever I have to."

"That's a good idea. Good luck, Katreena. Talk to you soon."

As soon as she hung up with Dusty, Katreena looked up the Norchak number in Zelena. A very young sounding voice answered the phone almost immediately.

"Hello. I'd like to speak to Ed or Sandy Norchak, please."

"This is Sandy Norchak. May I ask who's calling please?"

Katreena identified herself and asked if she could meet with them sometime to talk about Kaydee. Sandy Norchak sounded delighted to hear that Kaydee's grandmother wanted to discuss Kaydee's progress with them.

"Oh, Mrs. Banaduk, we are so glad to hear from you. We would love to meet with you and discuss this subject further. Ed and I have been hoping to get together with someone who would listen to our ideas." They made a date for half past two on Monday afternoon and hung up.

Great! It sounded like Sandy Norchak and her husband were very interested in Kaydee's welfare and were quite willing to do whatever was necessary to help. Katreena's hopes soared. Somehow, she felt she now had allies in her corner, the Norchaks, Dusty, and, of course, the ever present Janine and Vance. She could hardly contain her excitement.

A light rain was falling when she got up Monday morning so she busied herself in the house but she was restless and time seemed to crawl. Noon finally arrived and Katreena prepared a light lunch of soup and a sandwich but she was just too nervous to eat. She put on a long sleeved blouse and a pair of casual slacks, brushed her hair for the twentieth time, checked her makeup and glanced at the clock. Twelve twenty-five. Still too early to leave for Zelena. Katreena felt too agitated to sit still. The rain was still pelting down on the sidewalk so she couldn't go putter in the garden or the flowers. She glanced across the street and wondered if Janine and Vance had finished with lunch. Well, finished or not, they were getting company! She needed a diversion to help pass the time. What were friends for if you couldn't impose on them when you needed to? Grabbing a jacket and umbrella, she walked across to their house.

"I hope you're finished with lunch," Katreena told Janine when she answered the door. "I'm too antsy to wait at home alone so you just have to put up with me for an hour or two until I leave for a half past two appointment with the Norchaks in Zelena."

Janine laughed and pulled her inside. "Come on in, you crazy nut."

Time passed quickly there as Katreena briefed her friends on the reason for her anxiety.

"Helen told me that the Norchaks suggested that Kaydee should go to Lawn Haven Academy in Portmont because she is 'gifted,' but Michael wants Kaydee at home to look after the kids. He will never believe that Kaydee is special. I want to talk to the Norchaks myself and hear what they have to say. They seem genuinely interested in Kaydee. I need to talk to them. Kaydee deserves a break and this may be it."

Vance and Janine listened as Katreena informed them of the possibilities and the ramifications of this new development. With surprise and enthusiasm, they discussed the situation. At twenty minutes to two, they wished her good luck and Katreena left for Zelena.

Katreena arrived at the Norchaks a few minutes early but they were already waiting for her. The modest white bungalow with the aqua trim and shutters was easy to spot and the small sundeck on its east side was neat and cozy. The wrought iron settee and two chairs at the matching white table left limited space for extras. The house, though not exactly new, was well maintained and the landscaping was pleasing though unpretentious. The perfect starter home for a young couple, Katreena decided. The flowers around the house bowed under the weight of the rain but the grass was lapping up the moisture eagerly.

As Katreena approached, Ed came out to meet her, his hand extended in greeting.

"Welcome to our humble abode, Mrs. Banaduk. We are so glad you were able to come." He held the door for her and she entered the homey country kitchen with lacy white curtains and white painted cupboards complimenting the soft pastel of green stripes on the wallpaper. A round oak table and chairs sat in the middle of the room with a crystal vase full of fresh garden flowers. Beyond an arched doorway, a contemporary looking living room beckoned with its heavily padded couch upholstered in a delicate miniature-rose-print on an off-white background.

"Make yourself at home," Ed invited, motioning Katreena to one of the chairs in the living room as he sat across from her. Sandy followed with three glasses of iced tea on a tray.

"Somewhat of a dreary day, but it gives us a chance to get caught up with housework. We try to spend as much time outdoors as possible in nice weather, even if it means doing paperwork on the deck. Summer time is too short and too precious to waste but the gardens and flowers, and, of course, the lawn, require rain." Sandy spoke casually, obviously at ease with her visitor and Katreena was glad of the spirit of friendship this opportunity presented.

"Thank you," Katreena accepted the beverage and rearranged the cushions behind her back. "I will not take up too much of your time, but I understand you told Helen that Kaydee has a special need and I would like to hear more about it. Perhaps I may be in a position to do something in that regard."

"Kaydee is special and we would like to help her in any way we can," Ed said eagerly with a cautious look at his wife. It was easy to see that the couple had discussed the issue before and they welcomed the opportunity to test their ideas on a receptive and supportive audience.

"We think that Kaydee is very bright but has trouble expressing herself. She seems very apprehensive and timid, but she is definitely not retarded." Ed Norchak added that last part emphatically. Careful not to overstep his authority, he was hesitant and wanted to know Katreena's slant on the subject before proceeding.

"I have always thought that Kaydee was bright. But I agree with you that she has been very timid and almost backward in articulating her thoughts. Her apprehension is understandable if you knew her home situation." Katreena spoke candidly. She wondered if she should disclose the truth about what Kaydee was going through. Then, realizing that this was probably the only chance that Kaydee may have at a good life, she plunged forward.

"I'm not sure if you are truly aware of the situation. You see, my son-in-law is very rough on Kaydee. He is something of a control freak and he terrorizes her and belittles her constantly. I am afraid his endless verbal abuse has forced her to suppress her emotions and repress her mentality just to maintain a semblance of peace in her life."

Ed and Sandy Norchak exchanged knowing glances. "We suspected as much." Sandy's eyes were riveted on Katreena. She had obviously worried about criticizing Michael to Katreena, not knowing how that kind of accusation would go over. Now she seemed visibly relieved to find that Katreena herself, had volunteered this information.

Ed was also relieved that he could finally voice his opinion openly. "In this past year of working with Kaydee, we have learned many things, some from Kaydee's inadvertent remarks and some from people in the neighbourhood. We weren't being nosey, honest, but we did not wish to make any judgments or decisions until we had checked out all the facts. We also talked at length with Mrs. Boyer. We feel that Kaydee suppresses her feelings so much because of her preoccupation with her fear, anxiety and a conviction of her own worthlessness. We think that if we can break through that barrier of unease that is troubling her, she could do very well in school. She is a voracious reader, but her reluctance to mix with other children has earned her a misguided reputation of being mentally deficient. That, she is not! We believe that if she were in a different environment, she might have a chance to excel. We are quite convinced that her academic lack of progress stems from her situation at home."

Katreena sighed. Here was someone who shared her conviction. Perhaps by pooling their knowledge and resources, they might be able to ease Kaydee's burden and maybe even tap into her latent learning potential. Certainly the possibilities were very encouraging.

"I agree with you whole-heartedly. I have always felt that Kaydee was capable of much more than what we've been giving her credit for, but I must confess I've been totally impotent when it came to doing something constructive to remedy her situation. I have talked to Helen many times but she remains loyal to Michael and I hate to cause more friction in that home than there already is. Michael is very authoritative and he views any criticism of his behaviour as an attempt to undermine that authority. Consequently, he retaliates with more abuse. Every time I try to help, I create more problems for them. I honestly don't know what to do anymore." Katreena finished helplessly. She had never analyzed the situation this thoroughly, even to Janine who was a longtime friend. Now, here she was, baring her soul and exposing her ignominious family secret to total strangers. She felt disloyal for revealing Helen's weakness but relieved to have the problem out in the open.

"We understand your position, Mrs. Banaduk, and we sympathize with your difficulty, but there must be something we can do to lessen the damage this is doing to Kaydee. She has already lost more than a good couple of years of her education. It's unfair to let that continue. She's a good girl and she deserves a decent chance." Ed Norchak was pleading now. Katreena felt an overwhelming sense of gratitude to this stranger who viewed her granddaughter's plight with such sincere compassion.

"Do you have any suggestions on how to deal with this?" Katreena felt confident that this generous couple had already discussed solutions to Kaydee's dilemma, and were eagerly waiting for an opportunity to explore them.

"Well, like we told your daughter, one option would be to take her right out of that oppressive environment and send her to Lawn Haven Academy in Portmont. That would be a drastic move and may be quite stressful for her, especially at first. As well, we realize that separating her from her siblings may be traumatic. You know the bonds that exist there. Would you consider that a viable option?"

Katreena took an absent-minded sip of her tea as she pondered the consequences of such a move. "Those kids are very close. Kaydee adores Alvin and the girls and she would miss them terribly. And Jaynee worships Kaydee. Their bond is much stronger because of Michael's behaviour. I honestly would hesitate to separate them. I don't know what to think."

"I certainly wish there was a better solution, and perhaps there may even be one. Sandy and I have only become aware of the situation within the last year and we really have very few facts to go on. Kaydee has only recently started communicating and trusting us, but even then, she is very timid about discussing her home life. We have gleaned scant information from various sources, some rather unreliable, so we cannot formulate solutions based on speculation, but we would like to help." Ed's tone was pensive but Katreena knew his empathy was genuine.

Then she remembered her last conversation with Kaydee. She related it to the Norchaks. "Kaydee was quite impressed by the information that Helen had kept a journal and that she wrote poetry. She was going to question Helen about it. I was hoping that perhaps if Kaydee started a journal herself, she might be able to purge herself of some of those suppressed feelings and obtain some emotional release by doing so."

Ed Norchak brightened. He was encouraged by the news. "You may be right. That might provide her with a kind of buffer against her father's scorn." Sandy agreed enthusiastically. "Has she talked to her mother yet?"

"I don't know. I have to go there and speak to her personally. We can't let Michael know we are even talking about it. He'd berate all of us for it, or do something even worse."

"There is little we can do at this time anyway," Ed concluded. "Why don't we see what develops with the journal, and then we can discuss the situation again. Would you keep us informed and let us know if there is anything we can do to help?"

"I most certainly will, and thank you ever so much, Mr. and Mrs. Norchak, for your concern and your offer to help. I appreciate that very much. I feel so powerless and frustrated sometimes. It is nice to know I have allies in this cause." Katreena got up, shook hands with the couple and took her leave.

Driving home, Katreena was excited. True, no decisions were finalized, and no real progress made, but she was not alone anymore. She could hardly wait to tell Dusty. She had three other people to help her carry the burden and it didn't feel so heavy anymore.

The rain had stopped by now and the air was fresh and clean. Janine was out among her flowers again, pruning some, inspecting others that the heavy rain had brought to their knees. Janine's flowers were her pride and joy and her yard was always the exemplar of the block. Janine and Vance had no children and Katreena knew that depravation left a gaping hole in their lives, but they were not ones to dwell on the negative. With both of them teaching, they devoted themselves to their work and their students, took on a more active role in the church and community and immersed themselves in the beautification of their home. Katreena knew that Janine would rejoice with her about the Norchaks' constructive concern, so she parked her car and walked over to tell her neighbour about the latest developments. As they sat on the settee on the porch, Janine listened calmly to Katreena's account, then when she finished, she got up to give her friend a big hug.

"I'm so happy for you, Katty. I just know this is the beginning of something good and wonderful for your family."

"Thank you, Janine. I think so too, but I just don't know how we are going to get this past Michael. He seems so much more demanding and explosive now. It's like his hatred for Kaydee is so all-consuming that I'm afraid he'll pop a cork at the slightest provocation."

"That might just give you the perfect opportunity, you know." Janine suggested thoughtfully. "Maybe then, even Helen will be willing to go along with you in separating him from the family."

"Perhaps. As long as he doesn't hurt someone in the process, and I mean physically!"

They talked for a few more minutes and then Vance arrived home from his fishing trip at Lake Aggassee with his buddies. The rain had not reached that far so they had had a good day. Proudly raising a stringer of fish high in the air for them to inspect, he crowed haughtily.

"Me catch-em, you clean-em, woman, so hop to it!"

"In your dreams, buddy! You catch-em, you clean-em. Me, woman. Me cook-em baby!" Janine retorted. The girls laughed as Vance proffered a groan of mock injury.

"You two fight it out. I'm going home to a peaceful meal of tuna." Katreena said.

"You sure you don't want pickerel?" Vance called after her.

"Only if it's headless," she called back.

She knew that Vance would be calmly filleting the fish as soon as he got near the sink. He was good at it and he never minded doing it. They all teased each other about their fishing prowess but they always shared their catch. They still used the sixteen-foot Deep V Brunswick boat Vance had bought from Katreena after Daniel had died. They had replaced the cumbersome big motor with a smaller, modern, but equally powerful one, and added a collapsible canopy to the unit but Katreena still felt the vessel's pleasing familiarity whenever she went fishing with them.

She was still bubbling from her visit with the Norchaks and was eager to share her good news with Dusty, but right now, she was hungry. Still, she knew that Vance would be at her doorstep with a pickerel within the next fifteen minutes so she decided to wait. Nothing like fresh fish for supper. She went to the garden for salad greens. She'd call Dusty later tonight.

Dusty was delighted when she told him about her discussion with the Norchaks.

"That's wonderful news, Katreena," Dusty exclaimed enthusiastically. "We'll conquer this problem, you'll see. Have you talked to Kaydee about the journal yet?"

"Well no. I have to do it in person. We can't take a chance on Michael hearing us. I thought I'd take a drive out there tomorrow and see how things are going."

"Good idea. You've got a great start there. I'm sure you're very excited. Don't let him bully you now, Katreena."

They talked for a few more minutes, made plans to meet the following weekend and hung up. Katreena's heart was pounding like a drum. She was excited all right, but she was also nervous. She knew she was embarking on a potentially dangerous course, a course she must pursue, there was no question about it, but she was worried about the repercussions that might follow, for Kaydee, for Helen, for the other kids and consequently for herself.

"Why had this come to such a head now?" Katreena asked herself. Michael had been a brute for more than ten years. Why, then, was it so much more acute now? Sitting there on her comfortable rocker, she examined the events of the last few months. Michael had not been pleased with Katreena's desertion of the family at the crucial seeding time. He had begun to rely on her help since she retired. Perhaps Michael harboured resentment about her leaving in May and staying away for two whole months. Now as Kaydee grew older, she had been harnessed into many more duties around the house and yard. Michael's already bitter humiliation about Kaydee's problems in school intensified his scrutiny of her and he burdened her with more impossible demands. This set her up for more failure and disappointment. Yet it was those very failures that hampered her learning potential which, in Michael's mind, justified his embarrassment and therefore his hatred of her. It was the proverbial "*catch twenty-two.*"

The situation was getting totally out of control and Kaydee was extremely vulnerable. Something must be done and Helen obviously would not do it. The burden of that action had to rest on her, Katreena realized. The Norchaks would help and perhaps even Dusty might be in a position to assist, but it was she who had to make the decision to move things along. A heavy sigh escaped from Katreena's throat as she got up and went to the bedroom.

Chapter 9

Tuesday dawned bright and sunny, with the meteorologist promising a high of twenty-eight. Katreena would have loved to go boating or just lie on the beach, but she was on a mission. Resolutely, she donned a pair of light Bermuda shorts, a light cotton shell and her white sandals, and took her toast and coffee to the deck for breakfast with the finches and pinesiskins. After cleaning up, she grabbed her sunglasses, got in her car and headed for Zelena.

Her arrival at the farm was poorly timed. She had hoped that Michael would be in the field by now or, at the very least, somewhere in the shed so that she wouldn't have to run in to him. Instead, Michael was just leaving the house when Katreena walked up. It was clear that he was on a rampage and he was just finishing his tirade by getting in his last few barbs.

"And you better make sure that lawn is mowed today. None of your damn fooling around. And remember to clean that mower after you use it, or I'll make you scrape it out with your bloody teeth. Last time it took you an hour to clean that dried grass from underneath it. There better not ever be a next time, hear? And don't look at me like that. You better show some respect or you're gonna wish you damn well had! I don't want any more attitude from you, damn it!" Michael almost spat the words out as he slammed the metal gate behind him.

Kaydee stood in the middle of the room, looking after her father. She held her head high, her back straight, but instead of fear in her eyes, there was something else. Something new. Was it defiance? Anger? Mutiny? Was there a look of hatred in those hard hazel eyes? Katreena was stunned. Never had she seen Kaydee appear so bold, so unmoved. Katreena looked questioningly at Helen. Helen shrugged her shoulders helplessly and looked away, busying herself with the breakfast dishes.

"Hi, Granny." Kaydee planted a quick kiss on her grandmother's cheek. "I'm going to mow that lawn." Then, without looking back, she walked purposefully out the door. Something unbelievable had just happened here. Katreena was shockingly aware of it, but she could not comprehend what it had been. She turned to Helen.

"What in heaven's name has been happening here?" Katreena stepped firmly in front of Helen, forcing her to look up.

Helen seemed frightened, vulnerable. "Kaydee found out that Michael destroyed my journal. She's been furious at him ever since." Helen's face was haggard with anxiety.

"Have they been fighting about it?"

"No, but Michael can tell she is angry and it makes him livid because he feels she is being insubordinate. I've tried talking to Kaydee but she won't listen. She says it's time we started standing up to him. She calls him a bully, not to his face, of course. It's like she's a completely different child. She doesn't talk back to him, but she doesn't cringe any more either. She just stands there and waits until he is finished ranting. It's almost as if she's daring him to do something drastic and Michael knows it. Oh Mom, I'm afraid for her. He is so raving mad, I'm afraid he may become physically violent. I don't know what to do."

Katreena put her arms around Helen. "Let me talk to Kaydee and see what I can do but I'll let her finish the lawn. No point in antagonizing Michael with outright disobedience. Do you have fieldwork today?"

"No, the hay won't be ready for baling today and the summerfallow and spraying are all done. Michael said he was going to crimp the brome on the Jansen quarter today so I was going to check the garden. I know there are strawberries ready to pick and the peas need picking."

"I'll go pick the strawberries. You take care of the meals. If I get a chance, I'd like to take Kaydee for a ride later, but right now I'd like to talk to you about something."

Katreena had always been strong in dealing with her family problems, but Michael's recent behaviour had shaken her sense of security. She no longer felt strong; now she felt helpless and overwhelmed by her inability to come up with a viable solution to a problem that seemed to be accelerating and quickly getting out of control. Perhaps it was time to bring Dusty into the picture. If things should get out of hand, they might need his help much sooner than expected. Having a man around might make Michael back off.

"I have met a man, a very good and kind man, honey. His name is Dusty Duganyk." Katreena told Helen how they had met, about Dusty's patience, his sense of decency, his sense of humour. She told her about his concern for her family and his willingness to help.

"He has a very big heart and he wants to meet you," Katreena finished, watching her daughter carefully to determine her reaction to the news. "Dusty's presence will not create problems for anyone in this family. It may even help Michael to calm down abit, having another man around."

Helen remained silent for several minutes, then slowly, weighing each word carefully she spoke. "Mother, in all the years I have known you, I honestly don't think you have made any serious errors in judgment. If you think that this man is someone you want in your life, then I think that is where he should be. Daddy has been gone for almost thirteen years. You have made us your life but it's time you started to live your own. If he makes you happy then he's got my backing. I'd love to meet him, but Michael might be another matter. Are you sure Michael won't scare him away? You know what Michael is like."

Katreena gave Helen an impetuous hug. "Thank you for your concern, sweetheart, but I doubt anything will scare Dusty away. I must admit, I didn't know how you would take it."

"I'm happy for you, Mom," Helen exclaimed with atypical enthusiasm, sounding surprised that her mother would have even questioned it. Yet that simple unaffected statement, coming from Helen was like manna for Katreena's hungry soul. These last few years, Helen had been so withdrawn, so distant that it had seemed that she was devoid of any emotion. Yet today, both life and emotion, seemed to have returned to her. Today, Helen had openly expressed fear, worry, and concern for her daughter and now empathy, understanding, and happiness at her mother's good fortune. She had even hinted at an awareness of Michael's shortcomings! Something was happening here and, if it wasn't for the possibility of potentially terrible consequences, it might even be a cause for rejoicing.

Somehow, that journal was the key that had set in motion a sequence of developments that were having far-reaching effects. Was Kaydee's fury at her father for the senseless destruction of the journal going to wake Helen up? Helen seemed more animated today than Katreena had seen her in years. What did Kaydee say to her mother that brought her back to life again? Katreena was eager to find out.

"We better get to work and finish our chores." Katreena said almost sharply. "Then we'll have some time to decide what we do next. Let me get at those strawberries, and if I have time, I'll go pick the peas." Taking a plastic pail out of the cupboard, Katreena hurried to the garden, her stride purposeful, her expression dogged. Helen stared after her.

As Katreena worked on the strawberries, she could hear the lawn mower busily rumbling at the far end of the yard near the shelter belt. The front part was all finished. Lethargy was definitely not going to be a problem today. Kaydee was clipping with determined speed. She still had the edge trimming to do but Katreena was certain that she would be done by noon. If she finished the strawberries and peas quickly, and prepared a picnic lunch before Michael returned, they could escape a confrontation between Michael and Kaydee by simply not being around. She could even take Alvin along with them, just so Michael didn't accuse Kaydee of shirking her duties. If they gave him things to do, they may have time to talk privately.

By eleven, Katreena had the berry patch stripped. She took the berries to the house, picked up another pail and hurried to the pea patch. She couldn't hear the mower anymore, so she knew Kaydee was either cleaning the mower or trimming around trees. Within half an hour, she had a pail of fresh peas. Michael would be back by fifteen after twelve, she knew. She wanted Kaydee far away from the house in order to escape a row again. She'd leave the shelling for now. Perhaps if they got back in time, she may help Helen with that later. Right now, she needed to get a picnic lunch ready. Helen was fixing lunch for Michael but Katreena told her she was taking Kaydee and Alvin out. Helen agreed thankfully. Katreena worked feverishly. She assembled drinks, napkins, blankets, plates and glasses into a basket, then grabbed muffins, wieners, buns from the freezer, and stuffed them into a picnic cooler. As she sorted

Alvin's toys, Kaydee came in, sweaty and flushed.

"Quickly wash up, and get ready for a picnic," Katreena told her. Questioningly, Kaydee looked at Helen. Helen nodded. Kaydee picked up the cue and rushed to the bathroom and returned fresh and clean in a few minutes.

"Load up the car. I'll get Alvin." Katreena was brusque. Kaydee grasped the urgency and snapped into action. At twelve minutes after twelve, after a quick hug and kiss for Helen, they were in the car and on the road. In the rear view mirror, Katreena could see Michael's truck turn the corner and approach the yard.

"Phew, that was close," Katreena breathed silently. On the seat beside her, Kaydee sat rigidly, holding the bewildered Alvin in her lap.

"All right, everybody. Relax. We are going for a picnic in Casey's Park, and we are going to have a wonderful time, aren't we? Why is everybody so glum?" Katreena tried to diffuse the tension by sounding casual and teasing. She knew that their hasty departure had confused the kids. Well, Alvin anyway. Katreena was sure Kaydee understood her reasons and shared her purpose. Kaydee was probably a lot more anxious to get away from her father than her grandmother was.

"How are you feeling, Alvin? Does it hurt a lot?" Katreena attempted again, seeing her first try did not produce any response. She knew that once they got to the park, both the kids would loosen up but it was twenty-six miles away and that meant almost half an hour's drive. She had to get them to unwind soon or it would be a long and boring ride, and she certainly did not want to start explaining why they had left in such a hurry. She wanted to keep the atmosphere light-hearted and free from anxiety.

"It doesn't really hurt anymore, Granny." Alvin told her bravely. "I'm all right."

Katreena knew that Alvin was not himself yet. He slept more during the day and was content to amuse himself with playing quiet games or leafing through picture books. That was not the Alvin of two months ago before Katreena left for her holidays, but his efficacious smile told her his uneasiness had begun to dissipate.

"Are we going to go into the swimming pool, Granny? Did you take my bathing suit? Are you going to come in to the pool with me?"

"No, honey, I didn't bring my bathing suit. But I did bring yours. You'll be able to play in the pool. Kaydee and I will just wade along the edge." The "pool" was actually a shallow wading pool for children to play in, and Kaydee could cross it without getting her shorts wet. Katreena had deliberately chosen Casey's Park, because this pool would provide Alvin with a safe play area while she talked with Kaydee and watched him at the same time.

"Did you bring your bathing suit, Kaydee? You'll get your shorts all wet if you don't put on a bathing suit. I hope you brought the big green beach ball, Granny." Alvin was chattering away. Soon he and Kaydee were laughing and teasing each other, and planning their park activities. Katreena smiled, knowing that the children had already forgotten the tension at home.

At the park, Alvin took his beach ball, and the small pail with his toys and waited patiently, while Katreena and Kaydee unloaded the picnic supplies from the car. They chose a picnic table near the pool, and Katreena spread the blanket, near the edge, as a sitting area. Then as Kaydee brought in the rest of their store, Katreena lit a fire in the little iron fire box that the park provided near each table. Katreena knew the kids would be hungry. It was almost one o'clock. As the wieners cooked on the grill, Kaydee took Alvin to the change room to get his bathing suit on. The sun was already hot, and the huge old maples provided welcome shade. The air smelled fresh, and clean, but the humidity was high after the recent rain, and Katreena found the atmosphere rather muggy.

After lunch, they all lay down on the blanket and watched the sun's rays filter through the leaves of the trees, listening to, and watching a red headed woodpecker hammering away at a quarry somewhere beneath the bark of an old maple. Very soon, Alvin got restless and headed for the pool. Taking his menagerie of unsinkable toys with him, he sat in the sun heated water and made himself comfortable among his flotilla of rubber boats, and ducks, and things that squeaked and swam around him.

This was the moment Katreena had been waiting for. Turning on the blanket to face the pool, Katreena got to the point almost immediately.

"You want to tell me what's been happening since last Thursday?" They had to cover a lot of ground in precious little time and distractions may lie ahead. Kaydee hesitated, her emotions obviously creating some inner conflict. Then, anguish, reactions, opinions and frustrations poured out, tumbling over each other in a headlong rush to escape from their imprisonment.

"I did as you told me, Granny. I waited till Father was out on the field, and Alvin and the girls were asleep. Then I asked Mother about the journal. She *cried!* Granny. She cried because Father burned her journal. Granny, he *burned* Mother's journal! All her poems, all her thoughts, all her stories, all her ideas. He just burned them. She had no other copies so everything is lost. She has not written anything more since. Oh, Granny," Kaydee moved into Katreena's welcoming embrace. "I so wanted to read it. And I could tell she felt very bad." Then just as suddenly, Kaydee pulled away. She looked straight into Katreena's eyes and announced vehemently. "I *hate* him, Granny! He hurt Mother so much, and he's always so mean, and now she is always so unhappy. She's the one who looks and acts like a retard. And it's all because of him. *I hate him*! I can't help it Granny. I know it's a sin but I *hate* him!"

Katreena put her arm around Kaydee's shoulder. She was stunned. Never had she thought that this quiet girl was capable of such fierce emotions. Never had she imagined that docile, obedient, child concealed such all-consuming passion, or such a protective instinct towards her mother. Was this the same sweet, vulnerable, youngster that recently had cowered when Michael had yanked Alvin's bike away so harshly? Completely incensed and unbridled, her voice shaking with fury, Kaydee continued her denunciation.

"I won't let him get away with it. I promised Mother I would start writing my own journal now, and I will. But Father will never, ever, see it. He will never destroy me like he destroyed Mother. I wish she would start writing again. I wish I could read her writing. I wish I could get to know Mother the way you knew her. She never talks much and she is always so sad. I didn't know she could write poems. I wish I could have read them. I wish I could write poems." Tears were spilling down Kaydee's cheeks as she huddled in Katreena's arms, tears of frustration, despair, and anguish. But there was determination in that anger too, and Katreena knew that Kaydee's passive and submissive behaviour was now a thing of the past. Rightly or wrongly, this child was ready to stand up and fight. She had just grown up.

Katreena had said nothing throughout Kaydee's invective. She allowed Kaydee to vent, partly out of consideration for Kaydee's need to do so but probably even more because she had been so shocked by the passion with which the invective was delivered. She was still at a loss for words when Kaydee fell silent. She had spent herself. She had expelled her pent-up emotions, purged herself of their poison, and now she was done. She threw herself back onto the blanket and stared up at the heavens. Silent tears ran down the side of her face into her ears, but Kaydee didn't wipe them away. She was in a different world, one where tears didn't matter.

Katreena gently wiped Kaydee's tears, caressing the soft cheeks with her fingers. She wanted to lighten her burden, isolate her pain, absorb it herself. Kaydee's hatred of Michael was completely justified, and Katreena could not bring herself to chastise her for it or to soften her articulation of that hatred. Katreena just could not be that much of a hypocrite.

"I understand how you feel, sweetheart, and I don't blame you for feeling that way. You and your mother have taken his harassment for so long, and I couldn't protect you from it. I've been feeling awful about that for a long time but I didn't know how to help. Perhaps now, by working together with the help of other good people like the Norchaks and even a new friend that you will be meeting soon, we may be able to make your life easier. But you must promise me something, sweetheart," and she turned Kaydee's face to face her, "you must not disobey your father. You must not do anything to make him very angry. It worries your mother and we don't want him to hurt you. Please, please, honey, just be patient a little while longer. I'm working on a plan and I need your help. But you must not make your father angry in the meantime. Will you do that for me, please?"

Katreena had to make Kaydee understand the importance of not antagonizing Michael. It was absolutely imperative. He might become violent, and that could have horrific consequences. "Please, honey. This is very important. Promise, honey?" Katreena persisted.

Kaydee could not discount the urgency in Granny's voice.

"I promise, Granny. I'll try to do it for you and for Mother, because I don't want you to worry. But I hope you succeed with what you are trying to do soon."

"Thank you, sweetheart. You just hang in there for a little while longer. I promise you, things will get better."

Katreena watched Alvin as he played contentedly in the water, totally oblivious to them. "Great," she thought. This was a good time to introduce the subject of Dusty to Kaydee. Situations were arising that might require the cooperation of all concerned parties and it was time these parties united forces.

"I want you to meet someone, honey, someone who is honest and kind and thoughtful. I have told him about you and he wants to help." Katreena studied Kaydee's face as she told her about her new friend, and their possible ally. The girl listened attentively, not interrupting, her eyes wide with wonder, her previous outburst forgotten as she listened to her grandmother describing what she quickly realized was "Granny's boyfriend."

Impulsively, she gave her grandmother a big hug. "Oh Granny, I am so excited. I can hardly wait to meet him. He sounds just wonderful."

Katreena smiled. "Yes, he is, and you will meet him soon. He wants to come out to the farm as soon as I can arrange it. Maybe this weekend." She was glad her family, at least the two most important members, were happy for her. The rest were irrelevant. She thought about the Norchaks but decided not to divulge the subject of her meeting with them. Not yet, she thought, not until they came up with some specific strategy toward a solution to the problem.

Alvin had become bored with his floating toys and had gone to the sandbox to work on sand castles, but he was still peacefully occupying himself. The sun was hot and there was virtually no breeze so the heat was becoming oppressive, even in the shade of the big trees. Still, Katreena felt an overwhelming sense of gratification. She had accomplished her mission. She had helped Kaydee purge herself of the venom of Michael's mistreatment; she had elicited a promise of peaceful behaviour from her, hopefully acquiring at least some reprieve from Michael's wrath; and she had introduced the subject of Dusty and received two favourable responses. For the first time in a long while, she felt the lift of an onerous burden from her chest.

Answering Kaydee's eager barrage of questions about Dusty, Katreena felt happy and light-hearted. The afternoon passed quickly and when Katreena looked at her watch, it was already ten minutes to five. Nobody had even considered a mid-afternoon lunch, not even Alvin, the country's indisputable bottomless pit.

"Hey, you guys, do you know it's coming close to supper time and we still have to drive home? Your mother will think I kidnapped you two and smuggled you out of the country. Come on, let's load up and see if she'll still feed us."

Katreena got up quickly and the two children scrambled after her, gathering the picnic supplies, toys and other paraphernalia and loading everything into the car. As they sped towards home, both kids were quiet, tired probably, and Alvin was soon asleep in Kaydee's lap. Kaydee winked at her grandmother, indicating her brother's drooped head on her shoulder. They both smiled and drove on in silence.

Katreena had hardly slept all night. She had spent the evening on the farm just to see the interaction between Michael and Kaydee. She was also curious about Helen's behaviour in light of the emancipation of feelings she was obviously experiencing. When Michael had come indoors, he plopped himself in front of the TV, and said nothing to anyone. Katreena had whispered a reminder to Kaydee of her promise not to antagonize Michael and Kaydee had obliged by either staying outside of Michael's range or by being one step ahead of him in the chore department so he could not find any fault to pick on. With Michael in the house, Helen had remained calm but very quiet. After the kids were safely all in bed, Katreena had felt confident enough to leave. She had arrived home at twenty after eleven and had gone to bed immediately but it had been a restless night. Imagined events and their repercussions tumbled over each other in her brain, presenting one scenario after another without any definite direction or solution.

By seven o'clock, Katreena had had it. She got up, made her bed and jumped into the shower, taking her time and thoroughly enjoying the powerful spray washing over her, cleansing, she hoped, all the apprehension and negative forces from her mind and body. Then she dried and brushed her hair, sprayed it lightly to hold the set, and applied makeup to her face with careful precision. She needed to look and feel her best today. She dressed quickly, and she was ready! Worry about Kaydee and Helen plagued her and she had no idea how to deal with it so she dialled the number to the farm.

Helen answered. She sounded relatively calm. Katreena was relieved.

"How is everything going?" she asked. She had to find out.

"Everything is fine. Michael's gone to crimp the alfalfa in the west corner. Kaydee is staying out of his way so things are peaceful. I don't know what you said to her, but thanks, Mom. Don't worry. I'll call you if we need you. We may be baling that brome tomorrow." Helen hung up. This was rural Manitoba and their phones were still on a partyline. Too much information or long chats were unnecessary.

Satisfied that all was well on the farm, Katreena made her coffee and toast, put everything on a tray and took it out on the deck to enjoy breakfast with the birds.

These moments always helped to clear her head. Those birds only had one purpose in life and they fought over perches at the feeder as if they were the most important things in the world. How lucky they were, Katreena thought. They had no relationships to worry about, just their next meal. What a carefree existence! Humans were always complicating their lives with relationships. Every relationship carried with it a responsibility, a set of duties and roles and problems and pain. Pain because you can't live up to the responsibilities; you can't carry out the duties; you can't fulfill the roles; you can't solve the problems; ergo the all-pervading pain.

That was the downside of relationships. The upside! Oh, there was an upside, she had to admit that. First and foremost was her relationship with Daniel. Just thinking about him gave her great pleasure and intense pain – pleasure for the good times and pain for his loss. Life with her parents had been good, but it always seemed to Katreena that her life began when she met Daniel. As a child she had never been exposed to the avant garde issues of the day, so her aspirations were simple and her goals attainable. She got her degree without too much aplomb and decided to become a school teacher to earn her own living in the world. That was the logical thing to do.

Then she met Daniel, dear sweet, fun-loving Daniel. They shared a love for music and dance; a love for people; a spontaneity for fun; and a purpose for the future.

She smiled as she recalled that first Christmas at the Banaduks before she and Daniel were married. Daniel had insisted she come carolling with him and his friends but Katreena hadn't brought enough warm clothes for such an outing. However, Daniel was sure she would be fine because they were going to be riding in a small hand-built wooden "caboose" that was mounted on the sleigh and it would be heated by a metal fire box. As an extra precaution, Daniel's mother had insisted they take the "pyryna," a goose feather duvet that they took off the bed. Everything would have been great except the horses took a corner too sharply over a snow bank, flipping the caboose on its side. As the young people scrambled to get out through the door above them, the ensuing fire from the overturned firebox had to be smothered with the pyryna. For years after that incident, everyone had teased Katreena that Daniel's mother had purchased a wife for her son, and the price had been her best pyryna!

It was Daniel who taught her to relax and coaxed her out of that "prim and proper" posture that she had considered essential to a teacher's position. She remembered their first dance together. "You're stiff as a board. Loosen up. Bend those knees. Enjoy yourself." They both laughed but she did learn to relax. Dancing became one of their passions and they soon became known and admired for their grace and their synchronization of movement.

Daniel was never one to be plagued by indecision. If a thing needed doing, he didn't waste time mulling over it. After Helen was born they were so happy, Daniel had been adamant that their child would have a regular family upbringing and he insisted that Katreena take time out from teaching until Helen was well established in school. They took the baby with them everywhere, and if some outing was not suitable for a baby, Daniel always found an alternative excursion that was even more interesting and fun. Having a baby was never an impediment to their lifestyle; it was an introduction to a more exciting one!

Chapter 10

Katreena's reverie was interrupted by the shrill ring of the telephone. It was Dusty.

"I hope I'm not making a nuisance of myself. If I am, just say so and I'll back off."

Katreena smiled. There goes that insecurity of his again. If he only knew! He really had no reason to be insecure.

"Not at all! It's nice to hear your voice! How could you say that?" she scolded.

"Thanks, Katreena." He sounded relieved and Katreena could almost see the happy glow in his eyes. "What are your plans for the day? Did you get to the farm yet?"

"Well, actually I just got back from Zelena late last night. There have been some significant developments but I'd rather not go into it over the phone."

"Well, if you have no special plans, I was hoping you might join me for the day. I thought I'd hook up the boat and we could head out to Lake Aggassee. We could do some fishing and just enjoy the weather. It sounds like it's going to be a hot one but it will be nice on the water. I have a canopy so we won't be baking in the sun. What do you say?"

"Sounds great to me. Shall I meet you in Portmont?" Lake Aggassee was ninety miles north of Portmont and there was no sense in Dusty driving sixty-four miles south to Lanavale just to pick her up and then driving back the same way.

"That would save us some time. How soon can you get here?"

Katreena promised to leave immediately and hung up. Excited and humming to herself, she flew into action packing food and drinks into the big cooler, lotion, hat, sunglasses, plus a pair of slacks and a sweater in case it got chilly later. After checking to make sure nothing important got left behind, she locked the house and, still humming, left for Portmont.

Dusty's house was a sprawling low-set bungalow, with a stone front and attached double garage. Corkscrew evergreens stood like sentries guarding the short driveway and a neatly pruned hedge extended from the front to the back of the property where a mass of color acknowledged the essence of a lovingly-tended garden. A tall wooden bower covered with climbing pink roses arched over the walkway that led to the front door and a terraced crescent-shaped rock garden flowerbed adorned the alcove between the house and garage setting off a statue of a Greek goddess in front of it.

Dusty was outside, loading fishing equipment into the truck that was already hitched to the boat. He came over to meet her as she parked her car on the street.

"Hello, Katreena," he greeted as he opened the car door for her to get out. "I see you found the place with no problem. I've got everything packed and ready to roll. Come on, and I'll give you a quick tour of the house and garden before we go."

The house was neat and modern but not lavish. It was tastefully decorated throughout in a subtle shade of blue. Pleated white sheers and drapes extended from wall to wall giving the living room an elegant but airy look. Rich golden oak woodgrain accentuated the kitchen cupboards and the rest of the wood framing around the doors and windows. A wide archway led into the dining room from where the garden presented an array of color through the big glass patio doors that opened onto the small wooden deck at the back.

"Dusty, it's beautiful" Katreena breathed in awe. Dusty swelled with pleasure and pride.

"I'm so glad you like it. I find it comfortable and homey but let's go in the garden. That is where my passion lies."

As they walked through the garden, Dusty pointed out the diversity of plants, carefully arranged to provide a state of constant color throughout the season. Dusty was obviously in his element here. This garden was a labour of love and pleasure.

"Would you like some lunch before we leave?" Dusty asked suddenly, looking at his watch and realizing how quickly the time was going by.

Katreena also glanced at her watch. "Wow, eleven o'clock already. Actually I'm not hungry, unless you are. I packed us a picnic lunch which I thought we would eat on the boat."

"Super idea. Let's pack it in and head out then."

Within five minutes, they pulled out of the driveway and were on the way. Manoeuvring his way skilfully through the busy traffic of the city, Dusty pointed out his favourite reading bench in the middle of Portmont's Shilladay Gardens.

"I love my own little garden, but sometimes in the mornings, I like to take long walks and I usually stop here just to admire the flowers. Every year they bring in new and unusual varieties and I always find those fascinating. Often I take a book with me and I enjoy the beautiful fragrances of the blossoms while I read. The early mornings are always so quiet and peaceful here. Very few people like to get up at five or six in the morning, but I love the freshness and exhilaration of a bright morning."

"I know just what you mean," Katreena agreed. "There's something about the tranquility of a crisp morning that seems to evaporate like dew when the sound of rushing humanity charges onto the scene."

"So you don't like to sleep late in the mornings?"

"No, I don't though I certainly would appreciate the freedom to do so if I felt like it. However being 'on call' as the farm 'babysitter' does not allow me the luxury of setting my own personal routines whether it be about sleeping in, or scheduling my work, or planning special social outings. When I am needed on the farm, I basically drop everything and go."

They conversed comfortably as they drove down the highway, observing and enjoying the scenery and the little pieces of information they gleaned about each other's interests. Dusty exuded a carefree passion for life which was like a soothing balm for Katreena's permeating worry about her burdensome family.

Out on the open highway, they drove along lush green fields of grain undulating in the refreshing western breeze that carried with it the faint perfume of wild flowers. As the miles sped by, Katreena brought Dusty up to date on the events that had taken place on the farm during the last few days. She told him about Kaydee's anger at Michael, about the journal and how that anger had changed the girl's attitude and behaviour toward her father.

"Kaydee was fascinated when I told her that Helen had written poems and stories before she met Michael. The truth is Kaydee knows so little about what Helen was like when she was young. She sees Helen as she is now. She cannot imagine her being normal. All she sees is an unresponsive robot devoid of thoughts, emotions, intelligence or opinions, performing her tasks in a knee-jerk reaction without enjoyment or distaste or even evidence of boredom."

"Did you never tell her this about Helen before?"

"I'm ashamed to admit that we never talked about it. Somehow that subject never came up. I realize now that I could have, and even should have, but my preoccupation with their immediate problems always pre-empted any discussion of the past. Now I see that as a major oversight. Kaydee was totally blown away when I told her that Helen was editor of the school newspaper, that she was in drama clubs and choirs and that she was well liked in school."

Dusty gave Katreena a rather disbelieving look and Katreena winced.

"I know. It seems unbelievable but honestly life in that home is not normal. It's almost like everything we do is reactionary; like it's all just survival tactics. I know that's merely an excuse, and a bad one, at best, but it's all I have."

He shook his head and told her to continue.

"Journaling just does not fit in with the kind of person that Helen has become. When Kaydee realized that it was within Helen to be these things, she was eager to read that journal. Then when she heard how carelessly Michael had destroyed it, she became totally incensed. She sees Michael's denigration as the cause that brought Helen to this state and she hates him for it. He senses her resentment and it infuriates him."

She told him about Helen's concern for Kaydee's safety and how much such concern deviated from her usual behaviour of late.

"I extracted a promise from Kaydee not to antagonize Michael because it worried Helen and me about her safety. I told her that I had a plan to solve the problem, but that she would have to give me time to put that plan into action. I just hope she can maintain her cool around him if he goes into one of his unprovoked rages. Honestly, the situation there is positively explosive right now. He has always been authoritative but lately his dislike, actually more like his hatred, for Kaydee has made him almost menacing. It worries me, a lot!" Katreena concluded.

Suddenly serious, his eyes probing hers intently, Dusty queried. "You say that Michael is 'almost menacing.' Do you think he's likely to physically hurt Kaydee? Or Helen? Are you worried about him getting violent?"

"I really don't know. His rages have always sounded violent but he has never struck either of them before. Kaydee would have told me. He storms and yells a lot but his punishment of Kaydee has been limited to yanking her by the hair or by the arm and forcing her to kneel in a dark corner behind a big chair under the stairway. I have not personally seen this because Michael doesn't dare to send her to that 'sinhole,' as Kaydee calls it, while I am there but I know this to be true. I've tried to talk to Helen about it but she refuses to defy him. She said he wouldn't physically hurt her, but lately I think even she is worried. The fact is that lately he is so angry all the time and now with Kaydee's belligerence, I almost don't know what to expect."

"All the more reason we should get some sort of safety net in place for Kaydee, just in case something should erupt. Did you get a chance to talk to them about me yet?"

"As a matter of fact, both Helen and Kaydee are eagerly looking forward to meeting you. I told them separately, but they were both delighted and each one was enthusiastic about the idea. I'm not too sure how Michael will take it. I am dreading that confrontation. Helen also expressed reservations about it. In fact, Helen was afraid that Michael might scare you off."

Katreena watched Dusty's face for his reaction.

"You tell Helen to relax. I don't scare off that easy." Dusty sounded irritated and disgusted. "Sounds to me like you girls need a voice of reason in that household, if only for the sake of sanity. I cannot see Michael being so powerful that he could get away with such tactics. He may have brainwashed Helen but he cannot intimidate everyone that way.

Don't you worry." His jaw set tightly, Katreena noted Dusty's resolve as he gripped the steering wheel so tightly his knuckles went white.

Katreena suddenly realized that she had been talking almost non-stop since they left the city. What was even worse, it had all been a gloomy account!

Still, his concern for her family had remained steadfast and he was still anxious to become part of that family. Katreena felt humbly grateful for his patience and his offer to help.

"Thanks, Dusty. I really appreciate that. It's nice to have someone I can confide in. It has been such an oppressive situation." Then brightening, she added, "But I have good friends and allies now, you and the Norchaks. That's more than I had a week ago."

Katreena detailed her visit to the Norchaks and their belief about why Kaydee had been unable to function in school previously and their firm conviction of her intellectual potential.

"I really think they have a point there. Kaydee is not retarded. She is obsessively intimidated and insecure. She has been told to 'Shut up' so often she believes it to be a universal law. All those kids feel that way, even Alvin. That's not a normal household where kids fight or play with each other. They only talk to each other when Michael is not around, and then they are so suppressed that they feel only protective toward each other. Also Michael has told Kaydee she is stupid so often that she probably subconsciously believes it but she is an avid reader and she simply devours any book she can get her hands on, though she doesn't have many opportunities to just sit and read other than at school. There, she is too fearful to play with the other children and that has made her appear intellectually inferior. She is unable to articulate or communicate freely. She is somewhat unresponsive to questions, particularly oral ones, but she is open with me and has started to open up with the Norchaks this last year. She seems to have learned to trust them now. They are fond of her and have obviously bent over backwards to provide her with a secure environment where she has flourished. They suggested that she be taken out of the home, well, away from Michael anyway, and placed in a boarding school. But Kaydee is fiercely attached to the smaller kids. She adores them and they adore her. A separation from them could have serious consequences on the family. While fixing one problem, it could create another one, perhaps even a bigger one. I don't know what to do." Katreena finished helplessly.

Dusty reached for Katreena's hand and gave it a squeeze. "Let's not worry about it today. You said Michael was taking Alvin to the circus this week so they would be alright for a few days. Let's plan a trip to the farm for this or next weekend. We could spend the day with the family and see how things turn out. I'd like to talk to that son-in-law of yours. Maybe I can diffuse the situation somehow. Failing that, perhaps we may be able to take Kaydee to stay in the city with you for a while, even if we have to take Alvin as well since Michael is so determined that Kaydee should always be looking after him. But before that, I think you should let Michael know that I am going to be coming there with you. Phone and talk to him yourself. He may be angry at Helen if she tells him, but he can't blame her if you tell him. Today, we are going to relax and catch some fish and we're not going to worry, okay?" Dusty gave her fingers another squeeze and took his hand back to the wheel to make the turn onto the lake access road.

Chapter 11

The day was bright and warm and the slight breeze off the lake caressed their skin with a velvet touch. They had to wait for two other boats to be launched before they got their turn but, by half past one, they were in the water, roaring towards a small rocky island some distance from the shore. As they anchored the boat and dropped their lines into the water, Dusty secured the canopy that would offer them shelter from the scorching sun above. After baiting their hooks, they clamped the rods into place in the special locking pockets on the side of the boat.

"I didn't have much time to prepare anything fancy," Katreena apologized as she opened the cooler and handed him the ham sandwiches and the cold colas, then opened the container of marinated fresh veggies.

"So who said that a picnic lunch had to be fancy?" Dusty scolded, with a twinkle in his eye. "Don't you know it's the company that makes a meal into a feast?"

The tinkle of the tiny bell attached to the tip of Dusty's rod told them they had a fish on the line. All conversation ceased as he turned his attention to reeling in his catch.

"Do you come out here often?" Katreena asked, picturing him relaxing in the sun.

"Not as often as I'd like. Coming out by myself is no fun and it seems that when I'm free, my buddies aren't. What I really need is another retiree to keep me company, preferably a good looking female one," he winked mischievously.

"Preferably one who enjoys fishing with a good looking man, I hope," Katreena countered with a smile.

"Oh absolutely," Dusty replied with mock solemnity, then continued.

"Seriously, Wayne and Della and Jessie come out with me once in a while but they are rather tied down with their business."

"What kind of business does your brother own?"

"Wayne and Della run a small publishing house and spend long hours at the office. I invested money in the venture, but I don't spend time there. I am a silent partner except for my involvement in the administrative side of it. They employ fourteen people and during the summer holidays, Jessie spends time in the office. She loves it so they probably couldn't keep her out of there if they tried. If they let her she'd probably quit school to work there full time."

"How old is Jessie?"

"She's just fourteen and they have big plans for university for her. She's a good kid, makes good grades without too much effort so that should not present a problem. She can't wait to be a 'working girl' though. She loves literature and the publishing business and can lose herself in books, so we'll see what the future holds for her."

"Do they have any other children?"

"No. Just Jessie."

They spent a pleasant afternoon, relaxing and getting more acquainted with each other. By five o'clock, the sun had dropped down enough that its rays were not so scathing and Dusty unsnapped the canopy and folded it back so they could enjoy the sights of the rocky cliffs and green hillsides that bordered the lake. Katreena had been on this lake before, first with Daniel, then with Janine and Vance, but today was different. Today, the lake seemed to exude a subtle aura of beauty that enveloped Katreena in a cocoon of serenity that she did not want disturbed. She basked in its splendour and revelled in its liberation. Life was to be lived, and, after more than twelve years of vacuity, she felt alive again!

Katreena watched Dusty reach into the water to wash his hands after unhooking the last fish, noting every small detail of his physique. He was a 'hunk' as Janine had so coarsely put it but he certainly was no wolf and he was definitely no chauvinist. He was kind, gentle, considerate and above all, patient. Katreena appreciated that. In the future, well, who knew what the future held. Now, life was good and she knew that Dusty felt the same way.

They arrived at Dusty's place at nine and Dusty insisted that she stay for a fish fry. After he filleted the fish, Katreena washed them in the sink and got the pans ready for frying. By the time he had finished cleaning the rest of the fish, she already had the first couple of pieces sizzling in the pan on the stove. It felt good to be working alongside of Dusty,

Katreena thought to herself. It felt right, natural. Before they sat down to enjoy the sumptuous repast, Dusty brought out a bottle of Chablis. They toasted and congratulated each other on a great day. The sun was just on the horizon, ready to drop out of sight when they finished the dishes. Katreena picked up the container with the six fillets that Dusty had prepared for her and turned to thank him.

"Wish you could stay for a while," he told her, a note of regret in his voice. "We could just sit out there in the garden and do something romantic." He winked teasingly and added, speaking surreptitiously, "like listen to the crickets. It can be very relaxing, really." Then, "Seriously, I hate to see you work and run."

"I know, Dusty, and I'd love to stay, but it is getting late. Next time. I promise, okay?"

"That is one promise you are going to have to keep, Katreena. I'll hold you to it."

"Oh you will, will you?"

"Now, **I** promise." They both laughed.

At the door, Dusty took her in his arms, standing silently, holding her close. Then, ever so gently, he took her face into his big hands and covered her lips with his. "Till the next time, Katreena," he whispered huskily, before letting her go.

As Katreena drove home, her emotions were churning. That kiss had touched a nerve deep within her that she had forgotten existed. It spawned a genus of euphoria that superceded doubts or problems. She analyzed the events of the day detail by detail. He had been the perfect gentleman all afternoon. Other than some shy, hesitant, but sweet compliments, he had not made any overt moves that she might find presumptuous. He was attentive and candidly concerned about her and her family and made no secret of wanting to be part of that family unit. She wanted him as part of that family unit, too. But she wanted more than that. She pictured herself walking beside him along park pathways, his shoulder tight against hers, his arm around her. She envisioned waking up in the mornings, safely curled up in the crook of his arm, the smell of his body in her nostrils lurking in her mind like forbidden visitations. She fantasized quiet evenings sitting next to him on the couch, his arm around her, her head resting contentedly on his shoulder as they watched some movie on TV or listened to soft music on the radio. But she was getting ahead of herself. "Patience, now, girl. Patience!" she told herself happily.

Thursday morning, she woke up to a drizzle but Katreena checked with Helen regarding their need for a babysitter for the kids anyway.

"That hay won't be ready unless the sun shines and that doesn't seem likely. Michael is gone to town for some repairs. He'll be working on the equipment today," Helen informed her.

"Is everything alright?"

"Everything is fine." Helen knew what Katreena was referring to but for obvious reasons, preferred not to discuss it over a partyline telephone. Katreena had hoped to tell Michael about Dusty today but was not about to pursue that subject over the phone either. She hung up, deciding to wait and see what the rest of the day looked like.

As she busied herself with chores around the house, she tried to envision herself telling Michael about Dusty. She was stymied. The scene just would not materialize. She knew she was not ashamed of her relationship with Dusty and she certainly did not have enough respect for Michael to worry about his opinion, so why did his disapproval matter to her anyway? She knew she should have been stronger and not allowed Michael to bully Helen and Kaydee all these years but that was done now. It was too late for recriminations but what would Dusty think of her if Michael started to berate Helen or Kaydee in Dusty's presence?

Suddenly, Katreena felt very vulnerable and insecure. A wave of frustration washed over her, leaving her in a cold sweat. She had been weak! She saw that clearly now, but she could not change the past. Perhaps she did have the power to redirect the future, however. Of course that would take time, but things were looking up. Opportunities for change were looming up from several directions, the Norchaks, Dusty, Helen's behaviour and even Kaydee's belligerence. All these positives could alter the course of their lives in spite of what Michael did. Determined not to give in to defeat just when the possibility of change appeared on the horizon, Katreena left for Janine's house. She needed to talk to someone. When the time came, she would deal with telling Michael but she had to secure an objective viewpoint of her position first.

As she brought Janine up to date on the latest developments, she felt her insecurities lift. Putting it into words also put it in the proper perspective. Janine didn't even have to say much. What was done was done. Regrets were unproductive. It was time to move on and do what needed doing now and cover the bases as they came along.

"Thanks for listening Janine. It all seems so clear now. I'm going drive out to the farm right now and talk to Michael. On Sunday, I am going to introduce Dusty to my family." Katreena told Janine as she took the last sip of coffee and got up to leave.

Janine gave her a quick hug. "Atta girl! Good luck. I know you'll do great."

Katreena hurried home, opened a can of mushroom soup, made herself a tuna salad and within an hour, had finished her lunch, cleaned up her kitchen and was headed for Zelena. She would get this unpleasant obligation out of the way and then she would relax, knowing that the rest of the events would fall naturally into place by themselves. Still, her heart was pounding as she turned into the driveway at KD Acres. Kaydee had Alvin and Jaynee on the swings and immediately took them both down when she saw Granny drive in. As the kids all came running towards her, Katreena lost herself in their eager embraces and their exuberance neutralized her inhibitions about the impending confrontation with Michael.

The drizzle had abated but the clouds hung low and intrusive, a kind of dismal threat that permeated atmosphere and emotion alike. Helen was busy baking pies in the kitchen and Katreena chatted with her for a few minutes, then told her she wanted to talk to Michael, and left the house. Helen nodded knowingly and the kids backed off, puzzled, because Katreena never sought Michael out on purpose.

In the shop, Michael was tugging angrily at a wrench locked onto a nut that refused to budge off a rusted bolt on a set of harrows. He looked up with surprise and, obviously uncomfortable with her witnessing his frustration, immediately released his grip on the wrench.

"What brings you here on such a dreary day?"

"Well Michael, I have something I need to talk to you about and I don't want to put it off any longer."

Michael stared at her, dumbfounded. **She** wanted to talk to **him**?!? This was a new situation and Michael had no idea how to respond to his mother-in-law's peculiar declaration. Totally at a loss for words, he waited for her to break the awkward silence.

Katreena swallowed hard. There was no easy way to do this. She simply had to spit it out and put herself out of this miserable suspense. Whatever his reaction, it could not be any worse than what her imaginative mind was conjuring up.

"I have met someone, a man, who will probably become a big part of my life, and subsequently part of the lives of all my family. I have already told Helen and Kaydee. Now I wanted to tell you. We will be coming down this Sunday so you can all meet him. His name is Dusty Duganyk. I met him on the tour and have seen him several times since." Katreena stopped, exhausted. There! She had done it. Her heart was thundering inside her chest, her lungs were so constricted she was afraid she would suffocate. She waited for Michael's response.

Michael stared speechlessly at his mother-in-law. Caught completely off guard, he just stood there, unmoving, his hand suspended in midair just above the wrench.

Katreena waited for some feedback. Her task was not completed until she heard and saw his reaction. Whatever he said or did about the news would set the tone for their future dealings and she needed to know what she was going to have to face.

After what seemed like an eternity, Michael seemed to come out of his stupor. "Well, what do you know? The lady's got herself a boyfriend," he sneered disgustedly and then he laughed, a raucous, mocking laugh intended to taunt and belittle his mother-in-law. Suddenly, he stopped and methodically turned back to his harrows, picked up a hammer and began pounding on the stubborn bolt with a vengeance born out of what? Anger? Frustration? Disgust? Katreena didn't know, but neither did she care. He can scoff all he wanted. It didn't matter to her anyway. She had told him. What he did with the information was irrelevant. She turned and walked back to the house, relieved that this unpleasant moment was now behind her. She would tell Dusty about it and let the chips fall where they may. Dusty would deal with it in his own way.

Helen was waiting for a report of the discourse. She, too, had found the suspense oppressive. "How did he take it?"

Katreena told Helen of Michael's reaction. Helen was astounded. "That's awful Mom. I'm so sorry."

"That's all right. I expected something like it." Katreena soothed her.

Helen pondered over Michael's ill-mannered comment. "What do you think?"

"Quite frankly, I don't care what he thinks, Helen. I'm glad it's over." Then, with a shrug, she added, "Could have been worse, you know."

Helen sighed. A weight had been lifted from her chest. "Yes, it could have been worse," she repeated.

"You'll meet Dusty on Sunday, you know. He's very eager to meet you." Then as a word of encouragement, she added. "You'll like him, I'm sure of it."

"Oh, I'm sure I will. I just hope he can like us!"

"Don't you worry, sweetheart, he will."

Katreena decided to stay for supper. She wanted to see the dynamics that would come to play at the supper table. This would be the test of Michael's reaction to her news. The weather was still dreary and threatening but no actual moisture was touching down. The kids came in from outdoors where they had been rough housing with Rusko, the dog. As they took their jackets off, Katreena noticed the small notebook that Kaydee surreptitiously transferred from the folds of her jacket to her sweater and then immediately left for her bedroom. She was journaling at every opportunity, Katreena realized with gratification. Katreena washed the two smaller kids, then helped Helen with getting supper on the table. Kaydee came back, washed up and ready to help.

Michael came in and without a word went straight to the bathroom to clean up, then just as wordlessly he sat down and helped himself to the meal. Silence at mealtime in the Boyer household was normal. Sensing this to be a prerequisite to harmony everyone adhered to this rule. Katreena had long ago accepted this as the essential avenue to peace and had even condoned it. Now she wondered if she should have tried to modify the situation somehow. Probably wouldn't have helped anyway and perhaps may even have created more friction, she decided. Still, she wondered what Dusty's reaction would be to such stringent mealtime discipline.

When Dayna started slapping the spoonful of pureed peas away that Helen was trying to feed her, Helen quickly mopped up the green blobs with a wet washcloth and patiently tried again. Dayna was determined and flailed her tiny hands out in protest, upsetting the bowl and the glass of milk all into one oozing mass on the high chair. Helen started cleaning it. Alvin and Kaydee exchanged fearful glances and Dayna started crying. Michael roared at Kaydee.

"Why are you sitting there stupid? Clean the damned thing up. Do I have to look at that disgusting mess while I eat? Move!"

Katreena sensed Kaydee's body go rigid for a split second. She noted a flash of fire flare up in her eyes but she glanced at her grandmother and saw the silent plea etched on her face. Kaydee remembered her solemn promise to maintain peace at all costs and wordlessly got up to get another washcloth to clean up. Helen, in the meantime, quickly took Dayna to the other room until she was placated. The tension at the table froze the group like a huge iceberg. Michael seemed to be waiting for someone to cross him but no one did and the moment passed. With a low grunt, he resumed eating clanging his fork angrily as he ate. Hesitantly, Alvin and Jaynee followed suit, apprehensive and silent, and Katreena picked up where she left off although the food had lost all flavour. Helen finished feeding Dayna in the bedroom and Kaydee finished cleaning up the mess, brought the pie to the table then wet another clean washcloth and went to the bedroom. Michael seemed to be watching for them to come back but when neither Helen nor Kaydee returned, he finished his meal without another word, and promptly left for the shop.

When they heard Michael leave, Helen and Kaydee returned with

Dayna but nobody said anything as they silently cleared the table, cleaned the kids and washed the dishes. With Alvin and Jaynee in the room, the subject was just too loaded to open up. Not a word had been said about Dusty, and Katreena was unsure whether she was relieved or disturbed about that. When the dishes were done, Katreena whispered to Helen that she wanted to talk to Kaydee.

"You go with Granny, sweetheart. Alvin and Jaynee will stay here with Dayna and me." Helen dismissed Kaydee into Katreena's care.

They headed out on to the road. Katreena didn't relish walking anywhere close to where Michael was so that put the meadow off limits. Besides, the recent rain had probably soaked the ground to mud anyway. As they walked along, Kaydee told Katreena about the journal.

"I'm trying to write some poems but I don't know if they are any good. Mostly it's just about stuff that I see and what I think." Kaydee explained.

"That's great, honey. Sometimes journals end up being best selling books you know."

"Oh I could never try to write a book for someone else to read. I just want to write for you and Mother. And maybe Jaynee and Dayna someday."

With a pang, Katreena noted the absence of Alvin's name from the list. Kaydee adored Alvin, but Michael's favouritism of his son put Alvin's loyalties in question, regardless of whether that mistrust was warranted or not.

"Never you mind. You just keep writing. Perhaps you can read them to Dusty and me. Dusty will be here with me on Sunday so you can meet him. Would you like that?"

Kaydee's eyes glowed with excitement as she gave her grandmother an impulsive hug. "Oh Granny, I'd love it. I hope he likes me." Then her face clouded. "But what about Father? What will he say? Did you tell him about Dusty?"

"Yes, sweetheart. I told him today. I think Dusty will be able to handle whatever your father does. Don't you worry your pretty head about it. You just keep that journal of yours going, because Dusty is as delighted about it as I am. Right now, we'd better get back. I have to go home. Your father is taking Alvin to the circus this weekend, but come Sunday, Dusty and I are going to be here right after church. In the meantime, you remember what you promised. Don't do anything to get your father angry. Okay?"

"I promise Granny, but sometimes it's hard. You know what he's like." Kaydee spoke solemnly, "But I promise, Granny. Honest. And if Father says awful things, I'll just think of you and Dusty and how happy I am. I can hardly wait to meet him. Oh, I sure do hope he will like me."

"He'll love you sweetheart. You can bet on it."

It was still daylight when Katreena pulled into her driveway. She was exhausted. It had been such a stressful day but the worst was over. She had paved the way for Dusty's introduction to the family and that was important. Shared with him, this oppressive burden would be lighter.

Janine and Vance were on their deck watching the sunset.

"How did it go?" Janine was eager to hear the details.

Katreena sighed. She would have preferred to just go in and sack out, but Janine was a true friend and had her welfare at heart. It was only common courtesy to keep her informed after having spilled her guts out to her this morning.

Katreena crossed the street and sagged heavily into the padded blue lounger. Janine and Vance exchanged concerned glances and waited patiently for the account. It was Vance who spoke first when Katreena had finished her account. His disgust was in his voice.

"You shouldn't be worrying about that jerk's opinion. He's just that, a dumb jerk. If Helen and Kaydee approve, that's all that matters. You've done your part. You told him. He's just trying to spoil it for you with his disparaging remarks. Don't let him, for heaven's sake!"

"Vance is right, Katty. You must know that." Janine added emphatically.

"Oh I agree, though I must admit I didn't expect to be spoken to like a silly teenager. Scorn is not beyond Michael, it's just one of his natural vices, but it cut because of the way I feel about Dusty. It cheapens the relationship somehow even though I've never respected Michael's opinion. In this situation, especially, his assessment has absolutely no value. I guess I'm just tired. Anyway, that supper ordeal was the clincher. Sometimes I can't believe that man is real. If I didn't see and hear it, I probably would not believe it."

Then she brightened. "At any rate, the worst is over. I promised the family I'd bring Dusty over to meet them all on Sunday. I just hope Dusty can take it. This family of mine is a handful." Katreena sighed wearily.

"From what you've told me, that hunk of yours is a pretty solid rock. Lean on him and enjoy." Janine reassured her.

Katreena thanked them and took her leave. She just wanted to get into bed and forget about everything for a while.

She decided to try washing off all the unpleasantness by stepping into a hot shower, then got into bed and mercifully and immediately fell asleep. The next morning she awoke, still in the same position, totally refreshed and feeling cleansed and rejuvenated.

The day loomed bright and sunny and Katreena thought of the brome on the farm that would probably be ready for baling today. That meant another trip to Zelena again but she didn't mind. The practical thing would have been to spend last night on the farm in anticipation of this because it had started to clear up before she left for home. Yet yesterday she just couldn't do it, she needed the peace and tranquility of her own home and her friends. Now, fortified by the encouragement of Janine and Vance, and safely ensconced by Dusty's positive reception about the upcoming weekend, she was ready for anything.

She called Dusty. She needed to tell him about yesterday.

"It's all set up now," she told him. "I told Michael about you and that you are coming out to the farm to meet him on Sunday. So you're committed. There's no backing out now."

"How did he take it?"

Katreena hesitated. Should she shield Dusty from Michael's sarcastic opinion or was it wiser to be honest and give him time to prepare defence tactics should the need arise? Dusty picked up on her hesitation immediately. He sensed her reluctance to be open about the incident.

"Come on Katreena," he coaxed gently. "I can take it. Give it to me straight. I'm not some wimp that you need to protect."

Katreena swallowed. Best to be honest about it. She owed him that if she wanted him to make an informed decision about getting mixed up with this family of hers. "You have to understand that Michael is very conceited. Other than himself, he doesn't have any respect for anyone," she warned.

Dusty listened wordlessly as Katreena related the encounter with Michael. When she finished, he remained silent for a moment, then as if expecting more, he asked in surprise: "That's it?"

"Pretty much, but it was the way he said it that spoke volumes. And I purposely stayed till after supper to see if there was any other fallout from the incident, but he just totally ignored me. The only flare-up was about the kids."

"Then what are you afraid of?" Dusty was unperturbed. "If this is the worst he can throw at us, then relax. Nothing short of a shotgun is going to scare me off, silly, and even then, I have a suit of armour that I've been saving for just such an emergency. Don't you worry, honey, everything will be fine, you'll see. Tell you what, let's celebrate. What say we head out for supper tonight and end the evening with dancing?"

Katreena was elated. Dusty didn't seem fazed by Michael's scornful attitude at all. He was just glad that Kaydee and Helen were enthusiastic about their meeting. Everything else seemed insignificant to him.

"I'd love to, Dusty, but judging by the promise of a sunny day, I expect a call from the farm because Michael will probably want to finish that hay today. Can I call you back later and let you know if I can make it, please?"

"No sweat. Let me know when you're available. I'll be around home." They hung up on a happy note.

Just as she had anticipated, the call from the farm came before she finished breakfast. Helen was apologetic about making her mother drive out to the farm again, but Katreena assured her it was not a problem. Quickly, she cleared the few dishes and left for KD Acres. She knew the hay wouldn't be ready till about eleven but she didn't want Michael to have any delays to complain about. It was best to maintain as much harmony as possible at this time.

She arrived at KD Acres to find Helen already in the shop helping Michael setting up the equipment for baling the hay. Katreena took over her house, a familiar routine for everyone since her retirement from teaching. Kaydee was now a great help with the smaller children but she was still too young to be left alone with them so Katreena continued to assume the responsibility of staying home with the children when Helen went out into the field.

The day went along smoothly enough but Katreena was glad when the drizzle in the evening offered her the perfect excuse to escape back to the sanctuary of her own home. When Michael and Helen came in from the field wet and chilled, Helen immediately went to take a hot shower. Michael picked up Alvin, set him on his knee and started talking about the circus coming up, promising to take him out for a "fun day tomorrow, come rain or shine." Alvin was understandably excited. He'd been looking forward to this since his accident with the tractor.

As Katreena drove home, her thoughts turned to Dusty and an electrifying tingle raced up her spine spiking with a flush in her cheeks. Perhaps they might get to go dancing tomorrow after all. To Katreena, it mattered little where they went or what they did. She just wanted to be near him, to feel the thrill of his loving gaze on her, his husky voice shyly tantalizing her with compliments, his hand on her arm gently guiding her forward.

She called him as soon as she got to the house. When he realized it was her, his voice immediately softened and she could tell he was genuinely glad she called. Since it was already too late to do anything that evening, they made plans for an early supper on Saturday, followed by dancing "somewhere," as Dusty put it.

Saturday was a blur of excitement for Katreena as she prepared for her date with Dusty. She made a three o'clock appointment to get her hair done then pampered herself to a luxurious bubble bath and lay there enjoying the sensuous Diorella perfume that she had purchased in Europe last month. Katreena wanted everything to be perfect tonight. At half past four, she meticulously applied makeup to her flushed face. That flush made her look like a painted doll, and she tried to envision her complexion from Dusty's perspective. He'd probably think she had just applied too much rouge. She could hardly tell him that he was the cause for that natural glow. Try as she might, she just could not tame it. Still, at quarter to five, as she confidently met Dusty at the door, she was ill-prepared for his reaction.

"Pheweewe," Dusty whistled when he saw her and instantly Katreena felt that infuriating flush return to her face. "I'm not sure I want to take you out in public, lady. I don't think I have the stamina to fight off competition. You can knock the socks off a man looking like that."

Feeling suddenly overwhelmingly self-conscious, Katreena could only mumble a simple "thank you," as she took the bouquet of garden flowers he offered.

Dusty sensed her consternation and as Katreena went to put the flowers into a vase, he came up behind her, wrapped his arms around her and kissed her cheek. "Relax, honey," he whispered, "let's just go have fun tonight and forget about everything."

Katreena leaned thankfully against his solid chest, her cheek glued to his in silent surrender and nodded. They stood that way for several minutes, just enjoying the moment. Finally, Dusty broke the spell.

"I didn't make a reservation for supper. I wasn't sure where you'd want to go. Should we try the Olive Garden and the Jade Palace again or would you rather try that new Caribbean Club that just opened on Tobago Circle last month? I hear it's quite elegant and the food is great. What do you think?"

The question was so matter-of-fact that it put Katreena at ease and she grasped at the opportunity to get on to a safe topic.

"Let's try the new place and see what it's like."

"You got it," Dusty smiled and extended his hand towards to door. "Let's not waste any time. Your carriage awaits, milady."

Both seafood connoisseurs, they were pleased to find that the Club featured an ample menu to satisfy their passions. They ordered escargot appetizers and wine, then, as they waited for the main course of wild rice, lobster tails, breaded jumbo shrimp and stuffed mushroom caps, Dusty told her about a trip to Toronto he and his brother Wayne were planning to meet with other publishers. As they talked about the different books and genres of writing, they got on the subject of Kaydee's journal and her love for poetry.

"Kaydee writes poetry, eh? What does she write about?" Dusty wanted to know.

"I really don't know. She only started. I know she has been writing a lot lately, but I haven't read or heard any of it myself yet."

The supper was delicious and time passed quickly and pleasantly. The arrival of the dessert wagon interrupted their discourse and Katreena started to protest, but Dusty insisted they had to top the meal off. They finally settled on a light fruit medley parfait, and savouring it slowly, they continued to discuss the interests and allure of the literary profession.

The sound of music signalled the arrival of the band. Katreena glanced at her watch and noted with surprise that they had been there for over two hours. Time had gone by so fast. She felt at ease now and was enjoying the calm atmosphere that their casual camaraderie created.

"Shall we?" Dusty held out his hand to her. "I just have to show off this beautiful lady to the public. It's not fair to keep you hidden any longer. I feel like shouting from the rooftops, 'Look at me. This lady is mine!' Or am I being too presumptuous?" Dusty's smile was less shy now, but he still seemed to be pleading, belying his playful teasing self-confidence.

"You're not being presumptuous at all," she murmured huskily as he led her to the dance floor. He held her tight as they swayed wordlessly to the slow music and she felt a warm glow spread through her body as she abandoned herself to the wonder of the moment. The band asked for requests and Dusty asked for Elvis Presley's "Love Me Tender" which the band very obligingly struck up. As the band started to play, a young couple, obviously Elvis Presley fans, emerged from the floor, walked up to the microphone and proceeded to sing. They were actually good singers and harmonized beautifully. Dusty and Katreena swayed to the melodious strains, totally engrossed in the romance of the lyrics and in the wonder of their togetherness. All the dancers on the floor seemed to enjoy the singing. When they finished, the applause was deafening. Somebody requested "Blue Suede Shoes" and the band again obliged as did the singing couple. After that more requests came for Elvis' songs, "Wooden Heart," "Love Me Tonight," "Fools Fall in Love," "Don't be Cruel," "Tutti Fruiti" and "Jailhouse Rock." The band and the singers complied. It turned out to be an Elvis Presley night with resounding applause for the singing couple whose renditions of the Elvis tunes obviously more than pleased the crowd. Then the band announced a break and walked off the stage, much to the disappointment of the crowd.

Katreena and Dusty returned to their table for a refreshing drink and a rest. When the band resumed after the break, the singers did not return so the band played on alone, fulfilling various requests from the crowd. Dances melded into each other as the evening sped by, a blur of happiness, tender compliments, and blissful contentment.

Katreena's heart was singing when Dusty seared her lips with a passionate goodnight kiss when he dropped her off shortly after eleven. Tomorrow was a big day. Tomorrow Dusty would meet Katreena's family!

Chapter 12

Katreena was smiling as she walked into the house but the thought of tomorrow suddenly cast a shadow on her euphoria. She felt a pang of guilt about being so happy. Tomorrow might bring that to a sudden halt if Michael created a scene. Suddenly she felt an uncontrollable urge to check that everything was still alright with the family. Putting her keys and handbag on the table, she hastily dialled the number for KD Acres.

Helen's "Hello" was immediate, her voice hoarse with emotion. Katreena felt the tingle of goose bumps ripple all over her body. Premonition, like a glacier, gripped icily at Katreena's heart.

"Helen, what's the matter?"

"Mom, please come." Helen's whisper was barely audible. Then louder, as if for someone else to hear, she said, "Sorry, you must have the wrong number," and the phone went dead.

Not even stopping to think, Katreena grabbed her purse and keys and bolted out to the car. Terror and anxiety made her nauseous but she didn't have the luxury of time to succumb to it. As she raced out of the city, she cast her eyes ahead and to the side streets, hoping there were no police cruisers to monitor her illegal speed. Once out on the highway, she gunned the motor well above the speed limit, and thanked God for the modest volume of traffic that made it possible.

She couldn't imagine what had happened at KD Acres but she knew that something had to be very wrong – someone was danger. She wished she had invited Dusty to come in. He might have been with her now. She had a feeling she was going to need his help, but she had no time to stop and call him now. She shouldn't have gone away for the whole evening. She should have stayed close to home. The situation on the farm had been mutinous this whole week. She had known that when she left there the other day. What if something terrible had happened? What if Michael had hurt Kaydee or Helen? The thought of that possibility almost made her lose control of the car. She gripped the wheel firmly, squared her shoulders and leaned forward. "Concentrate on your driving and find out the facts before jumping to crazy conclusions," she admonished herself.

She missed Dusty. She needed his rationalism. She fought to maintain a calm composure but visions of terrible disasters assailed her brain. Never had the farm seemed so far away as it did tonight. "Please Lord," she prayed desperately, "let things be alright there."

As she pulled into the yard, the lights were all on in the house and so was the yard light atop the tall pole, illuminating the yard with what Katreena thought was an eerie glow. She dashed into the house, her heart hammering a staccato beat.

Helen met her at the door. "Thanks for coming, Mom." Her voice was a hushed whisper, as if she was trying to keep someone from hearing her. No one else was in sight. Then, with a wink at Katreena, as if for someone else's ears, she said aloud, "Hello, Mother, I see you made it out tonight after all."

Taking her cue from Helen, Katreena hesitated then forcing calm into her voice, she said casually. "Well, I thought I might join you for church here tomorrow but I got home later than I expected so I'm sorry it's so late." Glancing around to make sure Michael wasn't in sight, she mouthed silently to Helen, "What's going on?" then followed Helen's glance towards the dining room door, where Michael had appeared, his expression sullen, but his face flushed with agitation.

"Hello, Katreena. Helen told me you were coming out but when you didn't come by ten, I thought you weren't coming."

For some reason, her daughter had used her as a shield, and if Helen needed a shield, then it was time to bring Dusty into the picture as a shield for them all.

"Dusty and I went out to supper at the Caribbean Club and when the band started up, we stayed for a few dances." She stopped there, hoping that one of them would make a comment that would clue her in on how to proceed from there. Katreena's mind was racing. Nobody seemed to have been hurt so far, judging by Helen's composure, but...

"Who's Dusty?" Michael's voice was sharp, his manner abrupt.

"Dusty is a man I have been seeing. You remember. I told you about him on Thursday when I was here. You will be meeting tomorrow. I invited him to come and meet the family."

Katreena spoke boldly but casually as if she was unaware of anything unusual happening here. Whatever was going on, if Helen wanted buffers, she was going to get them. Michael always had more respect for men than for women, so the prospect of meeting a potential new man in the family might be enough to stabilize whatever unpredictable eruption was brewing here.

Michael grunted in antipathy but said nothing more. He turned and stomped back into the living room where he stopped, then with purposeful steps, came back to the dining room, his right fist pounding his left palm. Glancing up, he seemed surprised to see Katreena standing there, as if he had forgotten their conversation of less than a minute ago. Distracted, he turned again and walked out to the other room again. Out of sight, Katreena could hear him pacing angrily back and forth, but he did not enter the kitchen or even the dining room any more. Helen appeared apprehensive. She shook her head sideways and shrugged her shoulders at Katreena, as if to say, "Don't ask me. I don't know either."

Obviously, Helen felt that having her mother come out to the farm at this time would diffuse some kind of situation. What was it? Helen seemed to be alright, but she was definitely not in control here, frightened but not physically hurt and this did not seem the time to be asking her questions. Suddenly Kaydee flashed across Katreena mind and her heart lurched. She had to see her, make sure she was alright.

Mustering a casual enunciation she winked at Helen, "Well, I'm pretty tired. It's been a long day. I'm going up to kiss the kids goodnight." Whatever had happened, she could not get answers from Helen at this point but it seemed as if the threat of her impending presence had brought the problem under some semblance of control.

She had to force herself to climb the stairs reasonably, instead of racing up two stairs at a time as she would have liked. Katreena closed Kaydee's door quietly but firmly behind her as she walked in. Instantly, the light snapped on. Kaydee had been lying there in the dark, pretending to be asleep, but she sat bolt upright as soon as she saw her grandmother.

"What happened?" Katreena whispered as she crossed the room to embrace her.

"I don't really know," Kaydee whispered back, wide-eyed. "Father and Alvin were at the circus, and when they came home, Father was furious about something. He kept yelling something about nosy neighbours, and that Archer and Drapanik should 'mind their own business.' I was picking peas in the garden, and I heard him yelling at Mother so I came running, but before I could say a word, Mother made me take Dayna and Jaynee and Alvin outside, and told me to finish picking and shelling all the peas and beans. I put Dayna on the grass with Jaynee, while Alvin and I worked in the garden. I think she didn't want us in the house because Father was so angry. It was dark when I finished. When I came into the house, she just told me to put Jaynee and Dayna and Alvin to bed and then, go straight to sleep. Granny, Mother didn't do anything. But he was so angry at her, I was afraid for her. *I hate him*! I hate him, Granny! It's not fair that he yells at her all the time. I *hate* him." Kaydee whispered, her whole body shuddering, and then, defensively, she emphasized. "But I kept my promise to you Granny. I didn't make him angry. Nobody did. Honest."

"I believe you, sweetheart. It's okay." Katreena reassured her wrapping her arms around the trembling girl, holding her tight. "Did Alvin say what happened?"

"I asked him, and he told me a bunch of funny things. He said one man was telling the other men how Father was 'watching his wife pounding posts into the ground' and he was 'yelling at her because it was crooked.' Alvin said all the men were laughing very hard and they said Father 'has no leg' and something about Father 'living on his wife.' Alvin said all kinds of funny things that didn't make sense, but he said Father got very mad, and that he was swearing and yelling at them, and they didn't listen to him. He said Father was not having fun with those men because they were laughing at him. That was when they left the circus. When they got home, he was so angry, and he was just yelling and yelling, and he was swearing, Granny. I was afraid for Mother. I couldn't hear or understand exactly what he was yelling about. All I heard was something about 'those damn neighbours mind their own business.' And I heard him say Joe Drapanik and Fred Archer, and something like

Benson or Bedson so it must have something to do with them. Mother didn't want any of us in the house. I don't think she wanted us anywhere near the house. Granny, she was afraid, really, really, afraid this time!" Kaydee's eyes were fearful and her demeanour anxious. She was concerned about her mother having to endure Michael's unjustified fury yet again, but Katreena also sensed that Kaydee's hatred for Michael and her ferocity towards him had just reached a new and dangerous phase.

"It's okay, sweetheart. Don't worry. Everything seems to be peaceful now. I doubt that your father will do anything bad now that I'm here. I'll try and find out from your mother what this is all about. Maybe if we figure out the problem, we can figure out how to fix it. Dusty will be here tomorrow, and we'll deal with whatever it is. You go to sleep now. I'll be spending the night here so don't worry. Goodnight, sweetheart. I love you." Katreena kissed her on the forehead, and walked out of the room.

After checking to find the other kids asleep, Katreena went downstairs. Michael was still pacing angrily clenching and unclenching his fists, pounding his palm every now and then as if it were some mortal enemy he wanted to destroy. Helen was just giving the final touches of the iron to a pair of Alvin's pants. Anxiety and dread hung like a heavy fog in the room.

Katreena gave Helen a questioning glance, but Helen wordlessly shrugged her shoulders, folded the pants, and proceeded to put the ironing board away. Fearful that any questions might send Michael into another tirade, Katreena decided to make sure Helen was safely in bed before she went up herself.

Mouthing silently to Helen, "Go to bed now," Katreena was relieved to see her daughter nod agreement. Then to Katreena's silent "You going to be okay?" Helen added another affirmative nod.

Picking up her purse and keys from the counter where she had dropped them earlier, Katreena broke the silence. "Guess it's bedtime for this tired body."

"Yes, I'm ready to hit the bed as well. I'm finished here for today." Helen seized the opportunity to escape the ominous tension in the room and left for the bedroom, timing her pass through the living room so that

Michael was not in her path as she walked to the bedroom beyond.

"Goodnight, then. Goodnight, Michael." Katreena called from the stairs.

"Goodnight," Helen called. Michael didn't answer. His pacing didn't miss a beat.

Katreena left her door slightly ajar, listening for any noise from downstairs ready to fly to her daughter's defence if the need arose. She had no idea what the problem was and there was no way for her to ask any questions right now without stirring up the hornets' nest and risking a possible all-out assault on the family again. She could not diffuse the situation without knowing the details about it. Better to preserve the tenuous calm for the time being, providing that Michael goes to sleep without creating any more problems.

Only Michael did not go to sleep. Katreena could hear him pacing through the night. Sensing the hostility his behaviour indicated, Katreena could not sleep, fearful of what he might do. Michael's footsteps testified to his continued agitation and Katreena feared the worst. She conjured up various scenarios, inventing ways to cope with each and then discarding each solution as impossible, impractical, or unworkable. She should call the police. She should let them handle it. That is what she should do.

"And tell them what, Katreena?" she asked herself.

"My son-in-law is angry. Agitated."

"Yes, lady. What has he done?"

"Well, officer, nothing, really."

"Then how do you know he is angry?"

"Well, he's pacing the floor and pounding his fists."

"Has he hurt anybody?"

"No, he hasn't."

"Has he made any threats to hurt anybody?"

"No, he hasn't."

Katreena played this little dramatization over in her mind and realized how ridiculous it would sound to a police officer. She suspected, but had no confirmation, that Michael had been insulted or ridiculed by some men at the circus. She knew about Michael's monumental ego but this seemed melodramatic even for him. Still her fear was real and she knew it was not unfounded, but how do you explain a man like Michael to anyone? She would be the one that would come out looking like an idiot if she tried calling the police.

The pacing ceased finally and she dozed, on and off, a restless slumber, one ear still tuned for any unusual noises that might mean things were not at peace downstairs.

The glow of dawn embraced the room and Katreena checked the clock beside her bed. Five minutes after four. Something had awakened her. A sound. A sound of what? She held her breath and listened. Then a chair creaked downstairs. Katreena's body tensed. She lay rigid, every muscle of her body primed to spring into action if need be. Then footsteps. Someone was up. Michael? He was probably still in the living room. The footsteps continued into the kitchen, then stopped. A light shuffling, then a door opening and closing. Silence. Katreena waited. More silence. Someone had gone outside.

Silently grabbing a housecoat from the hanger in the closet, she tiptoed downstairs, unsure of what she would find there. No one seemed to be around. She tiptoed to the living room. Nothing. Dare she check the master bedroom? Nervously she stood there, contemplating her next move. Then she glanced out the window. In the shadows of early dawn's demarcated light she saw Michael out by the shed pulling at the huge door. Relief flooded through her veins like molten lava. She went to check on Helen. She seemed to be sleeping peacefully. She was safe. She was exhausted for sure, but safe. Thank God. Quickly she went to the phone, dialled Dusty's number and waited nervously for his answer.

"Hello," he sounded groggy, as if he'd been sleeping.

"Hi, Dusty, it's me. Listen," Katreena whispered quickly, not wanting to wake Helen. "I'm at the farm. Something has come up. Could you drive up here and meet us at the church in Zelena about tenish? It's on Zander Street. Just turn right after you cross the track. It's about two blocks down. You can't miss it. I'm sorry about this, Dusty. I'll explain later."

"Katreena, are you alright? Is everything okay with the family?"

Dusty's voice was sharp with concern.

"Yes, yes. We're all right. Do you mind terribly? I'll explain later."

"Of course I don't mind honey. I'll be there. You just hang tight. You sure you're all right?"

"Yes, we are. I'll explain when I see you. I have to go." She hung up without even waiting for his goodbye. She didn't dare risk having Michael coming in and seeing her. She still did not have a complete handle on the situation, and did not wish to exacerbate it. It was too volatile. Surreptitiously she crept upstairs. Church wasn't till ten and the family probably would not be up till eight if normal Sunday routine was being followed today. Given the events of last night, she had no idea what to expect, but she was willing to let someone else set the pace. She would just fall in where or when she was needed.

If there was anything that was inescapable, it was Michael's determination to be in church each Sunday. That was a given, an essential component of his façade, the impeccable family man. He always insisted on maintaining public image, no matter what. His father had been a regular in church before he died, his neighbours were regulars and there was no way Michael would be anything less. What he did at home bore no resemblance to what he heard in church. Love was something the preachers had to preach about but Michael Boyer was not committed to practice it. Still, judging by his pacing all last night, obviously a result of a humiliating experience at the fair with the neighbours yesterday, Katreena wasn't sure what to expect today. Well, if worse came to worse, she would just go to church alone to meet Dusty, but if things were that bad, would she trust Michael alone with the family? She didn't know. She would just have to wait and see. She settled down again to try to sleep.

That sleep took her into a dream world of savage snarling wolves bearing down on her as she struggled to cross a raging river of snow and ice crashing over jagged rocks that protruded out of the surging water slashing the huge chunks of ice into shards of flying icicles. Terrified, she woke up, cold and shivering, relieved to find herself in the safety of the house and then, as recollection of the events of the night before assailed her, her emotions plummeted again in response to the disconcerting memory.

A furtive rustle from Kaydee's room told Katreena that Kaydee was awake but there was still no sound coming from downstairs. It was getting on to eight o'clock and Katreena wondered if it was a good or a bad sign. She tiptoed to the door and opened it to find Kaydee stealthily heading towards her.

"Good morning, Granny," Kaydee whispered. Katreena held the door open for her to enter, then quietly closed it behind her.

"Good morning, honey. How did you sleep?" Katreena tried to sound nonchalant but she too, kept her voice at a barely audible whisper. "Are you hungry? I am starving but I guess your mother is still sleeping and I don't want to wake her yet."

"I don't want to wake them either. I hope Father will not be yelling again today. I wish we didn't have to be scared all the time. Is there such a thing, Granny? Why do we always have to be afraid of him? Why does he have to be so angry all the time? Sometimes I wish he would just go away and never come back, like Amy Gally's father did. I heard the kids talking in school and they said he just went away and never came home. Amy doesn't have a father now. I wish I didn't have a father!"

Katreena gathered the young girl in her arms, rocking her gently as they sat on the bed. She had no answers for her. No reassuring sagacious advice, no real promises that things would improve soon. Empathy with the girl's plight and her insurgent wishes made Katreena feel wicked. She was the grandmother. She should be teaching the child compassion, forgiveness. Instead, God forgive her, she was condoning this evil wish with her silence, secretly concurring, even reinforcing it, albeit mutely.

The sound of doors opening and shutting, water running in the bathroom told them that someone was awake downstairs and both grandmother and granddaughter held their breath. When five minutes had passed and only the normal sounds of kitchen clatter were heard, they both relaxed. Relieved, Katreena gave Kaydee a tap on the behind and whispered, "All's well. Let's get ready for breakfast." Kaydee smiled weakly and hurried to make her bed and dress.

Alone in her room again, Katreena realized she would have to go to church in the aqua coloured crepe she had worn last night. In her frantic rush to get to the farm, she had not stopped to think about clothes. She kept some clothes on the farm, essentials, work clothes, casuals, a nightgown and robe, but not clothes that were suitable for church. Those, she always brought from home if she expected to need them. Oh, well, the aqua crepe would have to do.

Breakfast was the usual silent affair. Michael was morose, obviously still angry, but with the whole family walking on eggshells, there was no provocation to bark about. It did seem to Katreena that he rather dragged his feet about going to church, almost as if he didn't want to go but acknowledging her own propensity to thinking only the worst of him, she decided it was probably her imagination.

Katreena decided not to take her car to church, planning instead, to come back with Dusty, so when Michael wordlessly left the house for the green sedan, Katreena joined the family and sat in the back seat with the girls, while Alvin sat between Michael and Helen. Silence and rigid inactivity dominated the ride to church but that too, was normal for this family.

Chapter 13

Dusty hung up the phone and sat there staring at it. Now what was that all about? She wasn't supposed to go out tonight yet she was at the farm now! She had said everything was alright, yet she was whispering. Was she afraid of being overheard? What in God's Holy name was going on there? It had to be Michael! What had that madman done now? She had sounded apprehensive, but not in pain. If somebody had been hurt, her voice would surely have conveyed it. He checked the clock. A quarter past four. It was the middle of the night, for heaven's sake. Their plans had been to go out to the farm together. What had caused those plans to suddenly change? She would have needed to let him know. But at this hour? Something was definitely wrong. He could sense it.

Dusty wondered if he should just head out now but no, she had said to meet them in church. If there was a problem, he might make it worse if he arrived at an unscheduled time. But what if they needed him? He was torn. Still, from what Katreena had told him before and this morning, he should probably stick to Katreena's plan. He checked his watch again. Six hours to go before meeting Katreena. Too early for his morning run but he was too agitated to sleep now.

He donned his jogging outfit and set out for a brisk and invigorating run. It always helped him clear his mind but this morning it did little to appease his confusion or assuage his worry. By the time he got back home, he had worked up a good sweat but the memory of that call, still gave him the chills. His jaw clenched, he stripped and stepped into the shower.

Katreena could hardly wait for Dusty to show up. She wondered how his arrival would affect the situation. Instead of sitting with Helen and Michael in their usual pew, Katreena sat at the back to intercept Dusty when he arrived. Kaydee looked at her with surprise at first, then realizing her grandmother was not going toward the front of the church, slid in beside her. Jaynee looked around and realizing Kaydee was not behind, quickly turned and toddled back to join her big sister. Michael gave Katreena an acrimonious backwards glance but decided not to make a scene and resolutely continued with the rest of the family to their regular pew.

Almost before they had settled into their pew, Katreena looked up to see Dusty sliding in beside Jaynee. Jaynee gaped at him and quickly moved to the other side of Kaydee and into the safety of her grandmother's arms. Hugging the child close, Katreena smiled a welcome to Dusty and Kaydee immediately realized that this was the man in Granny's life. Whispering a quick introduction, Katreena indicated to Kaydee that it was alright for her sit where she was, between Dusty and her grandmother. Beaming happily, Kaydee sat listening to the service just starting. Jaynee sat in Katreena's lap, watching the man who seemed to have so completely captured the ardour of her big sister.

As they exited the church after the service, Katreena introduced Dusty to Reverend Paul.

"Reverend Paul, I'd like you to meet a very special friend of mine, Dusty Duganyk. Dusty, this is Zelena's own genial shepherd of the flock, Reverend Paul Padaman, known affectionately to all simply as Reverend Paul."

"So nice to make your acquaintance, Reverend Paul," Dusty extended his hand as the crowd jostled around them.

Kaydee stood smiling proudly as the pastor and Dusty exchanged the brief amenities allowed by the surge of the crowd. Extracting a promise from Dusty to come back again soon, Reverend Paul turned to talk to the other parishioners patiently waiting to speak to him.

Moving out of the way, Katreena and Dusty walked down the steps and stood off to the side to wait for Michael and Helen. When they emerged, Katreena noticed that Michael did the perfunctory handshake with the preacher but did not stop to talk before striding purposefully down the steps. He was morose, obviously still affected by whatever had happened last night and seemed impatient to get away from the crowd. Groaning inwardly, Katreena decided this was going to be a grim day at the farm. Ruefully she determined to make the best of it.

Stepping in front of Michael, her hand on Dusty's arm, Katreena said, "Michael, Helen, I want you to meet Dusty." She deliberately said

Michael's name first, to put him off guard.

Michael gave Dusty an almost belligerent scowl, then resignedly, extended his hand. "Pleased to meet you. Katreena told me about you. Welcome to the family."

Standing slightly behind, Helen gaped, speechless. Katreena, too, was stunned at this unexpected about-face from Michael. Kaydee, who had been standing to the side, holding her breath with apprehension, now let it out almost audibly. She suddenly looked like she was about to start crying in relief, but Dusty, totally unperturbed, took Michael's outstretched hand and, in a completely casual voice, said "Thank you, Michael. I'm pleased to meet you too. Katreena has told me so much about KD Acres. I'm eager to see it for myself."

Michael didn't reply, he just dropped his hand, nodded dispassionately and started off towards the street.

Totally flabbergasted, Katreena could not even think what to do next. Once again, Dusty came to the rescue. He took Katreena's arm and followed Michael.

"You ready to roll Katreena? Is there a restaurant here in town? Can I take you all out for Sunday dinner? My treat."

Michael seemed to snap to attention. "We're not going to no restaurant. We will have dinner at home." Resolutely, he reached over to take Alvin's hand and left for the car.

Dusty glanced at Katreena but she merely shrugged her shoulders. Not wishing to antagonize Michael with word or action, Dusty took Katreena's arm and headed for his own vehicle. Kaydee, flushed red with apprehension but empowered by Dusty's effect on her father a few minutes earlier, asked quickly, "May I ride with Granny and Dusty, please?"

Dusty couldn't miss the mutinous look that crossed Michael's face as he fought for control. His mouth opened to say something, but Kaydee, determined to thwart the negative response before it was delivered, persisted, "May I, please, Father?"

Michael, not wishing to appear vanquished, muttered a somewhat half-civil "Go ahead," then rudely turned and strode toward the car, his hand tightly clasped on Alvin's little arm, practically dragging the reluctant boy along. Helen shrugged her shoulders at Katreena and followed, carrying Dayna in her arms. Jaynee looked pleadingly at Kaydee and then at Katreena, not daring to voice her wishes. Katreena smiled at her and held out her hand.

"You can come with us too, honey." Jaynee's little face lit up like a neon light.

On the ride to KD Acres, Dusty purposely kept the conversation light, focusing on Kaydee and her school activities and general interests. He would have preferred to have been able to question Katreena in private but that must wait now. Clearly Kaydee wanted to be away from Michael's presence and he wanted to put the girl at ease without interrogating her now. He needed to find out what was happening here but this was not the time to delve into it.

"Your grandmother tells me you like to read, Kaydee, and now you are even writing, and poetry, too. Is that true?"

Kaydee blushed purple. "I love to read and I have only started to write some poems because I enjoy it. I'm afraid my poems are not very good. I love poems like Tennyson's 'Crossing the Bar,' or Emily Bronte's 'Riches I Hold' or Browning, or Longfellow and all those guys but I can never write like them. I know I can't," Kaydee sighed wistfully.

"You shouldn't try to write like anybody. Be yourself. I want to read Kaydee Boyer's writing, not Tennyson or Bronte or Browning or Longfellow or any of those other poets. They have their place but you are going to need to have your own place, your own style."

"But they are so good," Kaydee protested.

"And I never said they were not good. But you learn from them and then you develop your own style. They wrote about things in their lives, the things they knew about and the things that affected them. Their things don't affect you. You write about things in your life. You write about Kaydee's life, now, nineteen seventy, not something from some other century."

"You make it sound so simple," Kaydee mused, smiling at Dusty's reflection in the rear view mirror.

"You just keep working at it and it will get easier as you progress. Just don't give up or get discouraged when things get tough, okay?"

"I won't. I promise." Kaydee vowed.

Dusty pulled in behind Michael and as the family disembarked from the two vehicles, Dusty saw the children's buoyant mood dissipate as they joined the rest of the family. Suddenly, sombre and uneasy, the children slowly followed the adults into the house. No boisterous running or laughing, no excited babbling that would be normal for children that age. Kaydee and Jaynee hung back to walk behind Katreena and Dusty looking apprehensive and wary. Dusty suddenly understood what it was that had Katreena so troubled about the family.

Watching Dusty's quizzical expression as he walked to the house, an intense feeling of shame and sorrow overwhelmed Katreena as she looked at her family through his eyes. He was right. It was incredulous. And the worst was yet to come. What would Dusty think of the silence at mealtimes, when only the most rudimentary comments or essential information was dispensed? Why had she not prepared Dusty for this aspect of the visit? Until now, she had not thought of how much her acquiescence had contributed to this deplorable situation. Her heart ached with this sudden insight into her own debasing weakness.

Helen immediately donned an apron and set to checking the oven roast that she had put into the automatic oven that morning. There were potatoes and carrots simmering in the juices around the roast and the appetizing aroma of the dinner filled the room. Kaydee immediately took the younger kids to change and Michael, without even looking at Dusty, wordlessly went to the living room, switched on the TV, and reclined in the big green tweed-covered chair in the corner by the stairway.

Dusty looked at Katreena as if to say "Now what?"

Speaking loudly so Michael could hear, Katreena said "Well Dusty, what do you think of KD Acres? Come on, I'll show you the rest of the house."

"We built this house the year after the war ended. Getting supplies was still slow and all too often delivery dates were unpredictable so we had several frustrating delays. In our eagerness to get it built, we had the basement poured and then the lumber did not arrive as promised. To make matters worse sudden heavy rains filled the basement before we could erect the framework."

"That must have been aggravating alright," Dusty agreed. "How long did you have to wait and how did you manage to get the basement dry?"

"Oh, it was quite maddening. Daniel was ready to hit the rails and bring the lumber in on his back. Then Drovner, our contractor here in town, pulled some strings and they brought the supplies in with a big truck all the way from Winnipeg, because Drovner was afraid that Daniel would bypass him if he went to fetch it directly from the supplier in the city. Drovner even brought pumps and fans to help us empty and dry the basement."

Dusty listened attentively, expressing interest in the conversation but obviously waiting for some direction as to how he was to proceed. Katreena was nervous and she knew she was rambling. She had expected that Michael would at least try to be civil, especially after he had "welcomed" Dusty to the family when he first met him but his behaviour now was totally rude and Katreena felt ashamed and ill at ease. When she showed him into the living room, Michael kept his eyes glued to the TV screen and did not even acknowledge them.

Now in casual attire, Kaydee came downstairs, took Dayna's playpen and Jaynee's toys out on the deck and set up the girls to play there. She then went into the kitchen to set the table as Helen mixed the salad. Alvin left the house to play with Rusko. Seeing that Michael was adamant about ignoring them, and dinner was still a few minutes away, Katreena led Dusty outside.

"To Hell with him," she muttered as much to herself as to Dusty. "If this is the way he wants to play it, so be it. Who needs his bullshit anyway? Just as well we don't have to put up with him."

As they walked among the flower beds and into the garden, Katreena filled Dusty in on the events of the previous evening and reiterated the story Kaydee had gotten from Alvin about Michael's humiliation at the fair.

"I'm not sure, but it almost sounds to me like Michael has had Helen doing the fencing at some time and it is totally possible that he stood there and yelled if the posts were not straight. Apparently one or more of the neighbours witnessed this and it's probably the community joke. If that is the case it would definitely set Michael up for a good deal of ridicule. Given his superiority complex, and inflated ego, it could sufficiently provoke this hostility. Helen has not told me about doing the fencing, but knowing Michael, it is entirely possible. The story seems far-fetched though, even for Michael, but Alvin is bright and I doubt he could have misquoted the words. I honestly don't know what to think." Dusty listened wordlessly, his face reflecting Katreena's own bewilderment.

"Have you had an opportunity to speak with Helen privately?"

"No, I haven't and Michael has chosen to pretend nothing is happening but Kaydee and the younger kids all feel the tension and are visibly apprehensive. His flare-up was evidently severe enough to frighten not only Helen and Kaydee, but Alvin and Jaynee as well, so everyone has been practically tiptoeing on eggshells all morning. Helen would never have summoned me so urgently without a valid reason. Kaydee said Helen was really scared. Michael is very vain so being the brunt of public humiliation that way would have been devastating to him but I don't want to aggravate the situation by trying to get Helen away from him to question her. From what Kaydee tells me, Michael has been rampaging from the moment he drove into the yard last night, but until I talk to Helen, I cannot tell if my suspicions are valid. He's quiet now, but with his temper, it's like walking a tightrope. We never know when it will snap. He's temperamental at the best of times, but this uncertainty is almost ominous."

"Is he likely to harm them physically? He appears to be brooding about something."

"I know. What I don't know is, is he about to explode or will he just fizz out?"

Kaydee came up behind them and linked her arm through Katreena's. "Dinner's ready." She was subdued, as if she were dreading the meal as much as her grandmother was.

Dusty noted her wariness with sadness. The girl was tense and fearful. Trying to cut the tension, he stepped across, and tucked Kaydee's other arm under his, and announced cheerfully, "Well, if dinner is ready, then what are we waiting for? I am starved, how about you?"

Katreena gave him a thankful smile but Kaydee was only able to muster a weak one, still afraid of what was waiting for them at the house.

When they walked into the dining room, Michael and the kids were already seated at the table. Michael did not even acknowledge Dusty's "You've got a lovely place here, Michael. Katreena showed me the garden and the flowers. After lunch, I'd like to see the rest of the yard."

Michael maintained a sullen silence.

Helen and Katreena exchanged glances at Michael's indifference. Then smiling at Dusty, Helen pulled out a chair at the far end of the table and said, "Here Dusty, why don't you sit at this end? This chair is always Mother's," motioning to the one next to it.

All through dinner, Michael remained morose and silent, reaching for the roast and the vegetables across Alvin and Kaydee as if they didn't rate being spoken to. Dusty kept up a running conversation, talking about fishing trips and the fish the lake always yielded. Katreena interjected comments here and there but Helen and the children all remained silent. Even Dayna fed quietly with Helen spooning food into her open mouth. When finished, she merely sat playing contentedly with the cheerios that Helen had put on the tray in front of her. It was as if everyone was holding their breath, not daring to disturb the probationary peace.

As soon as Michael's plate was empty, Helen brought out the dessert, bowls of coconut pudding topped with whipped cream and shredded coconut. Michael ate it, then retreated to the bedroom without a word. Within minutes he emerged, in jeans and a work shirt and went outside. An audible sigh of relief escaped from Kaydee's throat and the atmosphere in the room immediately changed. Alvin started asking Dusty about fishing, Kaydee perked up and even Jaynee took on an animated interest in the conversation. Suddenly, Dusty was engaged in conversation that included not just an audience, but participants. The transformation was unbelievable!

Dusty did not want to involve the children in any explanations. They were obviously very uneasy and he did not wish to alarm them further so he kept the conversation light.

"So what do you do for fun around here?" Dusty queried Alvin.

But Alvin was not interested in idle conversation.

"Do you have a boat?" Alvin asked excitedly, eager now to explore the conversation he had not dared to join during dinner.

"Sure, I do," Dusty said, laughing at Alvin's enthusiasm. "Do you like boats, fishing?"

"I don't know," Alvin's face went pensive. "I've never been in a boat before. Daddy said he might buy one and we might go fishing but he has to teach me first."

"Perhaps you can come fishing with me and Granny someday. Would you like that?"

"Yea!" Alvin breathed in awe, his excitement at the prospect clearly visible in his eyes. Jaynee had sat quietly listening, too shy to participate in the conversation herself.

As the table was cleared and dishes washed, everyone bantered on easily, but even as they worked, Dusty noted that Kaydee, Helen and Katreena all surreptitiously stole glances toward the shed checking that Michael was not heading back to the house. What a grip this man had on this family!

"Why don't you take the kids out to play in the yard," Katreena suggested to Kaydee. The young girl's face registered disappointment at being dismissed from the house but sensing that the adults wanted to talk, she gathered the smaller children and herded them outdoors.

Chapter 14

The moment the door closed behind the children, Dusty looked from Katreena to Helen. "Okay, would somebody like to fill me in on why everyone is tiptoeing around here?"

Katreena too, was looking to Helen for answers. Helen cast another quick look towards the shed and sighed.

"Well you know how proud Michael is. He has never had real respect from the other guys around here and you know how much he has always wanted it. Well it seems that one of the guys started telling some of the other guys about the time when we were fixing up that west fence line on the pasture. The guy must have been out there somewhere and heard Michael yelling when I pounded a post in crooked. Apparently it is the joke of the town and the guys were all mocking him for it. Michael accused me of telling the story to the neighbours to make fun of him. I didn't of course. You know I never even get a chance to talk to anyone. Anyway, some of the guys started saying that he 'married for the farm and that he lives off his wife because he doesn't have a leg to stand on.' Apparently they made some sarcastic comments that he couldn't handle the farm on his own and I guess they gave him quite a hard time. Sounds like he was the brunt of a lot of their jokes and you know how he hates that. Joe and Fred are usually pretty easygoing guys but I guess in a crowd, they just got carried away. I doubt they even realized how acutely it would affect him. They probably think it was just a big joke but it's us that have to live with him. Michael was livid about it. They just don't know!" Helen finished weakly, her voice trembling with emotion. "I'm sorry, Mom, but he was so angry, I didn't know what to expect. They must have said something about the kids also because he kept saying that he wished they would 'worry about their own family instead of looking at what I do with mine'. I was afraid he'd start picking on Kaydee and you know how she has been lately. I was just so scared so I told him that you were supposed to come down. I thought that would keep him from doing something really crazy. I'm sorry." Helen apologized again.

"Don't you worry about it, honey," Katreena soothed. "I'm just glad I thought of calling you last night. I still don't know what made me do it. I just wish you didn't have to go through this all the time. No one should have to live like this. I should have never let you marry that beast. But getting back to the fence story; is it true then? You pounded the post in while he was checking to see that it was straight?" Katreena could not believe this herself.

"I'm sorry, Mother. I never told you because I know how you feel about Michael."

Dusty listened in silence and awe as Helen explained the events and the causes that led to the final fracas. He could hardly believe the fence story himself but he could understand Michael's irritation about being the butt of that nasty joke. Still, he had earned it, in spades! What man lets his woman pound posts while he watches? If everyone was in such a state of fear of the man, this family was obviously in much more serious trouble than just being overworked. The family was terrorized and not just from last night.

"Was he being abusive to you or the kids?" Dusty wanted to know.

"Well, not really. He usually rants and raves, but last night, he was different. I was afraid that if anyone said anything, he might get physical. Kaydee has been really on edge since she found out about my journal and it's as if she's poised to defy him. He senses it and it makes him crazy. I made sure that she was not near him but he was yelling and going on and on and I was afraid she might come in anyway. That's why I told him you were coming out. I honestly didn't know what to do. He seems so angry and on edge all the time these days. It's worse now than ever before."

"Perhaps there is a physical problem that is developing. Has he been to see a doctor about those moods?" Dusty was pensive, trying to make sense out of the situation.

"Oh no," Helen was horrified. "Michael would never agree to that. He could never take responsibility for anything wrong and he would never accept imperfection in himself."

"Still it may be worth exploring, especially if you say there seems to be..."

Dusty never got to finish the sentence. A thunderous boom shook the house and sent all three adults flying to the door to check. At first they didn't know where it came from but Kaydee was beside them in a second, her face ashen.

"It came from there," she screeched, pointing to the shop. As they turned their heads in that direction, they could see flames inside the open door.

"Oh my God," Dusty pushed past the women and went tearing out towards the shop, both women at his heels. Kaydee stood rooted in her tracks, staring at the flames that were even now licking their way at the doorway. She gasped as she watched Dusty disappear behind those flames. Her heart was pounding in horror.

Katreena was screaming after Dusty to come back as she raced after him but Dusty didn't seem to hear her.

Alvin tugged at Kaydee's arm. "What happened, Kaydee?"

"I don't know," she whispered, leading him firmly towards the blanket where Dayna and Jaynee were playing. Thankfully, the house hid from their sight the drama that was unfolding at the other side of the yard. "We'll wait here until they tell us." Deliberately, she gave Alvin a surreptitious wink and immediately started a game of paddy-cake and loud singing to distract the kids and drown out the other sounds.

By the shed, Katreena was holding on tight to Helen. Her fear for Dusty's safety was overwhelming but her confidence in his judgment kept her rational. Helen was not rational. She was ready to follow Dusty into the blazing flames of the shop and Katreena had to prevent it. After what seemed like an eternity, Dusty emerged through the flaming doorway, Michael draped lifelessly over his shoulder.

"Call an ambulance!" he shouted "and the Fire Department!"

Katreena raced to the house to phone as Dusty lowered Michael to the ground, patting at smouldering remnants of the front of his shirt from which smoke seemed to be rising. Helen ran forward sobbing and trying to help.

Katreena had given the emergency personnel all the information she had. There was little they could do except wait. She ran to where the kids were and took Kaydee aside.

"Keep the kids here. Don't let them see the fire," she warned her earnestly. "The ambulance and the fire trucks will be coming soon. I'll come back as soon as I can."

Kaydee nodded and ran back to her post. She knew how important it was to keep Alvin distracted and behind that house. That scene had to be kept secret for at least a while longer.

Katreena hurried back to check on Dusty and Michael. Michael's still body was lying on the grass, his hair and eyebrows were singed, his face was burned almost black and red blisters were already appearing. His shirt was burned exposing his chest and shoulders which were red and raw. Some gray singed chest hairs remained at the left side of his chest and tattered remnants of his burned shirt hung under his arms. The rest of his clothes were splattered with soot and grease. Dusty was holding Helen who was sobbing and sagging limply in his arms. Dusty's own hair and arms were scorched and already some blisters were appearing on his hands and arms.

"How is he?" Katreena queried.

Dusty shrugged his shoulders and whispered. "I'm not sure. He's breathing. I think he got knocked out. He was lying against the shelving at the back of the shed. His shirt was on fire but I had no time to do anything but grab him and run. I guess I smothered most of the flames when I put him over my shoulder. There must have been some kind of explosion or something and that's probably what threw him back. The bench was all in flames and I didn't have time to check what else was burning or why. I just grabbed him and ran. He may have some serious injuries so I don't want to move him."

Katreena noticed blood on Dusty's now dirty white shirt and what looked like skin stuck to the shirt. She turned to check Michael to see where it had come from. Some parts of his chest were raw flesh where the skin had come off Michael and had adhered to Dusty's shirt. The sight of it made her nauseous but she forced herself to continue her inspection of Michael. Dusty nodded as Katreena noticed some blood on the side of Michael's neck. Dusty mouthed "Shhhhh" and Katreena realized that Helen had not seen it and Dusty didn't want her to know about it.

Katreena turned her attention to Dusty. "Your hands. And your hair. You have burns too." Katreena cried as she checked Dusty, but he shooed her off. "It's nothing," he shushed her, his eyes darting to Helen as he mouthed, "Hang on to her. Don't scare her."

Helen was sobbing brokenly. She tried to go to Michael but Katreena held on to her, telling her she mustn't touch him. "We must wait for the medics," she kept telling her, trying to calm her down. Dusty kept his eyes on Michael while trying to help Katreena calm Helen down.

Finally, they heard the sound of sirens in the distance and realized that help was on the way. Still it seemed like hours before the medics arrived. They rushed to them and immediately started working on Michael. The Fire Brigade drove in and the ambulance people put Michael on the stretcher to move him out of the way of the fire fighters who positioned hoses to douse the fire which by now was a roaring inferno.

The ambulance and fire trucks were too much for the kids to ignore and though Kaydee managed to get Jaynee and Dayna into the house, Alvin came running to see what was going on. He stared in awe at the burning shed and then spotting his father on the stretcher, ran towards him. Dusty swooped him up before he could reach him.

Above the noise and mayhem, Katreena walked Helen over to where Dusty was holding Alvin. "Your father got hurt so we must not move him. These people are here to take him to the hospital and make him well. You remember how they made you well. Now your father will have to go there and he will get well." Alvin listened attentively and allowed Dusty to hold him while the medics loaded Michael's stretcher into the ambulance.

As they prepared to leave, Katreena told Dusty, "You go with Helen. You need to get those burns taken care of too. I'll stay with the kids." Silently mouthing behind Helen's back, she added, "Don't leave her alone." Dusty nodded understanding, and led Helen towards his car to follow the ambulance to town.

Katreena carried the protesting Alvin to the house, explaining to him that the firemen could not do their job right with children underfoot. Inside the house Kaydee's face was a giant question mark begging for answers. Katreena didn't want to alarm the younger children so for their ears, she gave just a brief account of what happened.

"Well, your father was working in the shop and he had a little accident and he got hurt. The people took him to the hospital to make him better just like they did for Alvin when he got hurt. A fire started in the shop and these other men are going to put it out. There is nothing to worry about. Now who wants some cookies?"

"I do, I do!" Both Alvin and Jaynee were easily distracted with cookies. Kaydee knew there was more to the story but she would have to hear it later when the other children were out of earshot.

"Where is Mommy?" Alvin wanted to know.

"Mommy went with Dusty to the hospital to be with your father. They will come back soon." That seemed to end the question period for Alvin as he concentrated on the cookies and milk that Kaydee had placed before him. Jaynee took things at face value as usual and when Kaydee brought out the puzzles and the coloring books, a calm natural peace overruled the curiosity of the fire fighters whose sirens were now silent as the men attended to the task at hand.

Kaydee waited till the smaller kids were totally engrossed in play before she went back to the kitchen to once more question her grandmother.

"I honestly don't know how badly he is hurt, Kaydee. He was bleeding from the back of his head and he is badly burned. He must have been knocked out by falling on something but other than that I honestly don't know. Dusty thought it was some kind of explosion or something but he had no time to check anything because he had to get out of the fire."

Kaydee sat there thinking quietly. "You know, Granny. I said that I wished I didn't have a father. Do you think God heard me and He will now let Father die? I didn't mean that, Granny, honest. I just wanted him to go away or stop being so mean to us. I didn't want him to die!"

Katreena enfolded Kaydee into her arms. "Of course you didn't and

God is not punishing you. What happened was some kind of accident. Your father will probably be back in a few days, and mean as ever, so don't you go worrying about it, okay?"

Katreena considered Kaydee's remorseful statement. Michael had always had a volatile temper and Helen had almost lost her mind because of him. Recently, Kaydee's situation seemed to get worse and Michael had become more unpredictable and menacing. Both Kaydee and Helen became more aware of Michael's increased volatility of late but neither Kaydee nor Helen had ever voiced anything about it. Open criticism against Michael was not articulated till today. How ironic! Still, Kaydee's guilt about her reactionary statement was troubling, no matter how unfounded. And just when Katreena had started to see a glimmer of life coming back to Helen!

Dusty parked the car and quickly got out to help Helen. Together they hurried to the Emergency Department where the attendants already had Michael in the treatment room. As the crew rushed about their duties, Dr. Walley noted the burns on Dusty's hands. He examined them, then directed him to a treatment room to the left.

"They look like superficial burns but you better have them cleaned and bandaged to avoid infection." Turning to Helen, he pointed to a bench, "Wait for him there. He won't be long."

As soon as the nurse finished dressing Dusty's burns, he went out to find Helen standing helplessly outside the door waiting hopefully for some scrap of information on Michael's condition. She was in a state of shock. Dusty tried talking to her, but she did not respond, as if she didn't hear him at all. She seemed to be in a world all her own, oblivious to everything but her own anxiety. She stared into space, her eyes expressionless, her face ashen, a stone statue, lifeless and detached. Katreena had told him about Helen's withdrawal into her own misery and this was obviously where she was right now. Dusty only hoped that good news would draw her back to the real world. In the meantime, he was doing enough pacing for both of them.

Dusty did not know Michael but from what Katreena had told him, he was either some kind of sick bastard or just a raving lunatic. Or just plain psycho! But Katreena had said that he had been manipulative and mean from the day Helen had married him. That would rule out the "sick" part. Nobody could be medically "sick" for thirteen years and go undetected. He must be just a natural bully, a mean and heartless one. Still, he did not deserve to die, not like this.

Memory of the fire flashed through his mind. How did that thing start anyway? What had happened in that short time that Michael had been in that shop? Dusty tried to recall the scene in the shop when he had entered to look for Michael. All he could remember was that mass of flames at a kind of table in the middle of the room and the flames that were on the floor. That was it. There was fire on the floor! Some kind of fuel was burning on the floor because he had to avoid those flames when he was looking for Michael. He had found him slumped against the shelves at the west wall with his shirt on fire. Dusty had smothered the flames when he heaved Michael's lifeless body against his own to carry him out. The room had been an inferno except for the back and east wall. What had Michael been doing and what had he been using?

Finally, Dr. Walley came out to talk to them. "He's badly burned, by the fire, but also by a corrosive acid that is eating at his flesh. Do you know what kind of acid it was?"

Dusty swallowed. "I honestly have no idea, Doctor. We were in the house and we heard this big boom. When we got outside we saw fire in the shop. I assumed it had to have been some kind of explosion or something. I couldn't see Michael anywhere so I ran inside to see if he was there. He was lying against the side shelving and his shirt was burning. My first instinct was to get him out of there. I smothered the flames against my own body when I picked him up. There was fire all over the place so I just grabbed him and got the hell out of there. I have no idea what he was doing or what really happened. That's all I know. I had no time to check anything out. I have no idea what was in there."

The doctor looked pensive. "Hmmm." He stood there rubbing his chin. "Okay, I guess we'll just have to work from there then, but I think that acid is what is doing the worst damage. But wounds can heal. It will scar and disfigure him but that is not what has me worried. He's still unconscious. He has a bad gash on the back of his head. I want an X-ray to determine the possibility, and extent, of a skull fracture. There may be pressure on the brain. We'll have to take care of that as soon as possible to prevent permanent brain damage. Talk to you later." The doctor hurried back inside and closed the door behind him.

Helen just stood there staring after him.

Keeping his eye on Helen, Dusty stepped over to the counter at the other end and quietly asked the nurse if she had the number for the Boyer farm. The girl shuffled through some papers, wrote something down and passed a slip of paper to him, indicating the pay phone on the east wall. Dusty went over and dialled the number, still keeping his eyes on Helen.

"Katreena, yes, I'm fine… yes, they just cleaned me up and bandaged them up… no, I don't know how he is doing. The doc says he's still unconscious. He may have pressure on the brain. They're getting X-rays to see if there is a skull fracture... I don't know, they might have to operate I suppose… she's out of it, I can't reach her, but physically she's fine. How is Kaydee...? You bet honey... yes, I'll call you as soon as I hear anything. Hang in there."

Dusty hung up and went back to Helen. He squeezed her shoulder and she looked up at him with that wounded look in her eyes but said nothing. The treatment room door opened and Michael was wheeled out towards the hall. Tubes ran from his arm to the bags hanging from a pole that was being carefully pushed along side of him. His face was covered by a mask that was obviously feeding him oxygen from the tank on a cart that an attendant was wheeling along beside them. Helen watched them go but did not get up. Dusty's hand remained on her shoulder as they watched the entourage pass.

Chapter 15

It was almost ten when Dusty's car pulled into the driveway. The sun had disappeared behind the horizon but darkness had not quite overpowered the light. Kaydee and Katreena were beside the car even before Dusty had helped Helen out. The smaller kids were already in bed and Dusty was grateful that he did not have to sugarcoat any explanations. Kaydee, he was sure, would be mature enough to handle the facts if they were presented logically.

Helen seemed sullen and oblivious to her surroundings. Still in a state of shock, she had retreated into her trance-like state that had preserved her through her grief after her miscarriages. Dusty met Katreena's gaze and helplessly shrugged his shoulders. Kaydee, well aware of her mother's vulnerability when stressed, put her arm around her mother's shoulder, led her to the house into her bedroom where she helped her into bed. Helen did not resist, but her mind refused to face the painful situation.

When Kaydee got back to the kitchen, Dusty and Granny were at the table, discussing the repercussions of the events that had transpired since morning.

"What happened at the hospital?" Kaydee directed her question at Dusty. She wanted no part of secondhand information. Dusty was there. He knew, and now she had to know. Her mother was incapacitated. Her father was probably even worse off, meaning she was in charge. Hadn't Father always told her that she should be responsible? The children needed her and she would not let them down, no matter how stupid her father thought she was. It was now her responsibility to take care of the family. Her evil wishes had probably caused this and even though Granny called it an accident, Kaydee wondered if God had been listening to her thoughts and had granted her wish in a way that she had never intended. She wasn't sure God would do that but she would prove that she really was not that evil. She had to prove it! Not just to God, but to herself! To do that, she had to know what she would be facing.

Dusty swallowed. He and Katreena exchanged glances and Katreena nodded. Taking Kaydee's hand in his, Dusty spoke softly.

"Your grandmother and I both agree that you need to know the truth, as far as we know it. At this point we really know very little. Your father was burned very badly both by fire and by some kind of acid; we don't yet know what kind. That will take time to heal and will leave scars. However that is not the major concern right now. When the explosion, whatever it was, threw him backward, he hit his head against something that cracked his skull. Part of the skull penetrated his brain. Between that and the trauma of the pressure it caused, there is a possibility that he may have brain damage. To what extent, the doctor does not know. We don't want to lie to you, Kaydee. You have been taking care of your brother and sisters and you have done a wonderful job, most of it with little help from your mother, and all of it, in spite of your father. You are a bright girl, no matter what your father says. You must be strong now, for your mother and for your brother and sisters. At this time, we know very little about your father's condition. Dr. Walley is having your father flown to a hospital in Toronto for brain surgery and burn treatment. Hopefully, after the surgery, we'll know more, but for now, we will carry on as well as we can. Normally, your mother would be going with your father, but she is not well enough to do that. Tomorrow, we will go see Dr. Walley and he will try to help your mother get well. Tonight we get some much needed sleep. We will see what else needs to be done after that. That okay? Kaydee?"

Kaydee nodded pensively. Granny and Dusty trusted her and respected her enough to be honest with her, even down to the harsh truth and she appreciated that honesty more than they realized. There were so many more questions, but for now there were no answers to them. Tomorrow they would deal with whatever had to be dealt with. Today they all needed sleep.

Kaydee got up, gave her grandmother and Dusty a great big lingering hug. "It is more than enough. Thank you so very much for being honest with me. I won't let you down. I promise. I love you both so very, very much." Her voice was hoarse and emotional.

"You're very welcome, sweetheart. We love you too. Now goodnight, honey."

"Goodnight and thank you, again," she whispered as she left for the stairs.

When Kaydee left, Katreena and Dusty looked at each other with tears in their eyes. "She can handle it, Dusty, I know she can." Katreena whispered. "I told you, didn't I?"

"You know, Katreena, from the moment I saw her with those kids, I believed it, but when she took charge of her mother like that when we got back from the hospital, I knew she was special. I know we did the right thing by being straight with her about her father's condition. I think that by being honest with her, she will be able to rise up to her potential so much more freely. She is no retard. She understands and by telling her the facts as they are, she will be able to deal with the situation on a mature basis. You should be very proud of her, Katreena."

Katreena's pride was evident in her passionate, "I am."

Dusty got up to head out and go home. Katreena had suggested he spend the night but Dusty needed to make plans for the Toronto trip next week and doubted that Wayne could postpone it. In light of the events of the day, Dusty felt he should be on hand here at the farm until things settled down to a more rational routine so postponing the trip might be a practical idea if that were possible. Barring that, he might just forego it altogether and let Wayne go on alone.

"This is something I cannot discuss with him on the phone. Hopefully Wayne can reschedule because I really need to be there, but we have to discuss this in person."

"But it is so late," Katreena protested.

"I'll be alright, honey. Don't you worry about me. I'd rather get this settled as soon as possible so I can be here to help you. You're going to have a lot to contend with in the next few days. You'll need me more than Wayne will. Besides," he added, on a more positive note, "if the trip is postponed, we'll know more about Michael's surgery. We don't know how anything is going to play out at this point."

"I know," Katreena agreed worriedly. "The next few days could have all sorts of changes to a lot of lives. But please, honey, drive carefully. I need you." She choked.

Dusty took her in his arms and held her tight. He wanted so badly to shield her from all this distress. She had been walking a tightrope since the day they came back from the holiday. It had been one thing after another with her family and he felt powerless to protect her.

"I'll be careful, honey. I promise. But I have to go home now and clear this stuff out of the way so I can be here for you. You take care of yourself and the family. Get some sleep now. You'll need all the energy you can muster in the days ahead. And try not to worry. I'll be back as soon as I can. You can count on it."

Holding her tightly, he gave her a long lingering kiss then picked up his keys to leave.

"Call me when you get home, please. No matter how late. Please," she begged.

Seeing her look of despair, he agreed. "I will, I promise. Now go to sleep."

Katreena stood on the steps and watched him drive out into the night. With a heavy heart she went and checked on Helen who was sleeping the sleep of total exhaustion. Reluctant to leave her alone downstairs, Katreena went to the closet, picked up a sheet, a blanket and a pillow and went to sleep on the couch in the living room. In case Helen or Dayna woke up, she would be right there and unlikely to sleep through it. She put the phone on the arm of the couch so she could grab it immediately.

"Sorry, folks," she apologized silently, "but this call is important!"

She dozed off almost immediately but when the phone rang sometime in the night, she grabbed it even before it finished the first ring.

"Hi, it's me." Dusty's voice was husky. "I'm home and I'm fine. How is everything going out there?"

"Thanks for letting me know, Dusty. Everything is fine. I'm sleeping on the living room couch to be down here in case I'm needed, but so far so good." Katreena whispered, her hand cupping the receiver to capture her words more efficiently.

"Okay, that's good. I won't keep you. Call me in the morning. 'Night honey," Dusty whispered back and hung up. Katreena sighed in relief as she put the phone down. He was safely home. She relaxed and went back to sleep.

It was ten after nine when she heard Dayna's voice from the bedroom. Quickly, she got up and went to pick her up. Helen was still asleep in the same position she had been last night. Katreena's heart stopped. Holding Dayna close to keep her quiet, she stood watching Helen until she saw her chest moving that announced she was breathing. Relieved, Katreena tiptoed out of the room. She went to the bathroom and closed the door. As she washed Dayna and herself, she marvelled that everyone was still sleeping. It was late! It was not normal. But then this whole weekend had not been normal. They were all exhausted, emotionally and physically. Sleep is good therapy for many problems. Still, this silence, at this hour, was eerie.

The sound of running water in the taps roused the sleeping household and soon the breakfast ritual was in motion, but Alvin and Jaynee were obviously still sleeping. Helen came into the kitchen, her eyes red and bloodshot, but she seemed alert. She said "Good Morning" then went to the bathroom. Katreena was glad to hear the shower running. That meant Helen was functioning. Kaydee appeared at the foot of the stairs.

"Sorry, Granny. I guess I slept in. I didn't mean to."

"That's okay, sweetheart. I think we all slept in. I can't believe how late it is. It was Dayna that woke me up and that was just a few minutes ago. I guess we all needed that sleep."

Helen appeared in the doorway, looking refreshed but bewildered. Her hair was wrapped tightly in a towel, but she was dressed in a blue shirt and jeans.

"I had a terrible dream last night. I dreamed that the shed burned and that your Dusty got Michael out of the fire but that Michael was badly hurt in the fire." She spoke tiredly, as if she just woke up a minute ago, in spite of the shower Katreena knew she had had. Helen seemed normal, her demeanour almost surreal.

As she relayed her "dream" to Kaydee and Katreena, she sounded relaxed, controlled. Describing her "dream," she recalled it all, but she was detached from it, unaffected by it. It was merely a bad dream and therefore no stress was involved.

Kaydee and her grandmother exchanged puzzled glances. Thank heavens, Alvin was still asleep and did not hear her. With his childish candour he could have completely traumatized Helen, because she obviously did not remember that the events she had described, had actually happened. Kaydee and Katreena were totally at a loss as to how to deal with this bizarre situation. They listened in silence, nodding now and then, letting Helen go on, knowing full well that doing or saying the wrong thing might catapult them into something much worse than her denial. They were both aware that they desperately needed help, but from where? Frantically, Katreena searched her brain for some way to call for help without upsetting Helen.

When that bizarre breakfast was over, Katreena turned to Kaydee. "Why don't you and your mother go into the garden and pick some peas and strawberries? We'll need some for lunch. I'll get the kids up and feed them." She didn't want Helen anywhere near Alvin. A word from that child and who knows what could happen!

"Good idea," Helen agreed and went to the cupboard for the pails. Seizing the momentary opportunity, Katreena winked at Kaydee and silently mouthed. "Keep her there. I'll phone for help." Kaydee understood but Katreena saw the fear in her eyes.

Unnerved by this new twist of events, but determined not to worsen the situation, Kaydee linked her arm through Mother's and announced casually.

"Looks like we've been given our orders, Mother. Let's go get 'em." As they left the house, Katreena fervently thanked God for Kaydee's perception and wisdom. Surprised but deeply grateful that Alvin and Jaynee were still sleeping, Katreena quickly went to the living room to phone. She panicked. Who should she call first, Dusty? The doctor? She needed information from both and she had so little time. Dusty may be sleeping yet, but she needed his advice. Besides, if worse came to worse, he could call the doctor himself and save her precious time if something came up. With trembling fingers she dialled his number. He answered immediately.

"Dusty, we have more trouble... no I don't know anything about Michael. I haven't had a chance to call the doctor, but it's Helen. She has convinced herself everything that happened yesterday is a bad dream. She honestly believes it, Dusty! Kaydee and I don't know what to do. What's going to happen when she realizes the truth?"

"Where is she now?" Dusty wanted to know.

"I sent her and Kaydee into the garden to pick peas. Kaydee knows she has to keep her there to let me phone."

"Good girl. Try and get hold of Dr. Walley and tell him what's happening. He may be able to get some medication for her to prevent her from going over the edge. I just got back from Wayne's and that's all settled. I'm on my way and I should be there in about three hours. I'll step in to the hospital on the way. We'll work something out. Don't worry. Call the doctor now!"

"Thank you Dusty. I'm sorry for dumping this..."

Dusty interrupted. "Don't apologize. Just take care of yourself. I'll be there as soon as I can. Call the doctor," he repeated and hung up. She could feel the urgency in his voice. Quickly she dialled Dr. Walley's number, her heart hammering inside her chest.

The receptionist transferred her to the hospital. Katreena waited impatiently while they paged him. Finally Dr. Walley came on the line and Katreena quickly told him about Helen.

"Where is she now?" Dr. Walley asked.

"I sent her out into the garden with Kaydee. I know Michael should be the biggest concern now but I'm so scared about Helen. What's going to happen when she realizes the truth? What happens when she looks at the shed? We're sitting on a volcano here. What should we do?" Despair and apprehension made her voice shaky.

"Can you bring her here without arousing her suspicions? I have to see her before I can assess the problem."

Katreena thought about it. "Dusty will be coming here in a few hours, but I can't wait till then. The situation here is ominous. She's been like a zombie since her miscarriages and had just begun to emerge from mourning this spring. Her mental state is so fragile. What should I do?

Please Dr. Walley, you have to help us." Katreena begged, shivering at the repercussions that could result from waiting.

"Bring her in." Dr. Walley instructed. "Soon as possible. We'll take it from there."

Katreena felt better after talking with Dr. Walley. At least now she had an action plan. Problem now was how to implement that plan without arousing Helen's suspicion. Somehow, she had to get Helen to see Dr. Walley. She scanned her brain for ideas. Kaydee could be left with the kids for those few hours. She was dependable. Normally, Helen should be going to the hospital to see Michael but her condition pre-empted that. She could pretend to need groceries, but how would she explain going to see Dr. Walley?

Katreena's stomach churned. Her hands were clammy and her head was spinning. Katreena knew Kaydee would keep Helen away for a while, but there were the charred remains of the shed just behind that row of maples. Smoke and the smell of charred wood still permeated the air. The peas and strawberries had only been picked a couple of days ago, new ones would be scarce. They'd be done soon. And then what would they do? It was a calamity waiting to happen. This grace period they were in was so transitory, so unstable. "Think, Katreena, think hard!" she commanded herself urgently. Upstairs, she heard the pitter patter of little feet. Alvin and Jaynee were coming down.

At that crucial moment, Providence intervened. Kaydee came running into the house.

"I need a bandage. Mother cut herself with the knife while she was cleaning the strawberries. She wanted to come in and wash it but I got her to promise to stay there and wait for me. Did you get to phone?"

"Yes, and I have to take her to see Dr. Walley. This is my chance. Keep her there while I turn the car around. I'll pick her up on the road. Hurry!" Alvin and Jaynee had come downstairs and wanted breakfast but Kaydee sent Alvin to the bathroom to wash up first. Quickly, she picked up a wet washcloth and taking the puzzled Jaynee with her, she ran to the garden. Meanwhile, Katreena grabbed the keys and was already heading for the car.

The garden was right along the road, so it was a logical spot for Katreena to pick up Helen. As she stopped the car and got out, she could hear Helen and Kaydee arguing.

"But it's only a small cut. I don't need to see a doctor for it," Helen protested.

Katreena was beside them by then, inspecting the wound.

"Strawberry juice is deadly on a wound. We better get it checked out. We can't take a chance on it getting infected. Come on, Helen, let's go. We must go immediately. Kaydee, you take care of the kids. We'll be back soon."

Leading the bewildered Helen quickly towards the car, Katreena was thankful for her inspiration about the "deadly strawberry juice on a wound." Her urgent manner probably overrode Helen's better judgment to question the unlikely story. As she drove to town, Katreena kept the conversation flowing but her stomach churned with anticipation about Helen's state of mind and how the scenario would play itself out. She also felt intense relief that the "wound" had presented her with the solution to a problem that had seemed unsolvable.

At the office, Katreena gave Dr. Walley a surreptitious wink and "explained" about the "dangerous strawberry juice on the wound." The doctor nodded and left them for a moment. Soon a nurse came in with bandages and Dr. Walley motioned for Katreena to follow him out.

"I briefed Alice on the situation so don't worry about her saying anything detrimental to Helen. She will keep her busy for a while. Now you tell me what this is all about."

Katreena explained to him all that had transpired at home before and since the accident. "What do we do now?" she queried anxiously.

"I wasn't aware that her condition was so bad. I knew she was distraught about the miscarriages, but I never knew she was still carrying it till now. But you're right. We can't let this bring on a relapse, and we certainly cannot shield her from it forever. I'll get Maureen Phillips to talk to her. She is an extremely perceptive psychiatric nurse and is exceptionally good in her line of work. She can talk sense into an angry rhino. She may provide us with some insight on how to proceed. I'll go tell her to join Helen and Alice in the other room and take over when Alice finishes."

He left and was gone for a few minutes. When he came back, Katreena asked, "What is happening with Michael?" This was the first time Katreena had a chance to ask the question and she felt guilty at having ignored him till now.

"He was still unconscious but I couldn't wait. I had him airlifted to a burn unit in Toronto. We have one in Winnipeg but Michael requires crucial brain surgery immediately and Toronto is the only place that can provide that. The head surgery supercedes the burns, I'm afraid. Those will heal. That acid that burned into so much of his flesh also has me worried. Luckily, Dusty got to him in time so only some of the burns are deep. But those are mostly on his face and throat. The deep burns on his chest will be hidden under his shirt. There will be substantial scarring but that is of minor consequence at this point. It's a miracle Dusty didn't get any acid burns on himself when he brought Michael out. Michael will be hospitalized for a while but we may be able to bring him back to Winnipeg for that. How are Kaydee and the kids?"

"They are doing fine. Kaydee is such a treasure. She has just taken over. Michael always called her a 'stupid retard,' but she is anything but stupid or retarded. She's intuitive and responsible. She's a pillar of strength for our family. The smaller kids don't seem to understand. We told Alvin that his father had to go to the hospital to get well just like he had to after his accident and Alvin accepted that at par."

"That's good news at least. You'll be here at the clinic?"

"Yes, I will, Doctor. And thank you," Katreena added emotionally.

The doctor walked out. Katreena went to the phone and dialled the farm.

"Hello?" Kaydee's voice was eager, expectant. "Oh, hi Granny. How is Mother?"

Katreena told her everything she knew, about Helen and about Michael. It felt good not to have to pussyfoot around the subject, to be honest and straightforward and to know that Kaydee appreciated that honesty. She needed someone to confide in, to empathize with and

Kaydee had risen to the challenge, mature beyond her years and perceptive to the needs at hand. Dusty was wonderful but it was Kaydee that understood the anguish because she had lived through it. Kaydee had been oppressed and demoralized but she was more intelligent at twelve than Michael ever could be no matter what his age!

"Thanks, Granny. You stay as long as you have to. I'll take good care of the kids. Don't you worry! Is Dusty going to come in today?"

Katreena realized that she had had no chance to bring Kaydee up to date on that score and filled her in. After she hung up, she picked up a Chatelaine magazine and tried to get her mind off Helen by reading. It was no use. The words on the paper stayed on the paper. They refused to enter her mind. She tossed the magazine aside and walked down the hallway.

It was now forty minutes since she had left Helen in that office. She knew Nurse Phillips was with her and Katreena's mind was churning with images of the nurse frantically trying to restrain Helen after telling her the truth about the accident. It was torture not knowing what was going on. She knew that her mind was probably conjuring up the terrible images of things that may never even have taken place. Where was Dr. Walley and why didn't he let her know what was happening? She paced that hallway up and down and wished and prayed.

After what seemed like an eternity, Dr. Walley tapped her on the shoulder from behind. She hadn't even heard him come up.

"Katreena, I have some good news for you. Helen is alright. Like I told you, Maureen Phillips is very good and she was able to bring Helen about. We had given Helen a precautionary mild tranquilizer though, on the pretext it was an antibiotic. Anyway, Helen had the whole picture in her memory so all Maureen did was make her realize that it was not a dream. Helen is worried about Michael and distraught but I'm sure she will be alright. I will prescribe a tranquilizer for her to take in case she needs it but I think the best thing for her now is to be with her family where she is needed and loved. I told her Michael was airlifted to Toronto for surgery and treatment and she understands."

Katreena's knees buckled under her and she burst into tears. Dr.

Walley helped her to a chair. "Whoa there! I think you are the one that needs the tranquilizers. You've been under too much strain. Do you want me to give you something?"

"No!" Katreena cried out in alarm. Then taking a deep breath, she rallied. "Sorry, Dr. Walley. Now I'm the one that's being irrational. No, really, I'm alright. Thanks, I was just so worried about Helen. I'm relieved, that's all. Thank you so much." she repeated hoarsely.

Shortly after, Maureen Phillips led Helen out of the office. Helen's face was tear-stained and her eyes bloodshot but she seemed alright otherwise. She saw Katreena and came to hug her. Maureen Phillips and Dr. Walley looked on approvingly.

"It wasn't a dream, Mom. It was true. I did see Michael hurt. I wanted it to be a dream but it wasn't, was it?" Helen sobbed.

"No, honey, it wasn't a dream. But it'll be alright. He will get better and you'll be alright too. You'll see. We'll go home now, the kids are waiting for us. We'll all take care of each other. Everything will be alright, you'll see." Katreena soothed. She mouthed a heartfelt "thank you" to Nurse Phillips and Dr. Walley over Helen's shoulder.

Dr. Walley handed Katreena a slip of paper. "Get this prescription filled," then gently to Helen, "you take one of these whenever you feel overwhelmed. They will help you relax. Do not exceed four pills in twenty-four hours. And call me anytime if you need me, promise?"

"I promise," Helen nodded tearfully. "And thank you. Thank you both, very much."

After picking up the prescription, they left for home. Helen asked about the fire and how it had started. Katreena told her that they had no idea yet, that the firemen's report might offer them some clues. They talked about Dusty, how he had run into the shed and brought Michael out, and about what little he had noticed while he was there.

"Thank Dusty for me. We owe him a lot. He's a Godsend." Helen's voice choked.

"You'll be able to thank him yourself soon. He should be here in an hour or two. He's level-headed and he'll be able to get us set up so we can keep on going. Quite frankly, I personally don't know where to start." Katreena admitted candidly. Helen nodded agreement.

The kids were playing in the living room and Kaydee was busy fixing lunch when Helen and Katreena walked into the house. To Kaydee's unspoken query, Katreena answered aloud. "It's okay. Your mother is alright."

Helen added her own affirmation. "Yes Kaydee. I'm alright. I know it was not a dream. I know what happened. I'm so sorry I frightened you, honey."

"It's okay, Mother." Kaydee hugged her tightly. "I'm just so glad you're alright."

"Me too, me too," Jaynee squealed enthusiastically and they all laughed as Helen scooped her up into her arms. If there was anyone that could restore a sense of humour to a situation, it was Jaynee. Her world remained simple and her serenity was infectious. She was the model they all wished to emulate. In an ideal world, all its residents would be Jaynees and there would never be any strife or discord of any kind. *In an ideal world...*

Chapter 16

When Dusty finally drove in, lunch and cleanup were finished. Dayna and Jaynee were down for their afternoon naps and Alvin, now much better, was cautiously frolicking on the front lawn with Rusko. Katreena, Helen and Kaydee had walked out to inspect the damage in the shed and Dusty drove right up to the charred ruins to join them. He had obviously seen Dr. Walley and had been given the update on Helen's condition so he was not surprised to see them there. He kissed Katreena and Kaydee then walked up to Helen and, putting his arm around her shoulders, gave her a squeeze.

"I'm so glad you're doing better and I'm terribly sorry about this tragedy."

"Thank you, Dusty. I'm really grateful for all your help. Without you, it might have been so much worse. I can't thank you enough."

"That's okay, Helen. I'm just glad I was there. But let's forget the past now and concentrate positively on the future. I'd like to help in whatever way I can. Now are you sure you want to go inside that shed? It will not be a pleasant sight, you know."

Helen thought about it. She looked at Kaydee, so worried and full of concern for her mother. Memories of the past few years flashed through her mind: Kaydee, caring for the children; Kaydee, kneeling for hours in the "sinhole" so often; Kaydee patching Jaynee's knee when she fell off the swing. All those times when her young daughter had accepted a responsibility that should never have been hers in the first place. Yet Kaydee had borne it; suffered for it; even had been branded a retard for taking it so placidly! Even now, she was still concerned about her mother, taking responsibility for shielding her.

Helen nodded. "The nurse said I need to face things and look ahead, not back." With a wary look of sadness and some trepidation, she linked her arm through Kaydee's and turned towards the shed. "I need to see what I have to see," she said.

Pleasantly surprised, Dusty and Katreena fell into step behind them.

When they entered, Katreena and Helen especially, were shocked to see the shambles that used to be a well-organized shed. There seemed to be little that was untouched by the fire or the water that was used to put the fire out. Pressure from the water hoses had probably just completed the chaos that the explosion had begun. Tools that had once been so neatly arranged on the shelving and counters and hung on hooks on pegboard nailed along the west wall were strewn all over the place, many of them scorched or totally missing any wooden handles or parts. The beams above, though burnt to the point of being a safety hazard, still held up. The walls and shelving along the sides and back were just as bad. Parts of the roof perched precariously on the burnt rafters but it seemed like the slightest breeze could easily bring it down. Of the workbench in the middle of the shed, little remained, though an assortment of pliers, wrenches, empty hammer heads, nails, screws and such were scattered on the floor. The chainsaw, in the corner, had only some shards of metal attached where the gas tank had originally been. A blob of melted rubber and wire lay curled on the floor, the only reminder of an electrical extension cord. The metal housing of the welder in the middle of the shed was warped almost beyond recognition with barely a sign of the cord that had powered it. Other remains of tools and appliances were scattered about, possibly by the explosion, or the heat, or the water pressure.

"Phew," Dusty broke the depressing silence as they stood there amidst the charred ruins. "Unbelievable! This will all have to be cleaned up piece by piece and the shed will have to be rebuilt from scratch. Outside of some of the tools, there is little that is salvageable here."

He walked to the area of the shed where he had picked up Michael just twenty-four hours ago. A heavy vice lay among the ashes of the shelf that had once held it in working position. This was probably what Michael's head had smashed into when he was knocked out.

Dusty looked at Helen. She was surveying the scene with a kind of detached silence, almost as if she was testing her fortitude to face it. She didn't ask any questions or offer any observations and Dusty was glad she had not asked him where or how he had found Michael. That information might be too traumatic for her. For now it was "baby steps" for her and under the circumstances, Helen was doing exceptionally well.

Just being brave enough to view the scene of the tragedy must have taken a lot of stamina. That was a major step forward.

A thought occurred to him. Did the firemen determine the cause of the fire? Did they file a final report or was there still some evidence here that could be vital information to the cause of the accident?

"Before we touch anything, I'd like to talk to the Fire Chief. See if he has completed his report. They may still wish to come back here for a second look," he told the girls, "then we'll have to get some plan in place for you to get this all sorted out. You may have to hire someone to keep KD Acres going until Michael gets back on his feet. Dr. Walley thinks he'll be away for a couple of months at least and I know nothing about farming so I can't be of much good to you, even though I'd like to be."

"Thank you, Dusty," Helen choked. "We'll be alright. Right now, I just have to stand back and decide on how to proceed from here." She put her arm around Kaydee and squeezed her shoulder. With a grateful smile, the girl nodded.

Yes, they will be alright! Katreena agreed. She suddenly realized just how far Helen had come since this tragedy. She was actually starting to stand on her own two feet in spite of the bleak situation. Was it Maureen Phillips' magic at work here or was it the absence of Michael's domination that was shoring Helen up now? Helen had always been intelligent, yet since her marriage to Michael, she had become more like a... Katreena could not bring herself to complete the thought.

Katreena watched Helen standing there hugging Kaydee, giving her the respect and credit she had so long denied her. It warmed Katreena's heavy heart. Helen almost seemed ready to take charge of her life and of KD Acres! Just this morning, it had seemed all was lost and hopeless. Now hope loomed nearer on the horizon and Katreena prayed it was real.

Word of the catastrophe spread quickly throughout the community and people appeared from miles around with condolences and offers of help. In typical neighbourly fashion, the Drapaniks, the Ladducks and the Archers were among them, naturally and genuinely concerned about a tragedy that befell a fellow farmer. No mention was made of that fateful day at the circus that had precipitated the chain of events that culminated in this terrible catastrophe and Helen did not wish to pursue the subject in the face of their kindness because she was not certain that they had been guilty of any wrongdoing.

To Katreena, it seemed as if they were completely unaware of their involvement in the drama. Perhaps they were innocent, afterall. Perhaps Michael had created the tempest in the teapot himself with his bragging. How many times had Katreena herself practically bitten her tongue in two, trying to stifle a retort because she could not endure his obnoxious vanity? Perhaps when they challenged his overinflated ego and laughed him down in an effort to shut him up, they had touched a vulnerability that they had not foreseen. Katreena had witnessed his vulnerability before when she had compared Michael's farming practices with those of his neighbours in her attempt to make Michael ease up on Helen's workload during pregnancy. She wondered if this was what had happened on Saturday. Was being ignored then ridiculed openly in public so humiliating to Michael that it had provoked that traumatic ferocity that his psyche had been so powerless to quell?

"We'll help with the field work wherever we can," Joe Drapanik was saying to Helen as his wife Ellen hugged her. Dusty had just explained to them that Michael was not expected home for a couple of months.

"Don't worry, Helen, you just let us know when you need us and one of us will be around to pitch in," Tom Ladduck patted Helen's shoulder and both Joe Drapanik and Fred Archer agreed. "Sure, Helen, we'll all help. Don't you worry."

Katreena swallowed hard against the lump in her throat and fought against the tears that threatened to flood her vision. She was not too surprised at the generosity and compassion of these neighbours. The Drapaniks and the Archers had been in the neighbourhood for years, and had been friends to her and Daniel. They had wholeheartedly supported her during her bereavement after Daniel's accident. The Ladducks had moved in to the community after Katreena had moved away. They too, seemed like nice people though. Because Michael and Helen did not associate with any neighbours, Katreena had lost touch with them after she moved to Lanavale. Still, she found their charity towards her daughter very touching. They were not the type to be callous or tactless. If they had made any disparaging remarks to Michael, he must have aggravated them terribly.

Dusty spent the next two nights at the farm, sleeping on the couch. He wanted to see the pandemonium settle down before he left KD Acres. Neil Harris, the fire chief, and Judd Candon, from the insurance company, had revisited the shed on Monday afternoon and completed their report. According to their findings, a spark from the welder had ignited some gas in a container on the floor, causing an explosion which sent an open container with sulfuric acid flying, splashing and spilling the contents onto Michael's face and body, over the work counter, and over the floor. The gas that that released, just added fuel to the fire. The accident may have been preventable, had Michael been more safety conscious and kept all the containers closed and far away from the welder.

Hearing the report, Katreena was secretly surprised, because in spite of all his faults, Michael had always been meticulously conscientious and organized in the shop. Was his agitation a cause for this carelessness? Katreena kept her suspicions to herself. Judd Candon filed a report that it was an accident and the insurance would pay for the damage so no good would be served by analyzing the episode or casting blame on Michael. If he was the primary cause of the catastrophe, he was certainly paying a heavy price for it.

Beside the insurance situation, they had to deal with the logistics of Michael's transfer. All the while, friends and neighbours dropped in to pay their condolences and offer their support. Life assumed an almost hectic social pace at the house, though not an unpleasant one, Dusty noted. Katreena, Helen, and Kaydee just dealt with issues as the need arose. He was ready to assist if and when he was needed. He stayed at KD Acres till Monday of the following week and then left for home. He had joined the family for church on Sunday and was pleased to see that Helen seemed to be functioning remarkably well. Katreena was there, so Dusty felt comfortable leaving. Not an hour after Dusty's departure, Annie came to pay her respects.

"So sorry to hear about your tragedy," she gushed, hugging Helen sympathetically. "I only got home from Toronto yesterday. They told me you had a bad fire and that Michael was hurt so we rushed right over. What happened and how bad is Michael?" Words tumbled out of her mouth like marbles, colliding with each other in a babble of concern. Annie was always like that, bubbly and full of enthusiasm and emotion. What she didn't possess in physical beauty, she made up in personality. Her compassion was boundless and her heart overflowed with simple and unconditional love for everyone she knew.

Katreena, Helen, Annie and a young man who had come with her, sat on the deck, sipping tea and enjoying some of the cookies that had been brought in by neighbours. After hearing the story from Katreena and Helen, Annie clucked her shock and expressed her sympathy. Suddenly she remembered that in her eagerness to hear what had happened, she had forgotten to introduce the young man.

"Oh my goodness, Katreena, Helen, forgive me. This is my grandson, Joey Kerman. He came back with me from Toronto. The plant where he works has been closed because of some sort of takeover by another company and he has been laid off for the next few months but he expects a call back. He hates the city and decided to sublet his apartment and spend the summer here with me. Perhaps he can help you out while he waits for his call. He's good on the farm. He lived with his parents Amelia and Lawrence on the farm before he moved to Toronto three years ago. Amelia is my daughter."

She beamed proudly at the tall thirty-ish looking man at her side. He smiled back at her fondly and nodded to Helen.

"I have the time and I'm willing to help if you need me. It'll keep me from getting bored. There isn't much I can do at Grandma's other than cut grass and I'm afraid she'd have my hide if I touched a single one of her flowers."

They all laughed. Katreena chose to let Helen field that offer.

"We have not decided what we are even doing yet," Helen confessed. "Everything has been so crazy around here with the fire people, the phone calls, the doctors, and the visitors. We have been overwhelmed with all the offers of help and support. I truly appreciate everything but so far I have just been too busy and in too much of a shock to think rationally. I know I have to make a decision soon because I know I need lots of help. Let me think about it and I will certainly let you know soon. Thank you very much for your offer." She addressed this to both Annie and her grandson.

Only slightly surprised by Helen's now rational behaviour, Katreena was pleased with Helen's foresight and candour. It was still rather unbelievable, considering her feeble condition so recently. Nonetheless it seemed that, away from Michael's oppression, as well as feeling needed and in charge, she gained strength and confidence. Helen was almost reminiscent of her old self and Katreena's heart vacillated with concurrent gratitude, disbelief and melancholy.

Kaydee had just finished mowing the lawn and came in all sweaty and flushed. The sun was hot but a breeze helped to make the day comfortable. She had taken refuge in any shade she could find but now she came into the house for a welcome breather under a cool shower. She felt happy, and guilty. She shouldn't be happy. Her father was badly hurt. She had wished him to go away and now he was away. Had God actually heard her wish? Granny said "No," but Kaydee could not be totally sure. Try as she might, that guilt kept resurfacing. Still, she could not quell this feeling in her heart, this relief, this sense of freedom, and, yes, this euphoria!

She didn't miss her father. Nobody seemed to miss him. Mother was dealing logically with people and situations, confident and almost serene, so unlike the scared rabbit that she was a mere two weeks ago. Even Alvin, Father's pride and joy, seemed much more relaxed and happy than he used to be. It wasn't even two weeks since her father's presence had been removed from their midst and already the change in the atmosphere was remarkably healthier. Kaydee looked at her reflection in the mirror. Another hint of guilt sought to overcome her sense of peace but with steadfast determination, she refused to succumb to it. This was her first taste of serenity and she liked it. She was not going to give it up. She had earned it, and so had her mother! She thought again of her mother's journal and the poetry her mother used to write. Gone forever, never to be read or recalled. What an absolutely tragic waste! No! She was glad her father was out of the way, even if it would be only for a couple of months. If God could hear her secret wish, surely He must know that she did not want him hurt. She had simply wished he would go away! For once in her life, she was not going to apologize for a wrong she did not commit.

Chapter 17

Michael had been flown to Toronto on Monday. Tuesday, they operated on that skull fracture and reported, by phone, that he had come through the surgery alright. They still had to determine the damage to his brain but promised to let them know about his recovery soon. A whole week later there still was no word on Michael's condition.

Finally on Thursday afternoon, Dr. Walley phoned and asked Helen and Katreena to come see him at the office. Helen had just hung up the phone when Dusty drove in. He had a small bag with him, obviously a change of clothes and toiletries, in case he had to stay for a couple of days. Katreena marvelled at how naturally he had stepped into their lives and assumed responsibility for the well-being of the family! What would they have done without him this week?

Helen told Dusty about Dr. Walley's request. "He said he didn't want to go into it over the phone," she concluded, "but he wanted to see us as soon as possible."

"Would you mind if I came along?" Dusty asked, keenly watching her face for any expression of apprehension or hesitation. There was none.

"Quite frankly, I was hoping you'd come," Helen sounded relieved. "I don't know what he has to tell us but if it had been good news, they would have called us directly."

They informed Kaydee of the situation and promised to come back with news. Since the fire, Kaydee had taken on much more responsibility and Katreena, Dusty and Helen all realized just how mature and dependable she really was with the smaller children. She had proven herself by the way she stepped up to the plate with her mother and with the smaller kids each time a crisis arose. It was as if the tragedy had transformed Kaydee from a child into a responsible adult in just a week. More and more they relied on her to take charge of the household and smaller children. They gave her honest and frank information about what was going on and kept her in the loop about any new developments. She accepted this role responsibly and without complaint.

"How are you doing Helen?" Dr. Walley's eyes swept over her as he shook her hand. Her calm demeanour was unexpected and he glanced at Katreena and Dusty only briefly as he shook hands with them. Seeing no sign of apprehension in their eyes, he returned his gaze to Helen. He could barely recognize this woman, still thin and emaciated, but already the dark circles around those lifeless eyes seemed less prominent. Those eyes that had been so devoid of hope or expression a week or so ago now held an awareness of purpose. In front of him stood a woman who had been through a terrible tragedy but who now seemed prepared to accept what was coming without shrinking away from it. Was this the same woman who, just recently had been ready to crawl under a rock, there to cower and hide from the cruel world? The transformation was astounding! He knew Maureen had powers of reaching deeply troubled individuals in stressful situations but this seemed well beyond even her capability. Something more had happened to Helen, something deeper, more remedial. Dr. Walley saw before him a woman with a spirit in her eyes that was not derived from Maureen's expertise. It was a pleasant surprise though. He liked this woman so much more than the last one.

"Hello, Dr. Walley," Katreena began. "You remember Dusty Duganyk? I hope you don't mind him coming with us. He's been a pillar of strength for all of us since the accident. We are all anxious to know the verdict. Is it good news or bad?"

The doctor fixed an attentive gaze on Helen, hesitating for a brief moment.

"I didn't want to tell you this over the phone, but I'm afraid the news is not very good at the moment." He noticed Helen stiffen ever so slightly but then her reserve returned and she resumed that stoic determination that had surprised him so much when they first walked in. Watching her closely for any untoward reaction, he continued.

"Michael has not regained consciousness. At this time they have no way of knowing how much trauma his brain may have suffered in the impact. They have repaired what they could but it seems that it was the penetration into the brain of that piece of bone, as well as the blow itself, that may have done the damage. Sometimes a sudden and forceful crash like that can actually 'scramble' brain tissue. We don't know if that happened. The brain can heal itself over time if the damage is not too severe. Only time will tell if Michael can overcome this. In the meantime all we can do is wait and see. At this point they do not want to move him because it might create more stress and delay the healing process. His burn wounds are being treated in the best burn unit in the country, but the chemical wounds on his face and chest have literally eaten away a lot of flesh which will result in extensive scarring. When all that acid debris is cleared away, and depending on his progress of course, they may consider flying him back here. Until then, this is the best we can do. I am so sorry."

They thanked him and took their leave. Helen took the news quietly.

"Considering all that had happened, Michael is lucky to be alive. We owe that all to you, Dusty, for your immediate response in getting Michael out of there. You could both have died in that fire!" Helen shuddered, and so did Katreena as the image of that narrow escape engulfed them. They continued to discuss the implications and the near misses of the accident as they got into the car and drove toward home.

"I don't think the scarring is our biggest problem," Helen said in a low tone. "It's what Michael is going to be like when he does come home. I know he will take time to heal, but it's after he heals that has me worried. What will be his state of mind? Will he be angry?"

Katreena knew what Helen was talking about. That was the crucial issue. They can patch Michael's skin but can they fix his brain? That was where repairs were needed, much more than the damage from the accident. Although Helen did not say it in so many words, Katreena knew that Helen dreaded Michael's **return**, not his scars or his injuries. Katreena empathized with Helen's pessimism but she had no encouraging response to it.

"Let's not think about that now," she said. "We'll cross that bridge when we get to it. Thank heavens for Medicare. These next two months could have sunk us but as things stand, the biggest problem will be the upkeep of KD Acres." Katreena suddenly remembered Annie and her grandson. Could he be their answer?

"Helen, why don't you tell Dusty about Annie Dorozeck and her offer," Katreena prompted her daughter. She wanted to change the subject anyway, get their thoughts away from Michael, and alleviate the burden of gloom that the doctor's report had created.

"Annie Dorozeck has her grandson staying with her for the summer and he offered to help out on the farm," Helen explained. "He was farming till three years ago and apparently knows his way around the farm. He's been laid off from his job for a few months and is free to help out. It sounds like he might be a solution to my problem."

Dusty listened attentively while Helen outlined the pros and cons of the proposal. Deep in thought, he drove the last mile in silence. As they emerged from the car, Kaydee met them.

"So what did you find out?" she wanted to know.

Katreena and Dusty let Helen bring Kaydee up to date. It felt good to hear Helen's calm, albeit sad, voice explaining so naturally the fragile condition of a sick father to her daughter. Once again, Katreena marvelled at the miracle that had transformed her stricken daughter into this secure, almost confident woman who spoke with conviction and understanding. Was this a permanent modification or would it all dissipate the minute Michael walked back into the house? Katreena's heart lurched. She didn't want Michael to come back! She wanted him to stay away forever if it meant that it would prevent her daughter from sliding back into that black hole she had been living in for the last twelve years. This new-found peaceful haven was too fragile, too unstable to be tampered with. It could not withstand the impact of Michael's return.

Katreena gave herself a mental slap. "What is the matter with you? Michael is a human being. He is hurt and you are wishing he never gets well!" Still another voice within her argued: "Helen and the kids deserve a decent life but if Michael comes back they lose that opportunity." Katreena's emotions frayed as scenario after scenario presented itself. What if Michael came back brain-dead, a virtual vegetable, devoid of cruelty or anything else? What then? Katreena considered that image. That would be awful too, but less terrifying than the last. Resignedly she decided, "What will be, will be." For now, she would revel in Helen's current emancipation!

They began working on supper after Helen finished her explanation to Kaydee. Kaydee also had been having the same misgivings that Mother and Granny were harbouring and Helen tried to present hypothetical answers for all of them though it pained her mercilessly to even think in those terms.

"If Father has bad scars when he comes back, he will hate them and he'll be angrier than ever. He will want to blame somebody. He'll really have an excuse to yell then." Kaydee observed. Her rebellious belligerence was surfacing again but so was that unrelenting guilt. She clamped her mouth shut. Mother was doing well now and Kaydee did not even want to imagine what Father's rages might do to her again.

"Maybe it won't come to that, honey. Let's not borrow trouble, Kaydee." Helen begged, disallowing her own misgivings.

Dusty had come back from the shed where he had gone for another reconnaissance and now sat quietly listening to their conversation. When Kaydee left for the garden to get salad greens, Dusty brought up the subject of hiring someone to help on the farm.

"You know, I've been thinking. Your neighbours have offered to help on a job-by-job basis but I really think you need someone who is here to manage the whole operation. You have both the grain farming and the cattle operation to take care of. On top of that, there is the yard work, and the shed. As I told you before, I can help, but you need a farmer who knows what he is doing. This Joey Kerman, is thirty-ish, you say, and he farmed until three years ago. If he is as good as he sounds, I think you may be better off to hire him full time and that would take the burden off you for all the mundane decisions that go with a farm operation. Can you afford that?"

"I could probably swing it," Helen said pensively, weighing the possibilities in her mind.

"Of course, we can," Katreena offered quickly and firmly. "I'll pay his salary myself if you run short of cash. You need someone reliable. I have known Annie for years and I have never known her to make an irresponsible decision. She never would have suggested this if she thought Joey was not up for the job. This may be the perfect solution to your problem. Why don't you give them a call and see if you can work something out."

By Friday, they had worked out the terms and Helen had a full time farm manager. Joey seemed as excited about the position as Katreena and his grandmother were. Katreena was confident the arrangement would be advantageous to both. Helen and Dusty were somewhat more cautious, wanting to see Joey's performance before passing judgment but they were willing to give him a fair chance.

For his part, Dusty was relieved. Taking responsibility for a farm did not fit in with his line of qualifications. He'd been a stationary engineer all his life. That was his forte. He knew nothing about farming but he felt obligated to help. Now he could relax, knowing that the farm would be in the competent hands of a knowledgeable farmer.

They needn't have doubted Joey's farming capabilities. He assumed responsibility with alacrity. He had sought employment in the city when his older brother returned from military service and took over the farm. Joey had loved the farm much more than he ever liked the city. Getting this opportunity to actually run a farm made him feel validated. He was enthusiastic and eager to prove his worth. He immediately set out to familiarize himself with the operation by checking all the fields and crops, then the cattle and the pastures and in his spare time started working on the shed and its contents. His passionate approach to the job convinced Dusty, Katreena and Helen that they had made the right choice. Katreena in particular, was overjoyed. She was certain Michael could not have done better than Joey. To top everything else, Joey was always pleasant and treated everyone with respect. It was just too good to be true! If this was a dream, Katreena was sure she did not want to wake up. She felt like she had to hold her breath, lest this fragile bubble burst. He was the exact opposite of Michael and for the first time in twelve years, Katreena saw the sun shine on KD Acres again.

Joey was a tireless worker. He took over the farm as if it were his own, checking into every aspect of the operation and staying on top of every detail that required attention. Helen was not called out to work the fields anymore. Joey completed the haying and the summerfallow alone, often working after supper and late into the night. When Helen protested that he shouldn't be doing that, he countered with "But I love the work. It's not difficult or tiring at all. All I do is sit and drive. I enjoy it." And enjoy it he did. He actually whistled while he worked! Often he came home after dark, parked the tractor, got into the pickup and drove back to his grandmother's for the night. Next morning he arrived before anyone was awake, fuelled up and it was the sound of the tractor leaving the yard that woke the family up.

Life settled into a comfortable and peaceful routine around the farm. Dusty and Katreena went home, driving out rarely now but calling often to check on how things were going. Helen was doing well and looking better every day. Kaydee and the children were doing well also, although Alvin still asked about his father now and then.

"How long will Father have to stay in the hospital? When will he be better? When will he come home?" he wanted to know. Kaydee or Helen answered his queries as calmly as they could and he accepted their explanations, until the next time...

The only disturbing clouds on the horizon were the phone calls every few days that informed them of the minute progress that Michael was making and reminded them of his eventual re-entry into their lives. He had not awakened since the accident. When Helen failed to call the hospital, Michael's neurologist, Dr. Gorman, took it upon himself to inform her whenever they performed another test or proceeded with any new treatment plan or reached a new milestone.

"His burns are healing slowly but the scarring on his face will require surgery. His chest could be left as is since a shirt will hide it." Dr. Gorman had been there when they had operated on Michael to remove that bone fragment from his brain. When Michael didn't wake up, Dr. Gorman took on the case as his own personal challenge.

"I cannot tell if it is physical damage to his brain or emotional trauma that is keeping him unconsciousness but it is risky to move him. These cases are unpredictable; I have had patients who made a complete recovery after five months in a coma," he said. "We can see some kind of brain activity on the scan, but he is not responsive. We would like to trigger a response with a different stimulant."

Dr. Gorman hesitated before going on. He had apparently talked to Dr. Walley and knew of Helen's situation but Michael was his patient and his recovery was his priority.

"Would you consider coming to see Michael here at the hospital? I know it would be traumatic for you, but it may be the only hope we have of triggering a response from him."

Therefore, it was decided that Helen should fly out to Toronto to visit him.

"That Publishers' meeting that Wayne had rescheduled, is coming up next week," Dusty told Katreena "and Wayne and I have to go anyway. Why don't you and Helen come along with us? That way, Wayne and I can be there for you in case of any problems."

"That sounds like a good idea, Dusty," Katreena said. "Helen seems to be functioning well now but that's only because she is away from Michael. What will happen when she has to face him again? I don't relish seeing Michael, but I cannot risk Helen going alone and possibly suffering a relapse. And it would help so much knowing you're nearby."

Katreena and Dusty were standing in the kitchen at KD Acres waiting for Helen, Kaydee and Joey to come in from the shop. They had stayed behind to listen to Joey's plans for the shed.

Being at KD Acres these days was a pleasure for Katreena. The atmosphere had changed so dramatically, she often thought she was at the wrong farmyard. Everyone seemed at ease. Alvin and Jaynee chased Rusko around the yard, squealing with delight as Rusko tore around them in ever wider circles barking and snorting. Nobody worried about excessive noise or activity. Kaydee hummed as she did her chores and sometimes even joined the children in play. Memories of Michael's rages still plagued her and her guilt was like a phantom that hovered ever near but she was determined not to succumb to any negativity. She wanted to enjoy this period of grace while it lasted because she knew that all too soon her father would be back and her utopia would shatter and disintegrate. Most of her spare time though, was spent with her notebook which she now carried around openly, writing whenever inspiration occurred. She did not have to hide it anymore. She was relaxed, happy, and confident.

Mealtimes in the Boyer house were now boisterous and noisy events with conversation and jokes, especially when Joey ate with them. He initiated much of the easy banter and the teasing. His easygoing manner was a welcome change for the family. Laughter used to be an elusive dream here a mere month ago. Now it ruled the day and filled Katreena's ears with a jubilation she hadn't felt in years. This was the kind of family she had dreamed of and here it was, however temporarily.

Chapter 18

The following Wednesday, Dusty, Katreena and Helen left for Toronto and Annie went to stay at the farm until they returned.

At the airport, the trio were met by Wayne Duganyk, tall and handsome like his older brother with the same sandy hair and laughing eyes. There was nothing shy about this jovial fellow though. He seemed so sure of himself, yet he was not conceited or superficial. He saw them first and came striding towards them with a broad sincere smile, extending a long hairy arm out of the short sleeved polo shirt he was wearing.

"This has to be Helen," he grinned as he took her hand in both of his. "I'm so very pleased to meet you." Then on a more serious note, "Dusty told me about your misfortune. I'm so sorry. I hope that your visit will be a good one, and hopefully, productive. Sometimes the sound of a familiar voice can stir a dormant brain. It may make your husband wake up."

Helen thanked Wayne but Katreena thought she detected a note of angst-ridden panic in her voice. Dusty caught it too. "She is probably just nervous about flying, since she has never flown before." Katreena whispered to Dusty while Helen and Wayne exchanged pleasantries. Wayne's attention turned to Katreena.

"Katreena! I see Dusty did not exaggerate. You are every bit as beautiful as he said you were. I am so glad to finally meet you. That brother of mine cannot stop talking about you. There will be no problem meshing these families." Katreena blushed as Wayne shook her hand.

As they queued up to the ticket booth, both Dusty and Katreena watched Helen closely but she seemed to have recovered and was chatting casually with Wayne about the heat and the humidity in the air.

"You think this is bad. Just wait till Toronto! It's worse there." Wayne warned.

In mock alarm Helen countered, "Oh no! Dusty, you should have warned me to take that portable fan along," she admonished and they all laughed.

They walked through the airport to the gate where they boarded the plane. Dusty and Wayne sat together and Helen and Katreena sat behind them. While the men talked about the publishing business, Helen interjected questions here and there. Clearly she still carried a keen interest in writing. She seemed at ease and unconcerned through take off.

"I must have been imagining her apprehension before," Katreena told herself as Helen continued to converse effortlessly throughout the flight. No one mentioned Michael or his condition again, but it was obvious that Helen was not afraid of flying. Katreena relaxed.

Their arrival in Toronto was uneventful. Helen followed their lead, not knowing where to go or what to do, but she was relaxed. They cabbed it to the Kornova Hotel where Wayne and Dusty had arranged to meet with the other publishers. Instead of meeting at Ramada Inn as originally scheduled, Wayne had pulled some strings to move the meetings to the banquet room at the Kornova Hotel because Dusty wanted to be near the hospital for the girls' sake. Dusty did not want to leave them alone too much in case they needed help.

Their rooms were on the fifth floor, next door to each other but Dusty felt nervous when he walked away from their door after dropping the women off. Would Helen be alright here in the city? What would he do if she wasn't and Katreena ran into problems handling her? He really didn't know Helen too well. Katreena had described a timid, unstable recluse that used to be Helen but he only saw that side of her for a few hours. After that, it was another Helen he got to know, this confident, intelligent woman that Katreena seemed to find difficult to recognize.

Which was the real Helen here in the room next to theirs? What if she reverted to the frightened, dependent woman that Katreena had first described? He thought he had noted a hint of regression in Helen, back home at the airport and he knew Katreena had spotted it too. Hopefully they had imagined it, but what if it had been real? Could Katreena deal with the frightened Helen here in a city with such unfamiliar surroundings? Dusty really had very little time to help them in case a problem arose. As part owner of the business, he had a responsibility to attend any meetings involving its future. They had already postponed the meeting once to accommodate him. It was unfair, to expect them to do so again.

Dusty pondered over his predicament. After unpacking the bags, he called 508.

"How are you doing? ... Ready for supper? ... We're just going to the restaurant downstairs here in the hotel... Great we'll pick you up in five minutes."

"Everything sounds alright," he told his brother, "but I'm a little worried about Helen's reaction to some things – especially seeing Michael. She may still be fragile. We'll take her to the hospital after supper. In case of any problems we can still decide tonight how to deal with them. I don't want any last minute surprises tomorrow."

"There better not be any," Wayne admonished. "I told them you'd be there."

They had a leisurely supper and by seven Dusty, Katreena and Helen left for the hospital. Walking up the steps to the hospital, all three were apprehensive, but probably each for a different reason. Helen was nervous about facing Michael, Katreena worried about Helen and Dusty worried about Katreena. Helen's fear was probably most intense, because Michael had been so unpredictable and volatile before the accident. She had told herself and assured her mother that she was ready for this and that she could handle it, but each step brought her closer to something akin to a panic attack. Her chest felt tight and her throat constricted, almost cutting off her oxygen supply. Her stomach cramped from all those knots inside and there was this terrible loud whooshing sound that reverberated in her ears. She could feel her nails cutting into her sweaty palms.

How would Michael react to her? Would he be angry, belligerent? What if he started ranting again, or blaming her or something? How would she feel then? Dr. Walley had told them to expect a lot of facial scarring, but that was of minor concern to Helen. She was much more worried about his reaction than his physical appearance. That was where she was most vulnerable. She just could not face any more of his emotional abuse.

"Mother, can I sit down somewhere? I don't feel very well." Helen panted shakily. Spying a bench on the large landing outside the hospital door, Katreena and Dusty helped Helen onto it. They exchanged worried glances. This was what they had been afraid of, Helen's inability to face Michael's battered body. Or was she more afraid of Michael, the tyrant?

Katreena remembered the tranquilizer pills Dr. Walley had prescribed for Helen that fateful Monday just after the accident. She had taken them along "just in case." Helen hadn't needed them until now. But she had not had to face Michael, until now.

"Get a glass of water," Katreena croaked to the startled Dusty as she fumbled in her purse for the precious bottle. Dusty sped to the door of the hospital and disappeared inside. After a few moments, he was back with a styrofoam cup of water.

"Here, take this," Katreena offered the pill to Helen. Dusty handed her the water.

With shaking hands, Helen took the pill, swallowed it with the water then leaned back against the bench, panting and exhausted.

Dusty and Katreena sat on either side of her. Katreena met Dusty's gaze above her daughter's bowed head and mouthed a fervent "Sorry. And thank you!" Dusty nodded. He could see how worried Katreena was. He was glad he'd been there for her tonight, but what would she do tomorrow when he went to his meeting?

They had been there about fifteen minutes since Helen had taken the pill. They sat in silence, not wishing to disturb her, choosing instead to let the medication work its magic. People walked by, glancing their way, but few seemed aware of the conquest of distress that was taking place on that bench. Slowly Helen's panting had subsided and finally she stirred.

"Feeling any better, honey?" Katreena queried, her arm still around Helen's shoulder.

Helen nodded weakly. "I'm sorry. I don't know what came over me." Then turning to Dusty, she gave him a crooked smile. "Sorry for being such a wimp but thanks a million for being here. Seems like you're always there to rescue us from some catastrophe or another. You sure you want to be part of this crazy family?" she teased.

"No problem there, girl. You know what they say. Everyone needs to be needed. You're giving me a valid reason to keep coming back." She laughed rather shakily as he patted her arm. The gloom had lifted. The medication had obviously hit its mark, and Helen was back to normal, for now. She still had not seen Michael. That was what she had to do next. She could not avoid it forever.

They sat there for a while longer, giving Helen a chance to regain her strength and summon her fortitude. Katreena did not want to bring up the subject of Michael but eventually she had to. It was getting close to eight o'clock and visiting hours would be over in the hospital by half past eight. If they were to see him today, they had to make their move now.

"Do you think you want to go in tonight honey, or would you rather wait till tomorrow?" Katreena motioned toward the door.

Helen hesitated, then stoically, she got up and started for the door.

"It's not going to be easier tomorrow. And I'm feeling much better now. Perhaps it's the pill, but I think I may as well get this over with, and not put it off till later."

They were whisked up an elevator, shown through several hallways, followed various numbered doorways and finally came to a desk with two white uniformed nurses behind it.

When they asked to see Michael, the two girls exchanged glances. This was unusual. Michael Boyer never had visitors.

"Are you family?" the taller one asked, watching them with curious eyes.

"Yes we are," Dusty said. "This is his wife, Helen Boyer, and his mother-in-law, Katreena Banaduk. I'm Dusty Duganyk. We just flew in from Manitoba this afternoon."

"Oh, I'm sorry," she apologized. "We weren't told about your arrival. Follow me."

She looked at each one of them with pity in her eyes. "You are aware of his condition then?" It was a question and a statement; a warning perhaps? Be prepared for the worst?

Katreena nodded. "Dr. Walley has been giving us updates and we have also talked to Dr. Gorman on the phone."

"All right then, but it may be worse than what you expect. You haven't seen him since the accident?" Again that worried anxious gaze. Was she forewarning them? She led the way to a room where she gave them gowns, caps, gloves and masks to put on. "We have to keep the room sterile to prevent infections. He is very vulnerable," she explained.

They donned the protective gear then, like a flotilla of white ghosts, followed her to Michael's room. Just inside the door to Michael's room, Dusty stepped in front of Helen to block her view. "Are you sure you can do this, Helen?" he looked deep into those sad and frightened eyes. Katreena had her arm around Helen's shoulders, ready to lead her away at the slightest suggestion.

Helen took Katreena's hand and tucked her other arm through Dusty's and nodded. "I'm ready," she whispered. "I have to do this." Dusty stepped aside to walk her forward. The nurse stood by silently watching them. All three visitors, although they had been warned, were ill-prepared for what was before them.

The sight that greeted their eyes was grotesque, to say the least. The skin on Michael's face was like raw steak, the flesh stretched and gouged out where the chemical and the fire had eaten away at it. His eyes were narrow slits amid the barely recognizable other features and a thin layer of ointment covered the areas of thin-skinned reddish purple flesh making it appear shiny and stretched. An intravenous pole beside the bed held two plastic bags of clear liquid and tubes from these bottles led into a heavily taped arm. A loose white sheet covered a curved tent that kept the sheet off his chest and body.

Helen's breath caught. She cupped her hands over her mouth and screamed. "Oh my God, Michael!" She turned into Dusty's open arms her body convulsing with uncontrollable sobs. Dusty let her cry, holding her quietly. The nurse motioned to a chair and Dusty manoeuvred Helen into it then knelt down beside her, soothing her, comforting her as best he could. Katreena was still standing where she had stopped. Her face was a mask of shock and disbelief. She stood rooted to the spot, stunned, a virtual pillar of stone. She too, had not expected anything that terrible. Dusty wanted to go to her but he didn't dare leave Helen. He had no idea what to do next. Michael had either not heard them or had failed to react.

"Katreena?" Dusty called gently. "Katreena, are you alright?" The nurse brought another chair, put it behind Katreena and gently lowered her into it. Katreena suddenly realized where she was and groaned.

"Oh Dusty, I never knew it was that bad. I didn't know it could be that bad. It didn't seem that bad when you brought him out. This is unbelievable!" Katreena was practically incoherent herself. Dusty understood. Yes it was bad. He was shocked to see Michael's face too. He had served in France during World War II, so he had seen wounds before, terrible wounds and atrocities, but this one took even his breath away.

Helen's sobbing had subsided somewhat and only a pitiful whimpering was audible now. Katreena came and knelt beside her daughter, hugging her close. She was glad she had given Helen that tranquilizer before. Katreena had not realized just how bad the scarring would be. Perhaps she should not have brought Helen here, at least not until those burns had healed. But could she have, should she have, kept Helen away? Was Helen not entitled to know? Most women would have been there from the beginning, but Helen's fragile condition had precluded that. Still, had she been there from the beginning, this visit would have been less traumatic.

The nurse came back into the room and whispered. "It is now half past eight. We need to swab and cleanse the wounds for the night. I hate turning you out but he needs this treatment. I'm so sorry." She apologized. Michael had still not exhibited any reaction but Katreena did not wish to pursue that issue anymore at the moment. Helen had had enough for tonight.

"That's alright, Nurse. We understand. We will go for now. Thank you so much for your help here and for all you've done for Michael since he came here. We appreciate it." Katreena's voice was hoarse with emotion. Dusty added his assent. Then, tucking their arms under Helen's, they led her out of the room, purposely shielding her from the sight of Michael's ravaged face.

"Let's go back to the hotel now, Helen. We'll get a good night's sleep and we'll deal with the rest tomorrow. You need to rest now." Katreena soothed.

They took off their protective garb and Helen allowed herself to be led out of hospital and to the car. Once there, she collapsed into the back seat like a sack of potatoes. Katreena sat beside her determined to give her another tranquilizer when they got back to the hotel room if Helen appeared to need it. She wanted to wipe away that vivid image of Michael from Helen's mind. It was enough to rattle a healthy mind. Helen's was just barely functioning under the strain of years of abuse. And now this! It was just too much! Once again, Katreena sent up a thankful prayer for the grace of memory that made her bring those tranquilizers along.

On the short ride back to the hotel, they sat in stunned silence. There were no words to describe the emotions that were churning inside each of them. Tonight, they had observed the horrific result of the accident and they could not escape seeing it again tomorrow. But the real test of Helen's stamina would come when she had to try to wake Michael up. That had been the purpose of this trip. The surgeons hoped that might trigger Michael's consciousness. Only then could they determine the extent of damage to his brain. The scans they had done showed brain activity but unless Michael woke up soon, no one knew what kind of activity it was. What if Michael awoke in that irate frame of mind he was in prior to the accident and started ranting again? That vile mood combined with that appearance would be ghastly for Helen.

At the door of the hotel room, Dusty was the first to interrupt their brooding silence.

"Do you want me to come in for a while?" he asked and Katreena nodded gratefully. They seated Helen on one of the chairs and Katreena immediately left to get her a glass of water.

"You okay?" Katreena queried. Helen nodded but Katreena picked up her purse, took another pill from the bottle, broke it in half and handed it to Helen. "Take this. It'll help you relax. You need to if you're to get any sleep tonight. That was an awful jolt." Katreena was afraid to give her the whole pill. It was not even three hours since Helen had had the last one.

Helen accepted the pill without protest and obediently washed it down with the rest of the water in the glass. Dusty took the empty glass and refilled it for her. He was at a total loss for words. He felt utterly helpless. How do you cushion someone against an experience like that? He didn't want to leave the women alone just yet. They sat quietly beside Helen waiting for the pill to lift the misery from her face. Even after Dr. Walley's warnings, no one could possibly have anticipated the agonizing horror they had witnessed this evening.

After a while, Helen yawned and Katreena realized that the pill had taken effect. Mouthing to Dusty to wait, she led Helen to the bedroom, where she helped her to change and get into bed. Helen was lethargic and somewhat incoherent but Katreena knew it was the drug and that it would wear off eventually. Perhaps she had given the half of the second pill before the first one had worked itself out, but in view of her recent experience, Katreena felt justified. If it helped Helen sleep for the next few hours, it was the lesser of two perils because it would provide respite from the image of Michael. Tomorrow, Helen would have to talk to Michael.

When she heard Helen's deep breathing signifying she was asleep, Katreena tiptoed out of the bedroom. Dusty was still sitting on the chair, looking distraught.

"Do you think we did the right thing bringing her here, honey? I don't know. That was quite a shock. I almost lost it myself, and I saw horrors of war!" He shuddered at the memory.

Wearily, Katreena sank into the other chair. "I honestly don't know," she sighed. "I never imagined anything like it. But I still think that Helen's worst moment will come from Michael's reaction to her. Bad as his face is, I think she can handle his appearance, it's his reaction that has her traumatized. Problem is that the doctors' hands are tied with his treatment until they know if there is a person there to treat."

"What if he never comes out of this? What will you do then?" Dusty wanted to know.

"I honestly don't know. Maybe you're right. Maybe we shouldn't have come. But if she is the key to his waking up, do we have the right to stand in the way? Who do we sacrifice? Because that is the way I'm starting to feel. If she can't handle this, I may be throwing her into a vortex of despair that she may never recover from. Is Michael even worth that? I hate to admit this because it truly makes me feel wicked, but in my estimation, he's not! Yet who am I to judge whose life is worth more and who's less?" Katreena paused. "Should I just take her home on the next plane and forget about him completely? Is that even an option now that she has seen him? Will she ever be able to get that image out of her mind?"

Dusty listened in silence, letting her vent her frustration, purge it from her heart, hopefully forever, into some never-never land where it would remain eternally irretrievable. He wished he could whisk her away from all this and present her with a haven of peace and tranquility. But he could only wish. He felt ineffective and unable to offer any credible alternative to her dilemma. There was really nothing he could actually do to help. He had never felt so inept and useless in his whole life.

They sat there clinging to each other, till the phone rang at fifteen minutes after ten. It was Wayne from the next room. "Is everything alright there?" he wanted to know. He knew the three of them were going to the hospital that evening but this was well past visiting hours there. He knew the situation had been tenuous. Had something terrible happened?

Katreena whispered to Dusty. "It's okay. You go back to the room. Helen will sleep like a log, possibly till morning. I'm exhausted so I'll turn in too. Goodnight and thanks for everything, Dusty." She walked him to the door.

Dusty gave her a long slow kiss. He hated to leave her but tomorrow would be a big day for all of them. They needed sleep.

"Promise to call me if anything happens, okay?" He tilted her chin up to meet her eyes. "Anything! Anytime! Promise?" He paused, waiting for her answer.

"I promise! I promise!" she answered. She reached up, gave him a quick kiss then gently pushed him out the door. "Now go!"

Chapter 19

In the next room, Wayne was eagerly waiting for his brother when he walked in. "So how did it go?"

Dusty drew a blank. Where do you start with something like this? He crossed the room and sank heavily into a chair. Running his fingers through his sandy hair, he stared pensively at his brother, who stood watching his every move with great expectation.

"Well, what happened?" Wayne demanded, exasperated.

Stymied, Dusty admitted, "I don't even know where to begin!"

"Begin at the beginning, man. Begin at the end. I don't care, but for heaven's sake, start somewhere. You're acting like shell-shocked idiot, man." Wayne was getting uneasy. This was not like his brother. Dusty was always in control of any situation. He was never under the circumstances, he was always on top of them. What the hell was he struggling with?

"It's a long story, Wayne, and a damned ugly one at that. You got a couple of hours?"

Wayne sat down opposite Dusty and folded his arms. "Lay it on me, Bro!" he demanded.

Dusty had given Wayne few details about the family when he first told him about the accident but now he started with the history behind it all. He told him about Michael's character; his control over the family; his callous treatment of the family; especially Kaydee and Helen; how they cowered before him to the point of mental instability.

"I wouldn't have believed it had I not seen it with my own eyes, Wayne. I was there the day of the accident. I saw it!" He related the events of the day prior to the accident and how Michael's attitude may have been a contributing factor in the accident itself. He explained how the family had changed in Michael's absence, and Katreena's hopes for the future. Then he reiterated the prognosis of Michael's health and the reason they had brought Helen here. Some of the story, Wayne had heard from Dusty before. Now Dusty elaborated on the details.

"But Katreena and I both fear it may have been a mistake, bringing her here, I mean. It was incredible!" Dusty described what they had seen at the hospital, and Helen's reaction to it. "But his appearance is not even the major issue here. What if he lashes out at her? She's too fragile now to take that. Helen is on tranquilizers now and she's asleep, but what is going to happen when she wakes up? We can't keep her drugged forever. They're hoping that her voice will bring Michael back. Maybe it will and maybe it won't, but Katreena sees doom for the family either way it goes. Quite frankly, I myself, am afraid of what the future holds for that family! It was the war and France and Germany all over again, man. It would take Hercules not to crumble under that pressure and Helen is extremely fragile right now." Dusty finished miserably. "If truth is stranger than fiction, man, this is it!"

"Phew!" Wayne sat back to digest the information. He had listened attentively as Dusty had related the story. Now, dumbfounded, he understood Dusty's torment.

It was after midnight when they finally went to bed. It had been a harrowing day for everybody, even Wayne, whose only involvement in the situation was merely his empathy.

Katreena had slept like a log, though she was positive that Helen had not stirred much through the night outside of an occasional muffled moan followed by deep even breathing that attested to her sound sleep again. Katreena had listened just long enough to establish that fact and immediately fell asleep as well. Shortly after eight she awoke refreshed and ready for a new day.

As memory of the day before overwhelmed her and her spirits plummeted, she looked over at Helen who was still fast asleep. Katreena was relieved. Helen needed that mental breather. Heaven only knew she was in for another horrific ordeal today. Katreena tiptoed to the bathroom, taking care to close the door as silently as possible. While she washed up and prepared for the day, she wondered if the men had left for their meeting yet. In her concern over her own problems, she forgot to ask them when their meetings were. She wished that all four of them could have breakfast together. That way she could ascertain Helen's frame of mind in the comfort of background support.

As she opened the bathroom door, she was surprised to see Helen sitting on her bed. Her eyes looked tired and somewhat puffy.

"Good morning, Mother. What time is it? Did I sleep too late?"

Katreena walked over to her and kissed her on the forehead. "No, honey, you didn't oversleep. I only woke up myself about fifteen minutes ago. We don't have to hurry today. How are you feeling?"

Judging by Helen's movements and her somewhat dazed expression, Katreena noted some residual lethargy. That was possibly from the drugs, Katreena decided, but beyond that, Helen seemed alright.

"Groggy!" Helen replied with a weak smile. "That's probably from those pills you gave me. Guess Dr. Walley followed us here after all, didn't he? Thanks, for bringing them, Mom. I really don't know what I'd have done without them."

"You're welcome, honey. You remember what Dr. Walley said. You take them whenever you feel the need. All you have to do is ask."

"I know. Thanks again, Mom. Right now I better get into that bathroom and make myself presentable. I feel like I crawled out from under a giant-sized rock."

As the bathroom door closed behind Helen, Katreena sighed with relief. Helen remembered taking the pills! If she remembered those pills and dealt with that rationally, perhaps she may be able to cope with the rest. They would just have to deal with things hour by hour.

Curious about how the men made out this morning, Katreena dialled their room. Dusty's voice came before the first ring ended.

"Katreena? How is everything going over there? Is Helen awake? How is she?" Katreena gave him a brief resume of the morning and finished off with a whispered "She remembered the pills, Dusty. I think she's okay." Then out loud again, "Do you guys have time for breakfast with a couple of ladies or are you off to your meeting?"

"Actually, we were just sitting here talking about that. Our meeting doesn't start till one in the afternoon and we thought about you and breakfast, but I was afraid to call in case I woke you up. How soon can you meet us?"

"Helen should be out in minutes. We'll rap on your door when we leave, okay?"

"You bet, honey." Then, in a softer tone, he added, "I'm glad the morning started so well, Katreena. I hope that it continues that way. See you soon."

Katreena checked the temperature on the balcony. The day was already starting to get muggy so she changed into a light summer dress. Guess Wayne was right about Toronto's humidity range, she conceded. Helen stepped out of the bathroom, her hair still wet from the shower but she had combed it back and secured it with a big clip at the back of her head. Helen took in her mother's sundress and asked.

"We going out now?"

"The boys are still waiting for breakfast so I said we'd join them. I hope that's okay, honey. We can order room service if you'd rather not go out," Katreena offered.

"No, it's alright, Mom, I'll go. I can't hide from life forever."

"Put on something light then. Looks like Wayne was right about Toronto heat and humidity. We'll just rap on their door as we head out."

Breakfast was at "Yolandy's," a little restaurant about a block from the hotel. The boys said they often went there because of the homey atmosphere. The owner came to welcome them when they entered and it was obvious that the three men shared a very cordial relationship. Mr. Yolandy was a kind of Mr. Magoo figure, short and somewhat chubby, with a friendly face and squinty eyes that recessed behind puffy folds of skin. His cheeks sort of folded forward, and when he smiled those folds made his jaw and chin look like they were a separate part of his face poking out from behind. He chattered excitedly about how happy he was to see them again and asked about Wayne's wife and their daughter.

He showed them to a table that looked out onto a kind of miniature park, with raised flower beds, cobblestone paths and a duck pond. There were ducks, geese and a couple of white swans swimming lazily among lily pads. The edge of the pond was neatly lined with pastel coloured rocks and several benches were strategically located throughout the tiny park where one could sit and enjoy this little oasis in the midst of the bustling city.

Helen gazed in astonishment at the peaceful and demure haven.

"Oh, isn't that just the most beautiful little garden park you ever saw," she breathed in awe. "What a heavenly place it would be to spend the day!"

As the others nodded in agreement, the owner of the restaurant beamed with pleasure.

"That used to be my backyard when I moved here as a young man in nineteen twenty-eight. I created that park for my family. At that time there was much bush here and very few buildings. Then the city started building around me and they wanted big taxes for my property. I was not a rich man, so when they offered to buy it, I sold it to them. But I made them promise never to put buildings on it. It had to remain a park. They have kept their promise and I made my house into a restaurant because they said no more homes here. So now this restaurant is like my home anyway, and I can still look out at my park whenever I feel like it. My son, his wife and their children, they work here too," he finished proudly.

"What a wonderful success story!" Katreena marvelled. Mr. Yolandy bowed with appreciation.

During breakfast, they chatted about the publishers meeting and the schedules surrounding it. Dusty and Wayne deliberately avoided the subject of Michael and Katreena was glad they did. She too, was afraid to broach the subject, though she knew she could not postpone it much longer. Visiting hours were at two.

Dusty did not want to leave Katreena to face a potentially difficult situation alone so after breakfast he broke the subject of the afternoon activities.

"You don't have to leave for the hospital till after lunch, do you? What do you girls think about us going into that little park for an hour or two of relaxation before we face the rigors of rest of the day?" Surreptitiously he was watching Helen's face for any sign of instability or stress. He could detect none.

"Oh Mother, could we?" Helen pleaded enthusiastically, her face alight with anticipation. "I dread going to that hospital, but I know I have to. In the meantime, this park would be such a nice place to just collect and store some peace for later. We have the time, don't we, Mom?"

There, it was! That moment that they had all been dreading: Helen's acknowledgement of the painful ordeal ahead had come, had passed, and the world had not crashed!

"Of course we do, sweetheart!" Katreena wanted to hug Helen, and sing with the angels! She was elated! She hadn't even realized how worried she had been about facing that afternoon with Helen going to see Michael again. But Helen surprised them all. She was going into the situation with her eyes open, her heart vulnerable, her emotions fragile but her mind determined to conquer the mission and accept the responsibility. She had come a long way. Katreena and Dusty exchanged relieved glances as they headed for the park bench.

"Wait, wait," Mr. Yolandy came running after them, his wide pants flapping around his short legs. Even for that short distance he was panting. They waited for him to catch up.

"Here is something for the birds," he said, handing them a bag of dried corn. "I always have some of this for my good customers. My birds, they like it too," he added with a wink. The overhang of his lips stretched out straight as his smile slid behind the fleshy cheeks that jiggled when he spoke.

They sat on the park bench for an hour, then the boys said they had to go. Katreena and Helen stayed in the park, feeding the birds and enjoying the peace. Helen sat quietly, deep in thought and Katreena knew that she was worrying about going to the hospital. Helen's moments of reprieve were so few and far between and Katreena was powerless to spare her the agony.

"Penny for your thoughts Helen," Katreena prompted gently. "Perhaps talking about it may help alleviate some of the anguish!" Katreena was ready to try anything!

"I was just trying to imagine what this afternoon will be like," Helen seemed so far away in her own world. "You know, Mother, I was just trying to remember Michael ever being kind or gentle or loving. I suppose he must have been when we first married but I honestly cannot remember! Isn't that awful? I'm sure there must have been good times, so why can't I remember them? It seems like all I remember is that he was always complaining or angry about something. Ever since I married him! Why can't I recall a happy time of our life? Was it really that bad Mother, or am I blocking it out? I feel guilty, that somehow I'm not being fair to him."

She stopped and then absent-mindedly threw some corn for the geese. Abruptly she turned to Katreena, a look of alarm on her face.

"Mother, do you know something terrible? I'm not even sure I care if Michael wakes up! I don't believe it myself, but I don't think I'd care if Michael never uttered another word." Then, realizing what she had just said, she shuddered with the shock of it.

"Mom, I didn't mean it. Oh God, I didn't mean that! Truly, Mom, that was just some evil thing in me, talking." She suddenly seemed very distraught and disoriented. "I'm sorry" she repeated in confusion; but the apology didn't seem to be directed at Katreena anymore.

Katreena reached over and wrapped her arms around her daughter. "It's all right sweetheart. God knows you didn't mean anything evil. You just want peace for your family. God understands that." Katreena did not want Helen to slip back into that whirlpool of desolation she had just so recently escaped from.

"Listen, honey! It's alright, I understand. No one can blame you for being worried about his reaction when he, if he, wakes up. He's been so negative for so long that he probably cannot change. That's not saying that you have to be happy about it or that you have to go back to that way of life again. Think about your children. Think about Kaydee. You have all been so much more relaxed now since Michael has not been around. You're not evil for wanting some peace in your life. God knows you deserve that peace. So do your children, especially Kaydee! Remember how Michael always said that she was retarded? Well now you know she is not retarded at all. Just look at what she has become since he's been away. You have to be strong for her. She needs you, Helen! For God's sake don't desert her now. You're not evil for wanting to protect your children. Whether Michael wakes up or not, you have to be strong for your children. And if he does wake up in his usual nasty mood, you have to fight him to protect your children. You have to stand up for yourself and for your children. You have to! You cannot go back to being weak again!" Katreena emphasized with tears in her eyes.

Seeing her mother's tear-filled eyes, shocked Helen out of her melancholy. Her mother sounded so rational. She was also right. The last few weeks since the accident, she had experienced a sense of control over her destiny and it had felt good, had even given her peace. Yet now, the thought of talking to Michael again made that confidence evaporate. Suddenly Helen realized she could not give up now! She could not relinquish that sense of peace nor that awareness and stability that she had experienced in the last few weeks.

For the first time in years it seemed, Helen saw herself as the burden she had become, to her mother, and to her children. It filled her with a sense of shame! Even Michael had not respected her! Why would he? She was a wimp, completely unworthy of respect. She was not a mother to her children. Kaydee was more of a mother to her children than she was. Now when everyone needed her so badly, she would not abdicate her post as she had done before. It was she, as much as Michael that had been the problem in the past! She saw that clearly now. It was time to grow up and assume responsibility for her life, to take her place as a mother of her own children, and to earn her self-respect. What happened to Michael now, that was not under her control, what happened to her and her children was! This unexpected epiphany into her problems, and her shortcomings, was a revelation to Helen. Courage and determination vanquished her fear and empowered her with confidence.

"Thank you, Mother." Helen's calm voice surprised Katreena. She sat back and looked into Helen's eyes. There was no fear in them. Helen was in control again – she was dauntless!

"You're right, Mom." Helen spoke slowly but with firm conviction. "I'm sorry. You're right," she repeated. "I have to face this thing without buckling. I'm sorry for being such a coward. I realize now that it doesn't matter what happens with Michael. I have to do what I have to do to take care of my family. I am responsible for myself and it's time I stopped blaming Michael for my weakness. I'll be alright now Mother, but I may need a lot of help to stay on this rocky road. I guess I need a good shaking sometimes. Will you help me along?"

"Baby, you have got it!" Katreena voice was hoarse with emotion but firm with resolve.

Helen's smile convinced Katreena of her sincerity because she desperately needed to believe that Helen's determination would last. She wiped away her tears. They both needed to bring back that sense of serenity they had experienced when they first entered the park.

They stayed in the peaceful sanctuary till almost one, then grabbed soup and a bun at Yolandy's for lunch. Before they left for the hospital, Katreena asked. "Do you want a pill before you go in? It's going to be rugged in there, and you'll have to talk to him this time."

Helen thought it over. "I don't know. I can't rely on tranquilizers to get me through this forever but the thought of going in there makes my blood run cold. I have to learn to cope somehow, but it's just that it's so intimidating."

"Perhaps you better just take one, just to give you a little more courage for now. After today, we'll decide if you want more." Katreena handed her the pill and Helen took it.

Chapter 20

They arrived at the hospital just before two o'clock. There were different nurses on duty from last night but these had obviously been briefed on the events of the night before.

"We're very sorry about last night. We should have prepared you, but we had not been told you were coming and when you came, we thought you knew what to expect. You see, we don't keep his face wrapped all the time any more, the skin is starting to heal and it needs air. Too many bandages inhibit the healing. We're sorry you had to see him that way but we can't really do much to improve on that, at this point," the nurse apologized.

"That's alright, Nurse Gibson," soothed Katreena, reading from her name tag, "we understand. You're doing the best you can and we appreciate it."

Once more, they donned those ghostly white gowns and masks before proceeding down that formidable hallway. At the door of Michael's room, Katreena gave Helen an impulsive hug, trying to infuse her with inner strength, so vital for her to withstand the trauma awaiting her.

"You going to be alright, honey? It's going to be brutal in there, you know."

Stoically, Helen nodded. "I'll be alright, Mother. Just stay close by."

Michael was lying there very much as they had seen him the night before. Katreena watched Helen wince, then dry-eyed, jaw set and her head held high, she stepped up to bed.

"Hello Michael, this is Helen. I hope you can hear me. We flew here to Toronto to see how you are doing." No response.

Helen tried again. "Michael, can you hear me? Alvin has been asking about you."

Still nothing. Helen tried again, louder and more firmly.

"I hired a man to take care of the farm. I cannot do it myself so I hired Annie's grandson who was staying with her for the summer because he was laid off in the city. He is an experienced farmer. He farmed until three years ago so he is no stranger to farm work. Everything will be up to date when you get home so don't worry about the farm going to pot in your absence. Joey, that's his name, the hired man. Joey will have to go back to his job when he gets a call so you have to come home before then. Can you hear me, Michael? You must get well. You have to show the doctors that you're well enough to be moved closer to home."

There was absolutely no response from Michael. Helen sighed, paused, then tried again.

"Alvin is much better now. He is back to his normal self, running around and playing with Rusko like he used to do. He doesn't sleep in the afternoons any more like he did after he came home from the hospital. He asks when you are coming home."

Deliberately, Helen did not mention Kaydee, knowing how Michael felt about her. Then when there was still no reaction, she decided that perhaps she could elicit a response from him by doing just that. A response, even an angry one, would still be a response.

Swallowing hard, she tried again. "Kaydee has really stepped up to the plate. She is doing the yard work and taking care of the kids without being told to do it. She is responsible and is working like a trooper."

Helen hesitated, watching Michael closely for any sign that he was hearing her, but he never twitched a muscle. Positively nothing!

Helen reached for his hand and cradled it between her gloved ones. It suddenly struck Katreena that she had never seen Michael and Helen holding hands or expressing affection for each other. In all the years they had been married, short of the actual wedding kiss, she had never witnessed any demonstration of love, overt or veiled, between those two outside of that one impulsive hug they exchanged when they heard that Alvin was fine after his accident.

"How odd," she thought. She recalled Helen's words of the morning: "Why can't I recall a happy time of our life? Was it really that bad?" Yes, was it really that bad? Katreena could not recall a happy time in Helen's marriage either. Why in the name of everything holy had this marriage been allowed to continue to torment them all? Who was to blame here?

"Michael, listen to me. You must be able to hear me. The doctors told us you can do it. Please wake up and let me know somehow. I know you hurt, but you must wake up. Wake up, Michael! They can't help you unless you wake up." Helen's voice was strong, insistent. "We have to go back home tomorrow. I cannot stay here in Toronto. I'm needed at home but if you can wake up, they might send you to a hospital closer to home. I can visit you more often there, so please wake up. At least let me know you can hear me."

There was no response from Michael. Either he could not hear her or he could not, or would not, respond. Katreena recalled that terrible day of the accident. If Michael's mood was sealed in that irate frame of mind he was in on that fateful Sunday, perhaps he might refuse to respond out of spite. Certainly hearing Helen sounding so firm may make him want to defy her. But was it possible that in spite of the brain activity that the doctors assured them was evident through their scans, Michael's brain was scrambled beyond repair? Was it possible that Michael would be like this forever? Katreena trembled. Helen was still talking to Michael, rubbing his hand, the only part of him that didn't bear the scars of the fire. She pleaded; she encouraged; she goaded; she scolded; and she demanded. Nothing worked. Katreena hurt for her daughter, felt her helplessness. She stepped forward and added her pleas to Helen's.

"Michael, this is Katreena. The doctors told us that you should be able to hear us and should be able to respond. Dr. Gorman says that as soon as you show any signs of being able to respond, he will send you back to Winnipeg or somewhere even closer to home. Otherwise you have to stay here and Helen cannot fly out to Toronto again. You must realize that so you have to wake up, Michael." Still no sign of life.

While they were talking to Michael, Dr. Gorman had walked into the room. He stood there for a while, watching and listening and when it was obvious that Michael was not responsing, he stepped forward and motioned to the women to follow him. He led them down a long hallway to what was apparently some kind of sitting room with some chairs.

"I am Dr. Gorman and I take it you must be Mrs. Banaduk and Mrs. Boyer. Am I right?" he smiled, addressing them correctly. He had evidently been briefed by the nurses before he came in. "I am very sorry to have to meet you under such distressing circumstances but in my profession, this is how I often meet people."

They exchanged handshakes and pleasantries and then Dr. Gorman opened the subject that they all knew was uppermost in their minds.

"I see Michael didn't show any response. That is really too bad. We had hoped that the sound of a familiar voice would trigger a reaction from him. There was evidence of brain activity on the scans but we have no idea what it relates to. Perhaps he actually cannot hear due to damage between the ear and the brain but if that were the case, he should have responded to your touch. We know it was traumatic for you to see him this way but there is little we can do until those wounds heal. Between the acid and the fire, there was a great deal of damage to his face. That has only now started to heal but it will take a long time. How long are you staying?"

"Our flight leaves at half past eleven tomorrow night. We purposely made it late to allow us optimum time here at the hospital," Katreena explained.

She didn't want to reveal all the details about why they had chosen not to stay longer. She didn't want to tell this strange doctor about Helen's fragile state of health; how she was afraid to expose her to distress; how she worried about her reaction and ability to face the situation; and how she had been afraid to even bring her here in the first place. Hopefully, Dr. Walley had briefed him and he would not insist on something dramatic. Helen was doing fine and after this morning, Katreena hoped it would last but she could lapse back just as easily. Helen seemed to be all over the place lately. Katreena just wanted to get her back home where she could be at peace and not be bombarded by these bad memories, depressing problems or unpredictable situations. Michael was not the only one that needed to heal. They all needed it, just for different infirmities.

"That will be fine. We will try to rouse him again with each visit while you are here. If he does not respond, we will continue to treat him here for another month or so. It will facilitate the healing of the wounds and who knows, maybe even his brain requires more healing time. At the end of that time we will reassess the situation and decide what to do. I am so sorry we cannot give you any definite news at this time but medicine is not an exact science. Some things are still subject to God's will. I would like to make a suggestion though. When you come in tonight, I want you to wash your hands with that disinfectant soap that's there by the sink in the room where you pick up the gowns. Then when you put on the gown and head gear, I don't want you to put on the gloves. Go in with bare hands. Perhaps if he feels your hand maybe it will bring a response. Can you do that?" Helen nodded.

They talked for a while longer, then Dr. Gorman said he needed to get back to his patients. Katreena and Helen went to drop off their gowns. As they left the hospital for the hotel, they discussed Michael and his condition. Helen seemed totally rational but very subdued and physically drained. At the hotel, she lay down on the bed and almost immediately fell asleep. The room was cool from the air conditioner and Katreena found it refreshing but she took a blanket from the closet and gently covered Helen. Poor girl. She was emotionally worn out. Sleep was good for her; she needed to rejuvenate much more than she needed food. They would have supper later before heading for the hospital again. Katreena decided to call the farm. Ideally Helen should be the one talking to Kaydee but Helen would probably sleep late and Katreena knew that Kaydee would be on pins and needles worrying about her mother.

Kaydee answered the phone on the first ring. She had been waiting for the call.

"How is Mother?" she wanted to know immediately. Katreena gave her a brief resume of the events of the last couple of visits.

"She's actually doing quite well, though I have had to give her a couple of the tranquillizers that Dr. Walley prescribed right after the accident, just to ease the stress. But she is rational and fully aware of everything. It is very hard on her though. She's dead tired so she's sleeping now but she's okay. Don't worry. I'll let you know if anything new happens. Give my love to the kids."

Katreena hung up, then picked up a book she had brought along and settled down to read. The boys would not be back till late in the evening from their meeting and she didn't want to leave Helen alone in case she woke up disoriented.

It was just after six when Helen woke up. Bewildered, she looked around the room, then she realized where she was. "What time is it? How long have I been sleeping?"

"You've been asleep for almost two hours, honey. Are you hungry? We could order up or we could walk over to Yolandy's if you'd rather." Katreena was relieved to see Helen rational. This roller coaster of emotions Helen was on was upsetting and difficult for Katreena. They made her feel insecure and apprehensive. She did not like that feeling.

"Let's walk over to Yolandy's. I want to feel the fresh air. We'll still be able to make it to the hospital and it won't matter if we're a bit late."

"Alright but grab a sweater in case it cools off later."

It was a pleasant walk and Katreena was glad that Helen had suggested it. The fragrance of various blossoms from the park wafted softly on the breeze and they actually heard some birds twittering in the trees above them as they walked past. What a beautiful spot the park was, amid the tall buildings of the city skyline.

Mr. Yolandy was delighted to see them. He toddled over, cheeks jiggling, his smile crinkling up those folds of skin around his eyes and his mouth. "Katreena, Helen, how nice to see you come back," he gushed as he led them to the table. "What can I get for you?"

"We don't have too much time but we enjoyed your place so much this morning we just had to come back," Katreena was pleased when Helen took the initiative to answer him.

The old man's eyes lit up with glee. "We have some chicken cordon bleu that just came out of the oven. I can get a plate prepared for you just like that," he raised his snapping fingers and waved them high in triumph. "You like?"

"We like!" Katreena and Helen mimicked him, laughing and he scooted off chuckling. He looked pleased as punch. Within five minutes he was back with two salads, then followed it up with two plates piled high with the chicken and the vegetables.

"Enjoy!" He bowed low and trotted off with a smile.

"What a delightful little man!" Helen marvelled, "And so happy all the time!" They chatted easily while they ate and on the way back to the hotel. Just before leaving for the hospital, Katreena asked Helen if she wanted another pill.

"No, Mother. I think I'd like to try doing it without fortification this time. I have to be able to face this on my own. I don't want to take the easy way out anymore. I've been such a wimp for so long. I wish with all my heart I didn't have to go there. I feel so guilty and awful to even think that way because he is my husband and I should be a loving wife, but God forgive me, I can't help the way I feel. The doctors think this will help and we all need to know if it will. I'll try it alone but stand by, please."

"I won't leave your side honey, and if you need the pill, it will be there so don't hesitate to ask, okay?" Katreena gave Helen an impulsive hug. Helen smiled weakly and nodded.

They got to the hospital, and immediately went to the room to put on the gowns. Katreena squeezed Helen's hand for support. It was clammy. Beads of perspiration shone on Helen's face as she donned her gown and head gear. She washed her hands but following the doctor's suggestion, left her gloves off. Katreena slipped her own gloves on and together, they proceeded to Michael's room.

At the door, Helen hesitated.

"You okay?" Katreena queried. Helen gave her mother a doleful look, sighed dejectedly, and went in.

Inside the room, nothing had changed. Helen went up to Michael and took his hand into her bare ones. As she sat down in the chair beside him once again, she repeated all the things she had said to him that afternoon, begging him to wake up, to somehow communicate his awareness of her presence, but there was no sign from Michael that he heard her. Helen's voice was firm, determined. She did not give up. She even brought up the explosion and the fire.

"The shed has to be replaced and almost everything inside it. The fire and explosion destroyed everything so it has to be started from scratch. What were you doing there that caused that explosion in the first place, Michael?" There was absolutely no response from Michael.

Completely drained, she paused, at a loss for what to do next. Katreena sat in a chair near the doorway, feeling helpless and worse yet, useless. Then Helen started talking to Michael about when they first met, about their decision to marry, the wedding, the birth of their children. Once more she told him that Alvin was asking for him. Still nothing. Finally, totally worn out, she just sat there speechlessly looking at him.

After about ten minutes of silence, Katreena walked up to her and touched her shoulder. "Would you like to go back to the hotel? You look tired." Helen nodded

Wordlessly they left the room. They didn't see the doctor and the nurses were busy elsewhere so they dropped off their gowns and left for the hotel.

"Are you alright, honey?" Helen was so pale and quiet, Katreena was almost afraid to ask.

Helen nodded, "I'm just tired," she replied.

At the hotel, Helen went straight to the washroom to clean up, then with a "Goodnight, Mother. I'll see you tomorrow," she kissed Katreena and went to the bed.

Katreena dialled Dusty and Wayne's room. There was no answer. She picked up her book and settled down to read. Shortly before ten, she heard a light knock on the door. The boys were back. Quietly she slipped out the door into the hallway.

"She's asleep. I don't want to wake her," she whispered and followed them to their room. She gave them a report of the day's events with strong emphasis on Helen's positive resolve and determination.

"She's trying so hard, and it's playing her out. She is so fragile. I feel so helpless. She was worn out so she went to bed immediately after we got in. I need to be there in case she wakes up. She refused the tranquilizers tonight so she may not sleep as solidly. Goodnight, I'll see you in the morning."

Dusty walked her to the door, took her in his arms for a lingering goodnight kiss. "Take care, Katreena, and call if you need me."

Helen was sound asleep when Katreena got back so she quietly got ready and went to bed herself. The next morning, she woke before Helen, but when she got out of the bathroom, Helen was already up.

"Good morning, Mother. How did you sleep? I feel totally refreshed. I guess I must have been pretty wiped last night." Helen sounded revitalized, secure, and composed. "I hope we can spend some time in that park again today. It is so lovely and peaceful there. It's like home; you can't even tell you're in the city."

"We'll do whatever you like. I'll call the guys and see if we can hit Yolandy's for breakfast again." She dialled the adjoining room and Dusty answered. When she told him that they wanted to go back to Yolandy's, Dusty laughed and accused her of having a crush on the old man but they were glad to go back there to eat.

The day was pretty much a repeat of the day before; they spent some time in the park and when the boys left for their meeting, the girls stayed on to enjoy the serenity of the city oasis. Their remaining two trips to the hospital yielded no success in spite of Helen's earnest endeavours.

"Goodbye Michael," Helen said as they were leaving that evening. "We are going back home now. We probably won't be seeing you again till you get back to Manitoba. I hope that will be soon."

Dr. Gorman was very disappointed. He had had high hopes for progress.

"I'll consult with other neurologists and I'll keep you posted. I appreciate your coming in and trying to help. I'm sorry it was not more successful. I understand how traumatic it must have been for you. Have a safe trip home."

Chapter 21

The boys got back from their meetings and the four left for the airport. By half past eleven, they were winging their way home. Katreena and Dusty were looking forward to spending some happy times together but Helen was heading to something different. She wasn't sure what the future held for her, certainly not the distant future anyway. Her immediate future promised peace but it was temporary and therein lay the problem.

Helen closed her eyes and pretended to be asleep but sleep was far from her mind. She was remembering Michael as he was now: the Michael that could not hear or speak; the Michael that could not be mean or angry; the Michael that may never move or talk again. She recalled Michael telling her he hated being stuck with "a bunch of imbeciles," meaning her and the kids, of course; Michael forcing Kaydee to kneel in the sinhole so many times; Michael calling Kaydee a retard so often that they had all started to believe him, including Kaydee; Michael burning her journal because the baby was crying; Michael berating and blaming her for miscarrying her precious babies. So many memories, all of them bad. Her life had been a hell on earth for so many years. Perhaps there was potential for change now, but change to what? What if he never regained mobility or speech? Would she have to care for a vegetable for the rest of her life? Well, if he was silent and immobile... perhaps... what if he remained immobile but regained his testy nature and continued with the mental derangement on the family? How would she, and the children, cope with that? She didn't even want to go there. What if he never got well enough to come home at all? Life at home had been good these last three weeks, even pleasant. Perhaps... she would not allow herself to go there either because that scenario brought a heavy burden of guilt with it.

She knew she would have to be very strong if the worst came to pass. She had no intention of allowing Michael to ravage her emotions or her mental stability again. She was going to demand respect from him! She was entitled to it. True, she had to earn it, but earn it she would! No more would she be the passive, cringing idiot she had been in the past. She owed it to her children to give them a normal childhood. They had not known it till these last three weeks and they were flourishing now. She could see it in their faces. They were relaxed and happy now. She would make sure nobody ever took that away from them, no matter what!

They arrived at the airport, retrieved the car and drove to Portmont to spend the rest of the night at Dusty's place. It had been a harrowing day and it was late. Except for Dusty and Wayne going over some boring business details, there was little verbal interaction throughout the flight and during the drive to Portmont. Nobody even mentioned Michael and that was just fine with Helen. She did not want to go there. As for Katreena, she too, was happy to ignore that subject. Helen had said she was not going to let Michael upset her anymore and Katreena had no intention of testing that resolve.

Kaydee was nervous as a kitten in a roomful of dogs. She had not heard from Mother since they left though Granny had phoned that one day and said that Mother was alright. Nothing since then. Kaydee needed to know what happened since then. Mother had been in a pretty stable condition these last three weeks. She was even good when she left for the trip and Granny said she was rational after seeing Father again. Was it possible that Mother could survive the sight of Father as long as he did not lash out at her? Was Father's lack of response the reason that Mother was alright? Kaydee had been afraid that seeing Father might send Mother back into that catatonic state that was her trademark whenever Father was angry and went into one of his irrational tirades. Granny said Mother had held up well after the first visits when Father was unresponsive. But what about later? Did Father wake up yesterday? How was Mother now? Kaydee was dying to know. Why hadn't they called? Did something bad happen? Kaydee's mind was a blur of images and all of them terrified her.

Kaydee watched the minutes as she waited for news, but no more came. This morning, they only called to say they would be home in the afternoon. Nothing more! Kaydee had been in the garden and Annie had taken the call.

"We'll talk when we get there," Granny had told her and then she had hung up.

Mechanically, Kaydee had gone through the motions of chores around the house. She fed and took care of the children. She mowed the lawn and clipped around the trees and buildings. She cleaned the lawn mower till it shone like new. She fed the chickens, cleaned out their water trough and even relined the egg nests and spread fresh straw in the chicken coop. She picked vegetables for Annie and helped her prepare them but the hands on the clock refused to move faster. She had filled three pages of her journal with her anxieties but she knew that most of it was jibberish because she was so scatterbrained, but she just could not make herself think clearly.

Mother had been good lately but Kaydee knew how uncertain her mother's health was, especially if Father started yelling. Would Mother crumble again? Were they just trying to spare her by delaying the bad news for as long as possible? "Please God, let mother be okay," Kaydee prayed. If only they could be sure Father was never coming back. They would all be better off if he just stayed away! "There I go again, with those evil wishes." she scolded herself. She shouldn't think like that. "Please forgive me God, and bring Mother home safe."

They were due home any minute now and Kaydee could hardly contain herself. She was both excited and anxious. The only thing she was sure about was that she wanted her mother to be alright. As far as her father went, well she really didn't know what she wanted to hear about him: he's very bad; he's alright; he'll never get better; he will get better; he'll never come home... she honestly didn't want to think of the alternative to that last one, because it made her feel guilty for feeling that way and evil because she didn't care. She couldn't even talk to anyone about her feelings. Her mother and her grandmother were the only ones that knew her dark secret and she wasn't even proud to have them know it.

It was three o'clock and Kaydee was washing potatoes at the sink when she saw Dusty's car finally pull in. Dropping the half-peeled potato into the sink full of cold water, she was oblivious to the cold splash that soaked her, the cupboards, and the floor, as she flew out to the car.

"Are you alright, Mother?" Kaydee was breathless as her eyes swept over her mother's face when she stepped out of the car. Both Helen and Katreena were astounded at the extent of Kaydee's concern. They realized what the poor girl must have gone through these last couple of days, not knowing what was happening with each visit. Katreena felt guilty for not calling daily with updates of their visits. Kaydee should have been in the loop.

"Oh sweetheart, of course I'm alright. It was an awful experience, but honey, I promise you will never have to worry about me again. We are going to be alright now, all of us! I'm going to make sure of it. You will never have to go through that terrible kind of life again. I promise!" Helen held Kaydee at arm's length and looked her straight in the eyes. "I promise, Kaydee!" she emphasized solemnly. "No matter what happens with your father, whenever he comes home or in what state, I will be there for you. I will not let you down again."

"Oh, Mom," Kaydee threw her arms around her mother sobbing uncontrollably. Years of pent up love and longing released a flood of anguish and gratitude about her mother's fortitude. She had been ready to believe her mother mentally deficient, but it wasn't true. Mother was fine! Kaydee was euphoric.

Dusty and Katreena watched the display with tears in their eyes. To Katreena this was unsolicited vindication. Her daughter was intelligent and she was resilient. So was Kaydee. She had almost lost hope herself. Just one month ago, the future had looked dismal and bleak but this moment was nothing short of a miracle!

Dusty watched the scene with disbelief. In the short time he has known Helen, he had seen her waffle from a fragile, emotionally dependent weakling to a forceful woman determined to control her destiny and that of her children. Dusty didn't know if the transformation would last, but he found it heartbreaking to see Kaydee so desperately eager to believe her mother.

In her delight, Kaydee had forgotten the presence of Katreena and Dusty. With her arm tightly around her mother's waist, her head leaning against her shoulder, Kaydee led the way to the house. She had received the news she had wanted to hear. Beyond that, nothing else mattered! In the house, Annie brought them back to reality with her questions about Michael's condition.

Katreena took it upon herself to explain the state of Michael's health and his prognosis. She relayed the basic details about Michael's condition, but neither Helen nor Kaydee seemed overly agitated. Nobody was asking for specifics and Katreena wanted to leave it at that. She didn't want Helen to dredge up those harrowing memories. Helen was at peace with Michael's condition and prognosis and Katreena had no desire to rock the boat.

"Are you guys hungry?" Annie asked.

"Well we only had breakfast at Wayne's and then we left. We didn't want to stop for lunch on the road because I wanted to get home," Helen explained and Annie immediately set about preparing a lunch.

Helen checked on Dayna while Katreena and Kaydee went to help Annie. To Dusty this casual acceptance of Michael's condition seemed incongruous but, given what he knew of Michael's character, perhaps it was not abnormal. This was probably the only peace they had known in years.

While the women worked in the kitchen, Dusty excused himself to go to the shed. He was surprised to see that much of the tools had been sorted into groupings: the unsalvageable bits and pieces were on a pile near the door; the relatively untouched working tools were on a big piece of clean cardboard and on another piece of cardboard were parts and pieces that required cleaning or repairing. Joey Kerman had obviously spent some time here; his organizational skills were starting to show. Dusty was glad. He wanted Joey to be the answer to Helen's problem. She needed someone reliable around the farm. Dusty had neither the knowledge nor the motivation for it. He was retired and he liked the freedom retirement provided. If Joey Kerman was Helen's answer to a prayer, he certainly was Dusty's as well, because as long as things were running smoothly on the farm, he and Katreena would be free to spend carefree time together. If that was being selfish, then so be it.

As Dusty stood there surveying the debris, Joey drove into the yard on the big Massey tractor. The tractor cab windows were covered with dust but the ready smile on Joey's face was clearly visible. He descended from the cab and held out a sweaty hand to Dusty.

"Glad to see you back. How is Michael doing?"

"Hello Joey. I'll let the women fill you in on Michael's condition. I see you have been busy in the shop. That fire sure did a number there, eh?"

"Yeah, it sure did. I tried to sort out what was salvageable there. I guess we'll have to clean this mess away and start building soon. There is nothing worth saving of the structure. I'll have to talk to Mrs. Boyer and see what she wants to do about it. She may want to make some decision about it soon if she wants anything done before the winter sets in. It will probably not be practical to delay rebuilding till spring. A good workshop is essential on a farm. None of the other buildings on the yard can be converted into a temporary one."

Dusty nodded. This man knew what he was talking about. Dusty didn't even belong in his league. Helen was lucky to have Joey. The two men walked to the house where lunch was ready and waiting on the table. Joey quickly washed up and joined the family.

The adults discussed Michael's condition, taking time to answer questions from Alvin and Kaydee here and there. "If Michael were here, Kaydee would have been kneeling in the sinhole by now for having the temerity to even open her mouth!" Katreena thought. Now here she was, calm and comfortable, participating in the discussions like any adult, without fear of chastisement. She hoped Michael would never ever come back here! And she refused to feel guilty for feeling that way! Yet she did offer up a silent "Sorry Lord!"

After lunch, they took their coffee out on the deck where the balmy afternoon breezes caressed their cheeks and the perfume of the flowers assailed their nostrils. Joey wanted to go right back out to the field but Helen coaxed him to stay and relax for a while.

"You don't have to work every single minute of the day, you know," she told him. "Take a break. You're not a slave you know."

"Oh no, Mrs. Boyer, I don't feel like a slave at all. I love the farm and

I enjoy the work. I know I can take a break and I will, but I want to go back out this evening. I don't want to get behind. In the meantime, thank you very much for inviting me."

"You're very welcome," Helen smiled and curtsied as she offered him a chair. Joey bowed and sat down dutifully. Everyone laughed.

When the receding sun's rays cast flickering shadows from behind the trees, Dusty and Katreena said they had to leave for home. Annie asked if they would drop her off. Joey was going back out on the field and it would be pointless to stay and wait for him, she said.

Kaydee was somewhat disappointed to have them leave so soon. She wished she could have spoken to her grandmother alone to find out what really happened there at that hospital, but the opportunity had never arisen and to have asked for privacy away from the rest of the family would have been rude. For now, she was just grateful for the peace and harmony in her family. Her mother was back in body, mind and spirit. That was enough for Kaydee. She was glowing. As far as her father went, Kaydee still harboured that secret wish that he would never come back. The idea that he could come back a more pleasant person was too far-fetched to warrant consideration. Seeing Father would have been traumatic for Mother. Kaydee knew how vulnerable her mother was to his abuse but when she heard that he had remained unconscious, Kaydee was relieved. He wouldn't have been civil anyway, had he awakened.

Kaydee watched Mother's buoyant mood with interest. Judging by the reports, Father was not a pretty sight, but was it his **lack** of response that resulted in this unexpected stamina? Kaydee thought about it. If this condition was permanent, it certainly could have a positive effect on Mother. It certainly could be an answer to **her** own dream, Kaydee thought ruefully.

Katreena kissed the children goodbye, then gave Helen a hug.

"Hang in there, honey and call if you need any help, or even if you just want to talk. I'm just a phone call away, and I can drive up within the hour, Okay?"

Helen nodded. "I will Mom. I promise everything will be fine. And thanks for everything. Thanks for always being there for me. I love you

Mom!" she added fervently.

"You're welcome, sweetheart. I love you too. Take care of yourself."

Katreena kissed Kaydee and she said softly, "You, my girl, take care of your mother and the kids. If ever I thought I could trust anyone, honey, you are it! I'm proud of you sweetheart!"

As Annie, Katreena and Dusty piled into the car, Joey left for the back yard to fuel the tractor for the evening run.

"Joey really enjoys the farm, doesn't he?" Katreena said to Annie as they turned onto the road.

"Oh Katreena, he's gloriously happy. He loves farming. It's in his blood. When his brother came back to claim the family farm, Joey was devastated. In spite of knowing that the promise had been made before Vince left for the service, I think he had hoped that Vince would just remain in the city after he left the military but Vince returned to claim his birthright. Joey could not bring himself to be a part time farmer if Vince was making all the decisions. Vince paid him well for his share of the farm and for running it the last few years, but Joey didn't care about the money. Vince did not want to raise cattle. He was strictly into grain farming but Joey loved the cattle. There were no farms up for sale in the area so Joey sold every head of his herd of cattle that he loved almost personally. He was so heartbroken about it that he decided to move out. He knows that when Michael comes back he will have to leave again, but he feels in charge right now and he's happy even if this is only temporary. You should hear him! He's whistling all the time."

"He's doing a great job." Dusty put in. "Helen is lucky to have him. He knows what he is doing."

"Yes," Katreena agreed. "Helen is very lucky to have someone who is so conscientious. He is good for that place."

"Well I hope that Michael will get better soon. That was such an awful thing to have happened." Annie was sincere. Katreena was well aware of her generosity.

They had arrived at her yard by this time and she got out, thanking them profusely for the ride and went into the house. Dusty noted how immaculate the yard was. Annie's love of gardening boldly broadcast her devotion to her hobby. Crescent shaped flower beds overflowing with vibrant combinations of color and variety encircled a lovely stone angel fountain in the middle of the yard. Against the back fence were trailing colors of sweet peas that saturated the air with their magic fragrance. Beautiful shrubs, well-manicured, completed the aesthetic appeal. Just mowing that lawn around those flowerbeds would be a meticulous chore. Dusty was impressed. Even his well-kept flower garden would have a hard time competing against this setting.

They drove out of the yard and turned out onto the main road. It was a beautiful time of the year. Though much of the grain fields were still green, some of the early wheat now had a golden hue that meant it was starting to ripen. Fields of flax in beautiful blue blossom undulated in the breeze simulating lakes with the waves rolling in and fields of mustard radiated a vibrant yellow against the distant green tree belt. The sun was sloping toward the horizon but its warm rays still hung in the air. Katreena had always enjoyed evenings in the country. Evenings emphasized sights and smells of the outdoors, prompting the very soul to bask in the last remaining throes of a beautiful day, before the darkness made everything disappear. Birds sang more sweetly, flowers smelled more fragrantly, colors appeared brighter and every sound of nature bespoke of tranquility and peace.

Chapter 22

Katreena's silence told Dusty that she was thinking of Michael so he broached the subject himself. They had not had a moment alone together since Toronto, so outside of generalities, Katreena had not had an opportunity to give him a comprehensive report on the hospital visits of the last day. He was curious to know how that had gone.

"What do you think of Michael's prognosis? Do you really believe he will get better enough to come back to the farm? And if he does, how will that affect the family?" he asked.

"You know, I've been thinking about that a lot. To be honest, I'm having a lot of difficulty picturing him well enough to resume responsibility for the farm. But stranger things have happened. The doctors these days have been known to affect miraculous cures but, quite frankly, I think it almost would take a miracle to get him from where he is now to well enough to function again. I don't want to sound pessimistic but I have to admit to having serious doubts about his total recovery. It is very early in his treatment though, so perhaps it's too soon to make any assumptions." Dusty could tell that Katreena was trying to sound unbiased, but he knew all too well that she was anything but detached. Job himself, could not sound dispassionate under such circumstances!

Katreena continued. "My concern is for Kaydee and Helen. Helen seemed to grow up there on that bench in the park while we were talking. She even apologized for being a burden and for shirking her responsibilities. And she promised that she would never shrink from them again. Certainly at that hospital, she came through. Honestly Dusty, she stood her ground. You should have seen it. It was unbelievable! When Michael failed to respond, she tried everything, begging, coaxing, scolding. She practically bragged about Kaydee taking on full responsibility for the chores around the yard, hoping that might rouse him to respond, even angrily. She even went back through her marriage trying to dredge up memories to try to get to him, but nothing worked. That's why I have such a problem visualizing him well again."

"Kaydee accepted the prognosis quite calmly but I wonder about that," Katreena continued. "She is quite mature and rational but I just hope she doesn't harbour any feelings of guilt based on their last month together. She and Michael were in the midst of a cold war there and she was on the verge of mutiny. She even questioned me about whether God had heard her and granted her wish to make Michael go away."

Dusty thought about it. "From what you told me about Kaydee, I'd be more optimistic about Kaydee coping than Helen, even though Helen seemed so strong-minded when she talked to Kaydee. Helen's condition seems more tenuous and personally I believe that Kaydee is too concerned about her mother, to worry about herself. I doubt that she'll be a problem."

Before they even realized it, they were in Katreena's driveway. Dusty brought her suitcase into the house as she put some coffee on. Dusty still had a long drive ahead of him and he wanted to get going so he drank his coffee, kissed Katreena goodnight and left.

Helen's acknowledgement of the implications of Michael's poor prognosis did not seem to daunt her. If anything, it seemed to revitalize her. She took a more proactive role in the running of her household, enlisted Joey's help in investigating contractors to rebuild the shed, and of her own volition made the decision to man the bale wagon. When Joey protested, she countered with legitimate reasons why he should accept her help.

"We lost weeks after the accident. You've been working unreasonable hours and that is not fair. I should have been out there before now. We are far behind. There is no way that you can catch up before the onslaught of harvest. Besides, it's not as if I have never done this before. Ask your grandmother. Michael never did the haying alone. Or the harvest. Or the seeding. Don't worry," she teased him. "I won't tie myself up with the twine. I can handle any machine on this farm, you know!"

"And I don't doubt it for a second. It's just that where I grew up, women did not work the fields. They tended to the house, the garden and the children." Joey was almost blushing with embarrassment as he explained his reticence regarding her active involvement in the fields.

"Maybe in your world that was the way women behaved, but on this farm, this woman works in the field," Helen informed him matter-of-factly. "Besides," she added more gently, "I can't afford to hire more help and we need to stay ahead of the game. This is certainly not a reflection on you or your managerial capabilities, it's just that this is a big operation and we lost those crucial weeks of prime haying time and we have to get those bales picked up while they are in optimum condition. You have been doing a wonderful job and I do appreciate it, truly, but you can only be in one place at a time. What if you get called back to work? Do you understand my position?"

Joey cut in. "Mrs. Boyer, I would never leave you stranded. Even if they called me back to work, I would not leave here until either your husband was back to take care of the place or you had some other satisfactory arrangement in place. I don't walk out on responsibility. Please don't worry about my abandoning you. I would never do that."

"Thank you, Joey, I really appreciate that. You are a good man. I cannot imagine what I would do if you weren't here. But you have been working non-stop for a month now and you're entitled to some time to yourself but you never take it. I'm feeling like a slave driver instead of an employer. So let me help, please. If it weren't for the accident, I'd have been doing it a lot more. Harvest is just around the corner and when that starts we'll have time for little else. Now, instead of disagreeing with me, why don't you help me hitch up the bale wagon so I can make myself useful around here? Between the two of us, we can get this operation on track in good time and when we do, we'll do something frivolous, just to celebrate."

"Yes, Ma'am!" Joey snapped his heels together and gave a mock salute. "At your service, Ma'am." They both laughed.

"Your commandant speaks," Helen saluted him back and they headed for the machinery shed. She felt light-hearted and free, as if she had not a care in the world. It was so nice to have someone with whom she could share such a carefree moment. Joey was always so cheerful. It was nice to laugh and joke around again. She had forgotten how to laugh.

Over the next week and a half, they finished with the hay and the field work and, working side by side, they prepared the equipment for the impending harvest. With Helen working in the fields with him, Joey now started timing his refuelling stops to be home for meals.

Helen talked to Dr. Gorman regularly, but he had little to report, other than that Michael's wounds were healing slowly. He was still unconscious and totally unresponsive. No mention was made of his being transferred back. Helen felt guilty sometimes for adjusting so easily to a routine without her husband, but she kept those thoughts at bay. After all, the farm was well looked after, the children were happy and the household was suffering no setbacks. Michael's presence was redundant. Everything was functioning well and best of all, everyone was happy.

Kaydee, for one, was blossoming. Her cheeks filled out and there was now a healthy glow to them, not just in her cheeks, but in her eyes as well. With Annie there to help with the kids and the meals, Kaydee was cheerful, relaxed, and journaling and spewing poetry every day. She carried a small notebook in her pocket wherever she went and she jotted down notes, ideas, and impressions. Then each evening before she went to bed, she transcribed those scribbled notes into coherent poems, stories or just reports. Now that she did not have to conceal her writing, she utilized every opportunity and every brainstorm.

Much of her writing now dealt with the positive aspects of life. No longer was her journal full of anguish and acrimony. She kept those writings in a separate notebook entitled "My Blue Pages." She didn't even open that notebook anymore.

Helen and Katreena both knew that Kaydee was writing. Now and then she would read particular sections to them, often it was a poem, sometimes an anecdote of something that had happened or impressed her. Occasionally, even Joey and Dusty would listen to some special poem or story, but summer was a busy time and everyone had their own responsibilities to deal with. Kaydee's writing was not a priority, it was a pleasant diversion. It was Dusty who saw interesting possibilities in Kaydee's writing, but reluctant to give anyone any false hope, he maintained a detached façade after the readings. He resolved to get a second opinion though, one that came from someone who was not likely to be biased. He did not disclose his intention, even to Katreena, but the following Sunday, at Wayne and Della's, he broached the subject.

"I'm not very good at assessing good writing and I don't want to give them false hope so I can't just get the journals to you but I wish there was some way that you could read them and see what you think. Personally I think her writing is particularly insightful but I must confess to being prejudiced in this case."

Wayne, Della and Jessie were intrigued. "She has a lot of this writing?" Wayne asked.

"She apparently has quite a bit," Dusty answered. "I have only heard some parts of it, sections that Kaydee has read to us, but I think it is good, very good indeed. Problem is: I know I am biased. I like the kid. She's has had a rotten deal in life. What if I'm wrong? She reads it to us quite frequently, voluntarily, perhaps even eagerly, but she may be reluctant to just give me the journal to take home. After all, it is like a diary."

"I wonder if she'd let me read it," Jessie wondered pensively. "I know she doesn't know me, but what if I went to the farm and met her? She sounds nice and maybe we could even become friends. From what you tell me she doesn't have friends and everyone could use one."

"That might work provided she opens up enough. From what you have told me she's been somewhat of a loner and very guarded in her relationships with outsiders." Wayne was sceptical as he exchanged glances with the others.

"That's because it's been hammered – and I do mean 'hammered,' into her that she was a moron, and could never amount to anything worthwhile. Michael called her a retard and she had almost begun to believe him. Her own mother never stood up for her," Dusty clarified.

Della had heard about this before when Dusty had spoken of Katreena's family. The anarchy had seemed impersonal and remote, of little consequence, and the implications of such conditions had not been comprehensible. Now the repercussions of those conditions pierced her maternal instincts with profound impact.

"How could she do that? What kind of mother could allow such brutality to continue?"

In light of the situation, Dusty felt compelled to defend Helen. "Don't forget Helen herself was in the same boat. He was just as abusive to her. And standing up to Michael would probably have resulted in even more abuse."

Wayne was just as horrified as his wife. "Why in Heaven's name didn't she just get the Hell out of there and leave the bastard?"

"Leaving him would have meant forfeiting the family farm and home, though Katreena was willing to sacrifice that. However, for some distorted religious reasons and some stupid sense of loyalty to her husband, Helen refused Katreena's advice and continued to take the abuse even to the detriment of her own mental and physical health – and that of her daughter."

Jessie sat there, totally mesmerized by the revelations. She had never heard of anything so cruel; had never met anyone that had had to endure it. She felt an overwhelming sense of sympathy for Kaydee and her mother. She had to meet them, to see the kind of people they were to have survived such an ordeal!

"Mom, Dad, please let me go to KD Acres and get to know these people. Maybe I can help and maybe I can't but please let me try. I still have a week of vacation left before school starts. I'm not involved in anything very important here at home and you can get along without me at your office for a week, so maybe I can do something worthwhile elsewhere. Uncle Dusty can say I want a vacation away from the city and he can ask Katreena if it would be alright if I came to KD Acres. If she says it's okay, would you let me go? Pleeease."

Wayne and Della exchanged doubtful glances. There didn't seem any risk involved now with Michael gone and maybe – just maybe – this could turn out to be a good thing. Certainly, Jessie was eager to give it a shot. Jessie was level-headed and compassionate and they both knew she sincerely wanted to help. It certainly wouldn't do any harm to let her try. At this point, she was probably the only one in a position to do so.

"If that bastard were home now, I would not consider it for a moment. But from all accounts he will be out of the picture for quite a while yet, so I will agree to it, provided that Katreena is totally amenable to it. And you're right. To avoid putting pressure or expectation on anyone, we don't have to tell anyone the real reason for this mission. Just go there, have a good time and if things work out as we hope, everyone might benefit."

"Thank you Dad, Mom. I will be very careful, I won't push and I won't expect anything. I will just let things happen naturally but from what I hear, I think this Kaydee could use a friend and I think I'd like to be that friend. If it doesn't happen, we lose nothing. Now if Uncle Dusty would like to call Katreena and ask her, I will go pack some things for my vacation." Jessie dittoed two fingers above each ear on the last word and left to pack, unquestionably assuming an "Okay" from Kaydee's grandmother.

"She'll do it right, Dusty," Della assured him. "Jessie is sensible and has a heart of gold. If anyone can gain Kaydee's trust, it will be Jessie. And don't worry about Jessie's sincerity about helping Kaydee. She would never take advantage of anyone under any circumstances."

"Oh, I don't doubt that for a minute. You don't have to emphasize Jessie's good qualities to me. It's not Jessie I'm worried about. It's just that I am so excited and hopeful for big things that I don't know if I can control myself to sound rational. I hate lying to Katreena but she has had so many disappointments that I don't want to take a chance on giving her another one."

"Well control yourself, and go make your call already, you goof," Wayne scolded.

A few minutes later, Dusty came back to the living room and jubilantly called up the stairs, "You're going on vacation girl, so get yourself ready!"

Jessie came flying down the stairs breathlessly. "You mean it? Really? I've never been on a real farm before. Oh I just know this is going to be the greatest week yet!" Ecstatically she threw her arms around Dusty's neck. "Thank you! Thank you! Thank you!" She hugged her mom and then her dad. "You won't regret it, Uncle Dusty, Mom, Dad. I promise you!"

They all laughed. "I know I won't, princess," Dusty kissed Jessie on the forehead. "But we can't leave now. Katreena will call Helen to clear it with her but she's sure both Helen and Kaydee will be delighted. She'll call me back to confirm it. The best thing is to leave tomorrow morning. That way, we can have lunch in Lanavale and leave for KD Acres right after that."

Jessie scurried to call her friends and tell them she was going on a vacation to the country.

"It's a real honest to goodness farm," she told her friend Sheila. "I am so excited!"

Chapter 23

As they turned into Katreena's driveway, Jessie got nervous. Her confidence evaporated. What would they expect from her and would she be the kind of person that Katreena wanted her granddaughter to be friends with?

"What if Kaydee decides to freeze me out? Would Katreena blame me or hold me responsible? Would she be very disappointed in me?"

Dusty was flabbergasted. In all the years he had known Jessie, he never known her to be insecure about herself, but to see her nervous about impressing Katreena affected him strangely.

"Katreena will love you anyway, you silly goose. You could never disappoint her. Besides, Kaydee is a nice kid. She will love you because Katreena and I love you. How do you think I got into Kaydee's good graces?" he winked teasingly and Jessie calmed down.

"Hello Jessie," Katreena met them at the car. "I am so pleased that you came out. I know you and Kaydee will get along famously. Kaydee needs friends but things have not been easy for her until now and she just has been afraid to trust people. However, many things have changed this summer and so has she. I told her about you coming and she is excited beyond words. I know she will love you instantly. Come on into the house, I have lunch ready."

Dusty winked a smile of encouragement to Jessie as they followed Katreena into her home. They mounted the steps that led onto the roofed in deck where cushioned wrought iron chairs, settee and table made for a beautiful sitting area. From a bird feeder in the nearby tree, yellow and purple finches protested the interruption to their feeding frenzy. Jessie imagined lunch out here on this deck with the floral fragrances tantalizing their senses and the warm breezes kissing their cheeks as they ate. She always enjoyed eating outdoors and often suggested it when they were at Dusty's house because they did not have a deck at home.

"Oh Uncle Dusty, isn't this just ever so pretty?" she sighed and Dusty laughed.

Katreena glanced at them questioningly and Dusty explained.

"Sorry Katreena, it's just that I know what that sigh of Jessie's meant. You see, Jessie has a penchant for decks. She loves eating outdoors, often to the delight of the bugs and flying things that she has to share her meal with. They have no deck at their house, so whenever she's at my place, we have to eat outdoors or she throws a tantrum."

"I do not!" Jessie protested in horror. She swung around to Katreena. "You mustn't believe him, honest. I really don't."

Dusty tossed his head back and roared with laughter. Katreena picked up on the joke and shook a menacing finger at him. Jessie stood bewildered and hurt not knowing what to do next.

Katreena came and embraced her. "Don't you worry, sweetheart. Your uncle is having a laugh at the expense of both of us. He has told me so much about you that I know better than to believe such a ridiculous line. Let's just say we owe him one, a big one, and with us ganging up on him, he's going to wish he hadn't started this war." Katreena gave Dusty an ominous scowl and his eyes twinkled with mischief and mirth.

"But I must say that I think you have a fantastic idea about eating on the deck. I actually have breakfast here many times, and often I eat other meals here as well. Summer is short and we should take every advantage of the good weather before it turns cold on us. Those finches will be gone any day now, they're just fattening up for the long flight south. Let's enjoy them before they go. Let's just bring everything out here. And you, you big lug, are going to help so hop to it!" she pointed a threatening finger at Dusty.

"Reporting for duty, ma'am!" Dusty clicked his heels and bowed, first to Katreena then to Jessie. Jessie swiped at him in mock anger and he ducked, still chuckling.

They went inside and Katreena handed Jessie two dishcloths, one wet and one dry. "Just wipe the table," she said matter-of-factly. "The place gets dusty very quickly. The breeze, no matter how light, brings fresh dust for every meal."

Lunch was a pleasant affair. The bugs that Dusty predicted did not attend the banquet. Katreena knew they wouldn't. They had few problems with bugs in daytime. Katreena asked Jessie about her interests and that was the grand opening to an interesting exchange of ideas for all three. Jessie was passionate about books, about writing and thoroughly enjoyed her working hours in the publishing business. Those were her main hobbies but Katreena learned that she was also very active and involved with drama and the school paper.

"Just like Helen used to be," she said.

"Truly?" Jessie asked excitedly.

"Yes, truly." Katreena said proudly. "Helen used to edit the school paper and she was very active in the drama club." Then she added pensively, "that is until she met Michael. Then she dropped everything and got married," Katreena finished on a note of sadness and finality.

Jessie noted the regret in Katreena's voice. It made her even more eager to meet this intriguing family. She felt a comradeship with them already.

When they went in to wash dishes, Jessie admired the subtle tones of Katreena's home.

"I love that soft pink and muted grey combination. It is so restful. And that touch of maroon is like a happy giggle. I think I'd like to use these colors for my room next spring. Would you mind if I stole your decorating idea? It's so peaceful, kind of like a cuddly warm blanket. And you even have a skylight. I always think a skylight is the neatest idea. You can sit here at night and watch the northern lights dance through the heavens right from your living room. It must be wonderful to sit here in winter and let the sun warm you from above."

Jessie was chattering away, her brief moment of insecurity about Katreena long since forgotten. She was comfortable in Katreena's home and in Katreena's presence. Until today, she hadn't really got to know Katreena. Now she saw her as a warm and interesting person with whom she could share jokes, experiences and even dreams. Hopefully, she would enjoy Kaydee as much. The fact that Kaydee liked to read and write, fascinated Jessie. She had many friends in school, good and close friends whose company she enjoyed but none of those friends shared her passion for literature or writing. Having someone whose interests paralleled hers would be exciting and probably even motivational. It could prove to be beneficial to Kaydee, it was true, but that benefit could be reciprocal for her as well.

By two o'clock, they were on their way to KD Acres. With the hot sun beating down relentlessly from a cloudless sky, Jessie imagined even the name of the place sounded inviting, her mind conjuring up vast green fields and meadows. Still, Jessie could not totally control the butterflies in her stomach about meeting Kaydee and Helen, even after Katreena had told her that Helen used to harbour those very same ambitions that now connected her and Kaydee. Jessie had never actually met aspiring writers. She had read their work, read their bios, but had never actually met any of those people. Now she was vacillating between feeling excited about meeting Kaydee and Helen and nervous that they would find her incompetent or worse yet, uninteresting or unlikable somehow.

As they turned into the driveway, Jessie noted the neatness of the well-kept yard. It looked like a little park with the well-manicured lawn and flowerbeds setting off the buildings all surrounded by rows of stately maples. She'd driven through the countryside with her parents and even with Dusty but had never actually taken an interest in farmyards as they whizzed by in the vehicle. She had never actually been to a farm before and this place looked welcoming. She felt the peace here even as her heart churned with apprehension regarding the family's reaction to her visit.

A young girl with long blond hair came running out of the house as soon as they pulled in. Her heart-shaped face beamed with pleasure as she greeted Katreena and Dusty, then extended her hand to Jessie and smiled shyly.

"Hi, I'm Kaydee," she said hesitantly. "I am so happy you came." Jessie noted the somewhat cautious greeting and remembered Dusty telling them that Kaydee had never really had any close friends and how she had been berated all her life.

"She's more afraid that I will not like her than I am of being accepted," Jessie realized in astonishment. "This girl is convinced she isn't likable!" Right then Jessie determined to change Kaydee's perception of herself. No one should feel that insecure!

"Hi, Kaydee. I'm Jessie. Uncle Dusty has told me such wonderful things about you and I just could not wait to meet you. I am so looking forward to this week."

Kaydee blushed and was rather taken aback at the compliment but then regained her composure. "I'm looking forward to this week too. I hope you'll like it here."

Katreena gave Kaydee a quick hug. "I know you girls will get along wonderfully. Come on, where is everybody?"

The matter-of-fact question put Kaydee at ease because she could reply with confidence.

"Mother took the truck out to the field for Joey. He went with the tractor and the bale wagon but he wanted to have the truck there so he wouldn't have to drive the machinery back and forth. He will bring her right back. The girls are still napping and I just gave Alvin some milk and cookies because he said he was hungry. Honestly, Granny, he's forever hungry. I don't know where he puts it. He's like a bottomless pit!"

They all laughed. They were in the house by now and Alvin came charging from the other room calling excitedly, "Granny, Granny, Uncle Dusty!" At the sight of Jessie, Alvin stopped short and stared at her with his mouth gaping. His hair, scorched in his accident with the gunpowder, had been cropped to a close brush cut. Jessie smiled. There was something unnatural about an almost five-year-old boy with brush-cut hair! Alvin's face registered such bewilderment that Kaydee started laughing. It put the comical situation into perspective and everyone joined in the laughter, much to Alvin's chagrin.

"Alvin, this is Jessie, Uncle Dusty's niece," Kaydee explained with amusement, "now why don't you close your mouth and say hello to her?"

Before Alvin could collect himself, Jaynee came running from the other room.

"Me too, me too," she offered enthusiastically and toddled straight up to Jessie, her little hand extended in welcome. The whole scene was so delightful that Jessie stooped down to sweep the adorable little girl into her arms.

Alvin approached hesitantly with a "Hi, Jessie" and shyly extended his hand.

"Hi Alvin, I'm pleased to meet you," Jessie responded and shook his extended hand. Still holding the enthusiastic Jaynee with her other arm, she addressed Alvin.

"And who might this little girl be?"

"That's Jaynee, my little sister," Alvin declared proudly. "She's just two-and-a-half years old. I'm four-and-a-half. We also have another sister, Dayna. She's just a baby. She's sleeping now but you can meet her later." His shyness evaporated as he chattered on, making himself sound so superior and knowledgeable.

"I'm looking forward to meeting her." Jessie was enjoying this. Jaynee was beaming, content to just be held, and Alvin had obviously already accepted Jessie into the family.

Katreena and Dusty watched the interaction with interest and satisfaction. This appeared to be a mutually gratifying and friendly liaison in its budding stages.

Kaydee put some water to boil for tea and set some cups and saucers on the table while she conversed with Granny and Dusty. Alvin was monopolizing Jessie. He ran and fetched the tiny toy tractor that was so precious to him.

"The nurses gave me this when I was in the hospital after my accident," he proudly informed Jessie and then went on to explain all about how he had landed in that hospital in the first place. Jaynee was apparently enthralled with their new friend and Kaydee watched them through the corner of her eye, noting how patient Jessie was with the two kids. Jaynee was usually content to play by herself, yet she sat there on Jessie's lap as if she never wanted to leave it. Anyone that affectionate with kids just had to be a wonderful person!

The Boyer's blue one-ton truck pulled into the driveway, parked behind Dusty's Buick and Helen got out. Katreena could not help noticing the cheery smile on Helen's face as she bid Joey goodbye before he backed the truck out onto the road and drove off. Those two had developed an easygoing relationship and respected each other. Katreena's heart ached for Helen. She should always have been treated that way. Yet in all the twelve years of her marriage, this was probably the first time she was experiencing it. This was a transitory state for her, because when Michael... Katreena could not even bear to complete the thought.

Helen walked in, hugged her mother, shook hands with Dusty and then went up to greet Jessie, deliberately interrupting Alvin's prattle.

"Welcome to KD Acres, Jessie. Is Alvin hogging all your attention? We should have prepared you for this eventuality. He doesn't usually relinquish his hold on a receptive audience so you must demand liberation or you'll be in his clutches till midnight."

"Thank you, Mrs. Boyer, but it's alright, honest. I don't mind. They're wonderful children." Jessie gave Jaynee a tight squeeze and she responded with a giggly squirm. They all laughed and Jessie added, "I certainly don't get this kind of attention back home."

"Well, I hope you're prepared to stay for a while, because I don't think Dusty will be able to pry you away from those kids with a crowbar. You can stay, can't you?"

"I'd love to stay, if I won't be a bother to anyone," Jessie looked towards Kaydee.

"Oh, please stay," Kaydee's affirmation was instant. "I'd really love it if you stayed. We'll have fun, I promise."

And so began Jessie's country holiday.

When lunch was cleared away, Kaydee showed Jessie the yard, the garden, and the different buildings, explaining the roles and purposes of each. Alvin and Jaynee followed along excitedly, Alvin interjecting enthusiastic embellishments at every opportunity. Even Rusko tagged along for a while, then sensing his redundancy, left them and opted for a snooze in the shade beside his doghouse.

As they approached the charred remains of the shop Kaydee's voice became subdued and even Alvin's excitement faded away.

"This used to be the shop where Father did all his machinery repairs. He was working on something when an explosion caused a fire and he got badly burned." Kaydee said with finality.

"Daddy had to go to a hospital far away." Alvin added but even he fell silent as Kaydee purposely led them past the dark reminder of a past that seemed best forgotten.

They made their way towards the garden and Kaydee seemed to regain her calm as she told Jessie about hoeing and weeding the garden and flower beds, mowing the lawns, clipping the hedges and around the buildings, feeding the chickens and so on. Alvin and Jaynee had obviously lost interest and left Jessie and Kaydee to tour on their own.

"You mean you mow all this lawn twice a week?" Jessie gaped at Kaydee.

"It's not that bad, really. It's easier if I do it often. I usually do it on Wednesdays and Saturdays, but sometimes if it rains or something, I can't do it on time and then the grass is too big and it's more work, especially if the grass is so thick it has to be raked up. If I do it twice a week it only takes about four hours to do all the mowing and edging."

Jessie was fascinated. She had never had to be responsible for much more than cleaning her room and helping with the household chores. Keeping that much yard and garden seemed to entail so much work, yet Kaydee made it sound interesting and fun.

Kaydee glanced toward the sun in the southwest.

"We better get back to the house. Mother will be starting supper. I have to help."

Jessie could see no sign of Kaydee's predicted reserved or unsociable disposition. Jessie could already feel a comfortable camaraderie developing with her new friend. She could not imagine anyone not liking this quiet, obliging girl who didn't complain and who seemed to appreciate the simplest things.

The girls spent the evening getting acquainted with each other. They talked long into the night discussing school, teachers, books, various authors and other interests. Jessie could not understand how anyone would consider Kaydee mentally deficient. She found her to be fascinating. It was after midnight when they finally decided to call it a night.

Chapter 24

Tuesday morning dawned hot and humid. Everything took on a rather lethargic air and an almost ominous tone in the stuffy vacuum that surrounded them. Even the crickets ceased their chirping and the impatiens and petunias bowed their heads in the oppressive heat. Not a bird could be seen flitting among the trees. The air hung heavy with the humidity and there wasn't a whisper of a breeze. Life seemed suspended by the searing heat, waiting for a break.

After breakfast, Kaydee and Jessie set the small kids up with toys in the living room, then went upstairs to chat and read. Helen was just sorting some clothes of Alvin's when Joey's pickup pulled into the driveway and Joey came around the front to help Annie out.

"Good morning," they called in unison as Helen stepped out to greet them. "The weather is so muggy, and Joey thought that he could work on the shed today since he says he's caught up with the field work for a while. Me, well, I just ran away from home so I would have a legitimate excuse not to do any work. I hope you don't mind my dropping by unannounced."

"Don't you be silly! I'm so glad you did." Helen tucked Annie's arm under hers, welcoming her guest. "We don't seem to visit any time. It appears that everyone is always too busy but today I doubt that there will be anything much we can do with that humidity and heat outside. And there certainly is nothing that has to be done inside that cannot wait a while. Come on in. Can I get you guys a cup of coffee?"

"We've only finished a late breakfast back home, so perhaps later, but thanks anyway." Annie sank heavily into the kitchen chair by the window. She was grateful for the comfort that the Boyer's air-conditioned home provided. Her own place did not have air-conditioning, though the shade of the huge maples around her house offered a substantial degree of relief from the hot sun. Still, when it was this muggy, there were few places to hide.

"I expect that this humidity will be bringing on some kind of storm eventually though at this point it seems to be just hiding somewhere and trying to decide what to do," Annie observed.

Joey declined the coffee, made sure his grandmother was settled and comfortable, then excusing himself, announced that he was going to the shed.

Helen protested. "You don't have to work in this oppressive heat, Joey. That shed can wait. It's too hot out there for man or beast. Why don't you sit here and just relax for a while?"

"Thanks, Mrs. Boyer. I appreciate the offer, and I am not rejecting it entirely, but there are a few things I'd like to check and organize there and this seems like the day to do it. If it gets too uncomfortable, I'll duck back here, I promise." He raised his hand in mock salute and left.

Helen looked after him thoughtfully. "You know Annie, that man is an absolute treasure. I honestly don't know what I would have done without him. He's a natural. He is conscientious and knowledgeable about all aspects of farming. I am so lucky to have got him. I don't know what I'll do when he gets called back!"

"He's in absolute heaven, Helen. He's always loved farming. It's in his blood. He was devastated when Vince came back. It knocked the spirit right out of him. Now he's whistling all the time, even though he knows that this is temporary. He's prepared to leave when Michael comes back, but for now, he is enjoying every moment he has here. He's a good boy Helen, and he won't leave you stranded as long as you need him. I can promise you that."

"I know. He told me that. But as much as I want him here, I really would not want him to lose a good job on account of us. It would be so unfair," Helen said regretfully.

"Now don't you fret about that," Annie remonstrated quickly. "Joey is a grown man. He will make his own decision and I have no qualms about him making the right one. That city job is not his lifeline. He can pick another one just as good anytime, anywhere, but I can tell you with no trace of hesitation that he will never find one that will give him the same satisfaction that he gets from running a farm. Whatever happens with Michael and no matter how long it takes, you don't ever have to worry about Joey. He's a survivor and he'll make his decisions conscientiously and according to what is right and fair to all concerned."

Helen made some iced tea and brought some fresh doughnuts she had made the day before. Joey came in just then, sweating, his hands covered with soot and dirt.

"Just exactly what the doctor ordered," he pointed at the tall glass of iced tea that Helen set in front of his grandmother. "I'll be here to collect just as soon as I cool off with a shower. Man, it's hot out there! It's gotta be a hundred degrees in the shade. And that humidity! Phew!" He strode purposefully toward the bathroom, fanning his neck with the collar of his shirt.

Within ten minutes, he reappeared, looking refreshed and eager.

"I should have brought a change of clothes for after the shower but at least the shower helped," he said ruefully. "Okay, pass it to me. A whole gallon of it, if you have enough. I'm dryer than the Sahara. I must have lost five gallons in sweat out there. This has got to be the hottest day on record!" He emptied the glass in two gulps and set it in front of Helen for a refill.

"Hit me again, bartender," he drawled, John Wayne fashion and the women laughed.

After his third glass, he settled down, picked up a doughnut and bit into it with relish.

"There are some dark clouds rising on the northwest horizon. I hope it doesn't start to hail or something. This kind of weather is unusual and unpredictable. It's just too hot and humid. If a storm develops, I'd like to be here until it blows over. Also," and he looked straight at Helen, "if you don't mind, I'd like Granny to stay here till it's over as well. That way I can keep an eye on everybody in case of anything. Would you mind?"

"Of course, I don't mind." Helen was quick to reply. "It would be reassuring to have you both here. You don't even have to ask. For all our sakes, I hope we won't need protection, but it would be a comfort to know that protection is at hand if it is needed. Thank you so much for thinking about us, Joey."

The thick dark clouds continued to hang menacingly in the northwest, not advancing, just suspended in time and space, like a vulture hovering over its intended prey. The air was stuffy, it was as if they were in a barrel of some sort with no fresh air to be had anywhere. The heat and humidity were suffocating. While the women worked on preparing lunch for the family, Joey went out to the shed again. He kept watching that threatening mountain of dark clouds but they didn't move. He kept expecting the wind to whip up at any moment but none came.

Sweating in the sweltering heat of the shop, Joey felt thirsty again. He returned to the house for another drink, then went back outside but instead of going to the shed, he went out past the shelter belt to get a better view of the clouds. This day had been weird since morning and it seemed to be getting worse. This stillness was freaking him out. It was lasting too long. Storms came and went but they built up momentum quickly, ranted, roared, flashed and thundered and then they were over. This one seemed to be scheming or something. It was holding them in suspense while it plotted its course. Still, there was nothing he could do but wait. Wait for what? He felt strangely uneasy.

It was too hot to go outdoors so Kaydee and Jessie stayed upstairs in Kaydee's bedroom. Kaydee had not written in her journal since before Jessie arrived. She had been too busy getting acquainted with her new friend. They had worked together, laughed together and talked till every girly subject had been discussed but Kaydee had not yet mentioned her journal or her feelings about her father. Jessie was reluctant to broach those subjects herself, fearing that she would be treading on forbidden territory if she did. Yet she was undeniably curious and wondered if perhaps it had been presumptuous of her to think that Kaydee might open up to her.

As they sat there on the bed talking about school, they heard Joey come in and mention the impending storm. Kaydee listened as Joey asked Helen if his grandmother could stay there so he could keep an eye on all of them. She sat silently as her mother eagerly agreed. She remained silent and thoughtful after they heard Joey leave the house.

Jessie realized that Kaydee was brooding about something, something deep and profound. She was hesitant to break into Kaydee's contemplative world but felt an overwhelming need to liberate her from the distress she was obviously feeling. Still, she did not want to pry. This had to be Kaydee's call. She had to volunteer the information of her own free will or it would forever be reserved.

"Do you really think there will be a storm?" Jessie ventured.

Kaydee's head snapped back as if she had been yanked out of a trance. She stared at Jessie as if she hadn't seen her before. Then, slowly, reality set in and she became herself again.

"I'm sorry. What did you say, Jessie?"

"Joey seems to think that there may be a bad storm coming and he wants to keep an eye on everyone. Do you think it will be that bad?" Jessie felt the need to explain herself, to reacquaint Kaydee with the situation at hand so she could provide an appropriate answer.

"Oh, I don't know. But isn't it great that Joey even thought about it? That he wants to take care of us? He cares about us, Jessie! He really cares!" Kaydee's eyes were wide and teary with awe. She sat there staring at Jessie, speechless with incredulity.

"Of course he cares, silly. He wants us all safe. Why wouldn't he? What's so unusual about that?" Jessie said, surprised. She couldn't understand Kaydee's bewilderment.

"My father would not have cared." Kaydee said, her voice flat with conviction.

This time it was Jessie who was at a loss for words. How do you counter a comment like that? She gaped at Kaydee, pity in her eyes, pain and empathy in her heart. How could someone feel so uncared for? By her own father? For the first time since she had heard about Kaydee, Jessie understood what it was about the girl that no one could properly define. Unable to utter a word because of the lump in her throat, Jessie moved over and wrapped her arms around Kaydee.

They sat there rocking gently with Jessie's arms around her, as Kaydee struggled with her demons.

"Joey is so good to us," Kaydee finally broke the tension. "He's never mean or angry and he's always happy and kind to Mother and to all of us. My father was always angry and yelling and swearing, at Mother and especially at me. I think he hated me and Mother but I know he definitely hated me. He always called me a stupid moron and he kept telling us how much trouble we were and how trapped he was with us."

Once started, Kaydee couldn't stop. It was as if the flood gates had opened up. She poured out all her frustrations and aggravations. She told Jessie about having to kneel in the sinhole for any little provocation, about Father burning Mother's journal, about him beating Auggie to death, about being punished for not protecting Alvin from the rooster, about not being allowed to use the word Daddy, about being blamed for Alvin's problems, about all the times they had to keep silent for fear of triggering another one of his rages. Kaydee recounted how her mother had always been so afraid of him that she never spoke up for herself or for any of the kids no matter how mean Father got.

"Father always called me a retard, but the way Mother used to be, I honestly used to think she was the one who was retarded. She never laughed or cried or smiled or even acted like she cared about anything, including us kids. I didn't know she was a real person until Granny told me about how she used to be before she married my father."

Kaydee rested her head on Jessie's shoulder. With her arm still around Kaydee's shoulder, Jessie let her purge herself of this venom that seemed to have been bottled up inside her all this time. She could not fathom a life like Kaydee described! All through the exposition, Jessie's tears flowed like rain but Kaydee's eyes were dry, staring into that dark cavern full of memories where tears were unproductive and redundant, and hope was an impossible dream.

When she had spent herself, Kaydee sat up, looked Jessie in the eye and announced, "I'm sorry, Jessie but I have to be honest about it. I have an evil secret in my heart. I hate my father! I never even knew this myself until just lately! Before that I was just afraid of him. But now I know I hate him. It's my deep dark secret and only Granny knows it and now you. He always said how he wanted to be away from us and I wished that he would just go away and never come back. Maybe we both got our wish now, but you know the worst of it, Jessie? I don't even think I want him to come back. Isn't that awful?" Jessie could not speak for the lump in her throat.

Kaydee continued "Joey is good to us and our whole family is happy now and it feels good. It feels right, Jessie." She emphasized. "I know I shouldn't feel this way but I can't help it. I just want things to stay this way forever. I don't want Father to ever come back!" Kaydee's voice was strangely unrepentant, even as she pleaded for understanding, for forgiveness.

"It's okay, Kaydee. No one can blame you for feeling that way after all you've been through. Your father was a bad person and he made all of you suffer. Maybe it is his turn now."

Kaydee looked pensive as she reflected on that statement. "Maybe, but I still feel guilty. He is my father and I should care but I can't make myself care. I don't even dare tell anyone that I feel that way. I don't want to be evil but I know it's evil to feel like this."

"I don't think you're evil at all. I think you are very brave and strong to have put up with such abuse for so long. Nobody could think you are bad. You must believe me. But I do promise you that I will never tell your secret to anyone. You can trust me Kaydee. I PROMISE!" Jessie fervently traced a cross over her heart. "It's your secret and only you can tell people about it. I promise I will never tell!"

"Thank you Jessie. You're a good friend. I am glad Dusty brought you here. Outside of Granny, I could never talk to anyone before, though Mother is better since Father went away."

Suddenly Kaydee's eyes flashed bright and defiant and she almost whispered. "When Father was here, I started writing a journal. It was dangerous because if Father would have found out he would have gone into a terrible rage and I don't even want to think what he would have done. You remember I told you before that Father had burned Mother's journal? Well Granny only told me about that journal this summer. Granny said Mother had many friends when she was in school, that she belonged to drama clubs and was editor of the school paper and that she kept a journal and that she wrote poetry. I was very excited about finding out this stuff about Mother and I so wanted to read her journal. That was when she told me that Father had burned it during one of his stupid rages."

Kaydee paused and sat there staring into space, her eyes wide and cold but devoid of even a trace of tears. Her fists were clenched as tight as her teeth and her lips pursed while she fought to conquer the hatred rising within her heart again.

"That was when I started hating my father. Up until then I had just been very, very scared of him all the time, but when I found out that he had burned the journal I just became very angry at him. That was Mother's only copy and he destroyed it. That was cruel. I hated him for burning it and for all the other cruel things he had done to us all our lives." Kaydee paused, staring into space. "Do you know," she continued thoughtfully, "ever since I could remember, he has been telling us how he was smart and how stupid Mother and I were but he could only make himself feel smart by saying we were stupid. He burned Mother's journal because it showed Mother was smarter than he was so he destroyed the journal. He almost destroyed Mother too. She was so scared of him, she cowered and got that sad faraway look in her eyes as if she wasn't even there. I hated that he yelled and screamed at us. If we protested, he would become even more mean. Granny and Mother made me promise not to make him angry because they were afraid for all of us. I promised Mother and Granny that I would write all my feelings into my own journal and I would make sure Father never ever knew about it. I wrote a lot of sad and angry poems and things in my journal at first, but lately I don't write sad and angry things anymore. Ever since Joey came to work here, I write about more happy things. It's because Joey makes us all happy. He's never mean or angry or even unhappy and that keeps everybody else from being scared or unhappy. I've been reading some parts of my journal to the family. They seemed to enjoy it. Would you...?"

"Lunch is ready," Mother called from downstairs.

With a horrified start, Kaydee looked at her wristwatch. "Oh my goodness, is it lunch already? Where did the time go? I should have been helping." Flinging the magazines off her lap onto the bed, she rushed out and fairly flew down the stairs, oblivious to the fact that Jessie was left still sitting cross-legged on her bed. Jessie stared after Kaydee for a moment, not sure of how to take this unexpected abandonment. Then, realizing that Kaydee's sudden departure was not a rude action but probably a result of previously programmed behaviour borne of fear of chastisement, Jessie followed her friend downstairs where Kaydee was apologizing profusely.

"Oh Mother, I'm so sorry. I didn't realize it was lunch time already. Jessie and I just got talking and the time flew. I'm sorry."

"That's okay, honey, don't worry." Helen soothed gently. "Annie was kind enough to help out with the children so I just thought I'd let you girls visit for a change. It was no problem, really. You need time to get acquainted too and you deserve some time to yourself."

Then seeing Kaydee's flushed cheeks and her undiminished agitation Helen realized that her daughter was still cringing from fear of punishment. It was that involuntary response to years of accrued fear of Michael's relentless castigation. Helen thought the past few weeks had erased it but here it was, still holding them captive. Even from a lifeless bed in a distant hospital in a city half a continent away, Michael was still subjugating them to his will. Helen put down the ladle she was carrying and came around the table to put her hands on Kaydee's shoulder. Holding her at arm's length, Helen looked straight into Kaydee's eyes and, enunciating each word slowly she declared, "Kaydee, it's okay!!! Honest. I mean it. I would have called you if I had needed your help, but I really was alright with Annie. Don't worry! No one is upset with you. I am happy that you can get so involved with a friend that you can forget what time it is. It is a good thing, Kaydee. Understand? *It's a good thing!*"

Seeing her mother's eyes piercing deeply into her own that way, Kaydee nodded obediently, then impulsively, she gave her mother a hug and smiled. "Thanks, Mom."

Jessie watched this display with awe and imagined what horrible circumstances had created the requisite for this scenario in the first place.

"Good! Now relax." Helen kissed her forehead and went back to ladle the soup.

Still, deep down, Kaydee could not help feeling remorseful about her uncharacteristic forgetfulness. It was irresponsible to shirk her duties or to take her chores lightly. Father had drilled her "uselessness" into her for years and even though the threat of repercussion was not present with Father away, still she felt the oppression of it indelibly etched on her mind. As she finished putting the bib around Dayna's neck and slipped Jaynee into her highchair, Kaydee silently vowed never again to get so taken up with her own self-interest as to forego her obligations.

Joey had not lingered in the house after lunch. He was restless and went promptly outside. The women were still finishing up with the dishes when Joey came back in. They were too preoccupied with their own chatter to notice his furrowed brow, his sombre attitude, or even his abnormal behaviour. He had checked all the buildings outside, making certain all the doors were securely closed to the barns and the other buildings. There was little he could secure about that shed. He hadn't had the chance to tear it down, waiting instead for when they had more specific plans about rebuilding before he proceeded with any major reconstruction. He had put all loose tools and minor equipment inside the one grainery which he now utilized as a makeshift shed. He moved Helen's vehicles and equipment into the garage and the machine shed and secured the doors.

Still he felt there was something he should be doing but for the life of him, he could not figure out what else he could do. He checked the windows in the house, then quietly went upstairs to check the windows up there. He had been there only once before, when Helen had given him a tour when he first started at the farm. Everything seemed secure. He glanced out the window towards the west where those ominous clouds had been sitting the last couple of hours but they still had not moved high enough on the horizon to be visible above the tall maples. Too tense to relax, he went outside again, heading for the northwest corner of the yard beyond the shelter belt. Somewhere there was the key to this eerie silence, this suffocating atmospheric vacuum that seemed to be sucking the breath out of his lungs.

Chapter 25

Joey's heart lurched when he emerged into the clearing beyond the maples. The dark clouds had now turned into a greyish white mass that was churning within itself like a cauldron of fiercely boiling water. And the caldron was now advancing, swiftly. Almost instantly, the wind picked up. This was it. Joey took off on a run toward the house. How bad was it going to get? He didn't know, but he wanted to be in the house with the women, in case they needed him.

The women had not been aware that the wind had picked up. Helen and Annie were sitting in the living room, Helen had Dayna in her arms, and the women were talking casually. Jaynee was sitting cross-legged on the floor, lecturing her dolls on some imaginary misdemeanour but Alvin and the girls were not in sight.

"Where are the other kids?" Joey's voice was sharp with apprehension.

Surprised by the abruptness in his voice, both women looked up. "They are all upstairs. It's too hot to go outdoors. Why? Is anything wrong, Joey?" Helen wanted to know.

"No not really. It's just that the wind is picking up and those clouds are rolling up kind of heavy. I just don't want anyone to be outdoors right now." Joey answered lightly, not wishing to alarm anyone unnecessarily. It might just blow over without touching anything. Or it might veer off and turn in a different direction. Or it might...

As they stood there eyeing each other inquisitively, not quite sure what to say or do next, they heard a kind of sucking hiss of the wind. Putting Dayna into the crib, Helen went to the window to look out into a darkened sky where heavy clouds swirled in a vortex of ferocity that veiled the sun. The wind had now increased to a low growl, like the roar of an angry lion. The house began to creak under the velocity of the fierce storm that was attacking it. The room grew dark as a deluge of huge rain drops and hail stones suddenly started hammering against the house. Flashes of lightning lit up the darkened room, followed immediately by earsplitting crashes of thunder.

Joey rushed to the foot of the stairs. "Alvin, Kaydee, Jessie come on down here immediately," but they were already rushing down the stairs, alarmed by the sudden storm that had developed so ferociously without any warning.

"We may have to get to the basement fast, if it gets any worse, so why don't you take the small kids down now just in case things start getting really rough here." Joey addressed the startled women. Kaydee was right on it without a question. She grabbed Dayna and ran for the basement door. Jessie picked up the bewildered Jaynee in her arms, following right at Kaydee's heels. Alvin's eyes darted from Mother to Joey to the girls. Lightning flashed and thunder crashed and golfball-sized hail stones hurled down from the swirling mass somewhere above them.

"Hurry," Joey barked in alarm through the ever more deafening din of the storm. Helen grabbed Alvin and ran after the girls, reaching her free hand to Annie, pulling her along behind her as Joey pulled up the rear. Behind them, they heard glass shattering as the hail stones found their mark on the window panes.

"Get into that corner behind the freezer and be ready to crouch down if necessary. It may just blow over and everything will be alright but just in case." Joey told them when they were all safely downstairs. When everyone was settled, he walked cautiously up the stairs and closed the door, listening to any new developments. The noise out there was menacing but Joey held the door tightly closed to keep out the flying debris. He knew there was at least one broken window and perhaps more. Suddenly everything went dark. The power had gone off. Jaynee and Dayna started crying for the first time since the mayhem started.

"The lightning must have shorted the power out," Joey explained trying to sound calm and logical while the women soothed the children. "It's alright. It's just the storm. The lights will be back on soon. Mrs. Boyer, do you have a flashlight handy somewhere in the house?"

"There is one in the drawer beside the kitchen sink. But do you have to get it now? Wait till this blows over. Surely it can't last too much longer. Don't leave us alone, Joey. Please!"

"Don't you worry. I'm not going anywhere until this is all over. We're safe down here. There is really nothing anyone can do but just wait out the storm anyway. Is everyone okay there?"

A shaky chorus of nervous "I'm fine" emanated from the corner behind the freezer and Joey tried to relax. If he could maintain calm for them, and the storm vented its energy without creating too much destruction up above, perhaps they might come out of this unscathed.

"This kind of hot humid weather usually results in somewhat severe storms, so I've been expecting it since morning. It will probably blow itself out soon. These storms move fast. They don't linger in one spot for too long. It's really just an awful lot of wind moving at a fast speed, and it usually brings a heavy rain and sometimes hail, but that is where the major damage is going to be. We'll be out of here in no time." Joey spoke calmly, rationally, trying to make the storm sound like a natural happening that warranted nothing more than an inconvenient response and a mild schedule change in the routines of their day. Still, the next ten minutes seemed like ten hours as they waited in the darkness and listened to the howling winds, the crashing thunder and the roar of the rain and hail bashing their home above them.

Finally, after what seemed like an eternity, the terrible noise stopped short, as if cut off in mid air. At the same time, they realized that the thunder had become more distant also, though it had receded so gradually that they had hardly noticed it because of the din of wind and hail. There were no more sharp earsplitting claps, just rumbles that seemed to be directed at something remote and far away. The wind lost its menacing whine. The pandemonium had subsided.

"I think the storm has passed," Joey said from the top of the stairs where he had been holding the basement door closed. "I'll go look around first and then let you know if it's safe for you to come up," He opened the door and a ray of light illuminated part of the basement, as he disappeared upstairs. After a few minutes of reconnaissance, Joey came to the basement door and called, "You may as well come on up. The storm is gone and you'll have to face this sooner or later. Just give me a minute to sweep an area for you to stand on."

As they filed up the stairs one by one and emerged through the door, there was an audible gasp from each one as they took in the mess that used to be an organized household. Several windows had been smashed and there was shattered glass, water, and hailstones the size of tennis balls all over the floor, the counters and furniture where the wind had whipped them with obviously tremendous force. Ornaments had been flung from their perches and some were broken. The magazines that had been on such a neat pile on the rack were all over the house, their pages open, soaked or splattered. Pages of Alvin's coloring book were strewn throughout the house.

"Oh my God," Helen and Annie exclaimed in unison at the sight of the devastation. Kaydee and Jessie were completely speechless and Alvin just stared in shock.

"No one is to walk around barefoot here, so you guys just wait there by the door till I sweep this floor first," Joey ordered sharply. "Hold on. I'll get your shoes." Taking the broom once more, he carefully swept away the broken glass and the debris into the corner of the room then got their shoes out of the closet. As Kaydee's eyes took in the scattered pages of Alvin's coloring book, she suddenly remembered her journal sitting on top of her chiffonier.

Handing Dayna to her mother, she tore up the stairs two at a time. "My journal!" she called back to her stunned spectators who watched her wild dash up to her room.

But her room was intact. No windows had been broken, no damage had been done and her journal was where she had put it herself. Not a page had been touched by the storm. Relieved beyond belief, she clutched the notebook to her heart as a torrent of sobs overtook her and mammoth tears rolled down her cheeks.

Jessie had arrived by then and seeing Kaydee so overcome with emotion, yet unable to detect any visible basis for it, she put her arms around Kaydee's shoulders and asked, "Are you okay, Kaydee? What happened? What's the matter?"

Kaydee was crying so hard it took her a few minutes to calm down enough to answer. Then she quieted down, looked at her friend and smiled, big tears still rolling down her face.

"Actually, nothing is the matter," she hiccupped. "Neither my journal nor my room were even touched. And you know what? I have no idea why I'm crying!" They both laughed.

"You silly goose" Jessie hit Kaydee's shoulder mockingly. "You had me worried."

"I had me worried too," Kaydee replied. "I thought my journal would be destroyed, just like Mother's. But it's alright," she added firmly. "Now let's check the other rooms here then go downstairs and help with cleaning up the mess down there!"

Downstairs, Joey was in charge of operations. Jaynee was standing silently beside her mother, her mouth agape and her eyes wide with fear. Helen was still holding Dayna as she held on tightly to Jaynee's hand. Joey would not let her move until he was sure all traces of broken glass were removed from the area. Annie and Alvin stood quietly behind, too shocked, and perhaps still too frightened to do more than just stare at the mess.

"Can we help, Joey? Just tell us what to do," Kaydee spoke quietly but resolutely. Like Joey, she wanted to make things easy for her mother and the sooner they cleaned the mess up, the less stressful it would be for everyone concerned. There was no shortcut for this job. It had to be done slowly, methodically and thoroughly. Any remnant or tiny shard of glass left anywhere could spell danger to anyone in the house but most especially to the smaller children who spent so much time on the floor.

Joey would not let Helen or his grandmother join in the cleanup. "You guys sit down and take care of the children," he instructed them. "The girls and I will clean this up in no time."

Helen protested. "You don't expect me to just sit here and watch you guys work!"

But Joey was not taking orders. He was clearly giving them.

"Okay, but if you must do something, I'll tell you exactly what to do. You take those kids outside and keep them out of our hair while the girls and I make this house habitable. I mean it! It's dangerous here for them! Go check the garden, check the yard, check the chickens if you must. Do whatever you want to do, but get outta here, now! Please! I mean it!"

Helen turned to Annie in resignation, "I guess I cannot logically oppose him on that one. He just makes too damned much sense. Perhaps we ought to go check the yard and the garden like he says. I have to do that sooner or later anyway. May as well be now."

She put shoes on the kids, gave them jackets against the chill from the icy hailstones that covered the lawn and they left the house to let the crew attend to the cleanup. Gingerly, they picked their way over the thick layer of hailstones as they checked the yard and garden.

The storm had devastated more than just the house. Besides the broken windows, the shingles still hanging on the roofs were a tattered mess and pieces of them were strewn here and there on the yard. The garden had been demolished. Sticking out of the heavy layer of hail stones, only the barest centre stems remained of once sturdy tomato, potato, cabbage and corn plants. Where once used to be peas and beans and cucumbers, there was not even a trace of the vines. It was like someone had rototilled the garden, mashing the soil with the mulch of the vegetation and those chunks of ice, some of which even bore jagged corners. Even sturdy rhubarb stalks were broken and damaged beyond salvage.

The driveway, as well as the ground of the whole shelter belt, had a thick carpet of leaves, twigs and small branches which had been stripped bare off the trees and mixed in with a layer of ice. In fact, the trees presented more of a desolate winter scene than a summer one, they appeared so barren. Joey's truck had more dents in it than a pebblestone walk because it had borne the brunt of the savage onslaught of the hail. The buildings were intact but the shingles on the roofs would probably all require replacing.

The precarious tethers that had held the remnants of the shed together, had finally given up the ghost and the charred remains lay in various sized piles of mangled masses on the shed floor or scattered around on the yard, wherever the ferocious gale had wantonly opted to drop its cargo. Helen was thoughtfully contemplating one pile of that debris when Annie observed, "Quite a mess, isn't it?"

"Well there is one silver lining to all this. We don't have to worry about demolishing that shed anymore. The storm did it for us. Now all Joey will have to do is use the tractor to bulldoze it onto one pile."

As they passed the garage, Helen was surprised to find that its door was closed. During the day, when the car and the truck were out of the garage, the door was often left open.

"Annie," Helen exclaimed in shock, "Joey could have protected his truck by parking it behind the car. The door would not have closed, but so what? At least his truck would not have been damaged. If he drove in both my vehicles, and closed the door, why didn't he protect his?" With a pang of guilt, Helen suddenly realized that, anticipating a storm, Joey had purposely protected both her vehicles by closing the door, but had sacrificed his own truck to the elements. "I feel terrible about this. I must speak to him about this."

"It won't do you any good, Helen," Annie warned. "Joey is very conscientious and if he needed to protect your vehicles at the expense of his, then there is nothing you can say that will make him see it differently. He knows his place and he will never overstep his bounds."

"But he is so much more than just an employee, Annie," Helen protested, her voice hoarse with emotion. "He's my guardian angel. He is truly a Godsend. I mean it. I really believe he was sent to us by God Himself. I cannot even begin to imagine what I would do without him. How can I ever thank you for him?"

"No need, Helen. You have given Joey a reason to live. He has a purpose now, he is happy. And if he has done something good with his life then it is a good thing, for him, for me, and for you. Perhaps good things will come to all of us someday. If you must thank anyone, thank God. Who knows what God has in mind?"

"Yes, who knows," Helen sighed wistfully.

Taking a well-earned break from their labours, Kaydee and Jessie were outside by now, sitting on the steps, sipping on glasses of lemonade. They heard the conversation between Helen and Annie and exchanged covert glances at Helen's remark. Both girls were remembering Kaydee's last discourse about Joey's influence on the family dynamics, how much that influence impacted on each of its members and how much their new behaviour deviated from their accustomed routines when Michael was home.

When the women entered the house, the place was as clean and as organized as it could be, considering the circumstances. Joey had located gloves for the girls, then handed them shovels, boxes, a broom and a dustpan and set them up carefully cleaning the debris off each surface. When a box was full, he hauled it straight out onto the truck. As each area was cleaned, he checked meticulously, inspecting it to make certain there was no trace of glass left to pierce unsuspecting little fingers and toes.

"It should be safe for the kids to play here now, but I still wish we could get the power back on. I'll have to board those windows up until we can get the glass replaced so that will mean semidarkness even during the day."

Joey went to the phone and was surprised to hear a dial tone. "Hey, we're in luck," he called excitedly. "The phone is working!"

He dialled Manitoba Hydro but got a busy line. "Guess everyone has the same idea," he said ruefully as he hung up. "But at least we know the phones are working so help should be forthcoming. It just depends on what kind of damage we are looking at. If it's minor we should have power by tonight."

"Can you do supper cold?" Joey looked at Helen with concern. "You may have to, you know." Then, seeing the rather strained look on her face, he added, "It's all right, Mrs. Boyer. It could have been worse. Thank God everyone is safe. That's all that's important. As soon as I get in touch with the Hydro, I'll go check the yard and then I'll have to check Granny's place. Tomorrow, I will go out and check the crops. Don't worry," he added gently, "We'll make out alright. The insurance will cover it," and went back to the phone.

Kaydee and Jessie joined Joey on his surveillance tour. He noted which repairs would require immediate attention and which ones could be put off to a later date. When they got back to the house, Joey presented his conclusions to Helen.

"Our first priority of course, are the windows. I'd like to go check out the fields and crops, but that will have to wait. I'd like to wait till the power is back on but I have to go and check Granny's place. Depends on which way that cloud was heading. Maybe it missed you," he addressed his grandmother. "Anyway, I'll board up those broken windows right after I come back from Granny's. That should keep you safe for tonight. Don't you worry, Mrs. Boyer, we'll have this place good as new in no time. I promise you. I won't let you down. We'll make it through this, I promise."

Helen merely nodded. She had been watching and listening to him wordlessly, as were the girls. All were stunned by the devastation, unable to fully comprehend the impact of the afternoon's storm but Annie was the only one who had continued to utter incoherent exclamations as each scene unfolded before them.

"Granny, you want to come with me to check your place or would you rather wait here? There will really be nothing you can do and hopefully I'll be right back if everything is okay there. Are you guys going to be alright?"

Then watching Helen closely, his voice full of compassion, Joey added, "You hang in there, okay? We'll be alright, remember?"

Helen gave him a weak smile. "Thank you, Joey. I know we will."

Annie opted to go with Joey to check her place but before they left, she told Helen to call Katreena and inform her of the events of the afternoon.

As soon as they were in the truck, Annie told Joey, "I don't think we should leave them in that house alone tonight with the windows broken, especially if the Hydro men don't turn the power on. Helen hasn't said much but I know she is very shaken. If Katreena doesn't come out, perhaps we ought to spend the night there ourselves. At any rate, we have to go back there as soon as we check out my place."

As Joey had hoped, the storm had passed off to the south of the Dorozeck yard leaving all of Annie's flowers somewhat wind and rain beaten, but otherwise thriving. Annie felt bad for the people who had lost their crops but relieved that her yard had escaped unscathed.

After a quick inspection of the premises, Annie went out into her garden, got some vegetables and salad greens and then, loaded with bags, they drove back to KD Acres. Helen and the girls had made lemonade, sandwiches with cold cuts and preserves. Together, they all sat around the kitchen table to enjoy the feast. Without power, they could not cook or heat anything. Annie's vegetables and salad were a welcome addition to the feast but the sight of these items tore at Helen's heart. For the rest of this season, she would be totally dependent on handouts from her neighbours for vegetables since her garden would no longer provide for them.

They were still sitting at the kitchen table when the lights came on. A loud cheer exploded from around the table and smiles beamed on every face. Joey breathed a sigh of relief and raised a victory salute to Helen and to his grandmother.

"Okay! We're in business," he declared jubilantly.

The sun was half hiding behind the horizon, so it was too late for Joey to check the fields. Still, he was reluctant to leave the family alone till Dusty and Katreena drove up. Helen was expecting them to arrive at any time. For the moment, Joey just wanted to stick around to make sure that Helen was calm and settled; that she was not harbouring any unresolved fears or worries that would keep her awake at night.

When Dusty's Buick pulled into the yard, Joey felt more at ease. With Katreena and Dusty there, he knew the family would be alright and he felt secure enough to leave.

As soon as she was out of the car, Katreena put her arms around Helen. "Oh honey, I am so sorry. It must have been terrifying for you. I'm sorry we could not have been here for you when you needed us."

"It's alright, Mother. Honest. Joey was wonderful. He took care of everyone and everything. I don't know what we would have done without him. He had us all down in the corner of the basement, behind the freezer!" And then giving Joey a mischievous look of reproach, she added, "In the dark! I might add." Everyone laughed as Joey winked at Dusty and bowed low in a mock repentant confession.

"That I did, sir. That I did!"

Chapter 26

The next day was a day of inspection, not just for Joey and the Boyer family but for their neighbours as well. The storm had cut a swath almost a mile wide and about twenty-two miles long, starting from eight miles northwest of the Boyer place and arcing out to the southeast. Many of their neighbours had suffered extensive damage to crops and two even lost calves in the storm. All of them shared a common concern, all felt the same anguish, and all suffered the same pain. The Boyers were lucky that their cattle were fine. The pastures were outside the margins of the storm. Not only had it missed the Dorozeck property, it bypassed part of the Jansen section, which the Boyers owned. Even the far west corner of the home quarter was spared. However, the northeast corner of the section, along with the farmyard, was completely gutted.

Helen had accompanied Joey, Dusty and Katreena to assess the damages. It was a sombre-faced group that surveyed the mangled grain, most of which was unsalvageable, even for cattle feed. As they surveyed the devastation, Katreena watched Helen for any sign of weakness or loss of control, but outside of the normal shock and the sadness for the loss, Helen remained relatively calm. There was no sign of anxiety different from what they were all feeling. Helen seemed to find strength in Joey's confident manner and confirmation that they would come through this in fairly good form. On the road, they met and conversed briefly with two groups of neighbours on the same mission and swapped stories of the tragedy, but Helen maintained her rational equanimity. As they sat on the deck later having coffee, the men discussed insurance claims, salvage operations and priority proceedings. The next few weeks would be busy, to be sure, but it would be different work than what they had originally expected it to be.

"Our first priority will be to get the windows and roofs repaired," Joey said. "Everything else, like the shed, can wait. It's first things first. The storm has made sure of that. But we'll do fine Mrs. Boyer, don't you worry about anything."

Looking straight at Joey, Helen said, "Now I have one order I must insist you follow, Joey." Surprise and total silence befell the group. "I must insist that from now on you stop calling me 'Mrs. Boyer' and call me 'Helen.' Between the 'Mrs. Boyer' and the long hours you've been keeping, I feel I must be one heck of an awful boss."

Joey was aghast. "Oh, no, not at all. I'm so sorry. I didn't mean to give that impression at all. I was just... I only meant... I..." Totally flustered, with Helen's eyes locked on him, he stopped, looked around, and saw the others watching him with amused interest.

"Oh heck, just pass the coffee, Helen." They all laughed as Helen refilled his cup.

All through the morning, Katreena could not erase the picture of Helen and Joey from her mind. They were so in tune with each other. There was nothing covert in their relationship, just a comfortable, trusting friendship, no strings, no conditions and no limitations, yet Michael's stern countenance loomed morbid and foreboding in the background. Regardless of the outcome of his injuries, Helen was still married to the beast, like it or not, and her loyalty to her husband would not permit her to divorce Michael, even if his condition never got any better. Still, this was the life Katreena would have envisioned for her daughter and whether Helen admitted it or not, Katreena was certain that this was the life that Helen would have wanted as well.

During lunch, Helen had not volunteered any updates about Michael recently. Katreena was curious but it was Annie that broached the subject.

"So have you heard from Toronto recently? Has there been any improvement in Michael's condition?"

Helen did not seem her usual guarded self at the mention of Michael's name but Katreena thought she noted a tone of distaste in Helen's voice. Perhaps the memory of his presence and his demeaning behaviour was wearing thin at last.

"Nothing new to report," she answered matter-of-factly. "I spoke to Dr. Gorman on Monday but he said Michael is still completely unresponsive. They have done a couple more scans of his brain but they cannot tell if he is aware of his surroundings or if he is just unable to respond to them. His wounds are healing well and Dr. Gorman thought they may fly him back to Winnipeg in the next couple of weeks if his wounds continue to heal as they have been."

"I have to be honest with you, Helen. I'm really not looking forward to having him back in Winnipeg in his condition. It is just going to be so much more stressful for you. If there is nothing that they can do for him in Toronto, what hope is there in Winnipeg?" Katreena said.

"I know, Mother. I understand what you are saying and I must admit to having those same misgivings, but the doctors feel that at least here, we can visit him more often."

"You realize that those visits may not be easy for everyone, if you know what I mean." Katreena gave a surreptitious wink in Alvin's direction. "How are you going to deal with that?"

Helen stared at Katreena in horror. "Mother, I hadn't even thought of that!"

Katreena felt like the Devil's advocate bringing up such a weighty matter but she didn't want Helen blind-sighted either. If Helen was to handle this without falling to pieces, then she must face the reality now, and be prepared to deal with the issue when it arose.

Joey and Dusty exchanged glances. Helen fell silent as she considered the consequences of such an encounter. Finally, still hesitant with indecision, Helen broke the silence.

"I guess you're right, Mother. I don't know what I'll do when that happens. I'll have to speak to Dr. Walley and maybe even Dr. Gorman about the situation. Perhaps they will have some suggestions. I can't keep them –" her eyes indicated Alvin "– away from him forever, but at the same time, having them see what I saw, well I just cannot imagine what it would do to them. How can I prepare them for that kind of shock?"

Anxious to diffuse the tension for Helen, Dusty intervened. "Why don't we just wait and see what happens. First of all, we don't know when they will send him back, or what shape he'll be in when they do. Worry about it then." The warning had been posted. Dusty was sure Helen would follow up on the issue, no need to pursue the agonizing subject anymore at this time.

Driving home from the farm was a sombre experience. Katreena had insisted they drive through the country to see the extent of the storm's path of destruction, and it was a grim landscape indeed. Mile after mile, they observed a heartbreaking panorama of desolation where only a couple of days ago the fields had been lush, gold and rich with the impending harvest. Having been a farm wife herself, Katreena acutely experienced the despair of those people.

"You know, some of these people may not even have insurance on those crops. Not everyone buys insurance because it is expensive and adds to the operating costs of farm management. They just take their chances and hope they'll never be hit. I'm glad Michael believed in insurance because this year is certainly going to pay for all the premiums he has paid in the past years. I can only imagine how some of those other people are feeling at this point."

"I bet Helen and Joey have no idea how far this storm really extended and how much devastation it caused. They are one of the lucky ones because there are going to be many that lost everything and don't have any insurance. When I get home I'll call them and tell them how far it extended. I am sure that will be a big shock to them to hear it hit the Granden area too."

They got back to Lanavale shortly before five and as soon as they walked inside, Katreena went to the phone to call Helen. She dialled the farm. Helen sobbing "Hello" alarmed Katreena.

"Helen, what's the matter?" Katreena asked, frightened and convinced that something bad had happened.

Helen was crying brokenly at the other end. "Mom, something terrible has happened. We just got word that Fred Archer suffered a massive stroke. He was hitching up the tractor to the side rake and he just fell over. Josie had to call the ambulance. They didn't have insurance, Mom. They always took insurance but this year Fred decided to cut corners. Mom, they were wiped out completely! Ellen Drapanik said Josie called them. They don't know if Fred is going to make it. Oh Mom, I just feel so awful for them."

Katreena was thunderstruck. Her face paled as she sagged into a chair and listened in shocked silence to Helen's report.

Watching Katreena's reaction, it was Dusty's turn to be alarmed. "What happened, for God's sake? Is everyone okay?" he asked in exasperation.

When Katreena finally put down the receiver, her voice was choking with emotion as she related to Dusty the tragedy that had befallen their good friend and neighbour.

"The Archers are wonderful people. They were so good to me after Daniel died. I should go over and help Josie now, but she'll probably be at the hospital. Helen is so upset. I imagine the whole community is." Katreena was rambling, at a loss for any clear form of action.

Dusty knelt beside her and took her shaking hands in his. "Do you want to go back to the farm honey? Perhaps it would be better to be there just in case you're needed."

Katreena was too stunned to think. After a couple of minutes, she composed herself and rationalized. "I think you're right Dusty. For Helen's sake and for Josie's, I really should be there. This is such a traumatic turn of events. Maybe I can help in some way. I honestly don't know how at this point but I have to try."

"I'll drive you right away if you want," Dusty offered.

Katreena thought that over. "No, I think I should take my own car. I may have to do some running around and right now, I don't know how long I will have to stay there. Would you mind terribly if I went back there alone this time? There is little you can do anyway."

"Of course I don't mind, honey. I'll go home and you keep me informed if I can help in any way. I can be there in two, three hours if need be. You sure you're all right to drive yourself?"

"You're a sweetheart and I love you, but I have to do this alone. I'll keep you posted, I promise." Then, looking around uncertainly, she added "I guess I'll have to pack a bag with some clothes, just in case something really bad happens. What a tragedy! Oh, I so hope he pulls through this," she sighed audibly.

They stood up and Dusty wrapped his arms around her. She leaned against him for support. She was going to miss his strength but she was needed elsewhere. Kissing him passionately, she gave him a quick squeeze then pulled away.

"Can I fix us a quick supper before we head out? It'll be late before you get home. I have some perogies in the freezer and some headcheese in jars in the fridge. It won't take more than ten minutes. I can get some greens from the garden..."

But Dusty interrupted, "Don't bother about greens, let's just nuke the perogies and open up the headcheese. I saw some beet relish in the fridge. Let's open that up. That'll be faster."

Katreena spread the perogies on a platter and put them in the microwave then opened a jar of headcheese, a jar of beet relish and a can of corn while Dusty set the plates on the table. They ate hurriedly and soon had the few dishes washed and cleared away. Katreena apologized for the rush but Dusty shushed her saying, "Don't worry honey. I understand. We'll make up for this another time. Nobody plans on problems arising, but they arise anyway and we have to deal with them as they come along. You just drive carefully."

"Will do! I want to get back to the farm as soon as possible. I think Helen may need some extra help now with all that is going on in the community. She will want to return some of the support that Josie offered to her after Michael's accident. I, too would like to be on hand for Josie during this terrible time. They were always so kind to me and even to Michael and Helen in spite of Michael's standoffish attitude. Josie will be so devastated now. She'll need alot of moral support at this stage. I want to be on hand to give it."

"Take care of yourself, honey, and remember I'm just a phone call away. I love you."

Katreena hastily packed a bag, then phoned Janine and Vance and filled them in on the latest events. "I don't know when I'll be back but I'll give you a call when I find out what's happening." Janine and Vance had met the Archers and they knew how close Katreena was to them. They were shocked by all the bad news Katreena had to relate.

"Give Josie our best, and tell her we'll pray for Fred," Janine said as she hung up.

Katreena drove into Zelena and went straight to the hospital. When she asked at the desk about Fred, they only told her they were still awaiting results of tests and that he was being treated. Only family was allowed to see him. Feeling useless, Katreena went out and continued on to KD Acres. Helen's face was still tear-stained when Katreena got out of the car.

"Have you heard anything more?"

"Nothing," Helen answered, "I've tried calling the hospital but they just said that they're waiting for results of tests. Ellen said she was going to go to the hospital but I have not heard from her since. I just cannot imagine what Josie is going through, first the hail and now this."

"I know, honey. I stepped in to the hospital on the way in but I got the same line. Just that they're waiting for the test results and visits by family only. I didn't see Josie or Ellen."

"We'll just have to wait until we hear from somebody." Helen said helplessly.

Joey came around the corner of the house with a hammer in his hand.

"Hello Katreena. Guess that was the shortest trip you ever made home, eh? Everyone is completely stunned about what happened."

Katreena nodded. "You still working on the windows? I thought you had them done."

"I was just checking them for safety. I spoke to Jolson's Windows and Doors today and they said they can deliver and install these two windows tomorrow," Joey indicated the west side of the house, but they're ordering the others from the factory so it may take a while to get them. The roofers are another matter. Everyone's waiting for them. Hopefully we won't get too much rain before they get here. That could hurt."

"It will be a relief to get at least the windows done." Katreena sighed.

"Yea," Joey said. "Ned Jolsen told me that roofers from as far away as Winnipeg have already been contacted. There is a lot of work here for the next few weeks. Every contractor within driving range will be heading for Zelena over the next month. Everyone that got hit will be desperate to reshingle as soon as possible. A leaky roof can be costly in case of heavy rains. There is opportunity here for roofing contractors to make money.

Let's just hope we don't get any fly-by-nights with no conscience taking advantage of some desperate farmer."

Katreena thought that one over. "I guess that is another thing for us to worry about." It was depressing. But Joey seemed to be taking the events in stride, attending to each task casually without complaint or apathy. One more time, Katreena thanked the Lord for placing Joey in their path when they needed him most. He was truly a miracle! What would they ever have done without him these last few weeks? He had stepped into the void and with his buoyant attitude, taken full responsibility for the family and the farm as if they were his own.

Joey went back to the old shed to continue cleaning up debris left behind by the storm. Supper was finished, and the kids were playing peacefully. It was too late to start anything and there was no garden to tend, since it had been wiped out. In the house, Helen and Katreena felt tense and antsy, waiting for news that just wasn't likely to be positive.

"I'm going to go out to the shed and see if I can help Joey with something. Perhaps doing something useful will take away this feeling of hopelessness and melancholy I'm feeling." Helen announced finally.

"I may join you later for a look around. Right now, I want to see Kaydee if she's not busy." Katreena was glad Helen was joining Joey. She liked the idea of them spending time together. They got along so well and Katreena knew, from watching them over the last few weeks, that Joey had a very stabilizing and calming effect on Helen. She was getting her self-confidence back and her stamina towards negative experiences was definitely improving. The consequences of Michael's negative impact on her psyche were growing dimmer with each passing day. Whatever the future brought, Katreena was convinced that Helen would go a long way before succumbing to that catatonic state she had been in only two months ago. All this was thanks to Michael's absence, but it was Joey's presence and his positive outlook that really fortified Helen.

Katreena checked the kids one more time and made her way up the stairs to find Kaydee. As she approached the door, she could hear giggles coming from the room. Kaydee and Jessie were obviously having a "girl tête-à-tête" and Katreena felt reluctant to disturb them. These were precious moments for Kaydee; she had few friends with whom she could commiserate. Katreena turned and slipped quietly back down the stairs. She could talk to Kaydee later. Jessie would be gone next week and who knew when they might get together like this again.

She was about to leave for the shed when the phone rang. It was Dr. Gorman.

"Is Mrs. Boyer there, please?"

"She's outdoors. This is Katreena, Dr. Gorman. You remember me? I was with Helen when we visited Michael." These calls were always disconcerting to Helen, though she bore them bravely each time and tried hard to rise above the distress they continuously provoked in her. Katreena wanted to spare her at least some of that irritation. "Is everything alright? Can I give her the message?" Katreena was suddenly wary. This was an odd time for Dr. Gorman to call. Sometimes he called in the mornings, right after he had made his rounds if something important came up. Otherwise, it was Helen who called him. What was he doing at the hospital at this hour, and why was he calling them? It was after nine in Toronto.

"Actually, Mrs. Banaduk, it's probably just as well I speak to you first anyway and you can relay the message to your daughter. How is she really doing, by the way? I have spoken to her a few times since you left and she sounds different from what I saw of her when she was here. I certainly hope she is doing as well as she sounds."

"She is very well, Dr. Gorman. She had a traumatic experience there in Toronto, but she really is doing much better now. Thank you for asking. Now how is Michael?" Katreena was getting uneasy. What was this message she was to relay to Helen and why was Dr. Gorman concerned about Helen's condition in view of the news he would have her relay?

"Well, the truth is, Mrs. Banaduk, Michael has developed an infection and he is running a fever at the moment. We believe he has had moments of consciousness but so far, we have not actually witnessed any. Still, he has ripped at bandages and has actually scratched at his wounds so we had to put restraints on him for his protection. However, there are abrasions on his arms so he obviously struggles against the restraints and rips at the bandages when we are not in the room. We believe that he is aware of when we are in the room and he avoids giving us the opportunity to watch his efforts. The scans don't show us anything new in brain activity so we cannot determine what has changed. At any rate, the wounds have festered and infection has set in. We hoped to just ward it off quickly but he has actually developed a resistance to antibiotics. Controlling the infection is presenting a problem. I felt that Mrs. Boyer should be aware of it at this time. We have considered the fact that he may be trying to get home, but without his cooperation or response we cannot be sure. We will monitor the situation and keep her posted on the progress of our treatment."

"Thank you Dr. Gorman. I appreciate your honesty. I will inform Helen of the situation. Good luck with the treatment and please keep us posted on his progress."

Katreena hung up and with a heavy heart sat down to ponder the situation.

Jessie and Kaydee had retired to Kaydee's room for some private time together. They had had very little time for private talks since before the storm. Things had been pretty chaotic here ever since Jessie had arrived and Jessie had marvelled at her own false perceptions of farm life. In her limited scope of knowledge about farming, she had envisioned a boring routine existence, but this week had been anything but that. It had seemed that every new hour brought something traumatic or unusual. Even this latest development about the neighbour was not something that could have happened in the city. Unless you were closely related to the people, you were seldom involved this intimately with the neighbours. Here, a neighbour's stroke sent the family into a tailspin with dramatic consequences.

Not that Jessie resented the closeness of the neighbours. Quite the contrary. It was heart-warming to be a part of such a network of people who knew each other personally and cared for each other so deeply. She envied these people who shared each other's burdens. The news about the stroke had sent them all into tears! In the city, close friends were few and most of the neighbours were strangers who knew little about you and cared even less. Not because they were bad people but because they were used to a different lifestyle, a rather cold and distant one, Jessie realized. Ever since the storm had hit, talk had been about the misfortunes of this or that neighbour, always spoken with empathy and distress.

Jessie loved living in Portmont but she had to admit that it had its cool impersonal side. She pictured herself living on a farm, visiting with friendly neighbours, and playing with their babies. She could see herself sharing their lifestyles, rejoicing about their pleasures and triumphs or even crying over their heartbreaks. She slipped into a peaceful reverie of warm friendships, intense euphoria and unequalled tranquility and joy.

Chapter 27

Jessie and Kaydee sat on the bed, chatting and flipping through the magazines that Jessie had brought with her. Then Kaydee paused. "You know, with all that has happened, I'd like to put some of my thoughts into my journal. Would you mind terribly if I just kind of hole up in the corner for a while? I like to keep it as up to date as I can, and lately so many things have been happening. I feel like I'm boiling over."

"No problem. Go right ahead. I'll just check out some of these magazines."

"I have my book of poems there too, if you're interested."

"Really?" Jessie squealed incredulously. "Just like that? You would let me read your poems?"

"If you want to," Kaydee said nonchalantly. "They may not be very good. Sometimes I just get these ideas in my head and I write them down. Usually I do them on a scratch pad first because I scribble so fast that it doesn't make sense so later I have to change or rearrange things. I have several poems. Also some stories."

Jessie was ecstatic. "Oh Kaydee, may I really read them? I would love to read your work." Jessie could not believe her ears. This was too good to be true. Kaydee had just casually offered to let her read one of her notebooks! Just like that, without any fanfare!

Kaydee looked mildly surprised. "Only if you want to. You might find them boring or mediocre and that's okay. I won't be offended. You can go back to the magazines anytime."

"Oh, I'm sure I won't be bored! Thank you, Kaydee."

"Kaydee, I'm going to the shed so watch the kids," Granny called from downstairs.

"Alright, Granny." Kaydee picked up her notebook.

"We better go on the deck, just in case the kids need us. It's hard to hear them from here."

Jessie picked up Kaydee's other notebook of poems and stories and followed Kaydee out onto the deck where they could see Jaynee and Alvin frolicking on the front lawn with Rusko. Dayna wiggled contentedly in the jolly jumper.

Closing the screen door behind them, the girls put the books on the deck table.

They settled at opposite ends of the table, each busy with their own project. Kaydee immediately immersed herself in her writing.

To Jessie this was the realization of her secret purpose for being here in the first place. Now she would get a glimpse of the Kaydee that Uncle Dusty was so certain existed only in that traumatized world that was secretly locked away. Perhaps now she would discover the source of that diffident timidity she had noted when she first met Kaydee when she arrived here.

As Jessie read through the poetry, she was astonished by its depth. Had this girl actually been considered a retard? Was she really only twelve years old? She found it difficult to imagine someone so young and unsophisticated, writing with such profundity and passion!

"Where did you learn to write like that? Your words, and your expressions convey such deep feelings. My heart skips because your words reach into my very soul. How did you compose such poems? They're the best I've ever read." Jessie was utterly incredulous.

Kaydee looked surprised by the questions. She stared at Jessie, trying to think of answers.

"I don't really know. I guess they just come to me. When Father was..." she paused, then continued, "before Father's accident, writing that poetry was the only thing that kept me sane. Now I just write because I enjoy it. I don't really work at it. I just write what comes into my mind. I read a lot of books. I love reading and I admire the writers that write them. I wish I could write like them. Do you like the poems, Jessie? Are they any good?"

"Good? Kaydee, they're fantastic! I love them!" Jessie was exuberant. "Kaydee, I work with my parents in the publishing business and I read a lot of submissions. Your poems move me to the core. I'd love to read your stories too if you will let me. In fact, if it would be alright with you, I would like to show your poetry to my Mom and Dad. I am sure they would love to read them." Jessie was certain that those poems merited publication somewhere. They were deep, spellbinding. They were just too good to be hidden away in someone's back pocket.

Kaydee's face flushed almost purple but her face beamed with unexpected pleasure and astonishment. "You mean it?" she exclaimed. "You really think they're good?"

"Yes, I mean it. I cannot imagine why you are so surprised. Would you mind letting me read your other writings? If they are as good as these poems... oh, I'm so excited, Kaydee."

Jessie could not contain herself. She tried to sound rational but her mind was soaring into the future. She had stumbled upon something significant here and it had the potential to impact on all their lives. Aware that poetry was a subjective art form, Jessie could not imagine a soul that could remain unaffected by Kaydee's poetry.

Kaydee was blushing profusely but she took in Jessie's enthusiasm with disbelief. Never had anyone sounded so zealous about anything she did before. It was true that Granny was always giving her positive affirmation, but Granny was prejudiced. Although Kaydee appreciated and enjoyed the compliments, they did not carry much weight. Mother tried to be positive but she was still too overburdened with her own problems to give Kaydee's writings her full attention. Her encouraging adulation was often given by rote, therefore it was not authentic.

But Jessie seemed genuinely interested. She seemed excited, in spite of herself. This was no put-on. Kaydee was flattered and delighted. All those times when she had hidden her notebook from Father seemed validated now. The memories flooded over her like a cold shower. If her poems were good, could her mother's poems have been even better? An overwhelming sense of loss made Kaydee's whole body shudder. Had her father destroyed something beautiful and precious?

"Kaydee, are you alright?" Jessie noted that involuntary shudder. She was watching Kaydee's pensive reverie with concern and apprehension.

"What? Oh, yes. Oh, I'm sorry. I was just thinking. Of course you may read my writings if you're interested. I always hid them from my father because I was afraid he would destroy them. Like he destroyed Mother's writings. But I don't have to hide them from you or your folks.

I just didn't expect that anyone would be interested. I'm glad you like them. I wrote them almost in defiance against Father and I didn't expect them to be special. Father always said I was stupid and would never amount to a 'pile of shit' as he put it. I guess I just wanted to prove that I was not retarded, and then I started to like writing so I just kept it up."

Jessie was too stunned to reply. She just stared at Kaydee in disbelief.

"Oh, Kaydee," she breathed huskily past the huge lump that had lodged in her throat.

Kaydee appreciated her empathy but declined her sympathy.

"That's okay. I'm fine now that he's not here to yell at us anymore. When he comes back..." her voice trailed off, her face went hard and hostile. She turned to her notebook with dogged determination and started writing again. Jessie waited and then went back to reading.

Jessie fairly devoured the writings. She was extremely excited. When they had cooked up this little experiment of theirs last week, none of Duganyks could have dreamed of the pinnacle of success this venture would encompass. Instead of the naive, possibly mentally ineffective country girl she had expected, Jessie had found a soulmate in Kaydee. This girl was intelligent, sincere, and so genuinely altruistic, that Jessie could not help but admire her, particularly in light of the hardships she had had to overcome. Totally unpretentious, she didn't even recognize the value or the potential of her own talent. To Jessie, friendship with this girl, whose lifestyle had been so vastly different from hers, was made even more gratifying because of their mutual passion for literature. This was a different level of interaction and amity. Above all else, it created that bond that Jessie found lacking with her city girlfriends.

The adults were in the shed, and the smaller kids didn't require their attention. Kaydee took Dayna, washed and put her to bed then returned to her writing. Now they had some uninterrupted time to themselves. When Kaydee put her notebook down, Jessie looked up at her with new-found respect.

"Kaydee, you must never stop writing," she said solemnly. "You are too good. You have a tremendous talent. And you haven't even had any formal training in that field – in any field really, from what I hear. Just think of what you could do with some training! Have you ever thought of pursuing a career in writing?"

"I never thought of anything like that. I only started writing this summer after I found out about my mother's writings. I'm not very smart, you know, I go to Special Education class." Kaydee hung her head, embarrassed to reveal her shameful secret. "Before that, I was lucky to just have time for reading, let alone writing. Father hated it if he saw me with a book. He would always find something for me to do, even if it was only to follow Alvin around. I read only at school, during recesses and in my room before I went to sleep. I never thought ahead," Kaydee ended, sounding wistful.

"Are you telling me this is only a couple months' worth of writing?" Jessie was flabbergasted. "How did you do it? And don't go saying you're not smart!" Jessie was vehement. She was aware of the responsibility Kaydee was carrying on the farm. She knew she did all sorts of work around the yard, the house, the garden and helped with the younger children. How did she find time to turn out this much writing over and above all her other duties?

"Don't forget this is vacation time. There is no school and no homework," Kaydee explained casually. "Besides, since Father has been gone, things are a lot quieter around here and I can write almost anytime I feel inspired. Nobody minds if I write as long as my work is done. I think Mother and Granny both like to see me write. I read things to them sometimes and they seem to enjoy listening to it."

Jessie got up to give Kaydee an affectionate hug. "And who can blame them? You just keep it up girl!"

Kaydee hugged her back. "Thanks Jessie. You're great for my ego," she laughed as Alvin came bounding up the deck, Rusko in hot pursuit.

"Okay, you guys. Cool it. Stop with the ruckus. Dayna is trying to sleep, you know," Kaydee admonished affably. "And that is where you are going, as of now! Come on Jaynee. Time for a bath and bed."

The next morning, Joey arrived early and told them he planned to work around the yard in anticipation of the arrival of the window men who were to install the two windows. Helen was pleased about that.

"Then I guess I better plan my housework around men this morning," she smiled at Joey.

"Well, two or three, at least," he grinned good-naturedly.

Katreena had given Helen Dr. Gorman's news last evening and Helen had taken it with the usual heavy sigh, so typical of all her reactions to any news from Dr. Gorman these days. However her face had paled when Katreena mentioned that the doctors thought that Michael might be fighting to get home. Her expression had remained pensive the rest of the evening.

Kaydee and Jessie were up with the adults when the phone rang. It was Dr. Gorman.

Helen took the call this time. Katreena and Kaydee waited patiently for the conversation to end so they could get the report. Joey stood by, not exactly involved but just as concerned because he felt he had an important stake in this scenario as well.

Helen hung up the phone and turned to her anxious audience with an uneasy frown creasing her forehead. "Well, Michael's fever has dropped some overnight, but it is still high. Dr. Gorman says that if they can get it stabilized, they would like to fly him to Winnipeg and treat him there. He thinks that Michael is fighting to come home and that is why he struggles. There is no way he can come home of course, but Dr. Gorman feels that his treatment might go better if he got family visits. Personally, I don't think a family visit will help at all."

A dead silence fell over the group as each member mulled over this new development and the consequences that such a move would generate. Although nobody voiced it, neither Helen, nor Katreena, nor Kaydee, were pleased to hear that news, though each felt too guilty to express their displeasure with it. Things had just settled into a peaceful and very comfortable routine, so these proposed new circumstances promised limitless stress and anguish for them all. Still, no one dared admit to wanting Michael to just stay away forever.

Joey was the first to break the distressing silence. "Well, the doctors must know what they are doing. Perhaps Michael could recover faster here. From what you have told me, Michael was very close to Alvin.

Would you be obliged to bring Alvin to visit Michael? Can Alvin handle seeing Michael before he has healed?"

Joey's question was answered with grimaces and judging by their expressions, Joey suspected that none of the women considered Michael's transfer back as "welcome news." Joey wondered about the man that could generate that kind of reaction from his family.

"Oh Joey," Helen sighed forlornly as tears welled up in her eyes. For a fleeting moment, Katreena thought Helen was about go to Joey and lean against him for support. Katreena imagined Helen and Joey in a comforting embrace, but Helen remained stoic. She bit back her tears and turned to the cupboards to start breakfast, sighing resignedly, "I guess we'll just have to deal with the situation as it arises."

Joey watched in bewilderment but nothing else seemed forthcoming and only a dead silence ensued. After waiting a while, he left for the shed.

The next couple of days seemed normal on the farm with everyone tending to their own duties. Katreena spent most of her time at the hospital or with Josie Archer so she only came home to sleep. Helen dreaded another call from Dr. Gorman but she did not call Toronto herself. Kaydee was uncommunicative on the subject of her father's possible reintroduction into their lives. Jessie surmised that she was not looking forward to visiting her father either but, realizing that Kaydee was fighting her own demons, she decided to wait till Kaydee was ready to talk about it herself. Kaydee clung to Jessie's amity almost desperately, eager to commiserate on almost any subject except her father's eminent return.

The window men came, installed the windows and left, promising to return in a week or two when the rest of the windows arrived from the factory. The roofers left word that it would be two or three weeks before they could get to KD Acres so Joey returned to his fieldwork but he worried about Helen. She was morose, as if she were wearing a heavy dark cloud on her shoulders and each call from Toronto seemed to make that cloud more ominous.

Jessie's little vacation was fast drawing to a close, and she was surprised to realize that she had not felt a single pang of homesickness since she came to the farm. Even better, she had achieved vital success in her original purpose for coming here in the first place. She would be going back with Kaydee's precious writings for her parents to read. Kaydee would start a new notebook. Jessie would bring the old one back, but she already had permission to make a copy of each and every page so that each of them could have one. Jessie was confident that publication would follow but did not wish to promise it until her parents had reviewed it.

Katreena was excited in spite of herself. Today, Dusty would be arriving at the farm to pick up Jessie and Katreena could barely contain her anticipation. Their relationship had blossomed over the last few weeks into a tender love that they both knew could not be denied. Ever since Michael's accident, Katreena had leaned on Dusty for support and he had given it to her so unreservedly that now she could not imagine her life without him. Whether on the farm, at her place or at his place, they had shared their time together and their love for each other grew with every passing day. Not since her days with Daniel, had she known this kind of happiness. Even concern for Helen and Josie's problems, could not dampen her euphoria about seeing Dusty. Her life was incomplete unless Dusty was near and she marvelled at how completely her life had changed in just the few months since she had met him. She had never expected to feel like this again, yet here she was, at fifty-eight, feeling like her life was just beginning and everything ahead was exciting and wonderful.

Her heart swelled at the memory of that unforgettable afternoon before the storm when Helen's distress call had catapulted them into yet another traumatic trip to KD Acres. They had had lunch with Janine and Vance and then spent the rest of the afternoon at Katreena's. It had been too hot to sit outdoors, so they had opted to watch Susan Hayward in "I'll cry Tomorrow" on TV in the comfort of the air-conditioned living room. Nestled against Dusty's shoulder, his arms tightly wrapped around her and his lips against her hair, Katreena was in such a state of bliss she could hardly concentrate on the screen. During the commercial, Dusty had kissed her tenderly. Then, backing off an arm's length, he looked deep into her eyes.

In a husky voice, he had told her, "Katreena, you know, these last few months I have known more happiness than I ever thought possible. You have completed my life, given me a reason to be. I cannot imagine life without you. I don't want a life without you. I..."

That was when Helen's call had interrupted them, telling them that the farm had been devastated by a hailstorm. Katreena had been so distressed by the news that Dusty had just put everything on hold.

"Let's go. We'll talk about this another time." They had simply grabbed their keys and driven right out to the farm to be with the family. Over the next couple of days, there had been no opportunity to discuss personal matters, because first the storm and then Fred Archer's stroke had pre-empted moments alone. The subject, therefore, had remained in the background but Katreena knew that Dusty had been about to propose marriage before all the tumult began. Now, she could hardly wait to see him again. She knew they would still have no "alone" time for a while because they would have to take Jessie back to Portmont later today. Still, she would be with Dusty again and that was all that mattered.

Katreena felt good that Kaydee and Jessie had hit it off so well. Something about this friendship was magical for Kaydee. Katreena could see it in her eyes. Katreena knew that Kaydee had shared her writings with Jessie. She had heard them discussing the subject and she was glad that Jessie had been allowed that privilege. Katreena didn't suspect that the plan had been concocted by Dusty and his family to secure Kaydee's validation and to solidify her future. He had been afraid to mention the arrangement in case it failed. He was genuinely concerned for Kaydee and wanted to avoid disappointment for everyone.

It was just before ten when Dusty's Buick pulled into the yard. Katreena fairly flew out to meet him. Helen watched their amorous embrace with a mixture of pleasure and envy. She was truly happy for her mother but for the first time in years, she felt a yearning for that same kind of closeness. She tried to remember the last time she had felt anything akin to love and she honestly could not remember any. There must have been those moments, she was certain, otherwise why would she have married Michael in the first place? Even she could not have married in the absence of feeling loved or at least the pretext of being cherished. Yet, those moments vanished because the pregnancy was such a stark declaration of her sin. Michael was embarrassed about it and blamed her for the absence of his neighbours' respect. Still, she had been sure she could make him come around but Michael's arrogance and rigid upbringing defeated all hope of that. His wounded pride could not get past the jibes and he retaliated by lashing out at her. Now all she could remember of her marriage to Michael was his insensitivity and her own unreasonable submission to his scornful denigration. Try as she might, she could not recall one honest-to-goodness loving embrace from Michael. It saddened her because she realized how deeply it had been buried under the onslaught of abuse that followed the marriage. How could she have been so naïve not to have recognized Michael's insincerity? She wasn't that stupid, was she?

Now, she looked at her Mother and Dusty, so engrossed in each other and she knew she wanted that ardour in her own life. Even Joey gave her respect. Until now though, she had not even considered such frivolities. Always, she had been too busy, too distraught, too sick or in too much misery to miss them. Now, Helen felt an acute sense of loss and grief at how her life had turned out. She wanted that glow that made her mother a vibrant woman. She wanted to feel her eyes sparkle with happiness and anticipation. She wanted to feel pleasure from within. No longer was "being content" enough. She wanted to be cherished, adored, and fulfilled. She wanted what her mother had but she knew it was not for her. There in Toronto, lay Michael with his face disfigured, his angry heart cold and hard, his mind unresponsive and his body lifeless. Not that Michael's disfigurement would have mattered if he could just show some manifestation of kindness in his demeanour, but wishing for kindness from Michael was like asking for an orchid to bloom on the Manitoba prairie in the middle of January.

If Michael returned to Winnipeg she would be obliged to visit him, unconscious and expressionless as she tried vainly to rouse him. And if she did manage to rouse him, he would probably berate her anyway. He might be more miserable than ever. Regardless of how Michael fared, Helen felt trapped in a loveless marriage to an insensitive man or possibly worse yet, to an ambulant, angry and abusive man. Either way her future was dismal!

Katreena and Dusty walked up to the house hand in hand. Katreena beamed up at Dusty as he said something to her in a low tone meant only for her ears. Jessie came running down the stairs and flew into Dusty's arms.

"Uncle Dusty, I heard you drive in. How are Mom and Dad?"

"Well hello to you too, Pumpkin," Dusty grinned as he gave her a big hug. "Your folks are fine and they're looking forward to seeing you. They missed you. Are you ready to come home, or should I even ask? You look pretty happy. How did you like your country vacation?"

"Oh Uncle Dusty, I loved it! Kaydee and I had a great time. We all did," she added laughing, as Jaynee ran up to them for a hug with her usual cheery "Me too, me too."

"Well like it or not, you better pack for home. We'll be leaving after lunch." Then to Katreena and Helen, "How is Mr. Archer?"

"He's still in the hospital," Katreena said, "but he's totally immobilized. He won't be going home for a while, certainly not if he doesn't improve a whole lot."

"I'm sorry to hear that. How is his wife?"

Katreena brought him up to date on the community news as they sat sipping coffee that Helen had brought out. Dusty expressed his regret then informed them that they would have to head out soon.

"I'd like to make Portmont before nightfall. We'll go to church with Della and Wayne, then we're all going fishing to Lake Aggassee. That okay with you girls?"

"Okay by me," Katreena volunteered immediately.

Jessie hesitated. "Well, I'll have to think about that." She loved the lake country, but she found fishing boring unless a friend came along and she was reluctant to commit to going along with only the adults.

"I know," Dusty groaned. "You want your options open because us old folks are boring. Don't worry. I saw that coming and I was prepared for it. No offence taken, eh, Katreena?" He pulled Katreena close against him and planted a kiss on her forehead.

"None at all," Katreena confirmed smiling at the apologetic look on Jessie's face.

"Any more news about Michael?" Dusty wanted to know.

Helen's mood plummeted as she gave him the update which was weighing so heavily on her mind these days. "Nothing definite, but Michael may be in Winnipeg before too long. Apparently he is fighting to get here. At least that is what Dr. Gorman thinks. Michael has been tearing at his bandages but they have never caught him doing it so they think he is aware of his surroundings but careful not to let them know it. Michael is just devious enough to do that."

"Oh, oh," Dusty sighed worriedly. "That sounds ominous. Sounds like he's angry or plotting something. Maybe he's been aware of things all along. Do you think that's possible?"

"I've considered that too," Katreena offered uneasily. "It would be like him to do it."

Helen was silent and Dusty could tell it was causing her considerable anxiety. Okay change of subject, he decided.

"I see you're still waiting for the back windows," Dusty observed. "How much longer?"

"Joey made all the arrangements. They should be here next week. The roofers are on a longer list however, so let's hope we don't get any rain in the meantime or we may be in for much more trouble." Helen relaxed with this topic. She was not overly traumatized by the storm or the inconvenience. Joey was in charge and she was confident that he was taking care of everything. Dusty was glad. They could all relax because Joey was on the job.

Jessie went upstairs to pack and Kaydee offered to help her mother with lunch but Helen shooed her away. "You go with Jessie. Enjoy her company while she's here. I can handle lunch, don't worry." Kaydee gave Helen a quick peck on the cheek and with a grateful "Thanks, Mom," raced upstairs after her friend.

Dusty left for the yard and Helen smiled at her mother. "Go on with him, Mom. I know you want to. I have everything under control here. You missed him, didn't you?" To Katreena's nod Helen added, "It's good to see you happy, Mom."

Helen was slicing the roast when Joey drove into the yard with the swather. He pulled right up to the gas tanks, refuelled, parked the swather near the driveway and went to the house to wash up for lunch.

"That's a beautiful crop of wheat you got on that quarter, Helen. Should yield close to forty per acre. Good thing that storm bypassed it. You ought to come out and see it in swath. You'd be very pleased," he told Helen on his way to the washroom.

He came back refreshed, and stood watching Helen toss the salad.

"Can I help?" he offered and without waiting for an answer went to the cupboard, got the dishes and started setting the table. Helen could not contain the flush that spread through her body like a wild fire.

She smiled at him, muttered a shy "Thanks, Joey" and just hoped that he did not notice her flushed cheeks. She was not used to having a man help in the kitchen. Michael would never have stooped to such a demeaning task, but she liked having Joey work alongside of her in this way. It felt warm, comforting and wonderful!

"You're more than welcome, Helen. You know I'll help you in any way I can."

Helen was sure her face must be purple by now. She turned to the stove to attend to the vegetables and the potatoes.

After lunch, they took their tea and everyone gathered on the deck where they sat around the patio table discussing the latest events. Joey was the first to break from the group.

"This is nice, but I better get back out on that field if I want that swathing finished today. You guys have a good trip home and have a great day fishing. In fact, have such a great day that next time you come here I get a taste of what you caught, hear?"

They all laughed. "You got it man," Dusty promised.

Dusty was next to make an exit. "We best be going too." Then to Katreena, "You'll want to stop at home to check things out before we leave for Portmont?"

Katreena nodded. "I think I had better pick up a few things."

Jessie and Kaydee embraced tearfully as they bid their goodbyes. Then with apologies from Katreena, they left Helen and Kaydee to do the dishes. Kaydee felt sad to see them leave, but Helen was secretly relieved. She was agitated by Joey's help at the table and needed time to sort out these tingly feelings that were assaulting her whole being. She could not do that with people around. She needed "alone" time for that.

With the dishes done, Helen put Dayna and Jaynee down for their naps. Alvin went out to play and Kaydee went to mow the lawn. Mercifully, Helen sat down on the lounger on the deck to collect her thoughts and to make sense out of this restlessness she was unable to quell. She could not understand this agitation. It was not anxiety nor excitement, yet her body quivered with weakness and a tingle ran up her spine as she recalled Joey setting the table for lunch. He had said he'd help in any way he can, but setting the table? Joey, a man, helping her set the table? That was something that invoked very strange feelings in Helen's very soul.

Chapter 28

Jessie was simply bubbling with excitement. There was no way she could wait till she got home to share her good news about Kaydee's writings. Sitting in the back seat, she contemplated whether she should broach the subject in front of Katreena or wait to tell Uncle Dusty alone. Well, she rationalized, she didn't necessarily have to speak of their original plan to get the writings. She could simply omit that information. It wasn't crucial to the report. After all, Kaydee had offered to share her notebooks with Jessie out of her own free will. That was not a lie. Portmont was hours away, and private conversation with Uncle Dusty was highly unlikely considering that Katreena was coming with them and would be staying till at least Monday.

Jessie decided to plunge ahead. Katreena would probably be happy about it anyway.

"Look what Kaydee gave me," she held the notebooks out for Dusty and Katreena to see.

Katreena recognized them immediately. Like a schoolgirl who had just been asked to the prom, she practically squealed with excitement.

"Kaydee's writings! Jessie, do you know what that means? Can you even begin to imagine? She trusts you. She values your opinion and she's willing to share her most intimate thoughts with you. Jessie, that is wonderful. Kaydee is opening up! She's been locked up inside herself for so long and she's never shown any self-confidence like this before."

Katreena could have hugged Jessie had she been in the front seat. This was the ultimate triumph; the dream come true; the rainbow's end!

"I cannot believe this is really true. You have no idea how thrilled I am that you girls hit it off. Kaydee needed a friend so badly, but she's never been close to anyone before. Well, you know, with Michael around, she never had a chance. Maybe now... oh Jessie, I'm absolutely thrilled you came out."

"Thank you, Mrs. Banaduk. I'm glad I came out too. I really enjoyed the week with Kaydee. She is wonderful and so talented but she doesn't even realize it. I told her I wanted my Mom and Dad to read her work.

She was surprised to think it was any good. But it is. I know it is and I am sure Mom and Dad will think so too. Do you think she'd mind if we published at least some of her work? I didn't say anything to her because I'm not certain, but I think it's good enough for publication in a couple of our magazines – maybe even a book of her own."

Dusty had not uttered a syllable throughout this discourse. He had actually had no opportunity to stick a word in edgewise, but he was glad that he was off the hook. He didn't like doing things behind Katreena's back but Jessie had brought the subject up so casually that his part in the original scheme may never even come up, well-intentioned though it was.

Katreena was now considering the ramifications of Jessie's suggestion. "Kaydee would certainly benefit from such validation. Michael always reinforced her worthlessness and her lack of intelligence. He called her a 'retard' and constantly stressed her incompetence. Kaydee came to believe him but after she found out about him burning Helen's journal she's been seething with anger at him for cheating Helen out of her birthright. I personally, would like to see her prove Michael wrong on all counts but I realize that is a purely selfish wish on my part. However aside from that, I also think that getting published would be vindication for her, as well as a kind of atonement for her mother's grievance. I can't speak for her of course, but in my opinion, I think it would be wonderful – if it were possible, that is."

"I have heard some of her poems and stories and I thought they were good too, so I think it's a pretty distinct possibility myself," Dusty interjected.

"I can't wait to let Mom and Dad see these," Jessie was ecstatic. "I can't imagine how Mr. Boyer could say Kaydee was a retard. Besides being untrue, it was also very cruel."

"Oh yes, Michael was cruel alright. You can't even imagine how cruel! Anyway, that's water under the bridge now. We have no idea what will be happening to Michael but the important thing is trying to repair the damage he caused. Certainly the publication of Kaydee's work would be a start, if Kaydee allowed it. It would put her in the limelight though, and Kaydee has always been very shy and withdrawn. Till now, that is."

Katreena appended reflectively.

Jessie's insight into Kaydee's personality and the empathy she felt for her were both pleasant surprises to Katreena. The two girls had established a close personal rapport and Katreena was overcome with a profound gratitude to Jessie for – what? Being Kaydee's friend, confidante, aficionado, advocate, promoter? Yes, all of those things, and more. Jessie was the answer to all their prayers. Kaydee had opened up her heart, and Jessie was responsible for that.

Katreena did not question Jessie's sincerity. She knew it was sound. She had only got to know Jessie recently, but between what she observed and what Dusty had told her about the girl, she was convinced there was no guile in Jessie. She was true blue. It seemed almost too good to be true, Kaydee finding someone like Jessie to encourage and perhaps even advocate for her.

"She has only been writing since the beginning of July?" Jessie asked unbelievingly.

"As a matter of fact it was after she found out about Michael burning Helen's journal that she started journaling, as sort of an act of defiance against Michael, though Michael had no idea she was doing it. He would have destroyed it had he known about it."

"When did she have time and how did she get to be so good?" Jessie wanted to know.

Katreena pondered over that question. Then slowly, she replied, as much to herself as to Jessie. "Well, she has always been a voracious reader, and although she could not advance in class, her reading skills certainly did not suffer. Since she could not socialize with anyone, she spent her time with books. I doubt there are many books in that library that Kaydee has not devoured. She's a fast reader and she enjoys literature so I guess writing came naturally when she let herself go. Since Michael's accident, she's been writing at every opportunity."

"She certainly has done a lot of it," Jessica said pensively. "She's a natural!"

"Originally, it was a means of vengeful purging," Katreena explained. "She was so incensed at Michael that her writing was a sort of an emotional catharsis for her. It was a release that proved to be profoundly essential to her emotional stability. Now I think she does it simply because she enjoys doing it. With Michael out of the picture, the angst is not there anymore."

Jessie thought that over.

"I think I understand what you are saying," she said sadly. She was remembering Kaydee telling her how callous her father had been and how she did not want him to come back.

"Kaydee has had a lot to deal with in her twelve years but it's made her perception of the world much keener than other kids' her age. She may not be street wise but in certain ways she is very life savvy."

"Amen to that," Dusty cut in. "I can attest to that. The way she has taken over since the accident, sometimes I cannot envision the girl you used to talk about."

"She has come a long way, that's for certain. But frankly," Katreena ventured, "I'm still unsure how she would take to stepping into the limelight if she got published. Let's just hope that Michael does not enter the picture to ruin this for her. It would kill everything for her!"

They explored various scenarios regarding Kaydee's future, and time passed quickly. Before they knew it, they were in Katreena's driveway. While she went to pack, Jessie and Dusty sat on the deck to scan the pages of Kaydee's work. Dusty was surprised and impressed by the volume as well as the intensity of Kaydee's collection. Until this moment, he had not realized what it was that Katreena had been so excited about. Now it was starting to make sense. Katreena had always maintained that Kaydee was exceptional but he had not realized to what extent. For a twelve-year-old, these writings carried the weight of the world between their lines. Secretly Dusty made a vow to add whatever assistance he could to Kaydee's writing career.

Katreena was out shortly, toting a small overnight bag plus a garment bag with her clothes. They packed that into the car and left for Portmont. Della was expecting them for supper and Dusty didn't want to keep her waiting. Della was an excellent cook and prided herself on her culinary talents but she required precision timing to achieve superiority in her creativity. Her disapproval was difficult to conceal if someone's tardiness ruined her meticulous efforts. Her otherwise gracious nature sometimes got stretched too close to the breaking point if one did not have a legitimate excuse for being late. Dusty had learned that lesson very soon after Wayne and Della got married and he was not about to repeat that misdemeanour. He loved his sister-in-law dearly but he knew his parameters and he observed them diligently. It was just easier that way.

They arrived at Wayne and Della's shortly after five and while the women worked in the kitchen, Wayne and Dusty went out to the garage to pack the fishing gear for tomorrow's trip to Lake Aggassee. As soon as they were out of earshot, Dusty could contain himself no longer and went on to inform his brother about Kaydee's capabilities.

"Jessie has the writings with her and she will be giving you more info but I read enough to think that this could put DWD Publishing on the map. You'll be reading it yourself soon, but it's deep, man, real deep! And from a twelve-year-old! That kind of publicity could do big things for us – if Kaydee agrees to it. Katreena feels Kaydee might be too reticent to go for it. Katreena does not know that Jessie was a plant and frankly, I'd like to keep it that way. The two girls hit it off really well and Jessie is genuinely enthusiastic about Kaydee's possibilities."

Wayne listened attentively to his brother's raving. It was interesting because Dusty had never really taken that active a role in the publishing end of the business, preferring instead to be involved more in the financial aspect of DWD Publishing. Now he seemed to have acquired more than a passing interest in the publication. Not that Wayne minded input from Dusty. Spotting great talent was always an issue in this business and if Dusty had discovered something that could raise their profile, then it was good for everybody.

Jessie showed up at the door. "Supper's on the table and Mom wants you to come in."

Dusty and Wayne purposely kept off the subject of Kaydee during supper. Since Katreena was not aware of their original plans for letting Jessie stay on the farm to check on Kaydee, they didn't want the conversation to head in that direction in case Della inadvertently revealed it somehow. Wayne wanted to talk to Jessie to get her slant on things first and he also wanted to read Kaydee's work for himself. Right after the supper dishes were done, Dusty and Katreena prepared to leave.

"Jessie has some reading for you guys to do," Dusty told Della and Wayne. "Katreena and I will be waiting to hear your verdict, so we're going to leave you alone to form your own opinions." With a wink at Katreena, he linked his arm through hers and walked her out the door.

Back at his place, Dusty told Katreena to go sit in the living room and wait for him. She looked at him inquisitively but he put a finger to her lips to shush her, then in mock authority, pointed her to the couch. She stifled her question and, mimicking meek obedience, walked over to the couch to sit there with her hands folded in her lap. She laughed as he shook a finger at her, bidding her "sit" while he disappeared into the kitchen. She heard him go outdoors but she sat there waiting to see what he was up to. Within a few minutes, she heard him come back in. As he busied himself in the next room, she continued to sit and wait until he reappeared in the living room again, carrying a tray with a vase of pink day lilies, a bottle of champagne, and two glasses. Ceremoniously, he put the tray on the coffee table. With a big flourish, he uncorked the champagne, filled the two glasses and handed one to Katreena.

"We have some unfinished business honey, and just to make sure we are not interrupted this time, I have taken the phone off the hook. If you are considering a protest, let me make it clear that it is only for a couple of hours. I will not be keeping you incommunicado for the whole night, I promise." Dusty sat down next to her and put his arm around her shoulders, pulling her close against him. "I just want you to myself for now. Do you mind?"

Katreena snuggled against his shoulder. "No, I don't mind." She answered simply. "I have missed you. I didn't mean to put you off, really, it's just that things keep happening and I find myself torn in several directions sometimes."

"Don't apologize, sweetheart. I understand. I'm not blaming you and I'm not complaining. I just need to talk to you. I miss you when we're apart. I love you Katreena. You must know how much I love you."

"Dusty, sweetheart. I love you too. You know I do. I hate it when we have to be apart too. These last couple of months, you have been such an anchor for me. I cannot imagine how I would have got through it without you. Just four months ago, I actually thought that my life was fine. Now I realize just how empty it really was."

Dusty hesitated, swallowed and then plunged on. "Katreena, I have never met anyone like you before but I knew from the moment I met you that you were different. There was a chemistry there that I was unable to explain or control. That kind of chemistry is rare. I don't want to lose this opportunity and I don't want to waste time. I want to experience every minute of every day with you. What I'm trying to say is, I want to marry you. I can't picture my life without you. Would you agree to marry me and be my wife? Please say 'Yes' Katreena."

Katreena could not contain the tears of happiness that spilled from her eyes. She had wanted to hear those words so much; had waited for them so patiently. Holding her glass of champagne safely in one hand she put her other hand up to caress his face.

"Dusty, sweetheart! Of course, I want to marry you. I can't picture my life without you either. I've been waiting for you to ask me for weeks now but I was afraid my family problems might make you question taking on such responsibilities."

"Katreena, I want that responsibility. I want to lighten every burden you carry. I promise to do everything in my power to make you happy for as long as I live." Dusty could hardly contain himself. He forgot about the glass of champagne she was holding as he crushed Katreena against him, sating his hungry longing for her.

Suddenly Katreena pulled away from his embrace. At his look of shock, she started to laugh. "I love you sweetheart and I will marry you but first, I must wash this champagne off my dress and this couch, just in case we decide that we want to keep it as part of our home."

With a look of utter surprise, Dusty suddenly realized that in their enthusiasm, they had spilled the champagne onto Katreena's lap and onto the couch they were sitting on.

Katreena dashed to the bathroom for some towels. Dusty called after her.

"Maybe we'll just have to buy a new couch. As for that dress, I think I like the way it clings to you. Let's just keep it that way."

Katreena came back, swatted at him with the towel and started mopping at the spill but he grabbed at her again. "Aw forget the couch, woman. Come here where you belong."

Katreena stopped, then impulsively, flung the towel away and melted into his open arms.

Hours later, they were still making plans as they lay in each other's arms regaling in the sheer delight of their togetherness. Katreena was astounded that she could feel this complete again.

Chapter 29

"Mrs. Boyer, this is Dr. Gorman. How are you doing?"

Helen's heart stopped mid-beat. It always did when Dr. Gorman called. She knew it had to be more bad news.

"I'm fine, Dr. Gorman. What news do you have for me today?" she asked guardedly.

There was an audible gulp at the other end of line and Helen stiffened. An ominous shudder rippled through her body. She could tell by that gulp that Dr. Gorman was searching for words to soften the blow.

"Well, Mrs. Boyer," Dr. Gorman was hesitant. "We think that Michael might be ready to be moved back to Winnipeg, perhaps even as early as the end of this week."

"I see." Helen's heart was hammering in her chest and she felt the blood drain from her face. This should be good news, but she felt like she was suffocating. Her whole body felt weak and shaky. She grabbed the table for support and sank into the chair beside it. Kaydee was beside her in a moment.

"Mom, what's the matter?" she called out in alarm.

Doggedly, Helen fought for control. She had to be rational! "It's okay, honey. Your father is coming home, that's all." Then into the phone, "You were saying, Dr. Gorman?"

"Well Michael is regaining consciousness, though he's not rational. He's not speaking, at least nothing that we can understand, but he is definitely awake. He is incoherent but we think that he is fighting to go home, which he cannot do, of course. Since small country hospitals are not equipped to handle major cases like Michael's, he needs to be in a major trauma unit so we would send him to Bethune Sciences Centre. That's much closer and you can drive up there for the day and be back by night. We thought perhaps some family visits might help to calm him down. He struggles against the restraints, causing continuous multiple contusions to his body. In addition, he tears at the bandages, inflicting more abrasions to skin that can't heal from his assaults. We can only restrain him so much and drugging him into submission is not a good option. I have conferred with two neuro-specialists here and the consensus is to try sending him back. You can visit him more readily there and we hope that will pacify him so that he can concentrate his efforts on the healing process. When the wounds are healed, we would then bring him back here for surgery to repair the scars on his face." Dr. Gorman paused, waiting for Helen to make a comment.

Helen remained silent, Dr. Gorman spoke again. "Are you alright, Mrs. Boyer?"

"Yes. Yes, Dr. Gorman. I'm alright, thank you. We'll do the best we can when Michael comes to Bethune Centre. Is there anything else?" Helen was desperate to get this call over with.

"No, that is about all for now. You take care now Mrs. Boyer and good luck. I will call if there are any problems with the details of the transfer. Bye for now."

Helen hung up the phone and sat staring at Kaydee who had been rooted to the spot ever since Helen told her Michael was coming home. Kaydee's face was pale, drawn and expressionless. The news was only mildly unexpected, but it was extremely distressing to both of them! Neither one wanted Michael back in their lives but neither one dared to admit it because of the burden of guilt such feelings evoked.

Kaydee's hatred for her father had made her want him out of their lives. But not **dead** out of the way, just out of their lives. She still felt guilty for wanting him gone. And the worst of it was that even now, when she had the opportunity to forgive and move on, to purge herself of the guilt, she felt resentful about having that opportunity presented to her at all. How could she be so heartless, so unremorseful? That was her father's forte, not hers. Was she that much her father's daughter that she would revert to genetics so unmistakably? That would be the cruellest joke of all – to emulate her father. The very thought of that made her shudder with revulsion. Somehow, she had to make her peace with this situation. His return obviously was eminent. Could she just forgive and forget? Wasn't that asking too much? To offer her a taste of this freedom, this peace, this respect, only to have it wrenched out of her grasp. That was the ultimate injustice! Yet, she reminded herself, this situation had been inevitable right from the beginning. She had known it was coming. They all had! It had basically been a matter of "when." Wishful thinking was not a luxury she could afford. Kaydee sighed resignedly. Now it was merely a question of how bad it would get and how soon!

In the meantime, Helen was struggling with her own demons. For thirteen years, she had been loyal and obedient to Michael, no matter how badly he had treated her or her children. She had closed her eyes, had fenced in her heart and let evil rule their lives until it had sucked the lifeblood out of their very souls. She had buried goodness and decency without even a marker to indicate that they had once existed. She had allowed the ruination of her whole family in order to compensate for her acutely critical error in judgment and her failure to recognize the insincerity of this man, with whom she had committed the error.

She thought back – way back. Why had she married Michael in the first place? How could she have thought she was in love with someone who was so insensitive in his dealings with people? Even after discovering that she was pregnant, there had to have been some indication that Michael had serious character flaws. How could she have been so blind? She could have avoided years of heartache for herself, her mother and her children by walking away from the situation before she became irrevocably embroiled with the man. How could she have allowed the deplorable situation to continue for so long?

Then another image dawned on her. Would she be willing to go back to that situation again now? These last couple of months, she had had a taste of the good life. Was it going to be snatched away from her again?

As vivid recollections engulfed her, she felt a surge of overpowering anger – anger at Michael, anger at herself, anger at life and its injustice. Michael's irate countenance loomed before her and she shivered involuntarily. Goosebumps rippled over her body and cold beads of perspiration broke out all over her skin. Not again! She didn't want Michael to come back! Her life was good now. She didn't want anything to complicate it, certainly not the intrusion of Michael into it! But what could she do? A feeling of hopelessness overwhelmed her. She was trapped, trapped by a very bad decision made all those years ago.

Then a thought occurred to her. What if Michael had to remain in the hospital indefinitely? She could handle going to see him there as long as she didn't have to bring him home. Now she was being absurd, she realized. She was grasping at straws, flimsy straws to be sure, but everything she sought was not outside the realm of possibilities. When she had last seen Michael, he had been totally unresponsive. Now the doctor was saying that he was "incoherent and not rational." What if he never became rational? Surely she would not be obliged to take him home if he remained mentally unstable. Dr. Gorman's assessment of him was that he was angry and distraught. Little did Dr. Gorman know that he was describing Michael's "normal" state of mind. Michael was always angry and distraught. That was what had landed him in this condition in the first place and that was why she did not want him to come home! Unless Michael came back a loving and benevolent man, Helen could not picture herself welcoming him back. There were too many heartless memories to erase, too many demons to slay and too many emotions to conquer.

Michael could never be loving or benevolent. With a pang, Helen realized the void that Joey had filled in her life was the void that Michael's callousness had created over the years. Now there was too much pain and anguish that could never be forgotten. Helen knew she never wanted to go back to a life with Michael, regardless of his condition. Joey had opened a door, had shown her a new way and now she did not want to go back to the old way.

"Mom, are you alright?" Kaydee broke into Helen's reverie. She had waited for Helen to compose herself but Helen had remained silent for so long that Kaydee became alarmed.

Helen yanked herself back to reality. "Oh. Oh, Kaydee. Sorry, honey. I was just considering various possibilities of your father's return. To be perfectly honest with you, I am dreading it and I feel positively wicked about it."

Kaydee knelt down and wrapped her arms tightly around her mother. "I know, Mom. I feel that way too," she confessed.

Helen understood. She had paid dearly for her own teenage folly. She had earned the punishment that she so willingly took all those years, but her children were innocent victims. There was no denying that her folly had extracted an insurmountable sacrifice from Kaydee. How could any decent mother have allowed such abuse on her own child?

"When is he coming back?" Kaydee pulled up a chair near her mother. She needed to get the all the information. She had heard only one side of the phone conversation and that aroused a whole barrage of questions.

Helen repeated Dr. Gorman's words. They were indelibly etched into her brain. Kaydee felt relieved that "home" did not really mean "home" because Bethune was three hundred miles away. Still it was too close for comfort. They sat and discussed the various possibilities and scenarios. The potential for Michael to revert to form if he returned was looming dark and ugly in their future and they both felt powerless to stop its assault. Yet, for the first time in Kaydee's life, she felt she could bare her soul to her mother, could purge herself of that secret malice in her heart, and her less than charitable hopes for her father's permanent departure from their lives. It felt good to know that her mother was listening, not condemning. It felt wonderful to have her mother as a confidante.

When Joey came home for lunch, Helen watched him surreptitiously out of the corner of her eye. He strode across the yard toward the house and she could hear him cheerfully whistling a melody that Helen immediately recognized as the lilting old fifties tune, "There's A Bluebird On Your Windowsill" that Wilf Carter used to sing.

"Hi Helen, Kaydee," he greeted as he walked in the door and headed for the washroom to clean up. "How are you girls doing today?" As usual, he had come in early this morning, fuelled up and driven out of the yard before the family was up and about. Actually, Helen had been up but she had just got out of the shower. She usually didn't get out of the house till her morning ritual of house chores was complete and Joey never came into the house in the mornings. He routinely had his breakfast with his grandmother, who obviously got up at some unholy hour of the morning.

They had fallen into this pleasantly relaxed routine soon after Joey had come to work at KD Acres. Helen found the routine pleasant and reassuring because it was devoid of tension and uncertainty. However it had been too good to last. She had known this moment would come and yet she had permitted herself to be lulled into this false sense of security that allowed her to dream of a life that was different. The tranquility of the past few weeks was about to end. With Michael attaining even the most infinitesimal involvement in their lives again, the turmoil would be back. Even if Michael's negativity did not reach the vocal or physical stages, it was bound to have a disheartening impact on all their lives. The oppressive memories were all still there. They could not be obliterated. The grizzly apparition of their past life appeared before her like a dark shadow. If Michael returned, their future would revert to that unspeakable hell again. They would continue their atonement for that indiscretion she had committed thirteen years ago! A heavy sigh escaped her throat in spite of her attempt to stifle it.

Joey sensed something wrong in the atmosphere as soon as he returned to the room after washing up. Helen and Kaydee wore sombre expressions that could not be disguised or concealed and the cloud of gloom was unmistakably thick and heavy. Joey had gotten to know the family quite well in the last few weeks and this kind of anxiety was ominous. He felt his heart knot. Something was seriously wrong.

"What's happening?" he asked apprehensively as he looked from Helen to Kaydee then back again. "You look like the end of the world is at hand."

Helen hesitated, looked at Kaydee, then at Joey. There was no way she could make this sound like a casual announcement. She had to say the words to give credence to this issue, declare its reality, no matter how much she wanted to deny it.

"They are sending Michael back to Winnipeg at the end of the week," she stated, her voice sounding lifeless and stilted.

Joey froze. He had never met the man, but from all the conversations he had had with neighbours and friends, this man must have been some sort of merciless tyrant. Joey had heard via the local grapevine that Michael had almost literally destroyed Helen – body, mind and soul! Even his own grandmother, who never spoke evil about anyone, who was the most charitable woman he knew, had called Michael "a very hard man to live with." But beyond that, it was the family's behaviour at the mention of Michael that revealed Michael's character more clearly than any words could. It was their demeanour that told the unequivocal story. Their reticence to talk about him was enigmatic. This news, that should have brought joy to a family under normal circumstances, sent them instead, into this morbid depression. What kind of person was this man that had this kind of effect on his own family?

"Oh." Joey stared at them. He could not think of one decent word to add. He would have liked to comfort them somehow, tell them all would be all right, but that would be inappropriate and probably even untrue. Obviously, life with Michael could never be all right, Joey thought. He wished he could alleviate their despondency but he had no idea where or how to begin. Finally, all he could come up with was a feeble "Is there anything I can do to help?"

Helen's sad eyes met his. "Thank you, Joey. You're already doing it. Other than that, there is nothing anyone can do. Michael will not be coming home for a while anyway. He has to heal first. If, and when, he does come home, we will just have to deal with it."

"Promise you'll tell me if I can help." Joey's eyes bored deep into hers, imploring her to confide in him, allow him to be there for her.

Meekly, Helen nodded. She knew Joey was sincere. She knew he wanted to help and she dared not suspect that he could be much more than a sympathetic ear for her. But there was Michael. She was married to the man and no matter how much she fantasized a peaceful life with Joey, she had to resolve her personal commitment to Michael before she could even let herself think in any other terms.

By this time, Kaydee had everything on the table and they sat down to eat. Helen, Kaydee and Joey ate in silence. Alvin and Jaynee chattered on, oblivious to being practically ignored but they were a welcome diversion for the adults who were each engrossed in their own personal torment. Alvin had questioned his mother and sister earlier about something being the matter but had casually accepted their denial. Jaynee was her usual picture of serenity, blissfully unaware that life was anything but wonderful.

Joey was reluctant to go back out to the field immediately after the meal was finished. Normally that was what he always did but today, he could not bring himself to leave. This family needed consolation and he wanted to provide it but he felt inadequate and helpless. As Helen and Kaydee tended to the children, cleared the table and washed the dishes, Joey continued to sit in his chair contemplating potential courses of action. Alvin and Jaynee went out to play and Kaydee took Dayna for her nap. Helen sat on a chair at the other end of the table.

"Joey," she began gently, "I'm sorry if we burdened you with our problems. I don't want you worrying about us. It's our problem and we must deal with it. You have shown this family how good life can be and I appreciate that much, much more than you can ever even imagine but it is unfair of us to saddle you with our troubles. Please don't be upset."

Joey wished he could explain to Helen what was going on in his mind but truth be known, he didn't know himself. He had known this woman only a short time, but already he felt her pain deep down inside him. That was not explicable to him, to her, nor to anyone else.

"I'm not upset with you, Helen. It's just that I want to help and I don't know how to do that." Then realizing how ineffective he sounded, he said sadly, "I best get back to the field."

Helen watched Joey leave. He was such a caring man, deeply sincere and genuinely good. He was reliable, highly principled, sensitive and positive in his outlook on life. He was the kind of man she should have married, not a callous, self-centered egotist who relished putting everyone else down. How could she ever have thought she was in love with Michael? Why did she not recognize his shortcomings before it was too late? How could she have allowed him such control over her? What a waste her life had been! And poor Kaydee! Forced to endure such cruelty all those years with no sympathy or understanding from anyone, least of all her own mother.

Kaydee's arm on her shoulder brought Helen out of her reverie. "Are you okay, Mom?" Kaydee's eyes bored into hers, full of concern and sympathy. This child, for whom she had showed so little concern when

Michael's cruelty had so denigrated her, was now offering her sympathy and concern. What a paradox life could be! She realized that she had made a major faux pas in the management of her life and now she, and she alone, had to make a decision on how the rest of her life was going to evolve. She had seen a ray of sunshine these last few weeks with Joey and now she felt this urgent need to grab hold of it, savour it and never let it go. How she would do this, she had no idea, but do it, she must. That knowledge was irrefutable.

"I'm fine sweetheart," Helen wrapped her arms around her daughter. "I'm fine. Somehow, we have to get through this terrible time, but this time, I promise you that things have to be different. They **have** to be, honey. I don't know yet how, but we're going to make them better." Tears ran down her cheeks with wild abandon and Kaydee squeezed her as they clung together in their despair. In a week, she would be seeing Michael and only God knew how that would go, but she knew that no matter what, she would not let Michael ever intimidate her again. She would never allow herself to be that vulnerable. She had to take charge of her life and steer it in the direction which was best for her and for her children. It was time!

Chapter 30

Michael was being flown back to Winnipeg today and Helen's heart had been pounding ever since she had heard about it. She was emotionally exhausted. Aware of the turmoil this situation would create, Katreena and Dusty had come to KD Acres as soon as they had heard the news. They wanted to be there with Helen when she went to see Michael at the hospital for that first visit. Katreena could only guess at the anxiety Helen was feeling these last four days. Last night, Katreena had heard Helen get up several times. In fact, Helen had slept very little ever since that fateful call from Dr. Gorman when he had told her that Michael was being shipped back. She had imagined various scenarios of that visit and each successive one had stressed her out more than the previous one had.

She didn't know what to expect or what she should be prepared for. Would Michael respond to her with anger, his usual disdain or would he just ignore her, not acknowledge her at all? Still, Dr. Gorman said he was "conscious but incoherent," so she should expect some kind of reaction from him. How would she respond to him? She could not afford to capitulate to him again. She knew that. But was she strong enough to withstand his harangues without crumbling? And what if he was docile and happy to see her? Even that scenario set her up for an anxiety attack.

To be completely honest, Helen realized she just did not want to see Michael, no matter what his reaction was. She did not feel proud about that. She was his wife. She had promised to "love, honour and obey." But had she not exhausted that avenue during her marriage to him? How much more did God want from her? Could she forgive and forget now that he was ill? And even if she did, would it change their future? If the future was merely a continuation of the past, could she just bury those unresolved resentments which she bore towards Michael now?

Worst of all, Helen could not disclose her feelings to anyone. Outside of that initial outburst to Kaydee that first day, Helen had not articulated her secret wish for Michael's complete disappearance from their life. She was quite confident that her mother and her daughter shared that wish but she felt ashamed and sinful about harbouring it herself. She tormented herself with guilt and remorse, vacillating between wishful thinking and self-recrimination, fantasizing and self-loathing.

Breakfast was a quiet affair. Dusty and Katreena made feeble attempts at light conversation but only Joey responded and that was only half-heartedly. Even Jaynee and Alvin sensed the tension and ate in subdued silence, not daring to upend the tenuous peace that everyone deemed so transitory. The impending visit with Michael superceded all other thoughts and subjects and Dusty finally gave up all efforts to evade the topic and just fell silent. They did not want the kids to know about Michael's return so that subject was off limits. However, it was just too overpowering and no one could concentrate on anything else.

Kaydee kept watching Helen surreptitiously, half expecting her to burst into uncontrollable weeping or worse yet, crawl into that listless shell she had used as her refuge, just a couple of months ago. Of the two, Kaydee would have rather had her mother blubbering like an idiot than the alternative because showing emotion was healthier. It was a sign of a functional mind. Everyone was aware that Helen was going through an emotional upheaval, yet there was nothing anyone could do for her other than be available to listen to her, if and when she was ready to talk.

As soon as the last spoonful was done, the kids took off for the outdoors. Joey got up, ready to head for the field. Before leaving, he approached Helen, squeezed her shoulder and said soothingly, "Good luck Helen. I hope everything will go well for you. I have faith in your courage and stamina. I know you can make it through this. Be strong and take care of yourself, okay?" And without a word to anyone else, he walked out the door.

Katreena and Dusty exchanged guarded glances. Dusty knew Katreena was hoping for a liaison between Helen and Joey. This was an encouraging sign, though how to deal with Michael under those circumstances could present much more than just an awkward challenge. But that was not even the issue at hand. It was the uncertainty of this initial visit with Michael that was stressing them all out. It could introduce a whole new set of problems. Certainly Helen's distress about the visit seemed to presuppose the imminent dawning of more problems.

Kaydee had noted Joey's solicitous gesture but Mother had barely uttered an audible "Thank you," to him. She was oblivious to his gesture of support. Still, Kaydee could not help comparing Joey to her father, in whom kindness was such an unattainable trait.

"I'd better get ready," Helen said simply and left for the bedroom. Kaydee went to help her.

At the closet door, Helen seemed totally disoriented. "Kaydee, what should I wear?"

"Mom, don't worry. You'll be alright. You can do it. Here, why don't you wear this green skirt and this cream coloured top? They look good on you now that you have filled out so nicely. Come on, I'll help you."

Kaydee knew just how anxious Mother was about this visit. Hopefully this was not an omen of things to come. She wished she could spare her mother this ordeal but there was nothing she could do except try to imbue her with some inner strength to counter her father's negative effect.

"Just remember Mom, you're much stronger now. He can't hurt you anymore. Remember what we've been through these last couple of months. Look at our life now. Mom, he can't make you go back now! Joey believes in you. You can't let him down. We all believe in you. You can't let us down. Please Mom, don't let Father scare you like this. You're strong now, he's the one who's weak. Don't let him turn that around," Kaydee begged. Somehow, she had to erase this fear from her mother's eyes. She just had to! She would not let her father ruin their lives again.

Helen heard the anguish in Kaydee's voice. Her daughter was pleading with her to stand firm. Kaydee had endured such abuse at the hands of her father, without sympathy or intervention from her mother. She had as much reason to fear Michael as Helen had, yet here she stood, desperately beseeching her mother to maintain fortitude. Kaydee was right, Helen realized. It was she who had the power now, not Michael. If – and when – Michael came home, it was **up to her to reject** his cruelty. It was up to **her** to end this cycle of abuse.

"You're right, Kaydee. I cannot let him win. We have come too far. I will not give that up. I'm going to go there and face whatever he dishes out. I will show him that I am not afraid of him anymore and that I am as good a person as anybody else!"

Kaydee threw her arms around Helen's neck and hugged her tightly. "I'm so happy to hear you say that, Mom! I'm proud of you. And Joey will be too. He cares about us all, you know."

"Yes, honey, he cares about us all."

Katreena and Dusty were unprepared for the appearance of confidence in Helen's manner when she and Kaydee returned to the kitchen but Katreena breathed a sigh of relief at seeing it.

"I guess I'm ready to face the music," Helen said wryly. "It's half past nine now. That gives us four-and-a-half hours to get there and get the doctor's report before we see Michael."

The kids waved goodbye as Dusty steered his Buick out onto the road. Kaydee sighed then went to check on Dayna but the child was still napping. She got her notebook and sat down on the deck to enter the latest events into her journal.

Helen's silence was worrying Katreena and that made Dusty uneasy. They had made tentative plans for an October wedding – Thanksgiving Day weekend hopefully – but had not yet broached the subject to Helen nor to Wayne and Della. Now Michael's arrival on the scene could alter their plans. Dusty was not looking to give Katreena's family a hard time, but he was not willing to accept a postponement. He wanted to get on with their lives as soon as possible. Certainly Michael's situation should not be a complicating factor in their plans. He could acknowledge the fact that Helen would require support during this crucial time but he wanted to be at Katreena's side, as part of the family, not as an outsider, standing in line, waiting for the crumbs of Katreena's free moments. Michael was like an albatross around their necks and Dusty seriously wished he could shake loose of that impediment. However he was just borrowing trouble here and he knew that. They hadn't even seen Michael yet. Who knew how that would go? Dusty was pretty certain it would bring problems, but hopefully they would not be insurmountable. "Think positive," he admonished himself.

In the back seat, Helen relaxed as the car purred along on the smooth highway. Soon she had dozed off, her head against the pillow that Katreena had purposely put there just in case. Katreena winked to Dusty indicating the sleeping figure in the back and he nodded approvingly. They rode on in silence to let Helen catch up on those past lost nights. Helen slept for over three hours before Katreena noticed her sitting up straight, still pensively quiet.

"Are you alright, Helen?" Katreena could not take the suspense any longer. She had to know what was behind her daughter's silence.

Helen's head snapped to attention as if she'd been aroused from a dream. She looked absent-mindedly at her mother, collecting and sorting her thoughts into meaningful words.

"You know Mom, I'm dreading this visit for so many reasons. First of all, I know his face has not healed yet so that is going to be awful to see. But that is a minor factor. It is his reaction that I fear the most. I do want him to recognize me and to react to me. But what if he reacts with his usual anger? I cannot go back to the way things were. I owe it to my family to stand up to him and stop him in his tracks. But will I be able to do that? Can I honestly say to him, 'Stop it! I will not accept your abuse anymore.'...? Have I changed that much in the last couple of months, Mother? And what if he is a changed man now? I honestly can't say that having him remorseful has me excited either. Is it too late for us now? Have I lost the capacity to care for Michael after all these years of being afraid of him? I have no respect for him. Can there be love without respect? Honest Mom, I have no idea what I'm going to do there. I don't want to be there. If I had any choice in the matter at all, I would turn around right now, go home and stay there." Helen let out a heavy sigh. Helen's candour was directed at Katreena. If she was aware of Dusty's presence, she had either forgotten it or she had just accepted him into her confidence.

"Why must life be so unfair?"

Katreena was overwhelmed by a feeling of helplessness. She could not ease Helen's sense of oppression and despair nor help her carry the heavy load. She did not even know how to try.

It was Dusty who came to the rescue. "I know there is little anyone can do to help you at this point Helen. But just remember that today is probably going to be the worst. Take it one minute at a time, Helen. When you come out on the other side of today's visit, you will at least have solved two of your problems. You will know what Michael looks like for next time, and you will know what you are facing in terms of his reaction. After that, you will only need to decide how **you** are to react to **him**. Just one step at a time, Helen. One step at a time. Don't worry about tomorrow. Take care of today for now. Leave tomorrow, for tomorrow, okay?"

Katreena could barely speak for the lump in her throat. "Dusty's right, sweetheart. Take it in small doses. Baby steps, so to speak. Deal with the immediate issue at hand and solve just one problem at a time. Don't worry about anything else for now."

"Thanks, you guys. Maybe you're right. Maybe I can do it if I look at it that way. Things have to get better – someday. They have to!" Helen's voice was dejected but there was a note of determination in it, albeit a rather feeble one, and perhaps even transient one as well.

"Perhaps you should take one of Dr. Walley's tranquilizers just to help you get through this initial visit," Katreena offered. "I have them right here."

Helen hesitated then, "Perhaps I better take one. Who knows, I may need it."

She took it and Katreena passed her the bottle of water she had brought along for just that purpose.

"Thanks, Mom. Just this once. I don't want to become dependent on these things."

They had pulled into the hospital parking lot. As Dusty held the door for Helen, he gave her shoulder a quick squeeze. "Hold your head high Helen. Show him you're tough. Don't give him the upper hand. Keep that for yourself." Helen nodded at him weakly.

Chapter 31

Dr. Henderson, Michael's doctor in Bethune Centre, was in his office waiting for them when they came in. After the introductions were dispensed with, Dr. Henderson offered them chairs to sit on, obviously having been briefed ahead that the three would be coming in together. His face was sombre, as he checked the papers in front of him.

"Thank you for coming," he said cordially. "How was your trip?"

"Fine, thank you, Dr. Henderson. What kind of news do you have for me today?" Helen was following Dusty's advice, taking the upper hand, tackling any problem coming at her, dispensing with it quickly and moving forward.

Dr. Henderson seemed somewhat taken aback by Helen's direct approach, possibly expecting the timid Helen described in a report from one of the other doctors, but when Katreena and Dusty nodded their confirmation, he got down to business. "I thought you might want an update on Michael's condition before you went in to see him."

"There is an update then. Has his condition changed?" Dusty prompted.

"Well, I know you saw him in Toronto, so his appearance will not be a complete shock to you. That acid did a horrific number on him and it will take a skilful surgeon to make him look normal again, but at the moment, his appearance is not the major issue. It's his state of mind that has us worried. He is conscious but not rational and he is certainly not coherent. He's blabbering a lot but most of it does not make sense. The one thing we do know is that he is extremely agitated, and that seems to be because he is not getting the responses he wants. He has not seen his face yet and given his present frame of mind, we have not let him see a mirror. We hope that perhaps you may be able to clarify whatever issue he is attempting to communicate and give us some insight as to how to decrease his agitation and help calm him down. That would facilitate his healing process."

Helen's face fell. The bravado she had felt a moment ago crumbled as she felt the weight of responsibility that Dr. Walley, Dr. Gorman – and now Dr. Henderson, had dumped on her shoulders. Michael was "extremely agitated" and they were expecting HER to fix that?!!! Talk about misplaced faith! If he was that agitated, this was as close as she wanted to get to him, hidden far behind several sets of closed doors. She wanted nothing to do with his anger, his agitation, or his lack of rational behaviour. She had served her time in that state prison since her wedding. Surely, she deserved a reprieve now. Even criminals got paroled. In dismay, she looked at her mother, desperately pleading for some kind of way out of this horrid situation. However, Katreena too, was at a loss for words.

Once more, Dusty rose to the rescue. "Dr. Henderson, I hope you don't expect miracles from this visit. You may be asking for the impossible here. Michael has been abusive for years. He is a man who will, in all probability, continue to be abusive – now, and perhaps for the rest of his life. Expecting that to change may be an exercise in futility."

Dr. Henderson thought that over. He was aware of what Helen had been through, perhaps not all of it, but he had read the reports. However, he wasn't sure if he knew enough to judge whether Dusty was exaggerating or not. But Michael was ill now and not in a position to be a threat. Helen had done little to provide assisting insight into Michael's care. Short of that one visit to the hospital in Toronto, she had made no other effort to see her husband during his illness. Even if Dusty's evaluation was valid and Helen was too fragile to take on this angry beast, a doctor's first duty was to his patient and Michael was his patient. Perhaps Dusty was right about Michael continuing to be abusive even if he did get well, but he needed a prognosis on the future physical health of his patient at this moment.

"All right, I hear what you're saying and I agree with you. But we cannot leave the situation as is. If Michael continues to remain in this agitated state without showing improvement, then he would have to be committed to an institution where he will be cared for properly. However, if we can define a productive care plan to help him get better, we need to know that and deal with it. Helen can visit more often here. Perhaps that will have a positive effect on his recuperation. When Michael was in

Toronto, I can understand why she was unable to visit him. Dr. Gorman and I wonder if the lack of visitors may be a contributing factor to his agitation."

Dusty was quickly losing patience with this arrogant doctor who was convinced that he knew all the answers. "I understand, Doctor. But you must..."

Dr. Henderson continued, "It is imperative that we get this over with as soon as possible, so a proper assessment can be made and the necessary steps taken to provide proper treatment for the patient's future."

It was Dusty's turn to re-evaluate his position. Was it not better to face the inevitable now, rather than delay it in fear? If they could help Helen pull through this one traumatic experience, she may be in a position to resume some semblance of peace in her life.

"Just don't expect miracles," Dusty told him.

Dr. Henderson thought that over, then "All right, I hear you. I will get a psyche nurse to be present for this initial meeting to take the edge off any disturbing outbursts from Michael." He turned to the phone and dialled a number. While he waited for his party to answer, he turned back to Dusty. "I am certain we can achieve a workable solution to this problem."

The psyche nurse arrived to join them. Dr. Henderson introduced her to the visitors, then briefed her on the situation. Helen's hands were shaking and her face was flushed. Her heart was hammering in her chest so loudly it made her ears ring. She was sure that all the rest of the group must be able to hear its pounding. Her intentions to be strong and forceful seemed to have forsaken her. Noting her agitation, the nurse asked Helen about her family. Once Helen got on the subject of the family, she relaxed a bit, clinging onto the comforting images of her children. The nurse was concerned about Helen's relationship with Michael but each time she mentioned him, Helen seemed to freeze up. In the interest of keeping Helen calm, the nurse had to bring the children back into the conversation.

In no time at all, two o'clock had arrived and they were on their way to Michael's room. Helen felt less agitated and she had reclaimed some of the earlier bravado that she had mustered from Kaydee's pep talk back at home. Still, that step across the doorstep, was an apprehensive one and the sight of Michael's scarred and twisted face made all their hearts stop. Healing had obviously taken place since they last saw him. But instead of the raw flesh they had seen before in that Toronto hospital, they now saw paper thin strips of skin stretched across vast hollow craters not even resembling cheeks, where flesh was eaten away by the acid and the ensuing infections. This caused distortions to his face that made it unrecognizable. His forehead was a blotchy mess and his left eye seemed obliterated by the scrap of eyelid that was being pulled over by a stretch of skin. The mouth and chin were so off centre and twisted that it was no wonder Michael could not speak clearly. He had no normal lips to form words with. An audible gasp escaped Helen's throat, and was immediately echoed from Katreena and Dusty. The psyche nurse and Dr. Henderson watched for unusual signs that could set off a situation requiring immediate attention, but everyone appeared calm.

After a moment of hesitation, as if garnering her energies for the ordeal, Helen approached the bed. Michael seemed asleep and she lightly touched his shoulder to wake him.

His body jerked and his right eye popped wide open, his left one straining against the impeding flap that held it locked in squinting position.

"Hello Michael" Helen began cautiously, moving off slightly to a safe distance in case he decided to lash out. "How are you feeling?"

Michael lay there just staring silently straight into Helen's eyes, as if trying to figure out who she was and what he should do with her. He made no move at all but his eyes stayed fixed on their target. Once more Helen tried to extract a reaction. "Are you in pain, Michael?" she asked, still maintaining a safe distance.

Michael blinked and then he realized that it was Helen who was talking to him. "So ya crawled outta ya hole ta s see fe?" He drawled laboriously, forming his words with an unresponsive tongue and non-compliant lips that could not meet. Speaking obviously caused him considerable pain but that did not stop him. "Ya like dis, doncha, fech? Seein fe lyin here like dis. Ya t-tink yar so da a n good, showin up lak dis. Fel, I aint i-i-in-frest, ya da-an tufid f fech." He spoke very slowly, his words difficult to understand but his message was unmistakable, much to the astonishment of everyone in the room. Helen's mouth gaped in shock. "F fet ya f fesh fe now, eh? Ya can't h-handle it f-fitout da old f-f-fan ta t-take k-kar a ya, can ya? Da f-far n z a reel f-fesh now, I fet." To finish off, he actually tried to spit at her but his distorted mouth prevented even a half-hearted attempt. Even with his twisted speech, his vile personality was coming through loud and clear.

Helen saw red. She gained control over her fear, her hurt and all other emotions except her disdain. Even in pain, Michael could not be decent. It seemed to take every painful effort for him to talk, yet he used every one of those efforts to be vulgar and nasty. Well she was not going to cower before him anymore. Michael's nasty manner coming out at this point was just the trigger she had needed to prop up her sagging sense of security. "Don't give him the upper hand. Take that for yourself." Dusty had said. Well this was the time to take Dusty's advice and use it. She wasn't going to buckle to Michael's demeaning remarks. She was reminded of Joey's words: "I have faith in your courage. Be strong." Then for emphasis, she remembered Kaydee's "You can't let us down." She steeled herself against Michael's onslaught but then she decided to lash back at Michael.

Standing at a safe distance, her body tall and erect, Helen faced Michael. Then, voice strong and confident, she spoke. "No, Michael the farm is not at mess at all. As a matter of fact, the farm is doing fine. I hired a very good man to manage it and he is doing great. He has cleaned up the shed and we are planning to rebuild this fall. He has kept up with all the fieldwork and actually, he has done it with very little help from me. We had a bad hailstorm a couple of weeks ago and he took very good care of us by hiding us all in the basement until it was over. When the storm was over, he fixed all the windows and repaired all the damage that the storm had caused. He has started on the swathing and has all the graineries clean and ready for the new crop. No, the farm is not in a mess at all. In fact, it is looking very good indeed. The kids are all healthy –

and happy! All of us are doing just fine." Helen finished with a tremulous, albeit somewhat defiant glare.

"So there!" she silently triumphed. She felt good. She felt authoritative and free for the first time. She knew Michael had lost his power over her. She had taken it back!

There was a stupefied hush from Michael after Helen's proclamation. The four adults watching from the door noted Helen's firm narrative, but Dusty and Katreena were jubilant. Helen had come through! Michael was so shocked by Helen's bravado that he could not react immediately.

But the silence was short lived. Helen's last statement and smile made Michael even more furious. "Yar s-s-skroo- in da d-fash tad, ya fech," he yelled. "Yar skr oo -in da hi-ire h-h-h-and while yar ya hus-fan z lyin sik en f-fed. Ya deertee f-f-f-fukin hoor!"

Helen cut in forcefully, interrupting Michael's tirade. "No Michael, nobody is screwing anybody, but we ARE all doing fine and so is the farm!"

Michael started trashing about, fighting at the straps that held his body and his hands in position, screaming at Helen. "I keel ya, ya sona fich, I keel da fota ya."

The psyche nurse and Dr. Henderson jumped into action, trying to calm him down but he only trashed about more, screaming curses at all of them. The nurse barked at Dusty to help as she ran to get a tranquilizer needle. As the men struggled to keep Michael down, several of the wounds opened up, rendering them all bloody. Katreena led Helen out of the room and they passed the nurse in the hallway, hurrying back with a tranquilizing syringe for Michael. Michael's screams could be heard all the way down the hallway and two nurses and an orderly were already racing to the room to help. The commotion continued for a few more minutes and then quieted down as the tranquilizer obviously took effect. Shortly after, Dusty came out of the room, his clothes, hands and even his face spattered with blood. On his grim face, you could read the disgust as he headed for the bathroom to clean up. Helen was crying softly as her head rested on Katreena's shoulder where they were sitting on chairs nearby.

Chapter 32

"I guess we don't have to worry about taking the kids to visit Michael at the hospital, do we?" Dusty said grimly as he manoeuvred the car out of the parking lot.

Katreena shuddered. "Definitely not. I don't even want Helen going there either. He can rot in there by himself till eternity for all I care." Katreena added the last more softly so that Helen would not hear it, just in case she still retained some misguided loyalty or pity for that beast.

Dusty had looked so angry, when he came out of that washroom after washing Michael's blood off his clothes that neither Helen nor Katreena dared to ask him any questions. Without waiting for the doctor or the nurses, who were still in the room with Michael, Dusty grated through his clenched teeth, "We're going home," and the girls had meekly followed him out. It had been such a traumatic experience for all of them, they all felt drained. Explanations, plans, repercussions could come later. Right now, they just needed to be away from this awful place.

It was Dusty who voiced the thought that was uppermost in all their minds.

"Oh yea, Michael is sick alright, but more than that, he is mentally sick, very mentally sick. I hope that Dr. Henderson now realizes what kind of beast he has on his hands. That animal belongs in a psycho ward, not close to a family who are within his shooting range. Those doctors will have to lock that lunatic up and throw away the key because it is a cinch he is a menace – a dangerous menace – not just to his family but to society at large!" Dusty was so agitated he was shaking. He needed to distance himself from the scene of the problem in order to think rationally. That hospital was not the place to be right now.

Katreena turned to Helen in the back seat of the car. "Are you alright there, honey?"

"Yes, Mom. I just feel so wiped out, like somebody took all the energy out of me. If the wind blew at me right now, I would totally disintegrate because I have no substance at all. I just want to sit here quietly and forget about anything unpleasant."

"That's good, Helen. Don't even think for now. We'll put the radio on and see if we can find some good soothing music." Then, turning to Dusty, "Do you mind?"

"Not at all. I think it's a great idea. We all need some soothing music."

Katreena turned the dials until she heard Bing Crosby's crooning voice blending with Grace Kelly in their rendition of "True Love."

"Just what the doctor ordered," Dusty smiled in appreciation and Helen nodded her agreement.

They drove the rest of the way without a word but the radio kept the tunes coming: "Unchained Melody"; "Sounds of Silence"; "You'll Never Walk Alone"; "Save the Last Dance for Me"; "Let It Be Me." By half past six, Dusty was turning into the driveway at KD Acres.

Kaydee came running out to meet them even before they were out of the car. "How did it go?" She had obviously been on pins and needles worrying and she was anxiously scanning her mother's face for signs of distress.

But it was Dusty that broke the silence when Helen and Katreena hesitated. "Not good, Kaydee. I doubt we'll be making visits there again unless there is some miraculous improvement in his outlook which, for the life of me, I just cannot foresee." In bewilderment, Kaydee took in his bloody shirt, and stared at her mother and grandmother as they watched Dusty stride purposefully to the house. Wordlessly they followed. They heard the shower running as Helen again assured Kaydee that she was alright.

Since Michael's accident, Dusty always brought a change of clothes "for emergencies" whenever he came out to the farm. Now Dusty emerged from the bathroom where he changed after his shower. Kaydee watched him take his dirty clothes and toss them angrily into the garbage. Without a word, to anyone, he walked purposefully toward the shed for what was clearly some "alone" time.

Kaydee was even afraid to ask for any explanation. Helen put her arm around her shoulder.

"It's alright Kaydee. Come on, let's sit down and we can talk about it.

This is not going to be pleasant, honey, but you deserve to know the whole truth. Shielding you will serve no purpose. Besides, I desperately need your support and understanding now."

Kaydee listened in awe as Helen described Michael's appearance, his demeanour, his initial unresponsive attitude and then his vehement outburst and subsequent physical reaction.

"Perhaps I may have provoked his wrath when I told him that the farm was doing well without him, but honestly, Kaydee, when he sneered at me and made those disparaging remarks about how desperately we needed him and how everything would be a mess without him, well, I just saw red! I told him that we were doing just fine with Joey and we are not in a mess at all. I guess for just one moment in my life, I wanted to strike back. Knowing Michael though, I guess that was the ultimate insult – me striking back, that is. Anyway, we never even stayed to see what they did to him after all that. As soon as Dusty washed all that blood off himself, we took off for home, so I expect we'll be getting a call from Dr. Henderson anytime now."

Amazed by this account, Kaydee leaned over and gave her mother an impetuous hug. "Mom, I am so proud of you right now, I could just burst! I'm so happy that you stood up for yourself and talked back to him. He's had it coming!"

Katreena, who till now had been sitting wordlessly listening to the discourse, clapped her hands in approval. Taken aback by this sudden intrusion into their private dialogue, Helen and Kaydee gaped in astonishment at her. After moment of recollection, they all burst into laughter. The tension of the afternoon evaporated as they revelled in that single, but profound, triumph. The incongruity of resounding mirth emanating from the direction of the house stunned Dusty to the point of forsaking the calm seclusion of the shed and he came rushing back to see if madness had suddenly overtaken the household.

"It's a celebration," Katreena responded giddily to the puzzled query on Dusty's face as he stood in the open doorway. "Helen just told Kaydee how she saw red at Michael's assumption that the farm would go to pot in his absence and how she got mad and retaliated. Kaydee congratulated her on her first triumph in twelve years." The girls roared with laughter again. Dusty shook his head in disbelief as his eyes swept over the three strange females and their peculiar sense of amusement on this bizarre afternoon.

Then on thinking about it, he realized the significance of the occasion. While their hilarity was somewhat superfluous, he could well understand why Katreena and Kaydee would be euphoric about the development. He empathized with them. Helen's emancipating rebuke definitely did merit celebrating. It was time! In retrospect, the memory of the incident did undeniably relieve the stress and elevate the mood of the afternoon! Who could complain about that? Dusty smiled his approval as he sat down to join them.

The ringing of the phone shattered the moment and reluctantly Helen went to answer it. Kaydee and Katreena followed her with worried frowns. Most likely Dr. Henderson with a report on Michael.

"Yes, I understand, Dr. Henderson," Helen finished after a long period of silence which had obviously been Dr. Henderson's assessment of the situation. Her face was sombre when she returned. "They have him sedated and he's sleeping now but guess what? Dr. Henderson thinks it best if we don't come to visit for a while. Boo Hoo! And I was so looking forward to going back there too." Helen rolled her eyes in antipathy and continued, "Michael has stripped the new skin off much of his wounds and now they have to start him on antibiotics till that heals again. Anyway it doesn't sound as if Dr. Henderson is particularly impressed with me and my lack of concern for my husband." Helen seemed more disgusted than distraught.

"Have you guys had supper yet?" she asked, eager to change the course of their thinking.

"I made a roast chicken with potatoes and some vegetables. Joey came home, had supper and then went back out to the field. There's plenty left over for you guys though. I even have some dessert for you – raspberries and cream." Kaydee answered proudly.

Dusty brightened. "Did I hear somebody mention food? I am famished. And raspberries and cream for dessert! Girl, you are the answer to a man's dream!" He made a playful slap at Kaydee's bottom but she jumped out of the way and ran for the kitchen. Katreena followed Helen to put supper on the table.

Later that evening, Joey took the account of the visit with a worried frown. "He's going to make trouble for you, Helen. Would you prefer it if I left and you hired someone else instead?"

Helen was aghast. "Oh my God, Joey. No! You can't leave! Please! We can't do this without you. We need you. Please say you won't leave us."

"It's okay, Helen." Joey soothed quickly. "I promise you I will not leave as long as you need and want me here. I just thought it might be easier for you if I did. That's all I meant. I didn't say I wanted to leave."

Relieved but sorrowful, Helen went on to explain, "It will never be easier with Michael regardless of whether you go or stay, Joey. Michael is just being Michael. He was nasty long before you came here and apparently he'll continue to be nasty, probably for the rest of his life, but I need someone I can depend on to run the farm." Then, turning to Katreena and Dusty, she begged urgently, "Don't you agree? Tell him."

Dusty nodded to Katreena to respond for them both. "Helen is right, Joey. You may find this hard to comprehend but Michael is not a man that reacts with logic." Her voice level and controlled, Katreena continued. "We're not being callous or unreasonable here but Michael's disparaging remarks today are not new to Helen or to any of us. Don't let him scare you away. We all want you to stay. You have done a wonderful job and have had a very positive influence on the family. Michael is in no shape to take over for a long time and we all need you."

Joey's frown faded. "It's settled then. I don't leave till you tell me to," and with a little bow to Helen he did a mock salute, "At your service Ma'am, for as long as you want me."

"Thank you, Joey," Helen's voice was thick with emotion as she shook his hand.

"I'm hungry." Alvin came bounding through the door followed closely by Jaynee and her "Me too, me too."

Kaydee brought up the rear with Dayna in her arms. "Again?

Already? Honestly Mom, I did feed him supper. I don't know where he put it."

With a laugh, Katreena scooped Alvin up in her arms. "Well, go wash up, my little man and we'll see if we can find a nice little snack for you." Putting him back on the floor, she slapped his bottom as he ran off toward the bathroom. Jaynee, not to be outdone, reached her arms into the air to be picked up too. Katreena whisked her up, planted a big grunting kiss on her little neck as Jaynee squealed and squirmed in protest. "You wash too or no snack." Jaynee fairly jumped down from her grandmother's arms, grabbed Kaydee's outstretched hand and towed her toward the bathroom.

Chapter 33

The school year had started and Kaydee had gone back to classes with Ed Norchak still as her teacher. With his discerning eye, Ed had noted Kaydee's new perspective on life and her blossoming self-confidence. Remembering the conversation with Katreena and recalling his promise to Helen back in early July to offer tutoring for Kaydee, Ed had followed through on his proposal and had enlisted the help of his wife Sandy to coach Kaydee during spare time in an effort to bring her up to par with other kids her own age. Every lunch hour and after school Sandy spent time with Kaydee who was now enjoying school and devouring the extra lessons.

Either Helen, Joey or Katreena and Dusty would pick Kaydee up at the Norchaks after her evening sessions. Sometimes if Joey and Helen were busy, and Dusty and Katreena were unavailable, Ed and Sandy would drive Kaydee home. Kaydee was showing great promise and everyone was comfortable with the arrangement and happy with the progress.

Life had become peaceful and serene as everyone settled into this stable routine. Helen didn't call Bethune Centre to ask about Michael but Dr. Henderson took it upon himself to keep Helen informed via the telephone of Michael's progress though Helen wished he wouldn't bother. She dreaded those calls because they always aroused a depression deep within her that she just could not quell. She was trying so hard to cling to the peace that she felt was all too transient now with Michael only three hundred miles away and probably on the mend.

Michael was still angry, apparently not just spewing venom about his wife, but being just as spiteful to the staff that took care of him. Dr. Henderson never gave specifics of Michael's nasty remarks, but they were obviously unutterable. On several occasions, Helen actually thought that she noted tones of empathy in the arrogant doctor's voice. According to him, they were keeping Michael sedated as much as possible not just so his wounds would heal but also to protect the staff from his abuse. Dr. Henderson never mentioned visitations again and Helen relaxed because she did not have to think about it anymore.

One evening, Katreena and Dusty had driven down for a "friendly visit," as they called it and Helen had taunted them with a "What, you don't feel the need to check up on me anymore?"

"Not with this guardian angel looking out for you," Dusty had replied, pointing at Joey.

"Just attending to me duties, sir," Joey countered, and Katreena smiled affectionately at him. They had sat on the deck till after the sun had set and the evening chill sent them shivering into the house. Joey put on a pouting face and excused himself saying, "Now that you have these two capable people to take care of you, I guess my presence is redundant so I'm going home."

"Goodnight Joey, and thanks for everything," Helen answered. Dusty and Katreena echoed their "Goodnight" after her. "Guess it is time for bed for us as well," she observed.

Helen flicked on her bedside lamp. The clock on her bedside radio read twenty to three. Still half asleep, Helen stared at it wondering why she was awake at such an ungodly hour. Then the shrill ringing of the phone jarred her awake, rasping through her brain like a thorny branch of a rose bush against bare skin. That was it. That was what had awakened her. Who could be calling at such an hour? Groggily, she got out of bed and stumbled to the living room, flicking on the light switch as she passed it. She reached for the phone and noticed her mother just descending the stairs.

"Hello," Helen's voice was unsteady and somewhat hoarse.

"Mrs. Boyer?" The voice at the other end was that of Dr. Walley and instinctively Helen froze in panic. Her audible gasp automatically alerted Katreena to some kind of trouble.

"This is Helen Boyer. What is it, Dr. Walley? What is the matter? Why are you calling at this hour?" Helen's heart was hammering as she clutched the phone so tightly her knuckles turned white. Katreena leaned against Helen's ear straining to hear what Dr. Walley had to say.

"Mrs. Boyer, we have some disturbing news. I am actually calling on behalf of Dr. Henderson from Bethune Sciences Centre. He thought that it would be better for you to hear it from me. We want you to know that the utmost care was taken and all safety measures were observed by the hospital at all times but in spite of it, we have to report that Michael has somehow managed to escape from his room. All personnel have been alerted and they are conducting a thorough search of the hospital premises but so far, all efforts to locate him have been futile. We are certain they will find him soon. He cannot have gone far in his condition. However, Dr. Henderson felt it only fair that you should be made aware of the situation. I cannot begin to tell you how sorry I am to have to tell you this."

Helen's knees buckled and Katreena just managed to catch her in time to guide her fall onto the seat of the phone bench. The phone fell to the floor with a clatter and Katreena snatched it to her ear with her free hand, propping Helen's limp body with her shoulder to keep her from falling forward and onto the floor.

"Dusty!" Katreena's shriek cut through the air before she had time to consider the repercussions of her panic-stricken scream. Reacting simply on her protective maternal instincts, she struggled to help her daughter stay in the chair. She barked into the phone, "Dr. Walley, what the hell did you just say to my daughter?"

Dusty came running down and Katreena pointed to Helen mouthing "hang on to her" as she continued to listen to Dr. Walley's report about Michael's disappearance. Helen seemed to have lost all the strength from her body and sagged listlessly in the chair like a rag doll, her face an ashen, unreadable mask. Katreena's mouth gaped open in shock as she continued to listen to the phone. By this time, Kaydee had arrived and spotting her mother slumped over in the chair, immediately ran to kneel beside her.

"What happened?" she asked Dusty, not wanting to interrupt her grandmother in what was obviously an important call.

Dusty shrugged his shoulders to indicate he didn't know, nodding at Katreena as if to say "She has all the answers."

Impatiently, they both waited for Katreena to hang up and tell them what the uproar was about. Helen was hanging on to Kaydee like she was a lifeboat on a stormy sea.

"Are the kids asleep?" Katreena put down the phone, her anxious eyes darting to the stairs as she directed her whispered query at Kaydee.

"Yes. I purposely checked them before I came down after I heard you call for Dusty. What's happening?"

"Michael is missing from his room and the staff cannot find him," Katreena said flatly.

"What?" Kaydee and Dusty fairly exploded in unison.

"They thought they had him sedated as usual and they checked him at eleven o'clock. He was sleeping soundly, and he had the IV going so they didn't check on him till one o'clock. That was when they discovered that he was not in his room. He probably failed to take his sedative and the nurse never realized it. Apparently, he pulled the IV tubes off and left the room somehow. No one saw him." Katreena heaved a heavy sigh as she shook her head in disbelief. "He has to be there in the hospital somewhere. He can't possibly have gone far in his condition."

"I don't believe it." Dusty was incredulous. "How can this happen? I didn't think he could even walk. How could he just disappear from the room, for heaven's sake?"

"Actually, they had started him walking a couple of weeks ago. Dr. Henderson said they thought he should try walking so the nurses had him up each afternoon. He said Helen was told about it." She turned to Helen, "Did you know about it, Helen?"

Helen looked dazed. "Dr. Henderson told me that the nurses were walking him for a few minutes each day but it didn't sound like much so I didn't take it serious."

"Have they asked you to come see him?" Dusty was taken aback by this unexpected news.

"Oh no." Helen answered weakly. "Dr. Henderson told me that Michael was as belligerent as ever, even to the nursing staff, so they were giving him sedatives to keep him quiet. He said that he didn't want anyone visiting him until they thought he was ready to accept visitors. I was actually quite relieved that I didn't have to go."

"That means he's been stewing in his venom for over three weeks,"

Dusty reflected thoughtfully. "What can he be thinking?"

"Who knows what goes on in that crazy mixed-up brain of his!" Katreena scoffed uncaringly, but her eyes belied her offhanded remark. There was anxiety there, real fear that she was deliberately attempting to mask. Dusty picked up on it immediately. Kaydee too, sensed her grandmother's apprehension.

"Well, there is nothing we can do at this time anyway. It's the hospital's problem. Let's just try to get some sleep now and deal with it tomorrow." Dusty tried to sound casual and realistic. "Why don't you help your mother to bed, Kaydee. We'll deal with this in the morning."

Kaydee suspected they were being dismissed, but she also suspected the reason for it. Still she knew instinctively it was her mother whom he was trying to shield.

"Dusty is right, Mom. Come on let's get some sleep. I'll get you some hot milk and then I'll tuck you in for a change," she teased, deliberately being silly to avert any questions.

"I suppose you're right. There is nothing we can do tonight." She waited while Kaydee heated some milk in the microwave. Accepting the glass from Kaydee, Helen downed the warm liquid and meekly let Kaydee take her back to bed. To make certain that sleep would not be elusive on this traumatic night, Kaydee offered Helen one of those tranquilizer pills that Dr. Walley had given them after the accident. Helen did not resist and Kaydee was grateful she did not have to prod her into taking it. Her mother needed to sleep. Things might get a lot worse before they got better. Peace – and rest – might be a rare feat in the next few days.

Dusty and Katreena had gone upstairs as soon as Kaydee took Helen to the bedroom.

"He probably had this planned in that evil mind of his. He's trying to make it home." Dusty said as soon as they were out of earshot.

"Surely that would be impossible," Katreena looked at Dusty with fear in her eyes. They were whispering to avoid being overheard by either Helen or the kids. She was desperately pleading for affirmation of her last statement but seeing the look on his face she knew it wasn't coming.

"I think he **will** try to make it here but surely his condition would make that an impossible feat. Even if he did get past the hospital staff, he cannot have enough energy to walk far and his appearance would preclude anyone giving him a ride. I cannot fathom him getting here."

Dusty's logic was reasonable, but his demeanour was anything but reassuring. Katreena could almost hear the doubts that were hammering at his brain to defeat that logic.

Katreena voice was haggard as she considered the possibilities. "Michael is crafty but is he superhuman? That's what it would take to get here in his condition. He's mean, he's evil and he's mad, but is he determined enough to pull off such an act? I honestly cannot see how, but Dusty, I am scared out of my wits that he might."

Kaydee had just come upstairs and seeing the light under the door, knocked softly. Katreena went to open it and Kaydee slipped in surreptitiously.

"Look," she began, "I know there is something more than what you told us down there. I realize Mother needs to be protected because she is vulnerable, but I can handle it. Whatever it is, I need to know what's going on. Please don't keep any secrets from me."

Katreena wrapped her arms around the girl, holding her tightly. Behind Kaydee's head, she exchanged glances with Dusty and he nodded his endorsement for an honest reply.

"You're right, sweetheart. You have the right to know, particularly in view of the fact that if something should turn ugly, you would be in the middle of it."

"Turn ugly!?!" Kaydee's whisper rose in alarm. Eyes wide she stared at Dusty, then at her grandmother. "What is it that you're not telling me?"

"We're not sure, but we think your father is trying to get home. How he can get here in his condition, we cannot fathom. During our visit to the hospital, he was threatening to kill both your mother and Joey, because he assumed there was something going on between them. We think he has been planning this escape from the hospital for that very purpose and that he may be scheming to come here." Katreena watched the color drain from Kaydee's face as shock and panic sank in. Now Kaydee understood what Granny meant when she said that things could become "ugly."

Dusty cut in. "We cannot imagine how Michael can make it home in his condition, but honey, we cannot be too careful. We need to take precautions, just in case he makes it."

"Why doesn't the hospital call? What are they doing all this time?" Katreena groaned in exasperation. "Can't they at least give us an update?"

"Personally, I think it was pretty cowardly of Dr. Henderson to make Dr. Walley call here in the first place. I can appreciate that Dr. Walley is closer to the family, but this faux pas is not Dr. Walley's! It is a page right out of Dr. Henderson's book. It is his responsibility! I'm going to call them and see if they have any news. Do you know the number?"

"I can get it for you," Kaydee offered and ran off. Within a minute she was back with a piece of paper which she handed to Dusty.

"Hello. This is Dusty Duganyk. I am calling from Zelena, on behalf of the Michael Boyer family. Have you located Mr. Boyer yet?"

There was a long pause at the other end of the line, then the girl came back on. "Could you hold the line please? I will transfer you."

It seemed like forever before a man's voice came on the line. "This is Dr. Henderson speaking, Mr. Duganyk. I want you to understand that everything possible is being done to locate Mr. Boyer. So far, we have been unsuccessful. We have concentrated all our search efforts in the hospital and on the grounds. We find it difficult to believe he has escaped beyond those parameters. With daylight, we hope to achieve success and you can be assured we will call you as soon as he is located."

"What if he has escaped the grounds, Dr. Henderson? Have you checked for stolen cars?"

"We are doing a thorough search of all the premises. I am certain we will locate him soon. We will call you immediately when we do. Goodnight, Mr. Duganyk." The phone went dead.

"Damn the man!" Dusty slammed the phone down. "He hung up on me." Dusty could barely control himself. Katreena could see his teeth clench. "They said they'd call us when they find him," he finished in disgust. "I'd like to sue the pants off that bastard, him and his damned hospital!"

Kaydee suddenly jumped up as a horrifying thought struck her. "Joey!" she whispered anxiously, her eyes wide with fear as they cast frantically from Dusty to Katreena. "We have to let Joey know what's happening. He may be in danger too. He needs to take care of himself – and his grandmother, too. He'll help take care of us too, just like he did during the storm. We have to let Joey know!"

"But Michael doesn't know that the hired man is Joey. Helen didn't give Michael Joey's name, did she? I thought she only said 'hired man.' Help me out here Katreena, am I wrong?" Dusty looked perplexed but there was anxiety in his voice.

Katreena mulled over the idea. "I don't know Dusty," she said slowly. "I honestly cannot remember for sure. I know she said she had a hired hand and that the farm was doing well under his care but did she specifically mention Joey? I just don't know. But even if she didn't, Michael could find that out if he wanted to. In that sick mind of his, he probably would."

Dusty and Katreena exchanged concerned glances. "In which case, Kaydee just may have a point there, honey," Dusty rationalized. "Joey has earned a stake in this strictly by being in the wrong place at the wrong time. He is involved whether he wants to be or not. Given Michael's distorted mind, no one can possibly know what to expect. Caution may just be the best option here. I think we should call Joey and alert him to the possibility of that threat."

"Perhaps you're right," Katreena conceded; doubt still a plague she could not quell. "But now? In the middle of the night? You think it's that urgent?"

"Yes, now!" Dusty replied with determination. "I realize the probability is remote, but can we afford to take the chance? He could have left the hospital shortly after eleven for all we know. Until we get that call from the hospital that they have apprehended Michael, I think we should be taking every precaution. Want to make the call or shall I?"

"You call him, honey. I wouldn't know how to begin." Katreena could feel herself trembling in spite of her conviction that the threat was too impossible to be allowed credence.

Chapter 34

By four o'clock, the sun was still below the horizon but its glow was already beginning to dissolve the darkness. Joey's truck pulled into the yard and he ran over to the passenger side to open the door for his grandmother. Then he reached into the back and brought out a small suitcase which he carried into the house with them.

Kaydee, Dusty and Katreena met them at the door. Katreena and Kaydee exchanged hugs with the visitors, while the men shook hands. Katreena told them that Helen was still asleep, thanks to the tranquilizer Kaydee had given her and they were all grateful for that. They spoke in hushed whispers to avoid waking Helen or the kids.

Grimly, Joey set the suitcase down. "I have absolutely no idea where we are all going to sleep, but until that lunatic is either in chains or behind prison bars, we are all staying here!"

For the first time since she had met him, Kaydee was seeing Joey express anger. Although she knew that the basis for that anger was his concern for their safety, she could not help feeling a tinge of apprehension about it. Years of cringing from Michael's rages could not be obliterated that easily.

"I take it you haven't heard any more from the hospital? How can they have let such a thing happen for heaven's sake?" Joey wanted to know.

"No we haven't heard anything and as for your other question, well, that's way beyond my comprehension," Dusty retorted vehemently.

"We keep hoping the hospital has located him and will call us back soon so that we can all relax. Until then, we have to assume the worst, impossible as it may seem." Katreena's comment was meant for all of them, but she directed it at Annie by way of apology for disrupting her peaceful life. "I can't begin to tell you how sorry I am to drag you into this."

"Now don't you worry about that, dear. I'm here to help in whatever way I can though I honestly think I may be more of a hindrance than a help. Joey, however, wouldn't hear of me staying home. He made me come."

"I want everyone together here, where I – where we can keep an eye on everyone. Ideally, I would like to ship both families out to some kind of bomb shelter far away until this guy is apprehended, but we have neither the time nor the wherewithall to do any such thing now. Not knowing what we are facing is what makes this whole situation so perilous and unpredictable. I still have a tough time believing that he can make it this far in his condition but from what you tell me, he's capable of a lot of strange things. Besides, like you said, we can't take any chances. Anyway, we will have to maintain a constant lookout at all times until he's found." Joey finished as he looked out the window for traffic and anything else suspicious.

"You're right man. I'm just glad we came out. I'd hate to think what would have happened if Helen had been alone when that call came through." Dusty commented wryly.

Joey went outside, walked around the house, drove and parked Helen's truck into the garage beside her car then locked the garage doors. Then he drove his truck out of the driveway and parked it behind the machinery shed. When he came back in, he told Dusty to take his car and park it behind the shed as well.

"If Michael comes, I would think he will arrive in a vehicle, most likely a stolen one. I honestly cannot see him walking that far. And no one would give him a ride if he looks half as bad as you described him. So if and when that happens, I don't want him to see any other vehicles here. Hopefully he will not suspect we're waiting in ambush for him. I'm going to have to work out some plan for us to take care of everyone." Joey motioned to Dusty and Dusty left the house to move his car.

Joey went outside again to check something in front of the house. The two women and Kaydee stared at each other, wordlessly, just now finally comprehending the danger they might be in.

Joey followed Dusty into the house on completion of their respective tasks and immediately took charge of the situation like a drill sergeant.

"Okay. I want you guys to listen carefully. Hopefully none of this will be necessary, in which case we'll be able to chuck this all up to a bad memory but just in case Michael, by some miracle, manages to get here, we have to have a plan to protect ourselves. Granny and Kaydee will be in charge of the kids," He looked at Kaydee. "And your mother. I really don't think your mother will be in any shape to do very much, given her inherent fear of Michael. The safest place, I think, would be upstairs, but stay away from the windows. In fact, in case of trouble, stay close to the floor. I'm going to have to be frank here. I'm not trying to frighten anyone, but this is just the worst case scenario. I **need** you **all** to be prepared for it because there will not be time to explain later, if this should come up. In the unlikely event that Michael did get hold of a car or a gun, that is what we have to be prepared for. Dusty, Katreena and I have to keep watching for any signs that he's in the area – that means any vehicles driving up or any strange movement around the place. Rusko might help alert us as well but we cannot depend on the dog because he might recognize Michael and not bark, so it's really up to us. Now that is the plan. Outside of keeping our eyes peeled and our ears perked, there is really nothing to do now other than wait and hope this all passes. Until this blows over, I don't want anyone outside. If Michael is out there and has a gun that would be too inviting a target for that lunatic. I'm sorry, but this is for protection and not meant to scare anyone."

There was a stunned silence when Joey finished. Joey looked at each face in his audience, then convinced that they all understood, he left to look out the windows again. They were all still sitting there when he got back to the kitchen.

"There's one more thing. When I was out there, I noticed some of the telephone wire exposed where it enters the house. It was probably exposed while digging up the flower beds but it can be cut there, leaving us without a phone line. I don't know if Michael was aware of it, but I'd like to cover it up somehow, just in case. The only way I can think of, is to pile a bunch of wood on it. That way, if Michael wanted to cut the wires, he'd have to remove all that wood first, which would alert us to his presence."

"I'll go get the wood," Dusty offered, glad to be of some physical use. Dusty had never appreciated Joey as he appreciated him at this moment.

Joey was a lifesaver in more ways than one, Dusty realized. He could never have known what to do. All he knew was that real danger was a possibility – as remote as it was. By himself, he would probably have simply waited it out and hoped it would just go away by itself. But Joey... Joey knew how to organize everyone in the face of danger, what to do to minimize that danger, and how to protect everyone from that danger. Joey was truly "a treasure" as Katreena had once put it. Joey was able to put the whole situation in perspective and although he probably scared the daylights out of them by exposing the veracity of the threat, at least they now had a plan of action to protect themselves in its eventuality. As Dusty piled the wood over the exposed telephone wire, he felt a wave of relief to know that Joey was taking charge. Dusty wanted little to do with such heavy responsibility. He was only too aware of his own inadequacy in that field.

Helen woke up to the smell of bacon and the sound of voices coming from the kitchen. "Everyone must be up," she thought, glancing at the clock. Half past seven! She had overslept! Then she remembered the tranquilizer Kaydee had given her last night and the events that had precipitated the need for it. A feeling of fear and dread enveloped her as she recalled the context of Dr. Walley's call. Had they picked up Michael yet? Quickly she donned a robe and hurried into the kitchen.

"Have you heard from the hospital? Have they found Michael?" Eagerly she scanned the faces around the table. Annie! What was she doing here? "What's happened?"

Kaydee quickly got up and came to put an arm around her. "No, Mom. We haven't heard anything. Dusty called the hospital last night but all they said was they would call us as soon as they found him. We called Joey because we thought he should be aware of what's going on and he brought his grandmother here so we can all be together. Why don't you take a shower and get dressed while we get breakfast on the table and then we'll fill you in on what's been going on." Gently, but purposefully she led her mother back to the bedroom where she picked up fresh clothes and then guided her to the bathroom. "Have your shower and dress, Mom. Breakfast will be ready soon." School would be skipped today. Later she would call the Norchaks and tell them she'd be absent because she had a stomach ache or something.

Helen did not resist. It all seemed so surreal, last night, this morning, everyone in the kitchen, getting ready for breakfast, seemingly unconcerned; yet all the while something so bizarre was happening elsewhere. Mechanically, she showered, dried off, combed her hair, dressed; then walked back to the kitchen where she hoped to find answers to the myriad of questions that were battering her mind. Breakfast was on the table and everyone was sitting at the table waiting for her. The kids were obviously still all asleep.

"All right, stop treating me like an invalid. I may be somewhat dazed, but if I don't get some kind of clear picture of what's happening, my imagination is going to create a much more outrageous one!" Helen was being deliberately forceful. She had to know the facts because she was not exaggerating when she said her imagination was going wild. She was swimming in a vortex of nightmares and it was torturing her intolerably.

Joey and Dusty exchanged glances but it was Joey who spoke up. "I totally appreciate what you're saying, Helen, and believe me, it's not that we want to keep you out of the loop, but we were hoping to spare you some of the unnecessary drama of the situation. However, you're right. Imagination can be a ghoulish enemy and I really don't want you entertaining it. Honesty is the most viable defence against it so here is the situation as we see it."

Joey's eyes bored into Helen's as he continued. "I want you to take this rationally. I know you have the stamina if you muster it so please, for all our sakes, you must be strong because we all desperately need you to be. Hopefully, we will simply get a call from the hospital telling us they have apprehended him, but if that does not happen, we have to prepare for the worst. We think that Michael may be trying to get home. He has probably been planning it since your visit. None of us think he can actually make it here but we cannot take that chance. The only way he can get here is if he stole a car and drove it here himself. No one would give him a lift in his condition and his grotesque facial disfigurement would make him too recognizable so public transit is out of the question.

He wouldn't dare take such a chance. He must be aware that the authorities would be looking for him."

Helen stared at him incredulously and Joey continued. "We have taken certain precautions already because for all we know he's been missing since shortly after eleven last night. We have hidden our vehicles so that he would not expect anyone here, other than you and the kids. We have also protected the telephone line against being cut. I brought Granny here so that all of us would be safely together." Joey motioned to Dusty to check the windows while he continued. "We have to keep a constant watch for any vehicles coming into the yard or anywhere close to it. In the daytime, that should be easy. At night, hopefully he would drive with the lights on but we have to be prepared in case he drives without lights or leaves the vehicle farther away. I'm sure he cannot walk too far but you never know what he's capable of. Our biggest worry is if he stole a gun, so I don't want anyone going outside. Somehow, you are going to find ways to keep the kids entertained in the house. Like I told everyone before, I think upstairs would be the safest spot in the house, close to the floor. I don't want anyone near the windows up there. We're going to have to keep watch in shifts so that some of us can sleep. In case of trouble – and this is very important – you women head for upstairs with the kids and stay close to the floor. No ifs, no buts, and no maybes! Understand?" Joey's voice was insistent, authoritative, as he eyed each one individually, pausing for their nod of agreement.

"The others have all heard this before but it is very important that you all understand what you have to do. If Michael shows up, there will not be time for instructions. Between Dusty and myself, we can handle him, particularly if we have the element of surprise on our side, but we have to totally concentrate on what we are doing. We cannot – I repeat – **cannot** – be distracted by worrying about any of you, so remember what I said. Grab the kids, head upstairs and stay there, NO MATTER WHAT GOES ON DOWN HERE! UNDERSTAND?"

Helen's eyes were brimming with tears. "Oh my Lord, what have I done? It's all my fault for lashing out at him. Now I've put all of us in danger. I should have bitten my tongue off first. I'm so sorry! Oh Joey, thank you for being here. And to all of you. But don't you worry about me. I won't fall apart now, I promise you!"

"Atta girl, Helen. I knew I could count on you. We'll get through this. Don't you worry." Joey's voice softened in appreciation.

"Okay, enough already," Dusty countered with mock severity. "Let's eat!"

"I'll be right with you," Joey got up and went to check the windows before sitting back down. After a few minutes, breakfast was in full swing when the sound of Dayna's crying sent Kaydee racing to pick her up before she woke the other kids. Too late. Alvin came down the stairs followed closely by Jaynee, rubbing the sleep from her eyes. Kaydee passed Dayna to Katreena and took the two toddlers to the bathroom, while Helen went to get fresh clothes to change them into.

By half past nine, when there was still no word from the hospital, Dusty again dialled Bethune Centre in Winnipeg. He was incensed at their lack of communication. "They better not hang up on me again, or so help me, I'll... Hello. This is Dusty Duganyk from Zelena. What's the word on Mr. Boyer?"

Again a crisp feminine voice told him to wait. Finally, a very authoritative masculine voice came on the line. "Hello Mr. Duganyk. This is Sergeant Wilson speaking, from the Bethune RCMP detachment. We are well aware of your concern and we want to assure you we are doing everything we can to locate Mr. Boyer. Our detachment was informed of the problem two hours ago and a missing person report has been filed. We now have all available resources on the case. From our information about the man, we believe he is still in the vicinity but we understand your concern and the reason behind it so we are exploring all possibilities including mobilizing out of town and the highway patrols to be on the lookout. His condition is too fragile to really go far. He may already have succumbed to his wounds hours ago so he may not be a threat to anyone. However, just in case, we have alerted the Zelena detachment and they are on the lookout for him there. The radio networks have been informed and they are broadcasting his description so the net has been cast far and wide. Something should turn up soon. If he is still mobile, he can't hide forever and with so many people looking for him, we expect results soon. Don't worry. We'll get him. We're sorry for your trouble. We have your number and we will be sure to call you with any new developments. Your local detachment is covering your area just in case but we truly don't believe he is out of our area at all. Are you people all right there?"

"Yes, we're prepared here, but don't sell that man short," Dusty warned. "You never know what he's capable of."

"Don't worry, we won't. You take care now. I hope to have good news for you soon." Sergeant Wilson hung up.

"Well, at least that guy has a soul!" Dusty was grateful to get the comprehensive report. Now the police were involved and they were doing something constructive. In addition, they were kind enough to let them know how far they had progressed, not like that tight-lipped Dr. Henderson. Imagine hanging up like that! Unbelievable! Dusty still felt the gall in his mouth at the memory of that call to Dr. Henderson.

Being careful that Alvin was not within earshot, Dusty gave the report to the rest of the family. "Sergeant Wilson thinks that Michael may have succumbed to his wounds and may not even have survived long enough to implement any plans beyond getting out of the hospital. He might actually be lying there, dead, in whatever gutter he managed to crawl into!"

That idea spawned a whole new set of emotions for all of them, especially guilt for feeling relief. Still they all knew they could not rest. Michael was a dangerous man! He was angry, he was mean and he might just be extremely determined. One could go a long way on a pump of that kind of adrenalin! They could not afford to relax their vigilance until they knew his whereabouts for certain.

After breakfast, the women cleaned up the dishes while Kaydee took the kids to the living room to work on coloring books. Katreena decided to make some playdough for later, knowing full well that coloring books would not keep them occupied for too long – especially Alvin. Not surprisingly, after an hour, Alvin was bored with the coloring books, though Jaynee was still totally engrossed. Alvin wanted to go outside but

Kaydee managed to distract him for over another hour by making a kite out of some paper, wood, fabric and string. Helen and Annie started making cookies, producing different varieties and various shapes until lunch was around the corner. Half a day was gone without a major complaint from the kids. Dusty and Joey kept watching the road and the fields for any movement but all was quiet.

After lunch, Kaydee put the kids down for their naps. Joey suggested to Dusty, Katreena and Kaydee that they should try for one as well. "You three have been up most of the night and we'll need you sharp and awake to keep watch tonight. Why don't you try and get some sleep now while the kids are sleeping? Granny, Helen and I will keep watching and we'll call you if anything unusual turns up."

Dusty was reluctant but he couldn't argue with Joey's logic. "I'm not sure I can sleep in the daytime, though," he complained with Katreena and Kaydee echoing his concern.

"Have some hot milk or something, if you must," Joey insisted "but get some rest, man. I want you all alert tonight!" In the end, the three did go for a nap and actually all fell asleep. After all, they only had barely three hours of sleep last night.

Annie dozed off as well on the recliner she was occupying. She was used to an afternoon nap so she had no problem falling asleep. Joey and Helen kept watching the road, the fields, the yard, going from window to window, straining to see any movement that would indicate trouble, but everything remained peaceful. For Joey and Helen, things were both monotonous and stressful at the same time – boring, because nothing was happening but tense and edgy with the fear that something might.

"I can't believe this is happening. I cannot for the life of me imagine how he could get here in his condition, but he is so angry and so unpredictable I don't think anything is impossible with his frame of mind. He's just diabolical enough to make it. He's too mean to die quietly." Helen had given up on feeling guilty about Michael. Joey may as well know her true feelings.

"Let's just hope we spot him before he gets in here," Joey muttered. "Until we hear something to the contrary, we have to assume this is where he's heading with some evil plan of hurting you. We have to be prepared to foil that plan. With all of us working together, I think we have a good chance of outwitting him."

Helen was pensive. "He may have got out of the city last night, long before they started looking for him. Dusty thinks he may have been planning this for weeks and frankly, I wouldn't put it past him. He may be around here already for all we know."

"Maybe he crawled into some hole and just died there." Joey whispered hopefully.

"That would be too thoughtful," Helen muttered. "Michael does not do 'thoughtful'! It's just not in his nature!"

This was the first time Joey had heard Helen speak disparagingly against Michael. It encouraged him. Was this the emancipated Helen he had hoped to see these last few weeks? She sounded grim and resolved and he saw mutiny in her eyes. Joey hoped it would translate itself into rational action should a need arise in this crazy situation. She had apparently come through when she visited Michael at the Bethune hospital. Joey recalled the story as he had heard it and he still had a hard time believing it. Perhaps she can come through again.

"You must keep the kids safe. Promise me that no matter what happens, you'll stay with the kids. I anticipate the problem will come at night. Even if he is around here now, though I cannot see how he could have gotten close without us spotting him, I doubt he will try anything in the daytime. If he is as cunning as you all seem to think, he could be casing the joint now but he won't try anything till dark. Dusty and Katreena will be up by then and we'll handle everything, but you must remain with the kids and keep them safe. Promise?"

"When will you sleep?" Helen wanted to know.

"I got almost a full night's sleep last night, remember? Dusty only called me this morning. I'm fine. Don't worry about me. This won't last forever. Michael will show up within a day or two, you can bet on it. Either the police will nab him or we will. Maybe some concerned citizen will spot him and call it in. He can't hide out long in his condition. He needs his medication or he'll burn up with infections."

"I guess you're right," Helen conceded ruefully. "It's just that it feels like forever ago when we first got that call."

"It's only been about twelve hours, Helen. In another twelve this may all be history. Just relax. We have everything under control."

They walked from window to window, scanning the horizons, relieved to see nothing as they talked together in low tones.

They dared not put the radio or TV on because they wanted to hear every single sound from outdoors. The windows were left open for that specific purpose but all they could hear was the chirping of the birds and the crickets. Everything else was totally quiet.

Chapter 35

In spite of Dusty and Katreena's remonstrations that they could not sleep in the afternoon, it was actually the kids who woke up the household. Alvin had basically fulfilled his sleep quota and after nearly three hours of nap time, he was ready to roam. He sneaked down fairly quietly, knowing the ritual of not waking Jaynee and Dayna but it was his insistence to follow the rest of his routine that created the problem. Normally, he went outdoors to play and the girls continued to sleep in peace but this time his mother and Joey vetoed that practice and in his consternation, he forgot himself and wailed a noisy complaint which brought Jaynee downstairs to add her voice to the confusion and before long, the whole household was there to join in the confrontation. In the end, it was Katreena's foresight of having the mounds of colourful play dough characters that won out and returned peace to the household. Dusty was glad the mayhem had subsided. "Boy, we won't be able to keep this up for too long. They better get that guy and soon. This tension is going to make us all snap." Then aside to Joey, "I'm truly beginning to think that Sergeant Wilson is right. They'll probably find his stinkin' remains in whatever hole he crawled into to hide. He'll be half decomposed in this heat."

Joey grimaced at the image but nodded in agreement. "It can't be too soon for me, man!"

The waiting had them all on edge but the women were able to keep busy with the kids, the cooking, baking and other household chores. It was the men who bore the brunt of responsibility and tediousness. Joey was pensive, vigilant, ever watchful, talking very little, basically minding his business, which, at this time, was clearly to be steadfastly alert for any potential problems and to react instantly to quash them if they arose.

Shortly before six, Dusty's patience snapped. "Why doesn't somebody call for heaven's sake? This is like living a war zone, waiting for the bomb to hit. You'd think they would at least call and give us an update – any kind of update. Just some word they're still trying! This is not a case of 'no news is good news.' I'd take any kind of tidbit at this point!"

They all looked at Dusty with compassion in their eyes. Everybody empathized with him, but nobody had any solution to the problem.

Keeping her voice low key so as not to draw Alvin's attention, Katreena tried to explain. "It's only been about seventeen hours since they discovered th... – aw – this crisis. I'm sure they're doing everything they can. They'll let us know as soon as they find something. Let's just hang in there, honey, okay?"

"It seems like a century ago," Dusty grumbled.

"I feel that way, too," Kaydee interjected. "It seems 'normal' was forever ago. I'd give anything if we could just go back to this time yesterday."

"Amen!" they all agreed fervently.

Supper came and went and evening brought renewed tension. Dusty called Bethune Centre after supper and was told rather tersely that they had no news yet and they would inform them immediately if something should come up. The darkness intensified the cloak-and-dagger atmosphere and instinctively, they all knew that time was running out. Since the police had not been able to locate Michael during the day, it probably meant that he was either out of their vicinities or possibly dead somewhere. If Michael did somehow manage to get out of the vicinity and was to make an appearance here, it would have to be tonight! Surely, he cannot last longer than that in his condition!

All three kids were in bed and asleep upstairs before ten o'clock. Joey went outdoors "to take care of a couple of things."

"Please don't go out there. What if he's out there just waiting for you to show up?" Helen begged frantically but Joey insisted that he had to do something urgent.

"I'll be alright. Don't worry," he assured her.

Helen cringed for his safety as she watched him working on the yard and around the house. He was obviously checking something out and securing things. At one point Helen was ready to go and call him in but Dusty stopped her from going near the door.

"Leave him be, Helen. Joey is no dummy. He knows what he's doing.

Whatever it is, it must be important. Trust him. He has a reason for everything he does."

"But he's an open target out there," Helen wailed.

"Trust him, Helen. Joey knows what he's doing." Dusty repeated.

Helen had no choice. She stayed indoors and anxiously waited for Joey to come back in. It was quite dark when Joey came in, carrying ropes, a baseball bat and a crow bar. In the meantime, the rest of the adults took turns watching the windows, listening and talking in low tones, all nervously aware that this was probably going to be the longest night of their lives, though hopefully, the most boring. It was Joey and Helen's turn to go to sleep while Dusty and Katreena kept watch, but neither Joey nor Helen were ready for that. They paced the floor uneasily, waiting for something to happen and yet knowing full well that no action was the safest situation for them.

It was getting too dark in the house and Helen reached for the light switch. Joey lurched forward and was beside her in a flash, grabbing her hand to keep her from flicking it on.

"No lights!" Joey hissed emphatically as they all looked at him in surprise. He beckoned them to come closer. "If we were being watched, our best bet is to pretend we are all asleep. If we put the lights on he could see in, but we could not see out. If we keep it dark inside, we can see out but he cannot see in. We have to pretend we are all sleeping. I know this is going to be eerie, but this way we have the advantage. We can hear and see what's going on out there and therefore have a better chance to protect ourselves."

"God, I hope this is only some crazy dream," Helen breathed.

"I wish it was morning and this whole thing was just a bad memory," Kaydee muttered.

"Amen to that!" Katreena and Dusty echoed.

It struck Katreena rather sadly, and perhaps with an odd sense of guilt, that, although they were all churchgoers, none of them ever prayed aloud or together. Yet in the last few hours, she had heard the word "Amen" pronounced twice in a tone that was as close to a public prayer as any priest could pronounce it from any pulpit. It reminded Katreena of a saying her father had always used, "Lyudska tryvoha, zavyde ooseech do Boha" which translated "human tragedy brings everyone to God." Was that what was happening to them now?

"Granny, you and Helen and Kaydee go upstairs to bed. There is nothing you can do here anyway and you may as well get some sleep. Remember, no lights! Helen, can you get us a couple of bed sheets before you go upstairs? Then go to bed. I don't want you down here tonight. The rest of us will stay and watch." Joey spoke almost in a whisper but his words were authoritative. When Dusty started to protest that Joey should go to sleep as well, Joey silenced him with a determined gesture of his hand. "Perhaps later," he whispered. Dusty backed off.

Secretly, Dusty appreciated having Joey stay anyway. He felt comforted to have Joey's decisiveness as well as his definite plan of action in case the need arose.

"Come on Mom, please bring Annie upstairs," Kaydee said. Noting a protest formulating on Helen's lips, Joey instantly shushed her and she acquiesced, realizing that arguing with him would be futile. She went to the linen closet, got a couple of sheets, handed them to Joey and without asking why he wanted them, followed Kaydee upstairs.

After the women left, Joey unfolded the sheets and set them on the dining room table. "We may need to use these to entangle him. The ropes are for tying him up," he told Katreena and Dusty. Then the three of them resumed watch at the windows. All was quiet and only the crickets maintained their lonely serenade.

"Katreena," Joey asked softly. "Are you a heavy sleeper or would you wake readily if we called you?"

"I've always been a light sleeper," Katreena answered earnestly. "I don't wake up for a train whistle but when it comes to any unusual sound, I can hear a cat walk across the floor."

"That's what I wanted to hear." Joey whispered. "In that case, you go lie down on Helen's bed. Don't undress, just in case, but there is no point in you tiring out unless it's necessary. You go rest now. In case of anything, we may call on you to make phone calls or keep the rest of the family calm. Dusty, I'm afraid I want you patrolling here with me."

"No problem, man." Dusty kissed Katreena and she left for the bedroom to try and rest.

It was just after eleven. Everything was dark and quiet. The sky was shrouded with a thin layer of high clouds that partially obliterated the moon and stars but occasionally these would spread and let either the moon or some stars filter through. Joey and Dusty passed each other silently in the shadows as they walked from window to window. Their eyes had adapted to the darkness and the men had no problem manoeuvring around each other or around furniture.

Suddenly, they heard a low growl from Rusko which was immediately followed by a sharp bark. Then stillness. Then, more barking in quick succession. They could readily make out Rusko's dark shape standing on the sidewalk. He didn't move from the spot. He just kept barking. The men stood rooted to the window, their hearts arrested in mid-beat, their muscles coiled, ready to spring into action.

Dusty felt a light tap on his shoulder and involuntarily, he jumped. Katreena's scarcely audible whisper sent ripples down his spine. "What's going on? Can you see anything?"

"I can't see or hear anything, but Rusko obviously has heard something. He hasn't seen or smelled anything yet or he would have run after it by now. This is just his alert signal. Something or somebody must be out there. Rusko will let us know if it's anything. I just hope he doesn't wake anyone upstairs." Joey muttered worriedly as he fixed his eyes on the darkness and watched the dog for any signs of movement.

"I'll go check the other windows." Dusty announced softly as he moved away. Rusko was silent again but Joey could see him standing at attention in the dimness of the night.

"Wait here and watch the dog. I'll go check the kitchen windows. Stay very quiet." Joey whispered to Katreena and he hurried to the kitchen. Dusty was watching, alternating between rooms. "Anything?" Joey whispered. Both Dusty and Katreena answered negatively.

Helen descended the stairs, intending to ask a hushed question. Joey was beside her in a second. "Helen, please go upstairs where it's safe," he pleaded. "You're the target here, can't you see? With you here, our job is only going to be a thousand times harder. Please don't do this to us."

"Okay. Okay, Joey I'm going up. I just wanted you to know, the kids are all still asleep. Both Kaydee and your grandmother are awake and we'll all stay upstairs no matter what. I promise you." She emphasized the last part. "Don't worry about us. We'll do as you ask. Just take care of yourselves here. Please take care." With that she scooted up the stairs. Joey watched her in the darkness, relief flooding his veins. If it was Michael out there, the one thing they didn't need was Helen adding to the melee.

Rusko lay down and everything was quiet again, but by now everyone was strung out tighter than a violin string. With hearts pounding, and nerves taut, they listened for any possible sound but all they could hear were those ubiquitous crickets that never changed their tune.

Ten minutes went by. Joey was now constantly monitoring his watch. At this rate, that small flashlight that he kept hiding under his jacket was bound to run out of power by the end of the night. Then Rusko's sharp bark stopped them in their tracks again. Again, one bark, and then silence. Rusko was listening. In the moonlight, they could see Rusko standing, his body alert, his ears perked. They could almost see his muscles trembling with anticipation. Thank God for the dog's ears. Try as they had, none of them had heard a single sound but Rusko obviously had. Something was out there.

"If it is Michael, he will probably try to quiet the dog somehow. He may not be aware that we're watching for him but he won't want Rusko to wake up the household. We'll just have to wait him out and let him make his first move so we can overpower him when he enters the house. It'll be a war of nerves from here on in so be ready." Joey gave his instructions in whispers but with the confidence and authority of one who knows what he's talking about.

Seven more minutes passed by. No one had relaxed for one second during that time, not even Rusko. He stood there all that time, his body rigid as a statue, just his head turning from one direction to the other, his ears perked but he had obviously not heard a sound that was worth barking about. Joey's attention was now almost totally fixed on the dog.

He trusted Rusko's instincts completely and although he knew that the tactics of the defence had to be his own, much depended on Rusko. The element of surprise and ambush was an unfathomable advantage and it could tip the balance in his favour immeasurably. Joey was now almost eager for the confrontation. Let's get this mess over with and let everyone get on with living again!

Rusko suddenly took off toward the back of the house, barking all the way. Joey made a dash for the bedroom just in time to see the dog disappear into the darkness of the shelter belt.

Then the barking stopped, but Rusko did not come back.

"It's Michael!" Joey whispered sharply with conviction. "Rusko has recognized Michael and he's not barking anymore. Get ready and watch the doors and windows. He'll probably be coming through somewhere. Katreena, Dusty, get the sheets ready to throw over him and entangle him. Then when you have him in the sheet, use the ropes to tie him up. Use the crowbar or the bat if you have to protect yourself. Knock him out if necessary," Joey told them.

"Shouldn't we be calling the police?" That was Katreena's whispered question. It seemed perfectly logical to her that it was time to get them involved.

"And tell them what?" Joey scoffed through clenched teeth. His last conversation with Constable Jacobs still galled him. Joey had called the police after Dusty had first informed him that Michael had escaped and that there was the potential danger of Michael showing up at the farm with the intention of hurting the family. Constable Jacobs had laughed!

"I have coffee twice a week with Dr. Walley and from what he tells me that guy is in no shape to hurt his roommate much less come after the family three hundred miles away. Relax man and stop being such a worry wart. There is no bloody way that rotting pile of flesh is going to make it this far. He's probably already stinking up some deserted alley. Go back to sleep and tell the Boyers and the Banaduks to do the same." Then with an audible snort, he hung up.

Joey was furious! He couldn't believe a cop could take a potentially dangerous situation so lightly and so scornfully. It was incredible that people with an insensitive attitude like that were even allowed to take on responsible positions in a community. No! There was definitely no point in calling the police. Without proof that it was Michael out there, Jacobs would just laugh at them again and probably call them all "worry warts"!

"I'm sorry, Katreena." Joey whispered his apology. "I didn't mean to snap at you, but I spoke to Constable Jacobs last night and he laughed that we would even think of Michael showing up here in his condition. Unless we have irrevocable proof that it is Michael out there, he'll never take us seriously. I hate to tell you this, but we're on our own here."

Katreena backed off, feeling chastised. Perhaps Joey was right, especially if he had already tried to get the police involved and failed. Still, it seemed appalling to think that they could not call on the police for help when they needed it so desperately.

A muffled thud came from outside the living room window. Katreena and Dusty caught their breath, but Joey's triumph was unmistakable as he snickered, "He fell. I strung some blue twine on pegs around the house. I thought it might help to alert us and it worked! He must have tripped on it." In the darkness, Dusty shook his head in amazement. Joey was something else!

"Stay very quiet. He'll be coming in through the front door. Get ready with the sheet." Joey's whisper was barely audible as they scurried stealthily to get into position. Muffled grunts and groans told them that Michael was not having an easy time getting back on his feet. Then silence! Breathlessly, they waited. Then, the sound of the doorknob turning. Michael obviously was not aware that he had been observed. He still thought he had the element of surprise on his side. Slowly, quietly, the door opened. Katreena and Dusty were behind the door with the sheet. Joey flattened himself against the other wall trying to stay invisible.

Noiselessly, Michael's hunched figure turned and he closed the door behind him.

"Now!" Joey yelled and Katreena and Dusty threw the sheet over the hunched figure. Joey was ready with the rope and started encircling it. But Michael had a knife and with a hideous scream, he slashed at the sheet, cutting the sheet and slashing Joey's right arm in the process. Joey jumped back.

"Watch out, he's got a knife!" Joey yelled. Katreena ran for the light switch and in the light, Dusty tried to grab the figure from behind. Joey was still in front, grappling for the knife when a shot rang out. Joey folded forward. Dusty grabbed Michael from the back pinning both his arms at his side. Michael pulled the trigger again and screamed. He had shot himself in the foot. Michael struggled to get his hands free but Dusty held fast.

"Ya vastards, I kill you. I kill all a ya. Helen! Ver da the Hell are you, you fuckin vech. Ya ain't gonna screw around on ve, ya whore! I kill you! I'll kill all of you!" Michael kept screaming, profanities spewing from his mouth like venom from a snake. His speech was clearer, so his face must have healed some since they saw him last. Joey was holding his stomach but he lurched up and tried to secure the rope around the figure. Katreena ran to help. Michael kept shrieking curses under the sheet that was now getting bloodier by the minute. He was spitting, kicking and twisting, trying to get free but Dusty just held on, his arms locked tightly around Michael's sheeted form. Michael pulled the trigger again but the bullet hit the floor in front of Joey. They still could not see the gun or the knife. Both were somewhere under that sheet.

"Get that rope around the middle. Tie up his hands," Joey yelled. "Dusty, for God's sake don't let go. Hold on tight. Katreena, you have to help, I'm shot, I can't." Joey panted. He was bent over, bleeding profusely.

Suddenly Helen was there. Her face contorted with rage, uttering not a sound, she grabbed another rope and proceeded to wind the rope around the sheeted figure winding it in front of Dusty then snapping it tight. Again and again she and Katreena wrapped the ropes around the figure securing it tightly and soon they had Michael trussed up like a mummy.

Dusty was still holding Michael up and somehow Michael realized that Helen was now working against him. Shouting more profanities, he pulled the trigger again, but by this time, his hand was already held down by a tight rope. Once again, the bullet hit the floor, this time near

Michael's foot again. Helen flipped the sheet up, located the gun and as she tried to wrestle it out of Michael's hand, the gun went off again, hitting Michael's foot once more. Michael screamed in pain.

"Go ahead, Michael," Helen screamed. "Shoot! Shoot again! Shoot your damned leg off if you want! You can't point that gun anywhere else now, so go ahead, and shoot! Come on, pull that trigger and shoot, damn you!" she yelled, infuriated beyond control.

Realizing he was beaten, Michael dropped the gun from his left hand just as the bloody knife dropped into a loose spot of the sheet from his right. Katreena quickly jumped to get them out of the way, as Dusty threw the trussed figure to the floor in disgust. Helen ran to Joey and Dusty knelt down beside them. Katreena dashed for the phone and dialled the hospital. Joey was bleeding from a deep gash on his right forearm and a bullet wound to his abdomen.

"We have to get Joey to the hospital." Helen was frantic. "He'll bleed to death before the ambulance gets here. We have to take him now." Dusty looked around. He shared Helen's concern. There was no time to lose.

"Katreena, tell the hospital we're bringing him in. We can be there in fifteen minutes. Tell them to have everything ready." While Katreena barked the last few words into the hospital line and hung up, Dusty grabbed Joey and headed for the door.

"Watch out for the twine," Joey reminded them weakly, and Helen flicked on the yard light and followed Dusty. Katreena sped past them and headed for the shed where Dusty had hidden the Buick the evening before.

Dusty ran towards the driveway with his precious load, deftly stepping over the blue trip twine. Within seconds Katreena roared up with the car. Helen yanked the back door open and Dusty carefully deposited Joey in the back seat. Helen jumped in beside Joey, carefully cradling his head on her lap.

"I'll drive. You stay with Michael. Don't leave him alone!" Katreena yelled at Dusty as she spun out of the yard.

"Hang in there Joey. Please be alright. Oh please God, help us." Helen prayed as she had never prayed before. She had gone through so many tragedies that she had steeled herself into oblivion and ceased to feel. Now that she had learned to feel again, was she about to lose again? Surely, God would not take Joey away from her now. Life could not be that unfair!

Joey lay silently on the seat, his head cradled in Helen's lap. Helen did not know if he was conscious but his pain was evident as a low moan escaped from his throat now and then and he seemed to be drifting in and out of awareness. Wordlessly, Katreena sped along the familiar road like she had never even heard of speed limits. "This is getting to be a habit," she thought. How many times had she done this under such desperate conditions?

Finally, Katreena roared up the emergency ramp of the hospital to find the attendants at the door waiting for them. They whisked Joey away without asking questions. Apparently, Dusty had given them more details over the phone and they were prepared for them.

Helen and Katreena quietly went to the lounge to wait apprehensively for word.

Chapter 36

On the way back to the house, Dusty hastily removed the twine, threw it out against the caragana bushes and hurried into the house. He checked to make sure Michael was still securely trussed, made a quick call to the police, then called the hospital to give them the details of Joey's injuries, preparing them for what to expect when Katreena got there, thus saving them precious time. Upstairs, the radio was still blaring so loudly that he could barely hear the voice on the phone. His calls finished, he sank down on a couch. For now, things seemed fine upstairs but he needed to get his emotions under control again before talking to them. Wearily, he sat waiting for the ambulance. Michael remained quiet the whole time and Dusty considered the possibility that he had either passed out or passed away.

"He's too mean to die," he assured himself wryly as he looked down at the inert bloody mummy on the floor in front of him. He wanted to kick it to a pulp but just knowing that Michael was suffering from the knowledge of his ultimate defeat and entrapment gave him immense satisfaction. He eyed the trussed up figure now lying so still before him and spat at it in abhorrent disgust.

True to her word, Kaydee had stayed upstairs with Annie. When they heard the yelling, Kaydee put the radio on full blast and closed the stairs door to drown out the noise from below. The radio, of course, woke the kids from their sleep but Kaydee felt she would rather have the radio wake them than any noise they might hear from downstairs. At first, Mother tried to keep the kids entertained but she recognized the sound of the first gunshot above the noise of the radio and she fled downstairs, leaving Kaydee and Annie to tend to the kids and keep them distracted from the commotion downstairs.

The gunshots petrified Kaydee but she maintained her post and attended to her duties as she had been instructed. In an effort to entertain them, she put on a happy face and started to sing "Frere Jacques" as loudly as she could, encouraging the kids to join her. Even Annie joined them just to keep the kids interested as they laughed at her muddled words.

When the gunshots cracked above the other noise, Alvin looked in alarm at Kaydee and Annie but they just kept on singing so he assumed he was mistaken because Kaydee did not look scared. The radio music and the singing were so loud that the kids were unaware of the drama that was taking place below. Jaynee had not been happy to be awakened from her sleep at first but then she, too, gaily joined in the singing, taking her cues from the Kaydee and Annie. Dayna, who had been sleeping in Kaydee's room tonight, had been awakened by all the hullabaloo but Annie just took her in her arms and kept rocking her as she sang along so she quieted down.

Downstairs, Michael remained on the floor, too spent to struggle or yell anymore. He was wrapped tightly in the sheet and the ropes that held him captive. After Dusty finished with the phone calls and sat down, Michael started cursing again, shouting and demanding to be let loose, but Dusty ignored him and remained perfectly still. When it finally dawned on Michael that no one was listening, he quieted down again, assuming probably that he had been left alone. Now and then, he would call out but getting no answer, fell silent, too exhausted to do otherwise.

Dusty waited patiently for the ambulance and the police to come. They had both been informed and were on their way. Dusty still had not seen Michael's face or any other part of him for that matter and that was just fine with him. If he never saw Michael again, it would suit him perfectly. He wished he could forget he had ever met the beast.

His mind turned to Joey. Dusty wondered how he was doing. Hopefully the doctors could stabilize his injuries without encountering too much of a problem. He had lost a lot of blood, first from the gash on his forearm, then that shot to his abdomen but he just had to be alright. Joey was too good a man to lose. The whole family needed him, Dusty included. Joey was indispensable at KD Acres, and now, Dusty realized just how indispensable he was to the family. He truly cared about them and he had devoted himself completely, putting his heart, soul and life into protecting this family. Joey had to be alright, Dusty prayed.

Dusty thought of the twine that Joey had tripped Michael with. He almost laughed aloud. What an ingenious idea! It did thwart Michael's mutinous plan and must have provoked a significant amount of aggravation for Michael. Dusty smiled wickedly. He could not help relishing that imaginary scene in his mind. It was perfect! No wonder Joey had chuckled in triumph! It had alerted them to Michael's imminent arrival and given them the edge by depriving Michael of the element of surprise. Somehow, in spite of his anxious concern, Dusty had faith that Joey would come through this. God could not, would not be so merciless as to let a man like Joey die while letting Michael live! That would be cruel injustice!

The sound of sirens told Dusty that help was on the way and he got up to look out the window. Michael realized that someone was in the room and let out another barrage of curses and profanities. Dusty felt like kicking him in the mouth to make him shut up.

"Oh shut the hell up, Michael. You're in no position to squawk, and no one on earth would want to hear you anyway!" Dusty snapped in disgust as he walked around Michael. The sheet and the carpet were both a bloody mess and would both have to go in the garbage but, as Dusty saw it, it would be a small price to pay to permanently rid the world of Michael Boyer!

The ambulance attendants were first to enter the house running in with a stretcher and emergency equipment. Constable Jacobs was right behind with another officer. As the ambulance people attended to Michael, Jacobs stood aside, shocked and stunned, as he surveyed the scene. Sheepish and dumbfounded, he apologized profusely to Dusty.

"I am so sorry, Mr. Duganyk. Joey Kerman called me last night and tried to tell me this might happen but I honestly didn't believe him!" Jacobs' voice conveyed his disbelief. "Dr. Walley has been telling us how sick Mr. Boyer was so I just could not see him getting anywhere past the hospital steps let alone all the way here. There was definitely some grossly inaccurate communication there. This afternoon, Sergeant Wilson called and told us to keep our eyes and ears open, but although we did intensify our highway patrol, I must admit to total scepticism about the need for it. I cannot begin to tell you how much I regret not listening to

Mr. Kerman last night. I still don't know how Mr. Boyer made it. He didn't come down the highway, that's for sure."

Michael was out of the sheet by now and the other officer had already handcuffed his hands behind his back. Michael's grotesque facial scars were now clearly visible but the rest of his body was covered by janitorial green coveralls that he had obviously stolen from the hospital. Blood had soaked through the coveralls and it was evident that some his wounds had opened up. Still his hatred and fury clearly overshadowed his pain as he spat towards Constable Jacobs.

"Ya stufid assholes. Ya didn't efin know what yar were lookin for. I saw yar dam cruiser, ya jerk. I turned on the Assaily road, almost in fron of yar noses and you war too stupid to see me! Stinkin dumb assholes!" Michael spat in disgust. Dusty and Constable Jacobs exchanged astonished looks.

Dusty shook his head disbelievingly. Through clenched teeth, he hissed at the ambulance attendants, "Just get him the hell out of here!"

As they were leaving, Constable Jacobs apologized once again. "I hope Mr. Kerman will be alright. Tell him I'm terribly sorry for doubting him. I have to file the report but tomorrow will be soon enough. Would you be able to come in about tenish?"

Dusty just nodded. He could hardly wait for everybody to clear out. He wanted to phone the hospital to find out how Joey was doing.

The sirens were still whining when he got Katreena on the phone. "How is Joey?"

"We haven't any news yet." Katreena sounded like she'd been crying. "They have him on the operating table now. They had to open him up to get the bullet out. We don't know if it hit any vital organs. Helen is beside herself. She's blaming herself. I have to go back. I don't want to leave her alone." The phone went dead. Katreena had hung up.

Dusty felt helpless. He wanted to be there for Katreena and he was just trying to figure out his next move when Kaydee crept cautiously down the stairs. She had heard the ambulance leave and had watched the police follow them but was still unsure about what to expect downstairs, so she left Annie in charge of the kids and came down to investigate.

Because the radio had been blaring so loudly during the whole time neither she nor Annie were aware that Joey had been hurt or that he had been taken to the hospital. They had followed strict orders to stay upstairs away from the windows and keep the kids calm. Now Kaydee came to check.

In hushed tones, Dusty explained to Kaydee all that had happened.

Still in a low tone, Dusty continued, "Your father had a gun and a knife. Joey got cut on the arm and shot in the stomach. I don't know how badly he's hurt. He was bleeding pretty profusely so your grandmother and your mother took him to the hospital instead of waiting for the ambulance. We thought it would be faster that way."

Kaydee was distraught on hearing that Joey was hurt but Dusty quickly calmed her down.

"Kaydee, you must be strong now. We're all depending on you. For now, don't tell Annie about Joey getting shot. Just tell her he was cut on the arm with a knife and that he's in the hospital getting it stitched up. I'll go to the hospital and maybe they will know something by the time I get there. Right now, you go upstairs and turn that blasted radio down and try to get those kids to sleep. Then talk to Annie and try to get some sleep, both of you. I promise to let you know as soon as I find anything out. Can you do that, honey?" Kaydee nodded.

She went to bathroom, splashed some cold water on her tear-stained face, dried herself off and checked herself in the mirror. Satisfied that she looked calm, she went back to Dusty and whispered, "I'm okay, now, Dusty. Don't worry. I won't let you down. We'll be fine. Now go!" She waved her hand toward the door as she made her way up the stairs.

Dusty looked at his bloody clothes. He should change, but his clothes were upstairs. If he went up there, Annie would have all sorts of questions and he was not prepared to talk to her yet. What to do? He can't just walk into that hospital looking like this! Even in a hospital, this was far too inappropriate!

He went to Helen's bedroom and looked in the closet. Michael's clothes hung there as he had left them two months ago. It repulsed him to no end to put on Michael's clothes but what other choice did he have? He looked at his pants. There were two large stains on the pants. He hurried to the bathroom, grabbed a washcloth, soaked it in cold water and set about sponging off the blood stains. It didn't clean them off but it discoloured them sufficiently that the blood was not recognizable. Good enough! Could he do that to the shirt? In dismay, he gazed at his reflection in the mirror. The front of his shirt and the sleeves were all bloody, some of it was dried and grated in by the dirty rope when the girls were trussing Michael up. No way could he make that shirt look presentable!

Reluctantly, he went back to the bedroom, grabbed one of Michael's shirts off a hanger and gritting his teeth, he steeled himself against the revulsion that threatened to suffocate him as he put Michael's shirt on his body. "This is the ultimate insult!" he told himself angrily. He picked up Helen's keys, went to the garage, got in Helen's car and drove to the hospital.

Helen and Katreena were sitting on a couch in the lounge of the emergency department when Dusty walked in. Their faces were drawn and tear-stained. Katreena's arm was around Helen's shoulder and Helen's head was resting against Katreena. They were so engrossed in their misery they didn't even see Dusty come in. Dusty's heart sank.

"Did you hear anything?" Dusty's query was sharp with alarm.

Both heads snapped to attention. Katreena shook her head negatively and motioned him to sit next to her. She needed his strength to bolster her sagging spirits.

"Dr. Walley said he would tell us as soon as they knew something but it's been hours and we still don't know," Helen sobbed. "This waiting and not knowing anything is unbearable."

"Actually Helen, it's only been a little over an hour and perhaps a lot less since they actually opened him up," Dusty clarified soothingly. He could empathize with Helen. Time has a funny way of amplifying itself when life and death are battling for control. He had waited for word on injured buddies during the war and he understood Helen's desperation implicitly. Only someone who'd been there could feel the spectrum of time so profoundly. He wished he could alleviate Helen's suffering, but until Dr. Walley found that bullet and was able to ascertain the damage it had caused, there was nothing they could do but wait.

"How are the kids and Annie doing?" Katreena wanted to know.

"Well Kaydee came down and I basically told her everything but I told her not to tell Annie about Joey being shot. Kaydee will tell her that Joey's arm was cut by a knife and he's getting stitched up. I thought it best this way until we know something more definite."

"Good idea," Katreena agreed. "No sense in her worrying her about it now."

Dusty continued, "That Kaydee is a smart kid. She had that radio blaring so loudly, and she had them all singing so even Annie did not suspect any real calamity. Kaydee will take care of everything," Dusty declared with confidence, adding, "I promised her I would let her know the minute we heard something."

Katreena noticed Dusty was wearing one of Michael's shirts and rolled her eyes questioningly at him. He grimaced. "Don't ask," he warned with antipathy. "I decided this was better than going upstairs and explaining to Annie." Katreena understood. Putting on Michael's shirt would afflict Dusty with absolute disdain, but he sacrificed his own feelings to protect those of Annie. Katreena loved him for it. She knew what that sacrifice had cost him.

They heard a scuffle and Dr. Walley appeared before them. His worried frown had disappeared and he was almost smiling. All three of them jumped up so quickly that Dr. Walley involuntarily stepped back. He held up both palms to silence their enthusiastic questions.

"He's okay," he announced triumphantly. "We got the bullet out and it just barely grazed the upper colon but no major damage. He was very lucky. We've stabilized him and he's doing fine. I was afraid that the bullet may have punctured some vital organs because his blood pressure was so low, and I really worried about internal bleeding or that the bullet may have cut his spleen, but I guess he must have just lost a lot of blood during the fight. The struggle made his heart pump blood faster, causing excessive bleeding. We are giving him a transfusion now to replenish his blood supply. In a week or two he'll be as good as new."

Helen's knees turned to jelly and she sank onto the couch. Katreena was beside her immediately. They were both laughing and crying at the same time. Dusty pumped Dr. Walley's hand in gratitude. Until this moment, they hadn't even realized how much stress they had been under. Now, the knowledge that Joey would be fine made them all euphoric.

"May we see him?" Helen was tremulous and excited, her body quivering with relief.

"You may go and see him," Dr. Walley explained kindly, "but don't expect any response from him. He's still anaesthetised. Remember, he's just come through major surgery. But he'll be awake by noon tomorrow. You can talk to him then. Come, I'll take you to him. Don't stay long and don't try to wake him up. It's too soon."

They stood silently watching Joey sleep, just glad to see him breathing on his own. Blood dripped from a bag on a pole beside him and antibiotics fed directly into his left arm. His right arm was bandaged so the gash he had received from Michael's knife was not visible. Katreena winced as she remembered the blood gushing from the deep slash as he struggled to get the knife out of Michael's hand just before that fateful shot doubled him over. Even after that, Joey had tried to overcome Michael in spite of the pain he must have been suffering. That struggle must have cost him a lot of blood.

Helen could barely breathe for the lump in her throat. They had come so close to losing Joey and suddenly it hit Helen how much he meant to her. She could not even imagine life on KD Acres without him. She didn't know how Joey felt about her, but it didn't matter. As long as he stayed at KD Acres, she could be satisfied with that. Just knowing he was close by or was coming in each day would be enough to keep her happy. She had only begun to live since Joey came into her life. She thanked God for sparing him as she remembered again how close she had come to losing him.

They stayed in Joey's room for only a few minutes. He needed rest and quiet. Tomorrow they would come back and talk to him, thank him for all he had done for them. Tonight, there was nothing more they could do. Remembering his promise to Kaydee, Dusty went to the phone and called KD Acres. Kaydee answered before it even finished ringing.

"He's all right. He's sleeping now. We're on our way home now. Talk to you then." Dusty hung up. They thanked Dr. Walley once more, and left for home.

Everyone except Kaydee was asleep when they arrived at KD Acres. They brought Kaydee up to date about Joey's condition and then all of them decided to go quietly to bed and get some much needed sleep themselves. Over the last couple of nights, none of them had any decent shut eye – disturbed snitches and snatches of it here and there – troubled and uneasy, but nothing that could be classified as a relaxing sleep. They were all dead tired.

Dusty and Katreena worried about Helen walking through the living room to get to her bedroom because the living room carpet was stained with blood. After the ambulance people left, Dusty had taken the bloody sheet Michael had been wrapped in and thrown it into the garbage but there was nothing he could do about the carpet. That was a job that had to be left for another day. But they need not have worried. Helen seemed well in control of her emotions now. As she walked through the living room, she looked in disgust at the stains and remarked, "I can't believe I ever thought I loved that beast. I hope they never let him out! I'm going to replace that carpet first chance I get!" Then she went straight to bed. Katreena and Dusty exchanged grateful glances. Dusty gave Katreena's hand a tight squeeze and they went upstairs.

A habitual early riser, Annie was the first one up the next morning. She knew that the three adults were probably dead tired and still needed to sleep, so careful not to wake anyone, she crept quietly down the stairs. The sight of the bloody living room floor alarmed her even though Kaydee had given her the general basics about what had happened. Still, she needed to know how her grandson was doing and picking up the phone, she dialled the hospital. Trying to speak softly, she asked the receptionist to put her through to the wing where Joey Kerman was.

"May I ask who is calling please?" The professional voice of the receptionist sounded rather guarded and Annie could hear her questioning somebody near her about what to do next.

"This is Mrs. Dorozeck, his grandmother," Annie answered rather sharply. In her anxiety, she forgot about keeping her voice low.

"One moment, please." The phone got that distinct "on hold" sound and Annie was left to hold the line and wait. Helen, in the meantime, had heard Annie and was beside her immediately. Katreena and Dusty were awake, discussing the best way to break the news to Annie. They had heard the call too and raced down the stairs, their robes barely tied and still flying behind them.

Calmly Dusty took the phone from Annie, mouthing silently to her "Let me," as he nodded reassuringly at her. Meekly, and obediently, she let him take the phone from her, but her apprehension mounted as she gaped suspiciously at the concerned faces around her. "Hello... Hello?" Dusty spoke into the phone. Getting no answer, he waited and then "Guess we're still on hold." Then soothingly to Annie, "They had Joey sedated to fix him up last night. I didn't want them to wake him. That guy needs his sleep. He lost a lot of blood from that arm and they were giving him blood to replace what he had lost," Dusty explained rationally. At least he was not going to lie. They would add more of the truth later, but they would not have to retract any lies.

Finally, a voice at the other end alerted them again.

"Hello. This is Dusty Duganyk. We were with Joey Kerman last night. How is he doing this morning?" Dusty stood silently listening to the voice at the other end, occasionally interjecting, "Oh that's good," and "Oh, that's great to hear," then finally "Well, thank you for the good news Nurse Greene, we'll be down to see him later then. Thank you so much," and hung up.

"He's still sleeping. He's had a peaceful night and he was awake this morning. He took his meds orally but he is still groggy and went back to sleep. He had a total anaesthetic last night so it has not totally worn off yet." Dusty told Annie, then, glancing at Katreena and Helen, he plunged forward. "There is something else you should know before you go to see your grandson, Annie. We didn't want to alarm you until we knew Joey was okay but in the struggle with Michael last night, Joey took a bullet to the abdomen. That was why he was under anaesthetic, but they got it out clean and it did not harm anything. The doctor said he'll be good as new in a couple of weeks. They gave him a blood transfusion last night because he had lost so much blood but this morning they said all his vitals are back to normal. We'll give him till half past one to wake up from the anaesthetic and we'll see him then. I cannot begin to tell you how much I appreciated having him here and all that he did for us. He is an amazing and brave man! Annie. You ought to be extremely proud of him!"

"Thank you. I thought there was something more to it last night but I also knew that if it had been really bad you would have told me. Joey **is** a good man and I **am** very proud of him." Annie acknowledged as she wiped emotional tears from her eyes.

Kaydee heard the adults and came to join them as they sat talking for the next couple of hours. Dusty filled them in on the details of the night before. They were all shocked at Michael's determination and stamina to have accomplished that near impossible feat of making it over the three hundred miles from Bethune Centre to KD Acres and his cunning at avoiding detection in the face of the manhunt that was going on for him at the time. Dusty explained Constable Jacobs' disbelief when he recounted about how Michael had managed to steal pain killers, clothing, a knife, a gun and a car and driven down back roads to evade capture until he reached his destination. Everyone marvelled at his foresight, his perseverance and his grit to pull it off in spite of the pain he had to have been under, because surely, even with pain killers, he had to use discretion in order to maintain a balance between being pain-free and remaining alert and vigilant and focused on his objective.

Annie shook her head in amazement. "The Devil does not sleep. He plays with idle minds and hands. Michael had the time to plan. Evil lets nothing stand in its way. This was truly the work of the evil one! He could have killed everyone."

"Well, it is thanks to Joey that we are all alright," Dusty repeated again. "Joey knew exactly what to do. I must admit, I would not have known where to start. I cannot begin to thank him for all he has done." Dusty then repeated the story about the twine tripper.

"We didn't know what Joey meant when he said he had some important things to do last night but he'd gone to string a trip twine around the house. That slowed Michael down and also alerted us to his exact whereabouts and gave us time to prepare for him. That was pure genius! It was just so phenomenal, Annie. When we heard that thud when Michael fell over that twine and then the grunting and groaning when he was getting up, I thought Joey had lost it because he was snickering so hard! Now I know why. I can almost imagine Michael swearing. I think I would have had hysterics had I known!" They all laughed, imagining Michael's surprise as he fell. "That twine idea was pure genius. It tipped us off exactly where Michael was at the time," Dusty repeated, still in awe of Joey's ingenuity.

Annie smiled proudly. She was not one to laugh at someone's misfortune but she had to acknowledge that Joey's foresight had been brilliant indeed.

"Well I doubt that we will ever have problems with Michael again." Katreena reasoned. "They will not be taking Michael for granted anymore. He is a raving lunatic and I think that after last night, they will realize this and probably have him chained to the building for the rest of his life." Katreena did not try to shield Helen and Kaydee anymore. She was certain that both of them shared her disdain for him, particularly after the events of the night before.

As the morning hours advanced, Annie watched the clock impatiently. They had been up for more than two hours now. The kids were still sleeping, breakfast had not even been started and the visit to the hospital was still five hours away. She could hardly wait to see Joey. She wanted to talk to him, see for herself that he was alright, that he was on the road to recovery. But she had to wait. Joey would not be coherent enough now even if she did get to see him. Annie trusted Dusty. He would not tell her a lie, although they had not told her the whole truth before. She knew why. She was convinced that they were being straight with her now. Given the kind of surgery Joey had undergone last night, he would need time to recover from the anaesthesia. The best way to make that time go faster was to get busy.

Resolutely, Annie got up from her chair. “Okay, I don’t know about the rest of you, but as for me, I am going to prepare breakfast and we are going to get busy around here. This waiting around is driving me crazy.”

“You got that right, lady,” Dusty agreed. “Let’s get breakfast over with. Then I’m going to go into town. I promised Constable Jacobs to help him with the report on last night’s events. I’m not sure how long that will take so in case I’m not back by one o’clock, you may want to take Helen’s car to drive to the hospital.”

Dusty deliberately omitted mentioning that the back seat of his car was soaked with Joey’s blood from the ride to the hospital last night and he was going to try and get it cleaned as soon as he finished with Constable Jacobs. If that was impossible, he would have to cover it with a blanket. Helen’s car did not have such painful reminders of Joey’s traumatic injury and was, therefore, the car that must be used to transport Annie and Helen to the hospital.

Dayna’s crying announced that she was awake. Shortly afterwards, Jaynee and Alvin made their bleary-eyed descent down the stairs. While Helen and Annie attended to the breakfast, Kaydee and Katreena washed and dressed the children and breakfast was soon underway. Between them, the adults kept the conversation light and jovial. To the smaller children it was just a normal day. They had obviously forgotten the interruption of last night’s sleep.

After breakfast, Kaydee immediately took the kids outdoors so that the bloody carpet would not become a subject of curiosity. Dusty left for town and while Annie cleaned up the breakfast dishes, Helen and Katreena set about to disguise the blood stains from the living room carpet. Removing the carpet was impossible at this time but for now, all they had to do was camouflage it as some dirty stain and the kids would not question it. Neither one of them was willing to try to explain a bloody carpet to the always inquisitive Alvin.

Kaydee phoned the Norchaks and briefed them on the events of the day before, confessing that her “stomach ache” was a lie and giving them a short description of the night that prevented her from attending school today.

"I'll be there tomorrow," she promised, then added quickly, "unless something else happens. At this point, it can be anything. I will let you know if I cannot make it."

"We'll see you then," Sandy Norchak replied sympathetically. "We're so sorry to hear about all your problems. We know this is a bad time for you. Tell Joey we think he's a very brave man and that we hope he gets better soon. Give him our best. Also your family and Annie." Sandy Norchak felt sorry for Kaydee. She was dealing with so much. "We'll just try to make up your lessons the best way we can when we can. They are very important now if you are to catch up to your classmates. Good luck, Kaydee."

Chapter 37

"Give my love to Joey and tell him I wish him all the best. And so do the Norchaks," Kaydee called as Katreena drove Helen's car out of the driveway.

Helen did not wish to drive. She was too unsettled. Although she shared Annie's concern for Joey's health and was anxiously anticipating the visit to see him for herself, she felt nervous about seeing Joey. She could not understand it. She felt something unfamiliar, and that "something" had not been defined yet. It was an elusive shadow of a dream that was not quite formulated in its entirety. She felt its presence but each time she tried to grasp it, to focus on it, it evaded her scrutiny and moved just beyond validity so that she felt disoriented, mystified and bewildered.

In the front seat, Katreena and Annie chatted enthusiastically about Joey's recovery but behind them, Helen was in turmoil. Last night had made her recognize her total dependence on Joey, not just for the work that he did at KD Acres, but for his geniality and his rationale. His upbeat personality had become a constant in her life, the anchor of its existence. His positive outlook and perpetual good humour had captured her hungry heart. She needed Joey, Helen realized. She needed him because she loved him!

Her thoughts returned to Michael. He was her husband but insofar as love was concerned, Michael was not even a blip on her radar screen. She suddenly saw how empty her life had been all these years, so devoid of vitality, enthusiasm and passion. She had existed, but she hadn't lived, not until Joey came into her life and ignited that spark. The prospect of seeing Joey filled her with excitement and happiness. She could hardly wait!

Katreena parked close to the entrance. They were early, so she had a good pick of parking stalls. Helen was out of the car immediately, walking briskly up the steps, well ahead of the other two women. By the time they came to the elevator, Helen was already in, impatiently holding the door open, waiting for them. At the door to Joey's room, Helen did not wait for a discussion about who was going in first. Boldly, she walked right up to Joey with his grandmother behind her. Katreena stayed behind in deference to the rule of "two visitors at a time."

Joey was lying on the bed, his head propped up on a couple of pillows, his face slightly pale but smiling when they walked in. An IV needle still fed antibiotics into his arm but the blood bags had been removed. Annie walked up to him and planted a kiss on his forehead. "It's so nice to see that you're okay, honey," she said huskily.

"How are you feeling?" Helen asked before Annie had a chance to speak again.

Joey smiled mischievously. "Well, I wouldn't try for a wrestling match just yet, but give me a day or two and I may take you on."

Helen turned to Annie. "He's feeling fine, but we'll wait until tomorrow before we make him shovel grain," she laughed.

"Don't you go making me laugh now. I'm working on patching up my insides, remember? Besides, if you get too rough, I'll just go to sleep on you. I just woke up from a deep sleep less than an hour ago. It felt good. I may just wanna go back there, you know."

"I know," Helen retorted. "We saw you this morning but you were out like a light."

"Are you in pain?" Annie interjected. She wanted to know that much at least.

"Heavens, no! They have me on such a high with these drugs I could dance a jig," Joey assured them. "They told me the bullet didn't touch anything important. Dr. Walley says I should be good as new in a couple of weeks."

"Well, we won't be putting the harness on your back in two weeks, you can be sure of that," Helen said seriously. "You just concentrate on getting well. I'll get someone to take the harvest in, so don't you worry about it. Your job now is to mend. We just want you well again," she repeated, her voice throaty with emotion.

"That's right, Joey. You concentrate on getting well first and worry about jigging later." Annie reiterated Helen's concern.

They chatted on for another ten or fifteen minutes, but no one mentioned Michael's name and Helen was glad. She didn't want this wonderful time marred by the subject of that maniac. All conversation had been light and upbeat and that seemed to suit everybody just fine. If problems arose, they would deal with them as they came up. Right now, her heart was overflowing with gratitude and contentment and she wanted to keep it that way.

Dusty found Katreena in the waiting room and brought her up to date on what he had learned at the police station. The ambulance people had taken Michael directly to Bethune Sciences Centre where he had been immediately put into protective custody in a special section of the hospital for mentally unstable patients. There, he could be kept temporarily locked up with no chance of escape. However, his night of terror could not be ignored either and victims could lay charges to procure permanent custody service for him.

"He's a menace to society and he needs to be locked up permanently or else he'll come after them again and then he might succeed. Helen cannot live in fear for the rest of her life. Official charges have to be filed in order for them to keep him incarcerated while they try to heal him up again," Dusty said worriedly. "Actually, Joey can lay charges or any one of us can. Even the police report can make it stick with merely 'assault with deadly weapons' noted. A Restraining Order in this case would not be worth the paper it was written on. If Michael ever became mobile again, he would just ignore it. We'll all have to get together with Joey and the police to decide what would be the best way to handle this."

"Personally, I cannot see Joey pressing charges unless he does it to protect Helen and the kids. We'll have to see. I hope we don't have to deal with this immediately," Katreena worried.

"No, Jacobs said he would come by to talk to Joey in a couple of days."

Helen and Annie emerged from Joey's room, both smiling and relaxed. Katreena breathed a sigh of relief. They apparently had a good visit and were pleased with what they saw. Dusty and Katreena then took their turn at visiting with Joey but they only stayed a few minutes. When Joey brought up the subject of Michael, Dusty shushed him, saying that tomorrow would be soon enough to address the issue. For now, Joey should relax and simply concentrate on getting well. Everyone was pleased with his prognosis. Relieved and happy, they rejoined Helen and Annie in the lobby for a joyous tête-à-tête. Since there was little else they could do for Joey, they left the hospital and returned to the cars to head for home.

"You go with the girls," Dusty dismissed Katreena with a wink, "I have some things to attend to." Katreena grasped his wink as he motioned towards the bloody back seat of his car.

Katreena dropped Annie off at her place and then briefed Helen on what Dusty had told her about the hospital putting Michael in the special ward for unstable patients.

"He will be kept there under lock and key so there is no chance of him escaping again but that is only a temporary solution. We will have to meet with the police to provide a more permanent resolution to the problem. We could press charges and put him in a mental institution. That will be up to you and Joey."

"That would solve the problem, wouldn't it?" Helen said wryly, but her expression was grim. "If that hospital doesn't do something about their security, I certainly will. I blame Dr. Henderson. He was so sure that I was being a bad wife because I wouldn't visit Michael. He just didn't take precautions because he felt sorry for him. Now maybe he'll believe us."

When Katreena and Helen got home from the hospital, Kaydee was waiting for them with a million questions about Joey: his appearance; the extent of his wounds; his prognosis; his attitude; and when he was coming home.

Helen wrapped her arms around Kaydee and in a voice shaky with emotion, answered question after question after question. Helen was euphoric with what she had heard at the hospital and her tone unambiguously conveyed it. Katreena noted her exhilaration with approval sensing a budding chemistry between Joey and Helen. Kaydee noticed it also.

The phone rang and with a groan, Helen picked it up. It was Dr.

Henderson.

"I am so sorry, Mrs. Boyer. We had no idea Mr. Boyer was..."

Helen cut him off. "You think a simple 'I'm sorry' could make up for this? We've been to hell and back because of your negligence! As far as I am concerned, no amount of apologies could make up for what you put us through. You told us yourself, before that visit that first day that Michael was 'extremely agitated.' You saw Michael go wild. You heard Michael's threats with your own ears. Yet you did not take the precautions to ensure that Michael always swallowed his sedatives and that he was safe in his bed and in his room at all times! What kind of hospital is Bethune Centre, that Michael was able to walk out with a supply of pain killers and clothes? Nobody was even aware that he had left the building let alone the room! This constitutes gross negligence on your part. You are responsible for all of this. Michael was under your care and it was your duty to ensure that all precautions were observed. You failed in your duty and you think 'I'm sorry' can fix that? There is a man in the hospital because of you and our whole family was traumatized!"

Helen slammed the receiver into the cradle. If it hurt Dr. Henderson's ear, then so much the better! She was not going to waste pity on that man. "Ugh!" she fumed.

"What's happening with Michael," Katreena insisted.

"I didn't ask!" Helen snapped. "They should have had him in a secure ward from the beginning!" Helen could not control her exasperation. "Saying 'I'm sorry' just doesn't cut it for me. Joey is lying in the hospital with a bullet wound in his belly and Dr. Henderson just says he's sorry and we're supposed to be all happy and forget it all happened? That is beyond belief! I'd like to sue that hospital for everything they own!"

"Truth is, Helen, you have that option open to you. I am sure Dr. Henderson knows it and he is trying desperately to win your forgiveness. It's up to you and Joey, what you want to do about this matter." Katreena tried to sound empathetic but she was actually fascinated by this forceful daughter she was seeing. Helen was so full of verve and passion. How had Michael stripped Helen of that passion for life so completely? Helen had been intelligent, resilient, not foolhardy, but strong-willed, nonetheless. She had been well grounded with a ferocity of spirit and a solid sense of perspective. Katreena smiled as she watched the resurgence of those qualities.

Helen seemed to consider Katreena's proposal of her options and grimaced. Then, without a word, she went to the kitchen to prepare supper and set it on the table. Kaydee and Katreena tried to help, but they could not keep up with Helen's momentum. Dusty came home but seeing the women so involved, decided to seek solitude outdoors. He felt a pang of uselessness. Everyone had a purpose except him. Dusty knew nothing about farming, yet he knew that in Joey's absence, the farm work would be neglected. As he walked around the yard inspecting all the other earmarks of Joey's influences, he worried how they would fill the void his absence would create. It was a temporary gap. The harvesting was less overwhelming because of the hailstorm but this was still a crucial time on the farm. Joey had already started swathing the grain. They would have to make other arrangements for harvest now. Dusty hoped a workable solution to that problem could be found soon.

The breeze from the west carried a distinct scent of swathed grain. Even Dusty could identify that smell. The tawny golds and browns of ripened grain had already replaced the vibrant greens of the grain fields. The air had a hint of an evening chill. Occasional patches of dark green spruce and pine interspersed among the yellows, oranges and burgundies of the forests boldly announced that fall, though close, was not quite here yet. The crickets chirped frenziedly, bidding their summer friends farewell and only chickadees, jays and sparrows chattered in the trees. October would be here soon and with it, Dusty's marriage to Katreena. Dusty felt a warm glow engulf his body. His reverie was interrupted by Katreena's call to supper.

Dusty hurried inside. He had seen Helen eagerly working to get supper on. Obviously she had plans for the evening and Dusty did not wish to be the one to detain her. While they ate, Helen told them that she was going back to the hospital for the evening visit. She wanted to discuss the harvest plans with Joey and see if he had any suggestions for his interim replacement.

"The neighbours are willing to help out right now but they are already stretched to the limit trying to help Josie Archer. Fred is still in the hospital and Josie may have to make permanent plans for renting the land next year but for now, she needs help collecting what's left of this year's crop, and tilling the land. I'm sure Joey will have some good suggestions about what we should do."

"May I go see Joey too?" Kaydee was hesitant. It was always the adults that went. Her job was to take care of the kids, but she did want to see Joey also.

"Of course you may go see Joey," Katreena was quick to reply. Poor Kaydee had been treated like Cinderella. While they kept going here, there and everywhere, Kaydee had stayed back and babysat and she had done it without complaint. Now it was time to award her the credit that she was due. She had accepted responsibility like an adult. It was time to treat her as one!

"I will stay with the children while you and your mother visit Joey. How is that?"

Kaydee was ecstatic. "Oh, thank you Granny!" Kaydee threw her arms around Katreena's neck, hugging her impulsively.

"In fact," said Katreena, "I will also volunteer to do the supper cleanup so you can get away sooner. Do you want Dusty to drive you, Helen, or will you go alone?"

"I don't see why I can't drive myself," Helen answered nonchalantly. "We'll swing by Annie's and pick her up along the way. I'm sure she would appreciate seeing Joey as well. Thanks Mom." Then to Kaydee, "Let's go change."

After the girls drove off, Dusty helped Katreena with the dishes then poured a glass of wine for each of them. He took Katreena's hand and led her outside to sit on the deck to watch the sunset. Jaynee was playing on the grass, Alvin and Rusko were playing a vigorous game of tag and Dayna was laughing up a storm as she hopped around in the jolly jumper.

"Oh Dusty," Katreena sighed, her eyes filling with wistful tears. "This is what life should be like – should have been like – for the last thirteen years! So many wasted years!"

"Maybe we'll still have a chance to make them up, sweetheart." Dusty murmured as he squeezed her hand.

"I'm almost afraid to hope, Dusty. Over the last few years, but particularly this last summer, it's been crisis after crisis. I know that this time it looks more promising, but it seems every time I get close, something happens to snatch the good things out of my grasp. For once I would like to have things stable again."

"I – we will make them stable, Katreena. Together."

Katreena looked into his eyes. "I love you, Dusty Duganyk."

"And I love you, Katreena Banaduk."

Chapter 38

The next day Dusty went home to check things out there but Katreena remained at KD Acres to stay with Jaynee and Dayna and Alvin. Kaydee had gone back to school and Helen was constantly on the go now, between working on the swather, hauling grain from the combine and running to the hospital to see Joey every chance she got. She hardly had any time to herself anymore but she seemed to thrive on it. She had radiance to her which Katreena had not seen in years. After every hospital visit, she brought glowing reports of how well Joey was doing, how much he had improved and how much he was looking forward to getting home.

Joey had recommended one of the men that he knew from town to help out with the harvest and everything was going along smoothly. Elmer Sutton drove himself to the farm each morning and went back home for the night. He was efficient and knowledgeable, having done custom combining for farmers in the past.

It was barely seven in the morning when the phone rang. With annoyance, Helen stepped out of the shower, quickly grabbed a robe and ran to get it before it woke everybody else. Kaydee and Katreena also heard the ring and were just coming down the stairs when they heard Helen answer it.

"Hello...? Yes, Dr. Henderson, what is it now?" Helen's voice was apprehensive but sharp, her tone cold and discourteous. She listened for a couple of minutes then added tonelessly but matter-of-factly, "I see." She was unemotional and unsympathetic. Then she just hung up.

Katreena and Kaydee were at her side waiting patiently until she finished. "What was that about?" Katreena queried. Helen had been unmistakably rude and while Katreena could empathize with Helen's disdain toward the doctor, she was surprised at Helen's attitude. Aware that a lawsuit against him and the hospital could be pending, Dr. Henderson was eager to appease Helen. Yet according to Helen's logic, treating him like a world menace was justified.

"Michael's foot refuses to heal," Helen related. "He had several small bones shattered by the bullets and even though they tried to clean it up, it is still festering. They only have one other antibiotic they are going to try on him. Each time they start healing him, he does something that undermines the process. They are running out of options. Dr. Henderson says that if this new drug does not stop the infection, they will have to amputate the foot."

Katreena and Kaydee gasped in shock but Helen remained unmoved. Without another word, she turned and walked back to the bathroom to finish her hair.

Kaydee looked questioningly at her grandmother but Katreena simply shrugged her shoulders and went upstairs to change. Kaydee could do nothing more than follow.

The roofers came in and within the week they had finished shingling all the roofs that had been damaged by the hail. Joey was elated when Helen reported that they had finished.

"That's wonderful, Helen," Joey enthused. "Now we don't have to worry about the fall rains damaging anything. That's another thing off our 'to do' list. The next thing is finishing the harvest. After that it'll be the shed."

"The most important thing is getting you well, Joey. You'll be coming home soon," Helen beamed.

October drew closer but plans for Dusty and Katreena's wedding were put on hold because Joey was in the hospital. Harvest was incomplete but it was fast coming to a close thanks to Elmer Sutton. Joey was walking by himself through the hallways of the Zelena Health Centre, signalling his imminent release from the hospital. The police had filed a report on Michael that kept him under close guard and now that his leg was getting gangrenous, the threat of him walking out was diminished. Laying charges against the hospital lost its urgency because Helen didn't want to talk about Michael or Dr. Henderson now.

It was now five days since Dr. Henderson had called to tell Helen of a possible amputation for Michael's leg. Early Thursday morning, the phone rang and Helen reluctantly reached to pick it up. It had to be Dr. Henderson. No one else called before seven.

"Mrs. Boyer?" It was him all right. Helen bit her lip. Her mother had convinced her that being snappish to Dr. Henderson would only bring her down to Michael's level and no way was Helen going to stoop that low. But courtesy for the arrogant doctor was still beyond her limit.

"Yes, Dr. Henderson. What is it today?"

"Not very good, I'm afraid. We cannot control Michael's gangrene and we have to amputate as soon as possible. We were hoping you could come in to the city and sign the consent forms, perhaps even today, if possible."

"Why can't Michael sign them himself? He's conscious and coherent, isn't he?"

"Well, you see," Dr. Henderson chose his words carefully. "Michael is noncompliant. He refuses to have his leg amputated. He is still very agitated and he refuses to sign anything. We cannot make him understand that this is a matter of life or death for him. As his wife, you can sign the papers because it is a medical emergency. If need be, we can declare him mentally incompetent and in view of recent events that you are well aware of, the judge would have no qualms about signing such a declaration. Would you consider it? If we do not amputate soon, the poisons will spread throughout his whole body and then we have no chance of saving his life." The doctor fell silent, waiting for Helen's answer.

But Helen was not prepared to go there. "If Michael does not want to sign for the amputation and he is still 'very agitated' as you put it, then he would be even more furious with me if I overruled him, don't you think? You may not know the extent of his temper, Dr. Henderson, but I am only too well aware of it. That is strictly his decision to make and I am certain he is totally capable of making it. I will not defy him on this issue. I am sorry."

"You understand what this can mean, do you not?" Dr. Henderson persisted.

"Yes, Dr. Henderson, I understand completely. But this is your responsibility and I am not going to take it off your shoulders. You have a coherent patient there. You convince him of the urgency of this amputation. I refuse to shoulder a responsibility that is not mine. I will not expose myself or my family to his wrath again. I want nothing to do with signing that paper."

"Do you wish to be informed of when he signs the papers?"

"Not particularly. It is his call, not mine. You do what you have to do. Goodbye and good luck, Dr. Henderson!" With trembling hands, Helen hung up the phone.

Dusty, Katreena and Kaydee had all been heading down the stairs when they heard Helen's answer to Dr. Henderson. They stopped halfway down to hear what she was saying. They needed no explaining as to what was going on. They could easily fill in the blanks for themselves. They were cheering Helen even before they descended the stairs.

"Atta girl, Helen. You told him where to get off." Dusty was jubilant but exasperated at the same time. "Imagine the nerve of that man, trying to get the monkey off his back that way! He's a bloomin' coward! If Michael wants to commit suicide, it's his prerogative, but personally I think Michael is calling the doctor's bluff. He either doesn't trust that doctor or else if Dr. Henderson threatened to get you involved, Michael was giving him a dare so he'd get you there for him to scream at some more. You did the right thing, Helen, and I am proud of you!"

"So am I!" Katreena and Kaydee echoed. Kaydee raced past Katreena and Dusty down the rest of the stairs to hug Helen passionately and Katreena followed.

Dusty took Helen's hand and raised it up into the air triumphantly, "This has been a long time coming Helen, but I really think you have finally made it into the real world."

"I have never been more proud of you than I am at this moment, honey." Katreena told Helen fervently.

Kaydee merely managed to choke out a fervent "Me too."

"That was a Jaynee comment!" they all hooted in unison and then all of them started laughing. That not only changed the subject but broke the tension as well.

Dusty had to go home and check with Dwayne on some business about the publishing company and he asked Katreena if she wanted to come.

Helen agreed immediately. “Go ahead, you’ve been cooped up here for so long you’re starting to grow roots. I’ll get Annie to look after the kids for a few days. It won’t be long now anyway. You both need a break from this place. We’ll manage, honest. Go on, enjoy yourselves. I promise to call if anything comes up.”

“But...” Katreena started a question but Dusty cut in.

“Thank you very much, Helen. We’ll leave right after breakfast.” Though he was talking to Helen, he was looking into Katreena’s eyes.

Katreena laughed. “I was going to say if anything happens, be sure to...”

“She will, she will. You heard her promise. Now let’s get breakfast on the table and then let’s get going!” Dusty was so excited he could hardly contain himself. Helen had never seen him so animated. He had been so patient, so tolerant, so accommodating throughout this whole ordeal, Helen was afraid he had lost his zeal for life, but thankfully it had resurfaced. For her mother’s sake, Helen was glad. This summer had been so oppressive and they all had difficulty maintaining an optimistic attitude – even Katreena and Dusty!

Annie was delighted when Helen called her about babysitting the kids.

“I was beginning to feel quite useless already. I need something to help make the time go faster. Thank you for giving me this opportunity to do something useful with my time.”

Dusty picked up Annie while the women got breakfast on the table. They were barely finished eating when the schoolbus drove up. Grabbing her books and lunch bag, Kaydee gave everyone a peck on the cheek and went flying out to catch the bus. Annie stood there speechless, gazing at Helen and Katreena, a totally stunned expression on her face.

Helen laughed. “She’s been like this ever since school started. She loves school now and Mr. Norchak even called me to tell me how well she is getting along with the other kids. Sandy is coaching her in her spare time and Kaydee is sailing through her classes according to them. It’s too early to say how she will do in her catch-up lessons but the transformation in her personality is nothing short of miraculous.”

“I am so happy for all of you,” Annie gushed. “I knew that girl was no retard.”

Chapter 39

It had been two days since they had heard from Dr. Henderson. Everything on the home front had remained quiet. Helen had informed Annie about Michael's prognosis and the poor woman was dumbfounded when she heard that Michael was refusing treatment.

"Dusty thinks that Michael is calling the doctor's bluff. He thinks that Michael just wants Dr. Henderson to get me to come there to defy him so he can blame me all over again. Michael can sign those papers himself and we're pretty sure he will as soon as he realizes that no one is going to fall for his line anymore. He's stubborn and mean and he thinks he's making us suffer. Instead, he is causing his own misery. Truth is, I would not dare do something that he has already refused to do. He'd chop me up into tiny pieces and feed me to the dogs if I did."

"I know, my dear. I understand your position and I would do exactly the same thing if I were in your shoes. He must sign those papers himself. It is his body, his leg, and he knows exactly what he is doing. If he chooses to play these crazy games then it is his problem. Like you said, Michael is a stubborn man."

Helen was relieved to get the subject off her chest. To have Annie's unconditional support on this issue meant everything to Helen. It gave her incomparable peace.

Joey was scheduled for release from the hospital on Tuesday. Dr. Walley was pleased with his progress and both Helen and Annie were ecstatic about his imminent release. That Sunday evening, when Helen arrived home from her visit with Joey, she was exuberant. Kaydee met her at the door, her face sombre and anxious.

"Mom, Dr. Henderson wants you to call him back," she announced worriedly handing Helen a piece of paper with a number on it.

Helen tensed immediately. All her previous enthusiasm evaporated. "The curse of Michael," she muttered to herself as she went grudgingly to the phone.

Dr. Henderson answered on the first ring. "Mrs. Boyer, I understand that you were not particularly interested when Michael signed the paper but I thought I should still inform you that we finally got him to sign today. However, I'm afraid that I may still have bad news for you. The gangrene has spread to above the knee and we will have to amputate well up his thigh. He is very angry about it. He remains extremely belligerent, and I can see now why you chose not to defy him. My sympathies, Mrs. Boyer. We have scheduled him for surgery first thing tomorrow morning. I will keep you informed about the outcome." With that, Dr. Henderson just hung up.

Helen just stood there glaring at the phone in her hand. Kaydee came and took it from her, listened, and hearing no one there, hung it up. "What did he have to say?" she asked gently.

In a daze, Helen answered. "Dr. Henderson offered me his sympathies!"

"You mean Father died?" Kaydee whispered incredulously.

"No, that's not it. He signed the consent forms today and he's having surgery tomorrow morning. Dr. Henderson said that he realizes now why I refused to sign. He said that they have to amputate well above the knee and Father is very angry and belligerent. That's when he offered me his sympathies. I think he has just now got to know the man your father really is."

"Don't worry about it, Mom." Kaydee put her arm around her mother. "It is not your responsibility. Father made his own choices and he will have to live with them, that's all. How is Joey?" Kaydee deliberately changed the subject. She didn't want her father's problems to dominate her mother's thoughts and thus spoil the rest of the evening.

Talking about Joey was just what Helen needed. "Joey said he wants us to have tons of honey on hand because he will not drink his tea without it and he wants tea cakes baked fresh twice a day. He said he'll make us wait on him hand and foot day in, day out."

Kaydee giggled. She was just trying to visualize Joey being that demanding.

Helen told Kaydee how glad Joey had been that they had finished the combining.

"He said he owes Tom Ladduck a case of beer for his help when Mr.

Sutton ran out of fuel." They both laughed, because neither Tom nor Joey were that fond of beer in the first place.

Helen slept well in spite of the bothersome news from Dr. Henderson. She refused to let it bother her. Monday morning, she woke up feeling refreshed and excited. Tomorrow Joey was coming home! After breakfast, she decided to call her mother. She was not sure if her mother would care about Michael's surgery but Helen just wanted to talk to someone. The thought of getting another call from Dr. Henderson was too unpleasant so if she kept the phone line busy, she could defer the call!

"Hello, Helen. Is everything alright?" Katreena was never sure why Helen was calling these days. It seemed that bad events were the priority, social calls were few and far between.

"Well, uh, yes, it's alright." Helen faltered. "To be honest, I am finally making a social call. Well, that's not true either," Helen corrected herself and Katreena detected a note of apprehension in Helen's voice. "I'm actually trying to keep the phone busy to avoid getting a call I don't want. Guess I'm using you again. Sorry about that, Mom."

"No problem sweetheart. Okay, what is this call you don't want to take?"

Helen told her about Dr. Henderson's strange call the night before.

"He actually offered me his sympathies. They are amputating Michael's leg right now. I dread hearing detailed news about it, good or bad." Helen confessed.

Katreena empathized. "Can't say I blame you but you realize you are just delaying the inevitable, don't you?"

"I know but the mere mention of his name invokes horrific memories and pain."

"You could simply take the phone off the hook, you know," Katreena suggested.

Helen thought that over. "Nah, I just have to bite the bullet and get this thing over with."

"You haven't forgotten you are still on a partyline," Katreena reminded Helen gently.

"I know but at this point, I'm past the point of caring." Helen said cryptically.

"I wish I could help, honey." Then Katreena brightened. "Oh, by the way, I do have some good news for you. Dusty and I saw Wayne and Della yesterday and they said to give you their best. They also said they are thinking of publishing Kaydee's poems but they wanted to consult with Kaydee about a couple of things first so Kaydee will have to either go to Portmont herself or host some company one of these days. Jessie sends her love too."

"Oh Mom, you have just made my day! And I am sure Kaydee will be thrilled too. Somehow I can even face news about Michael at this point. He can't hurt me now. Thank you."

Helen had barely put down the phone when it rang again. It was Dr. Henderson.

"Just a short update, Mrs. Boyer. Michael is now in recovery. Surgery went well but he is still at risk. His cooperation and a positive attitude could go a long way in affecting the healing process, but you know Michael. I will keep you posted." He hung up.

After dealing with this amputation issue, Dr. Henderson got first-hand experience in communicating with Michael. He understood Helen's reservations about visiting him. Still, as a doctor, he felt duty-bound to keep Helen informed of Michael's progress and prognosis. He was well aware of Helen's resentment toward him so he kept his bulletins brief and to the point. After that escape fiasco, a lawsuit against the hospital was still a distinct possibility.

Chapter 40

Katreena and Dusty were busy planning their small and simple wedding ceremony with only family and friends present. They would be married by Father Rory Caddish at St. Joseph's Church in Lanavale as that was central for everybody. After the church ceremony, everyone would gather for a banquet at the Caribbean Club with the Five Minstrels Band providing dance music afterwards. They booked a barbeque of "pig on a spit" with baked potato and a variety of vegetables for the menu. For those that wished an alternative to the pork, they also ordered Cornish Hen on a bed of rice. Choices of red and white wines as well as a variety of beverages and desserts were included. So except for their wedding wardrobe and the flowers, all the arrangements were complete.

To stand as witnesses for them, they wanted Wayne, Della, Helen and Joey. They had already spoken to Wayne and Della, who were delighted of course. Vance and Janine were thrilled when Katreena told them about their plans but Helen, Kaydee and Joey still knew nothing about Katreena's impending nuptials. Helen seemed to be bouncing from one crisis to another and the time just did not seem right to spring something so incongruous into that mix. Michael's condition was still a thorn in their plans but Dusty was determined to go on with the wedding. Katreena and Dusty decided to drive to the farm for a face to face announcement.

"I wonder what she'll say when she finds out that we have told everyone about our plans without letting her in on them. We should have told her before this. She should have been part of our plans. I don't even know how I can explain this to her now."

"Stop beating yourself up, silly. She'll be so happy for us she won't think of blaming you for anything. Trust me." Dusty winked and gave her hand a squeeze.

"Perhaps you're right," she smiled uncertainly. Yet she could not help feeling that somehow she had shortchanged her daughter, that she had treated her with shameful disregard.

When they arrived at KD Acres, they found Joey and Helen walking out by the shed. Being idle was not his forte so Joey was here, checking out the yard and making mental notes of what he could do when he got back to work again. Dusty drove up to the shed so that Joey would have less distance to cover on his way to see them. Alvin and Jaynee came running after Dusty's car all eager for their hugs and greetings. When these were dispensed with, Dusty and Katreena faced Joey and Helen to find out how he was doing.

Helen looked at Joey with fondness as she explained "I'm here making sure he doesn't start to work immediately. He keeps telling me he's bored so I told him I'll let him take a mental inventory of the work that is waiting but he's not allowed to touch anything."

"Shucks!" Joey complained. "And here I thought she liked my company. All she is doing is policing me. Now isn't that just the most insulting thing you ever heard?"

They all laughed. And Joey continued. "I need work, man. I need to feel useful. I feel fine and there are a lot of things I can do, but no! Orders from headquarters," he pointed at Helen.

"We'll have you working soon enough, you can be sure of that, but Dr. Walley said to take it easy for the next two weeks. Remember? He made me promise to keep you away from work. I'm just obeying orders too, you know." Helen countered.

"You guys can finish your fight later, right now let's go to the house and we may have a different job for you both to do," Dusty cut in.

Joey looked questioningly at him, but Dusty's face was a blank as he checked around for the kids, got back into his car and drove it to its usual parking spot in the driveway.

Inside the house, Helen went to put on some tea and brought out some sponge cake that she had recently baked, while Katreena set the table. The kids grabbed cookies, gulped down their milk and were off outdoors again. Katreena was glad they left them alone as she really wanted privacy today.

"Okay, man. Spill it. What is this job you have for me? At this point I'll take anything you got." Joey said but Helen cut in. "Not 'anything' Joey! 'Anything within reason'."

"Oh stop it already, you two." Katreena scolded. "What Dusty wants to ask is would the two of you stand up for us at our wedding?"

Helen's mouth dropped open as she stared at her mother. "When?" she fairly shrieked in delight. Dusty let Katreena field this one all by herself. He wanted to know if her fears about the timing were grounded.

"How about two weekends after Thanksgiving Day?" Katreena ventured hesitantly. Helen flew at her mother hugging her so tightly Katreena could barely breathe.

Joey pumped Dusty's arm, congratulating him. "You lucky devil. If you want me there, buddy, you got me!"

"When did you guys decide this?" Helen wanted to know.

"Uh, oh here it comes," thought Katreena as her heart plummeted.

"Well, actually we started talking about it this summer, before Michael was moved back to Winnipeg. Our original plan was for the Thanksgiving Day long weekend, but one crisis after another kept coming up so we moved it over two weeks. Now it will be on the twenty-fourth of October. Anyway, I just could not find the perfect time to break the news to you before this."

Helen became thoughtful. "I guess I should be mad at you for robbing me of a whole lot of happy moments that would have broken up all that gloom. However since you asked me to stand up for you at your wedding, I guess I can forgive you. Welcome to the family Dusty. I am very happy for both of you. You know I want the best for you both."

Katreena brightened. "We haven't picked out what we are going to wear yet. Would you like to come and help us decide that?"

"I don't know how much help I will be in helping you in that department," Helen mused. "I am hardly the fashion expert around here but I do know that **I** will need help. So will Kaydee. So if you don't mind, we'd definitely like to come with you on your shopping spree. How about you, Joey? Why don't you come along as well? It will be a good break for you and whenever you get tired, we promise we'll find a place for you to rest. Please say you'll come Joey," Helen pleaded.

Joey accepted without much hesitation. "I may just take you up on it, you know. I could use a new suit. And to stand up as groomsman for a wedding? Well that warrants a new suit, doesn't it? You're on man!" and he gave Dusty a hi-five.

They made plans to leave for Portmont the coming Saturday. Dusty and Katreena would come back Friday afternoon, spend the night and early the next morning Helen, Kaydee and Joey would leave with them for the city. Helen would get Annie to stay with the kids with the understanding that if necessary she could stay the night until the next day. It might be too hard on Joey to make that long a trip in one day. They could spend Saturday night in Portmont and return home on Sunday. This would give Kaydee a chance to visit with Jessie and talk to Wayne and Della about the publication of her book. It all sounded too perfect. Helen was ecstatic and she was sure Kaydee would be too. Helen could hardly wait to tell her.

Dusty and Katreena decided to wait for Kaydee to get home before they headed back so they called the school and told her to take the bus home instead of going to the Norchaks for her extra classes. While waiting, they sat around chatting, making plans and enjoying the afternoon. Katreena asked how Kaydee was doing at school and Helen eagerly reported her latest conversation with the Norchaks.

"They have put her in Mrs. Jenkin's class now. That's a regular class but it's two grades lower than other kids her age. But Kaydee is getting along well with the kids now and with Ed and Sandy tutoring her every spare minute, they hope to help Kaydee advance to the level where she should be at her age. They are very optimistic that she can do it eventually and Kaydee doesn't mind the extra work. It is still too early to tell if this will work out but it looks promising and Ed and Sandy are so enthusiastic, I cannot help but catch the fever myself."

They continued discussing Kaydee until Dusty asked if Helen had any more news about Michael. Helen visibly stiffened and both Joey and Dusty noticed it, but she recovered and told them about Dr. Henderson's updates.

"They did the surgery on Monday and he was recovering well that afternoon but he was not out of anaesthetic yet. I haven't spoken to the doctor since. Dr. Henderson says that Michael's healing now depends to a large extent on his cooperation and his attitude. He has to improve from inside in order to cure the outside. And with Michael, you all know how successful that is likely to be!" Helen finished wryly.

"Well Michael can't blame anyone but himself for that," Dusty observed sardonically.

After a while, the conversation turned to the wedding plans again. Just then the bus pulled up. Kaydee jumped down and came running excitedly up the steps. She was understandably thrilled when she heard about Katreena and Dusty's wedding plans, and the plans for the weekend trip to Portmont had her positively delighted. She could hardly contain her euphoria about the wonderful news. The trip to the city was especially exciting.

"I could visit with Jessie again," Kaydee exclaimed happily.

"Which reminds me," Dusty interjected, "Wayne and Della want to meet with you about publishing a book of your poems. You'll have to fit in a business meeting in there somewhere."

"You mean they are really going to publish my work?" Kaydee was incredulous.

"Yes, really! So see you on Friday. Right now we better go."

Friday afternoon, Dusty and Katreena arrived at KD Acres but Kaydee was still at the Norchaks so they offered to go pick her up. Katreena wanted to see the young couple again who were such a Godsend to Kaydee.

"Mrs. Banaduk, you should be so proud of Kaydee. She is working so hard and she is catching on so fast. At the rate she is going, she just might catch up to the other kids by the end of this school year. She is such a trooper." Both Sandy and Ed Norchak were enthusiastic about Kaydee's diligence and impressed with her progress. Katreena thanked them fervently and they left for home. Kaydee chattered all the way with her praise for her benefactors.

They got back to see Helen's worried frown when they entered the house.

"Helen, what's the matter?" Concerned, they were at Helen's side immediately.

"I don't even know if this is something for me to be concerned about. It's just another case of the 'Curse of Michael' again. It seems that every time I start to feel good about something, Michael always has to spoil it for me."

"What is it now?" Katreena sighed.

"Dr. Henderson called again. He says Michael is not doing well and to be prepared in case he doesn't make it. Apparently, he has been so agitated and difficult to control that he may have created his own trouble again. They think that there may still have been some residual gangrene left in his blood and that by trashing around he may have exacerbated the problem and spread the poison through the rest of his body. Antibiotics don't seem effective on him anymore. Dr. Henderson said he felt it his duty to forewarn us in case we wanted to see him before anything happens."

"Do you want to see him, Helen?"

"No." Helen snapped with no hesitation.

"Even if he should die? This might be the last time, Helen. Are you sure?"

"Mom, Dr. Henderson said he is still very difficult. He is not at all repentant. He has not had a change of heart or disposition. Why should I go there to get yelled at and sworn at?"

"Good! That is exactly what I wanted to hear. Now relax. There is absolutely nothing that says you have to change your plans because of this new development with Michael. He has brought this all on himself. There is absolutely nothing you can do for him! Forget you even got the call. Unless something drastic happens before tomorrow, we are all going shopping to Portmont and we are staying for the weekend. Understood?" Katreena was deliberately authoritative. "Now put on a happy face and let's start preparing for tomorrow!"

"You're right, Mom. I don't owe Michael anything. I'm not going to let him spoil things for me again." Helen spoke with conviction and Dusty breathed a sigh of relief to hear it.

Plans had been made for Annie to stay with the kids. On Saturday morning, Joey would bring his grandmother to KD Acres. By seven, he would join the rest of them in Dusty's car and leave for Portmont. Everyone was looking forward to the trip. It would be a fun adventure for them all!

Secretly, Katreena worried about another phone call from Dr. Henderson. If something should happen to Michael, it could spoil their plans so she resolved to forewarn Annie about such a contingency.

The morning dawned bright and clear when Joey and his grandmother arrived, right on time. So far, so good. Katreena called Annie upstairs to her room so she could speak to her in private.

Katreena told Annie about Michael's condition, and of the possibility that it could get worse at any time. "If that should happen, they will be calling here again and you will have to answer that call. Don't be upset." Katreena prompted. "Just say we had to go out of town and we'll be back on Sunday. There is absolutely nothing we can do for Michael anyway and this trip means a lot to Helen, Kaydee and even to Joey. I don't want anything to spoil it. Can you do that? Annie, please?" Katreena pleaded.

"I sure can, Katreena. I will not let Michael spoil the only vacation Helen has had in her whole life. You can depend on me!" Annie said with determination.

"Thank you, Annie," Katreena breathed a sigh of relief. "Now here is the number for Dusty's brother in Portmont and this is their office number. This is just in case you need to get in touch with us for any sort of emergency. But remember, any news about Michael is **NOT** an emergency," she emphasized. "That news can wait until we get back, okay?"

"I understand Katreena. Don't worry. I will handle everything. You all just go and have fun. And congratulations on your marriage. You got yourself a very good man there."

"I know Annie. And thank you." Together they came downstairs and immediately sat down to breakfast that was already laid out for them. No one had even noticed their absence.

Chapter 41

The trip to Portmont was a blessing for all of them. The weather was beautiful. The slight breeze combined with twenty-four degree temperatures was perfect. The trees had donned vibrant autumn colors, and the air smelled of ripe cranberries. They zoomed past stubble fields and fields of brown flax still uncut, awaiting their turn to be harvested. The ditches were mostly brown and green where indigenous plants grew with wild abandon. Much of the vegetation was dried and brown, but here and there a stubborn goldenrod defied the season with its yellow plumes, or some patches of spiney yellow and purple flowers stood out among the rusty greens.

"Wouldn't it be nice if this was a convertible and we could put the top down and have the wind blowing in our hair? We could savour all the smells of harvest, distant pine and stubble smoke that must be just marvellous out there." Helen mused.

"Oh, tis wind in yar hair dat you vant," taunted Dusty imitating an Irish brogue. "Vell ladies, tis wind in yar hair you get!" He pushed a button, and the windows came down, sending a swoosh through the car. "Complete with the smells of harvest." Dusty added.

The girls all screamed as they grabbed for their hairdos and Joey for his hat. Then they all started laughing. Katreena ran her fingers through her hair deliberately mussing up whatever was left of her set. "Oh what the heck, let's just enjoy it." Helen and Kaydee followed suit, revelling in recklessness and the freedom from inhibition.

"You guys are nuts, but I like it. There is not another bunch of nuts I'd rather be with at this point," Joey teased. He meant it. He felt comfortable and at ease with this family. Best of all he felt like he belonged with them. It was a wonderful feeling. He had never experienced it before. Now this warm tingly sensation spread throughout his body making him feel content, pliant and exuberant. He loved it. But this was just a dream, he reminded himself. He would be going back to the city eventually. The pain in his heart made him stop there. He was going to leave this at God's doorstep. "Thy will be done" he thought to himself. Today had been granted to him and it was his to enjoy. He was not going to question it or waste it.

They drove on chattering, joking and laughing, without a care in the world. All of them were determined not to let any negative thoughts mar this glorious day. Kaydee was deliriously excited about seeing Jessie. She had never been to the city before and the thought of shopping with Jessie hopefully by her side, was exciting beyond words.

They arrived at Dusty's house first and the landscaping and gardens immediately caught Joey's attention. "My grandmother would swoon over all this," he declared, totally captivated by the meticulousness of the layout and the effort that evidently went in to keep it looking that way. "You must have a real passion for gardening."

"That I do, Joey, that I do," Dusty answered proudly.

They went into the house where Dusty showed Helen and Joey to their rooms. They brought in their luggage as they would be spending the night here. Kaydee stood waiting with uncertainty, not daring to hope that she would be staying with Jessie.

"You, young lady," Dusty pointed at Kaydee, "are going farther. Jessie would have my hide if I did not park you right within the walls of her room. That girl's got a temper, and I am not about to cross her!"

"Oh Dusty," Katreena scolded. "You're always teasing. Don't worry, Kaydee. Jessie hasn't got a hint of temper. You know that."

"I know, Granny, but Dusty, I'm going to tell on you and Jessie better at least take a strip off your hide for that lie."

"Uh, oh. Me and my big mouth again." Dusty cupped his hand over his mouth. They all laughed. Dusty opened the doors to the deck. "And this, my loyal friends," he waved his outstretched hand to indicate his deck, his house and his garden, "is the extent of my kingdom." Then turning to Kaydee exclusively, he indicated the deck specifically, "this particular part is the absolute envy of my niece, Jessie."

Stomping her foot for emphasis, Kaydee declared, "And I, for one, am with her on that."

"So are we," the others agreed. "It's a wonderful place to enjoy your Garden of Eden."

"Wayne and Della don't have a deck but they do have a more beautiful house than this." Dusty explained. "Come on, I will now show you their place." Then a thought occurred to him. "Are you tired Joey? Would you like to lie down and rest for a while before we continue?"

"Not on your life, man. I'm not wasting a single moment of this day lying down in a room somewhere. Rest is for home. Right now, I'm enjoying myself too much. Let's just keep on going." Eagerly, they piled back in the car and were on their way.

They drove through the city streets and Dusty took them the long way around as he showed them Shilladay Gardens, Greenwoods Park and Portmont's CN Park. Then he showed them the Winners Stadium, the City Hall and St. Mary's Cathedral, the Public Schools, Portmont University and lastly Portmont Academy. Dusty had deliberately left this for last.

"This is an exclusive school for specially qualified students. They cater to gifted students actually, those who excel in some specific fields and require specialized guidance that they cannot receive in a normal setting. Students here are usually scholarship winners or protégés of some professor. Their criteria for admission is high though, so if the student doesn't measure up to the standards, even money cannot get them in here." Dusty explained.

Katreena and Helen listened intently to Dusty's clarification about the school. It was interesting and informative news about this school that Ed and Sandy Norchak thought Kaydee could qualify for! They were both astonished. How was this even possible? Kaydee had been behind in her school grades. Was the Norchaks' belief in Kaydee's scholastic acumen so high that they felt she could overcome that handicap and still be accepted into such an elite school? That would be an unbelievable honour!

Kaydee, of course knew nothing about it. She had not been informed of the Norchaks' suggestion to have her attend the Academy. At this time, it was not relevant. The situation at home was changing so rapidly that there was no point in pursuing the Academy issue anyway. Since the threat of Michael's presence had been removed, Kaydee would likely now have the opportunity to close the gap between herself and her peers naturally. Portmont Academy may become a possibility in the future but there was no need for it at this point.

When they arrived at Wayne and Della's house, Jessie came flying out of the house to give Kaydee an enthusiastic welcome.

"Hi Kaydee," Jessie squealed. "I am so happy you were able to come!" Taking Kaydee's hand she led her towards the house and their girlish giggles faded with their departure.

Wayne and Della came forward to reinforce the warm reception.

"Welcome Helen, Joey. We have been waiting to meet this paragon of virtue we heard so much about these last couple of weeks. Dusty thinks you're quite the hero, man." Wayne pumped Joey's hand and Helen beamed.

"We all think he's a hero, Wayne. No, that's not correct. We KNOW he's a hero!"

"Hey, listen, you guys. You're making me want to turn and run because you're talking about somebody other than me. I'm no hero. I'm just a poor farm shmuck who happened to be in the right place at the right time. What happened was a whole lot of luck, not much hero," protested Joey self-consciously. He hated being the centre of attention and was obviously very uncomfortable in that role. Wayne realized this and relented.

"Be that as it may, welcome to Portmont and to our home. I guess you guys are at the mercy of the women today, being as I understand it, you are on a shopping trip. My sympathies, you guys. Better you than me." Wayne had skilfully changed the subject and put Joey at ease as he ushered them into the house. Inside Wayne felt concern about Joey's frail condition in view of his recent release from the hospital.

While everyone chattered on excitedly, Wayne discreetly offered Joey a quiet place to rest for a few minutes before they embarked on their strenuous shopping spree.

"You're in for a heck of a long and strenuous day man. You may want to recharge your batteries for a few minutes before they put the lunch on. You may not have a chance to relax later. You can rejoin the group anytime you feel like it."

Joey did not wish to make this a public issue but Wayne did have a point. It was going to be a long day so, expressing his gratitude, he slipped away quietly and followed Wayne to one of the bedrooms where he lay down to regenerate some energy for the stress he knew lay ahead.

In the meantime, still keeping up with the visiting, Della prepared soup, salad and sandwiches for the group. In just over an hour, Joey joined everyone for lunch.

It was agreed that Jessie would come along for the shopping spree. She was knowledgeable of the fashion trends for young teens and would be a tremendous help to Kaydee in selecting her wardrobe, not just for the wedding, but a few new outfits for school as well. Neither Kaydee nor Helen followed teen fashion trends, so they sorely needed guidance with selecting clothes to update her wardrobe. So while Helen had Katreena at her side, Jessie was going to assist Kaydee. Joey, on the other hand, needed no help. All he wanted was a new suit for the wedding.

Kaydee appreciated Jessie's assistance and suggestions in choosing her new wardrobe. For school, she now had several new outfits that she could mix and match, thus creating the illusion of abundance and variety. Also, she and Jessie were to be the two junior bridesmaids for the wedding and she wanted to look her best. For that special occasion, they had chosen matching dresses, with slim fitting princess-line bodices, modest sweetheart necklines and low backs in a stunning sapphire blue crepe. They would not likely be going to identical functions after the wedding so they could both utilize the dresses for other special events later. Since Katreena was wearing a very pale blue lace-top silk dress with a short bolero, Helen and Della both had outfits in light blue and the men all wore deep navy suits, the bridesmaid dresses complimented the bridal party to perfection. Katreena even bought a beautiful little blue dress for Jaynee and a navy suit for Alvin since they were going to be in the wedding party as flower girl and ring bearer. The wedding was now becoming a reality and excitement was mounting. Kaydee felt that all her dreams were being fulfilled and she was in seventh heaven. Life was wonderful!

At half past five, they met Della and Wayne at Arturo's Restaurant where they had agreed to rendezvous for an elegant dinner. Kaydee felt giddy with pleasure at this enchanting experience.

After dinner, Dusty, Katreena, Helen and Joey left for Dusty's place, with all the parcels in the trunk of Dusty's car. Kaydee wished they had let her take her clothes to Jessie's so she could try them on once more. However, she didn't want to be a pest, so she waved goodbye to them as they drove off and then got into Wayne's car next to Jessie.

Shortly after they got to the house, Wayne and Della brought up the subject of Kaydee's poetry. Wayne complimented Kaydee on her work and expressed his fascination about her captivating ability to present her readers with so much sentiment and vivid imagery.

"I have never read poetry which invoked such depth of emotions and inspired me with so much passion. It challenges the reader to delve deep into his own uniqueness. In addition, it conveys your own unique personality. You really have a gift there, Kaydee, and I know a book of your poetry would sell very well because almost anyone can relate to it in one way or another. Do you have any more poems?" Wayne asked hopefully. "We could compile a whole book of strictly poetry and leave the stories for a different book."

Kaydee was overwhelmed. She had written the poetry simply expressing thoughts and emotions that required purging at the time because they weighed so heavily on her spirit. She had never considered its effect on an unknown reader. To know that it could affect someone so strongly was a total revelation to her. Still, it felt exhilarating somehow, to find out that she, Kaydee, the girl that Father always said was dumber than a doornail and would never amount to anything, could write something that was appreciated by intellectual people.

"I, uh, I have more poems," she stammered, dumbfounded. "In another notebook – an old one, in fact, but I have written some new poems in it since I gave this new notebook to Jessie when she left my place. I don't know if they're any good though."

"We'd like to see them. If they are anything like these, they will fit in very nicely. Poetry books do not have to be very big. I understand you have only been writing for about three months. That is amazing. You have done extremely well. For now, I would like to see the rest of your poems and we will compile all the poetry you have written to date in one book. Whatever you do, don't stop writing!" Wayne tried hard not to sound as excited as he felt but he definitely wanted to encourage this child prodigy. Here was a twelve-year-old poet who had tremendous potential and he was confident that she would catapult his little publishing business into the big leagues.

Kaydee's stories too, warranted acclaim, but because many of them referred to Michael's cruel behaviour, exploiting such a painful situation at this time would be insensitive. Considering Michael's recent critical surgery and his unstable and erratic prognosis, Wayne preferred not to mention those stories yet. Promoting such a book at this time would be inappropriate. Still, Wayne wanted Kaydee to keep on writing those stories because someday such an autobiography would likely hit the bestseller list.

"Your poems and stories are excellent. I am certain that all your work will be published sooner or later. We will publish what we have now and then when you have enough for another book, we'll work on the next one. How soon do you think you can arrange to get this notebook to us?"

Kaydee thought it over. "I could give it to Dusty to bring to you," she suggested brightly.

"That would be great, Kaydee. In the meantime, I will draw up a contract and I'll have your mother, your grandmother and Dusty look it over. If everyone agrees, we're in business. That alright with you?"

Kaydee sat there staring at Wayne while he talked. She could not believe what she was hearing! "You mean you are just going to take my poems like I wrote them and put them in a book, and people will buy the book and read my poems?" she asked incredulously.

"Pretty much like that, Kaydee. We will have to reformat some of the poems, you know, maybe divide one line and make it two, maybe add some punctuation here and there, but we will not change the words. I promise you that. They will be your poems like you wrote them, your ideas, your thoughts and your messages. Absolutely no changes to the words, I promise. Okay?"

Wayne extended his hand and Kaydee took it dazedly. This was happening so fast but she forced herself to concentrate. "Okay," she agreed.

Della had remained silent throughout the interview. She had only come as a backup in case Kaydee felt intimidated or misunderstood something but Wayne was the brains behind the company and she was there strictly for support. She was glad that things went along so smoothly but she need not have worried. Kaydee trusted Dusty and Jessie implicitly and therefore she had no reason to mistrust Wayne. The impetus of the publication was strictly in Wayne's hands and Kaydee was content to leave it there.

After they had retired to the bedroom, Kaydee and Jessie talked well into the night. Kaydee told Jessie about her father's surgery, about all the setbacks and problems with his treatment and the prognosis for his recovery.

"So I don't think he will be coming home. I really don't care. I didn't want him to come back anyway. He would have killed us if Joey had not been there. So I don't feel guilty anymore about not caring. Dr. Henderson told Mother the other day to be prepared if he doesn't make it. I don't know if that means that he will die. I don't know how I feel about that."

"No, Kaydee, you should not feel guilty about it," Jessie retorted angrily. "Don't even waste time thinking about him. You have every right to live your dream so enjoy it!" Jessie just wanted to get Kaydee's mind off the subject of her father altogether.

"How is school? I hear you're doing well now."

"You know, I never thought I would like school. I was always so scared of the teachers and the other kids. But they're nice, Jessie! I don't know why I didn't see that before. I guess I just never gave them a chance before."

They talked on without rest, discussing school, clothes, friends, studies, hairstyles and numerous other subjects until they were so tired their words were slurring.

"Goodnight, Kaydee," Jessie said groggily,

"Goodnight, Jessie." And in no time, both girls were fast asleep.

Chapter 42

All the way home from the city, the next day, Kaydee was bubbling about all the exciting things she had seen, done, and learned. The most exciting, of course, was the imminent publication of her poems. Katreena and Helen both empathized in her revelling on that subject. Vindication was finally theirs. "If only," Katreena thought, "they could somehow let Michael know about Kaydee's accomplishment in this field, it would truly be the ultimate triumph!" She vowed that if she ever got that chance, she would somehow ensure this tidbit of news found its way to Michael's ears. Unbeknown to Katreena, these were Helen's sentiments as well. Having Kaydee produce a book of poetry for publication would be the ultimate irony to Michael. Helen could feel the sweetness of seeing Michael vanquished on this subject alone.

Dusty and Joey smiled at Kaydee's enthusiasm. They had abandoned attempts to converse with each other in the front seat because, in her excitement, Kaydee could not keep her voice down and it was difficult to talk over her. Genuinely fond of the girl, they did not begrudge her this moment of glory. She had earned it after overcoming such terrible adversities. They were glad that something positive was finally happening in her life.

They arrived at KD Acres just before four in the afternoon, still full from the big brunch after church. Annie had been expecting them home for supper and had just started peeling potatoes. A stuffed chicken was already cooking in the oven. Helen thought wistfully of her garden vegetables which were now just a sad memory since the storm.

Almost as if she were reading her mind, Annie spoke up. "Katreena, Helen, why don't you take over here so Joey, Dusty and I can drive over to my place for some fresh vegetables. There is no way I can ever use all that produce myself, especially since Joey is eating most of his major meals here anyway." As the three left the house, Kaydee was already on the phone filling Sandy Norchak in on the details of their trip, and the upcoming publication of her book.

Helen and Katreena laughed. "We may as well face it. Kaydee will be on a high here for who knows how long."

On the drive over to the Dorozeck place Dusty told Joey about the quiet girl that Katreena had described to him before his momentous introduction to the family that fateful day when he had carried Michael out of the burning inferno that used to be a shed. "It's not that I don't believe Katreena," Dusty asserted. "It's just that the Kaydee we are seeing since Michael is out of the picture is so different than the Kaydee that was under Michael's oppressive influence."

"And that is not exaggeration, believe me," Annie interjected.

"I understand what you are saying," Joey agreed. "I see glimpses of that oppression whenever they talk about that man. He had to have been quite the beast. You know, if we hadn't been there on that terrible night, he would have killed the whole family! You read about lunatics like that but you never think you'll meet one."

"When Katreena first described him to me, I have to admit, I thought she was exaggerating. I could not believe the things she told me about him. He used to call Kaydee a retard, you know. I wonder what he'd say now if he heard that she was getting published."

As they collected the vegetables, Joey told Dusty about the inquiries he had made about contractors to rebuild the shed. "I thought that since I can do little else these days, I can at least do some planning and organizing. Then when I get in motion again, I won't have to waste time with that aspect of it. I'd like to get the framework and the roof up before freeze-up."

"Good plan," Dusty agreed.

While the women worked to prepare the vegetables for supper, the men sat on the deck. Katreena set out glasses and a jug of juice for them to enjoy while they waited. When supper was on the table, Katreena called everyone to come in and eat. Alvin was soon bored with the subject of Kaydee's writing and poetry. As soon as he had swallowed his last mouthful he took off for the outdoors and Jaynee followed him. The rest of the family were still eating when the phone rang. Helen got up to answer it. They heard her voice change after she said "Hello."

"Yes, Dr. Henderson, what is the news today?" She listened quietly for a few minutes while everyone at the table held their breath. Finally, she spoke again. "Is he in imminent danger then?" Then, quiet again. "I see, but for now, he's fine?"

Katreena could take it no longer. She had heard "he's fine," and that was all she needed. She jumped up, ran to Helen and put her ear to the phone. They both listened. Then Katreena cut in, "Tell Michael that his daughter Kaydee is having a book of poetry published. I am sure that will give him something to look forward to." With a smug smile, Katreena left Helen and came back to the table. Without a word of explanation, she started eating, ignoring the rest of Helen's conversation and the questioning stare that Dusty was trying to pierce her with. When Helen finished, the others were all eager for news but Katreena remained nonchalant.

"Michael's infection is getting critical but they don't consider it life-threatening at this point. Michael is still belligerent, blaming the doctors for his infection and insisting that they should do something about his problems, instead of making him suffer."

"Dr. Henderson is getting concerned with Michael's insults. If he only knew what the real Michael was like before this, he'd just get earplugs." Helen finished laconically. "Little does he know just how insulting Michael can be! Considering he was barely able to talk a month ago, he sure can make his insults clear now. I really have no sympathy for Dr. Henderson. He was pretty insulting himself when this first started."

"He **was** pretty convinced that the family was not very sensitive to 'poor Mr. Boyer,' wasn't he?" Katreena added dryly. "Now he understands why. I'd give anything to be a fly on the wall when he congratulates Michael on his daughter's publication of poetry!"

Dusty could barely contain his admiration as he shook a mock menacing finger at Katreena. "That was pretty sneaky of you to slip that one in," he admonished but he was smiling.

"The devil made me do it," Katreena retorted as she continued eating. "Michael had that one coming after all the times he had called Kaydee stupid!" Katreena's sentiment was reiterated on everyone's lips.

After everyone left, Kaydee could not control her enthusiasm about her new wardrobe. One by one, she tried on her new clothes, modeling them for her mother, discussing the variables she could create with each and basking in the sheer luxury of their newness. Helen was just as captivated as Kaydee was. This was the first time she and Kaydee had shared a moment like this and Helen relished it. Her daughter was almost grown. In fact, she had a maturity about her that Helen could enjoy and respect. Here was someone who could be a daughter, a friend and a confidante; someone who could understand and relate to her own feelings of vexation, chagrin, hopelessness and now, this new-found sense of freedom and peace. Since her marriage to Michael, Helen had not had a single friend; she did not know her daughter and she could not even relate to her own mother as a confidante. Now, here she was discussing the best outfit her daughter would wear for her next school day! Helen felt warm and happy. Life was good. The years with Michael were just a distant bad memory.

Chapter 43

They were still in bed when the phone rang on Wednesday morning at a quarter past seven. Helen groaned. "The Curse of Michael" again! Groggily, she made her way to the phone. For two glorious days, she had not heard that aggravating voice and she had savoured every minute of that reprieve. Now here it was again and she knew instinctively that it would bode ill will.

Dispensing with all the preliminaries Helen went straight to the issue she knew prompted the call. "What is it, Dr. Henderson?"

Taken aback by her abruptness the doctor hesitated, his rehearsed introduction speech obviously arrested. Helen waited, tapping her fingers impatiently against the desk. "Uh, uh, this is Dr. Henderson," he recovered, then paused.

"Yes, Doctor. I assumed that. Nobody else calls me at this hour. So what is it this time?" Katreena had said "Be polite" but who cares about being polite when awakened from a deep sleep? Helen's patience was not even programmable at that hour.

"Well, Mrs. Boyer, I'm afraid Michael is not doing well at all this morning. In fact, he may not make it through the day. I thought you might wish to know if you want to see him."

"Is he conscious? Aware? Coherent?"

"I'm afraid so, Mrs. Boyer and as belligerent as ever, I'm sorry to say. It is unbelievable considering the infection is causing him to be so feverish. But yes, he is still coherent. I told him about your daughter's success with her poetry, hoping that would mellow him out but if anything, it has made him even more irate. We are doing everything we can to control his infection and his fever, but I am afraid that the gangrene has overtaken his body and we cannot reverse its progression." Dr. Henderson stopped, waiting for Helen to voice her opinion.

"Dr. Henderson, you are aware of Michael's state of mind and his recent history. Do you honestly believe that my coming there would serve any beneficial purpose?"

Dr. Henderson hesitated, then, "Quite frankly, no. I just thought you may want to know."

"Dr. Henderson, Michael's belligerence is not a new experience, nor is it a consequence of his illness. As for his critical condition, may I remind you that you have been very mistaken in the past. He has incredible endurance. As it is, let me just say: I will not be coming into the city to visit Michael. Goodbye Dr. Henderson."

Helen hung up but in spite of herself, she was shaken. Michael might be dying. She should feel some kind of sorrow, some sense of loss. Instead, all she could feel was annoyance at Dr. Henderson for bothering her with his phone calls! She didn't really want Michael to die, but she certainly did not care if he lived or died.

Kaydee came down still in her robe, but she carried a new outfit for after her shower.

"Was that Dr. Henderson on the phone?" She too, did not seem overly concerned.

"Yes. Seems that your father is not doing well and they thought I may want to visit him."

"You're not going?" Kaydee groaned in alarm.

"Yeah, right. I'm still short of a few more nasty insults for the heap! Dr. Henderson says he is still ranting and raving, in spite of running a dangerously high fever. Guess nothing will ever change him." Helen did not wish to add that the doctor had said that Michael might not last the day. Michael had fooled them before when they were so sure he could not go anywhere yet he had managed leave the hospital, equip himself with clothes, drugs, car, knife and a gun and come over three hundred miles to KD Acres with the intention of killing them all. Helen was not going to take that man's fragile condition for granted again. He was capable of unbelievable stamina when his anger gave him the motivation. She was determined to put the situation out of her mind and let the chips fall where they may.

Satisfied that her mother was on the right track, Kaydee showered and came out wearing her new blue slacks and white shirt with the flip collar that crossed over at the front. She looked neat and sharp. Humming softly to herself, she finished her breakfast, packed her lunch and excitedly raced out the door to meet the schoolbus. Helen was left to herself for the day, nothing stressful, just take care of the kids and can some tomatoes that somebody had dropped off while they were in the city. It had been this way ever since the storm. Every so often somebody – often total strangers – would stop and drop off some vegetables for them.

"We heard about the storm," they would say. "These are extras from our garden. We thought you might enjoy them."

Helen would thank them profusely but they just brushed it off. "It's nothing," they would say, "we have more than we can use."

When Joey came that afternoon to tell her about his plans for the shed, Helen did not tell him about Dr. Henderson's call. They sat on the deck, drinking lemonade and discussing the plans. The phone remained quiet all day and into the evening. So much for Dr. Henderson's doomsday prognosis! Helen thought silently. Joey had supper and then went to pick up Kaydee from the Norchaks after her special tutoring. He dropped Kaydee off and left for home. They went to bed as usual and got up the next morning without any more news about Michael.

The next day passed as uneventfully as the last. Helen had become complacent that Dr. Henderson had, yet once again, underestimated Michael's stamina.

It was after nine o'clock in the evening. The kids were in bed. Joey and Kaydee were not yet back from the Norchaks and Helen was just tying off the thread of some mending when the phone rang. Annoyed at the intrusive jangling, she stuck the needle into the pincushion and went to answer it. It was Dr. Henderson. Was that man ever going to give her peace?

"Mrs. Boyer, I have bad news for you." Helen's heart stopped! Michael had escaped again! But Dr. Henderson went on gravely. "I'm afraid your husband passed away a few minutes ago. He fought hard to beat it but after the pneumonia set in we were unable to help anymore. He just had too much infection in his system. I'm sorry."

Helen was dumbfounded. Michael had really given up the fight! She had thought about the possibility and Dr. Henderson had predicted it but she really did not believe it would happen. A million thoughts raced through her mind but she could not grasp one to give it veracity.

"Mrs. Boyer? Are you there?" It was Dr. Henderson. He was still waiting for her response. Helen snapped back to reality.

"Uh, yes, Dr. Henderson. I'm here. I heard you. Are you sure?"

"Yes, Mrs. Boyer. Michael passed away about ten minutes ago."

Helen suddenly realized what a stupid question that must have been. Of course, he was sure. He would not make jokes about something that serious. "I'm sorry. Dr. Henderson. I didn't mean that. I just – I, well, you – uh, I'm sorry, Dr. Henderson."

"No apologies necessary, Mrs. Boyer. I understand. Are you alright, Mrs. Boyer?"

"Uh, yes. Dr. Henderson. I'm alright. Thank you." Abruptly she hung up the phone and sank heavily into the chair. Michael was gone! He was gone for good this time. A wave of nausea and weakness spread throughout her body. Michael was actually gone!

It was not long after that that Joey drove up with Kaydee from the Norchaks. They found Helen sitting dazedly on the chair next to the phone, her face pale, her eyes staring into space. Kaydee's breath caught as memories of her mother from last spring engulfed her.

"Mother, what's the matter?" Kaydee rushed to kneel beside her mother. Joey came to stand in front of her, concern creased his features as he stood waiting for an explanation.

Helen stared at Kaydee, but no sound came from her open mouth.

"Mom, what's the matter?" Kaydee repeated, her voice rising in alarm.

Helen shook herself awake as if from a dream. "Your father just died." She announced.

Kaydee gasped in shock. There must be some mistake. People like Father didn't die! They lived on forever just to torment their victims out of spite. Yet the look on her mother's face told her it was no mistake. Kaydee could not believe it. She had not realized he was really that sick. Truth be told, she never bothered to question anyone that much about his condition. She was just glad that he was not around. Nothing else warranted consideration. Now he was gone and she would never have to worry about him coming back to wreak havoc on their lives again!

Joey was thunderstruck. He had known Michael was not doing well but was not aware that he was actually dying. The family spoke of him only if pressed to do so and Joey had been satisfied to leave it that way. To ignore the subject was just less disturbing for everybody.

"You better call your grandmother and let her know." Joey told Kaydee, watching Helen closely. Katreena would know best how to handle the situation. Joey didn't know if she had been forewarned about this but Katreena was level-headed and would take over.

Helen had refused to believe Dr. Henderson when he told her that Michael may not survive. Since his attempt to annihilate them, she had just lost interest in his well-being. Michael had always managed to extinguish her fledgling hopes for peace before with some incredible strategy he had cooked up in that scheming evil mind of his. She just automatically expected this to be another one his manipulative ploys again. But this was reality. She thought of a world without Michael in it. Peace! Eternal peace! Dare she believe this one? No more fear of Michael, and no more upsetting calls from Dr. Henderson.

Kaydee picked up the phone and dialled her grandmother's number. It rang five times but Granny did not answer. She would have to try again. Hopefully Granny was not out of town. She hung up and went back to Mother. Joey stood by helplessly, not knowing quite what to do.

"It's over, Mom. He'll never hurt either one of us again." Helen stared at her.

"I didn't believe him," she said simply.

"You better call your grandmother, too," Kaydee said to Joey. "She needs to know."

Joey thought about it. "Your grandmother isn't home now. I shouldn't tie up your line. You need to keep trying to get hold of her. Will you be okay for a few minutes while I go and bring my grandmother here?"

"Good idea Joey. We'll be okay. Bring her here. Thanks Joey."

She went back to her mother's side. "Did you know he was that bad?" she asked Mother.

"I didn't believe it." Mother kept repeating over and over again, her voice barely audible. She sat staring at Kaydee, unbelieving. Kaydee held her hand, telling her all would be alright but Mother seemed too shocked to comprehend the implications of what she was hearing. After a few minutes of silence Kaydee tried the phone again.

"I better try Granny again. Maybe she was just outside."

Katreena answered on the second ring.

"Granny, Father passed away a little while ago. Dr. Henderson called."

"Oh my goodness. Are you guys alright?" Katreena asked anxiously, hesitated for a second, then continued, "Dusty and I are coming right over. Hang in there, sweetheart."

Within an hour, Dusty's Buick pulled into the yard. Joey and Annie were already sitting at the table with Helen and Kaydee. Katreena wanted to know all about the preliminaries that had led up to this moment. Helen told them all about the call on Wednesday morning.

"I must admit, I just didn't believe he was really that sick. I even reminded Dr. Henderson about how wrong he had been about Michael's condition before he escaped. Perhaps I just didn't want to really listen to him. I guess I just didn't really trust Dr. Henderson's judgment or his attitude," she said wryly. "But when I really think about it, Dr. Henderson had given me ample warning that Michael may not make it. Perhaps I just didn't want to care."

"Well, that's all water under the bridge now," Dusty said. "What we have to do now is make the arrangements for the funeral. You say you didn't talk to Dr. Henderson about it at all? And he didn't question you about what to do with the body?" Dusty was incredulous.

"I hate to admit it," Helen answered sheepishly, "but I don't think I gave him a chance. I think I hung up on him."

"I better call him back. He's probably waiting. You will be using the Bedson Funeral Home, I assume?"

"Of course." That was Katreena. Helen nodded and Dusty went to the phone, dialled and waited to be connected to Dr. Henderson.

"Hello Mr. Duganyk. I have been waiting for your call. Mrs. Boyer was rather upset when I called so I thought you would be calling shortly with the arrangements." They exchanged information back and forth then Dusty hung up.

"He'll have the remains shipped here to Bedson's Funeral Home for the burial but we'll have to make the arrangements here with Bedson's."

"It's late," Joey observed, looking at his wristwatch "but Bethune Centre will probably be contacting them shortly anyway. There is someone around to take calls twenty-four hours a day at Bedson's but it might just be more practical to wait for tomorrow to make arrangements."

Kaydee sat quietly while the adults discussed the funeral arrangements. She felt strangely guilty about her lack of remorse but did not want to be a hypocrite by faking concern she did not feel. The funeral was not a significant event in her life. The significance had come when her father was taken away from the farm by that ambulance three months ago. That was when her life had changed. Today, merely the fear of his return had been removed.

The next day was Friday and it was a blur. Kaydee went to school as usual. She didn't want to miss out on too many classes. They were more important to her than her father anyway and it wasn't as if staying home would serve any useful purpose now. Annie stayed home with the kids while the rest of the adults all went to town to make the arrangements for Michael's funeral. Alvin was told about Michael's passing but he didn't seem overly affected by it. He didn't understand the impact of the event. He had become used to life without Michael and he had built up quite an attachment to Joey so Joey was able to distract him quite easily. Katreena and Dusty remained at the farm till the funeral which was scheduled for Monday. A few people stopped by the house to pay their respects but it all seemed hollow to Kaydee. Outside of their Sundays at church, their family had not really been active in the community affairs. Even after church, Kaydee had never witnessed anybody welcoming Father into their group. As far as her mother was concerned, her withdrawal from humanity had been so complete these last few years that few people had known she even existed. Some of the close neighbours had come after the fire and again after the hailstorm, to give their condolences and vegetables, but tragedy often brought empathy from people with like backgrounds. This time, often as not, it was people who knew Katreena or perhaps remembered Daniel who were trying to be kind.

It was when Wayne and Della came with Jessie that Kaydee was able to come alive again. Till then she had pulled away from the stifling niceties of the visits. Condolences were for the wife, or Katreena, whom they knew. Only a few of her school friends, along with the Norchaks, even considered a twelve-year-old girl's feelings. Kaydee just wanted this tiresome event to be over. She would much rather have preferred to avoid it altogether. Jessie brought reality to Kaydee. Jessie knew Kaydee's feelings about Michael. She would not be judgmental about her lack of sorrow. Kaydee could be herself with Jessie. She did not have to pretend concern and Jessie would know why.

"Please tell me you're not going home until after the funeral," Kaydee begged Jessie. "Please, Jessie, don't leave me alone now. This is just too bizarre. I need you."

"I'll have to check with Mom and Dad. Perhaps I can stay," Jessie agreed. She read Kaydee's desperation in her pleading. She understood Kaydee's torment. Missing a day of school was a small price to pay for Kaydee's relief from this trauma. Jessie knew Kaydee had not divulged her secret to anyone else so she had no one else to help her get through this. After the funeral was over, Kaydee could relax but in the meantime she desperately needed a friend. Once more Jessie marvelled at how Kaydee had managed to live through such oppression for so long and still come out sane and sensible.

Wayne and Della went home to Portmont with the intention of coming back for the funeral on Monday. They would miss the chapel prayers which were scheduled for Sunday evening. They consented to let Jessie stay with Kaydee when Jessie discreetly told them of Kaydee's disconcerting dilemma. They felt sorry for Kaydee, having to go through this all so alone. Katreena was concentrating on Helen getting through this without too much stress and even Joey was there for Helen but Kaydee was left to fend for herself. No one considered the fact that she had many of her own demons to slay and just as many to bury. She needed someone who would understand her battle with this ordeal.

After Wayne and Della drove away and left Jessie to spend the weekend on the farm, Kaydee experienced a calming effect that imbued her with a degree of comfort and self-confidence. Jessie's detachment from the issue at hand, her easygoing manner and her sincere camaraderie, had Kaydee completely relaxed and she was able to accept the preparations for the funeral much more easily. No longer did the funeral arrangements agitate her or fill her with guilt or misgivings about what she should or should not be doing or feeling. She devoted herself to spending time with the kids and with Jessie and helped with the preparation of food. Working beside her confidante, Kaydee did not feel so bereft. Kaydee counted the hours till the whole thing was over and they could assume a life that held no fear, no anger and no guilt. It was a dream and Kaydee would only believe the situation was real when she truly experienced it.

Kaydee expressed all these feelings and bared her soul to Jessie during the long evenings when they lay awake, listening to the adults rehashing memories from the painful past.

"You know, Jessie, I have not been able to write a single word since we got the news. I should be overflowing with emotions, recollections, ideas that require purging, but I haven't got a single thought in my mind. It's like I'm dead too; like I am suspended in some kind of vacuum without anything ahead or behind or anywhere around me. It's totally eerie; like he's holding me hostage in this black hole or something. I just wish this was all over and finished because honestly this waiting makes for a real sinister atmosphere around here."

"Don't worry Kaydee. After the funeral is over and you resume a normal routine, you'll be so full of ideas, you won't be able to write fast enough. Right now, there is just too much commotion for your thoughts to organize themselves into something coherent. Give it time. It will all be back." Jessie assured her.

"I hope so," Kaydee said worriedly. "It would be ironic if Father's passing accomplished in death what he wanted so badly to do in life – squelch all prospective literary talent within this family. Honestly Jessie, that would be his ultimate triumph and our ultimate defeat. I just couldn't stand it if that happened!"

"It won't! So stop worrying. It's just this oppressive funeral that is making everyone crazy. He was such a mean man and yet everyone is bending over backwards to 'say nothing bad about the dead'." Jessie mimicked, screwing up her face to match her ugly voice. "It would be so much easier if everyone just decided to be honest for once and say how glad they are that he's gone because he was a mean and hateful man that nobody liked or wanted around."

Kaydee thought that over for a minute then giggled. "What an epitaph! Here lies a man who made the world a better place by leaving it. May he remain forever forgotten!"

Grimly, the girls gave each other the hi-five.

Sunday morning they went to church, if only to have something normal to do for a change. The last two days had drained them all to the point of excruciating emotional exhaustion. They all needed a reprieve. After the service was over, however, it was more of the same, people trying to be polite and say good things. It was almost easier to listen to the few people who did not know Michael personally. They didn't have to work so hard at being polite.

The girls had it easy. They took the kids and escaped to the cars, leaving the adults to fend off the condolences. When they finally got back home, they all breathed a sigh of relief that that ordeal was over. There was no escaping the crowds these days but each hour of serenity was one hour less stress. Thankfully, most of the people had seen them in church so the afternoon was more peaceful. They made up veggie plates for tomorrow but the church ladies would take care of preparing food for the crowd.

The next ordeal was the Prayer service at Bedson's Funeral Home that evening. After the service, there were more condolences. Finally, they retreated to the cars and left for home.

"One more day." Kaydee breathed to Jessie. "Just one more day and then we can start living again. I feel like such a hypocrite," she confessed to Jessie for the umpteenth time.

Chapter 44

Monday finally arrived and everybody gathered at the church for the funeral. Michael had cousins in Alberta and one in Nova Scotia, but all sent their regrets about being unable to attend. Michael had no siblings and his parents had deceased when he was in the army so there were no members of his family present for the funeral. To assist as pallbearers, Dusty had asked Joe Drapanik, Tom Ladduck, Vance Warner, Ed Norchak, Elmer Sutton and his brother Wayne. Joey Kerman was still too fragile to carry any heavy weight so he was spared pallbearing duty but was assigned participation in the service by holding the cross for the short graveside service. Dusty stayed with the family. He wanted to be available to Katreena and Helen in case they needed him.

Reverend Paul gave a short sermon on Michael's history. Other than his regular attendance in church there were really very few pleasant memories he had of Michael but he touched on his pride in his son, citing the gunpowder incident as an example and then summed up his life with his unfortunate accident in the shop over three months ago that sent him to the hospital from which he never recovered. Although Reverend Paul was aware of Michael's escape from the hospital and his murderous intentions toward his family, he did not include it in his eulogy. Everybody knew about it though, and remembered. Zelena was a small community. There were few secrets here, especially about major events like a shooting.

After the internment, everybody gathered in the hall for the memorial luncheon and once more, the family had to endure the charade of regrets at Michael's passing. Finally, the last handshake, thank you and farewell had been dispensed with. The last guest left and the pretence came to an end. The family packed up the leftover food and headed home to KD Acres. On the way, they picked up Dayna where they had left her with young Angie Gohlane for the day. Jaynee and Alvin had simply gone along to the funeral with the rest of the family and outside of a few questions, took it in stride. Both kids stuck close to Kaydee and Jessie and watched the proceedings with fascination. The casket remained closed, of course, so even curious Alvin had no idea of the drama that had brought this day about. Annie, Joey, Wayne, Della, Vance and Janine had come back to KD Acres with the family. These were the true friends who knew the whole story and needed no explanation, no pretext and no apologies. With a heavy sigh of relief, they settled around the familiar dining table for some true camaraderie and honest fellowship. Everyone was exhausted but paramount was the relief that this era of life was truly over! Instead of making supper, Helen merely opened up the leftovers from the luncheon and they just continued visiting while they ate.

It was Wayne and Della who were the first to break up the gathering. "It is after six and we still have a long way to go. We left Gord and Patty to man the office for today, but I don't like to be away from the office too long. Besides, this young lady has to get to school tomorrow. And you, young lady," Wayne addressed Kaydee, "have a lot of writing to do. That is in addition to your schoolwork, not instead of. You promise?"

Kaydee hesitated. "I hope I can, Uncle Wayne. I've been pretty dry ever since this happened. I just hope Father doesn't score the ultimate victory over me now. His anger might find a way to get to me from beyond the grave." Kaydee worried.

"Now don't you let your mind even go there! He only has as much power over you as you designate for him. If you don't give him the power, he will fade into oblivion where he belongs. Your best way to rid yourself of his anger is to write about it, expose it, purge it out of your system, cleanse yourself and then forget about it. Try it. You'll find it works. And do it soon so you can go on to other things. He'll soon lose his hold on you if you shred his anger and discard it. Remember, I'm looking forward to your next book."

Jessie put her arm around Kaydee and gave her a squeeze. "It'll come, you'll see."

Kaydee smiled. "I will try."

She felt more confident now. Maybe Wayne was right. Perhaps if she refused to give her father any power to stop her from writing, he would simply fade into oblivion as Wayne predicted. She could almost feel his anger at being crossed. She remembered Helen's journal and her own anger returned. She would never let him win! She may not expose her secret desire for his disappearance from their life but she could expose his meanness. People only heard his bragging. They never got to know what his family had to live through every single day of their lives. "I will do it, Uncle Wayne, I promise," she said.

"Good girl. Joey, I'm putting you in charge. You take care of my girl here, Okay?" Wayne pointed an authoritative finger at Joey.

"Aye, aye, sir! I shall do my best." Joey drawled in mock seriousness and saluted.

Wayne saluted back and the girls giggled.

Kaydee hugged them goodbye then squeezed Jessie tight. "Thanks for everything, my good friend."

Vance and Janine decided to leave too. "It's been a long day," Janine hugged Katreena then Helen, then Kaydee. "You take care and start living a normal life now and ENJOY IT!" She stressed the last part purposely to give it emphasis. "Just remember that God Himself has granted you this reprieve. Appreciate it and make the most of it! Don't throw it back in His face by stressing over the past. You have served your time and now even God thinks you deserve peace and freedom."

"Thank you, Janine." Helen and Katreena echoed together as they choked back tears of relief and gratitude at Janine's empathy. Janine had been their confidante and co-sufferer through those many years of trauma and anguish when life had seemed so hopeless and stressful. Katreena had purged her frustrations on Janine and Vance's sympathetic ears more times than she could count. Now Janine could genuinely appreciate the liberation from the turmoil because she had been part of it for far too long. Helen and Kaydee's emancipation was a victory for Janine and Vance as well as for Katreena.

Joey and Annie were next to leave. Annie promised to keep closely in touch. Joey made sure Katreena and Dusty were staying for the night before taking his leave. "They shouldn't be alone tonight," he explained to Dusty privately. "I'd feel much better if you spent a couple of nights here for now. I can be here during the day but it would be great if you two could just stick around for a while. Just until things settle down to a routine of sorts."

"We'll be here for a couple of days at least but remember we have a wedding coming and I'm not postponing that on account of Michael. That lowlife did not deserve that kind of respect and I'll be damned if I'm going to let him spoil my big day. He's done enough damage to this family already!"

"Man, you got that right," Joey agreed. "And thanks. I'll see you tomorrow then."

When everyone left, the women washed up the dishes and corralled the kids in for baths and bedtime. Thankfully, not even Alvin protested. He too, was exhausted. Not completely understanding quite why, both Alvin and Jaynee sensed that it had been momentous day and they did not resist an early curfew. By half past eight, everyone was in bed.

Kaydee woke up early the next morning feeling light, and free, and strangely energized. Although she could see through her window that it was cloudy outside, she felt as if the sun had somehow broken through and was shining right into her world. She lay there for a few minutes just basking in this euphoria, trying to store it up for the time when it would vanish and the real world would again set in. But the lightness and the carefree feeling persisted, even intensified. This called for analysis. The funeral! She remembered it. Yesterday they had buried her father! They had put his silent, lifeless remains into a hole in the ground and had covered it with a heavy mound of dirt that would entomb him forever. He would never, ever, return to spread his venom and his misery on the family again. She was free. No more sinholes. No more being yelled at. No more being called a half-wit, stupid, or a moron! No more fear! Realization of that engulfed her like a cuddly blanket.

These last three months had been merely a peephole in the door to show them what life could be like. Father's eventual return had always loomed over them like that constant shadow that never let them relax. Now the shadow was gone. This time they were really, truly, free!

Kaydee jumped out of bed. Her mother! How was her mother feeling? Grabbing a robe, she went racing down the stairs, contorting her arms into sleeves that were flying somewhere behind her. There was no one in the kitchen. Quietly, Kaydee crept through the rooms to Mother's bedroom. The door was slightly ajar and Kaydee pushed it open a bit further to see inside. Her mother was sleeping peacefully and deeply. Kaydee just stepped back out of the room and tiptoed back up the stairs, careful not to waken anyone. At the head of the stairs, she met her grandmother. She must have heard Kaydee's mad dash down the stairs and came to investigate. Kaydee put a finger to her lips to silence her.

"What's the matter?" Katreena whispered in alarm. "Why did you go chasing down the stairs in such a hurry?"

Kaydee gave her grandmother a long impulsive hug, pulled her into her room and closed the door. "It's nothing, Granny. Honest. I just woke up with this wonderful feeling of freedom and peace. When I remembered the funeral, I got worried about Mother, so I went to check on her. Granny, she's sleeping like a baby. I think she feels it too, this peace and this freedom that I'm feeling. He can't ever hurt us again!" Kaydee finished in awe. "Never again!"

"I know, sweetheart," Katreena breathed, the lump in her throat almost choking her. "I'd rather not wake your mother up just yet. Let her enjoy her sleep. It's been a long time coming. Breakfast can wait. There is no rush. You still have an hour and a half before you leave for school," Arms around each other, they explored a future full of wonder, promise and joy.

Dusty and Katreena stayed for two more days, just to make sure everyone had settled down to normal, then they had to leave to prepare for their wedding. Helen and Kaydee understood Katreena's eagerness to get home. Katreena kept in touch by phone every day just to make sure everything was fine. She was encouraged by Helen's new carefree attitude and her positive outlook. Helen seemed to have buried her fear and meekness when they buried Michael. She was looking forward to life, not looking back and Katreena suspected that Joey played big role in that positive transformation. Whatever the reason, for the first time since Helen announced her pregnancy and her intention to marry Michael, Katreena felt relaxed about their future. Life was going to be good after all, Katreena could feel it.

Joey came down every day, puttering around the yard, itching to get well enough to go out on the field to cultivate the last stubble fields before the imminent freeze-up but he was glad just to stick around the house. Helen never mentioned Michael and Joey hoped that she had put all the bad feelings totally behind her. She talked about Kaydee's writing but never mentioned her own personal sojourn into the literary field.

Chapter 45

Joey was spending a lot of time at the Boyer farm now. He played with the kids and he became great pals with Alvin, though Alvin often alluded to the things he had done with his dad. Joey didn't mind that. Michael had probably been decent to Alvin, and Joey wanted him to retain those good memories. Jaynee often watched Joey, shyly checking him out as he held Dayna in his arms or played with Alvin, but unless Kaydee was there talking with him, Jaynee maintained a safe distance.

On Saturday, with Kaydee home to stay with the kids, Joey suggested Helen join him for the routine cattle check in the pasture. Helen had always done this with Michael, especially in the spring when the cows were calving but had never gone with Joey other than that first introductory time when Joey first started working at KD Acres back in July. Kaydee noted her mother's eagerness with satisfaction. That was definitely a good sign. It allowed Kaydee to dream...

As Helen and Joey drove out of the yard in his truck heading for the pasture, Helen opened the window to take advantage of the breeze. It was cloudy and veils of mist dipped to the ground then lifted, then dipped again as they covered the four miles to the pasture. The sweetly pungent aroma of cranberries, the mellow dampness of dead leaves, grasses and faint whiffs of stubble smoke wafted in the just slightly cool, moist air. Helen put her head out the window to breathe in the full impact of these autumn odours. Joey watched her contentment, empathizing with her delight. He loved the country too. He felt euphoric. Here was his soul mate! Right beside him, and she was sharing his pleasure too!

They checked the fences and the watering holes, counted the cattle, and checked them for hoof rot and other signs of stress or trauma. Joey talked gently to the cattle and they eyed him curiously as they grazed. Helen told him about how difficult the birth of a certain calf had been and how they had almost given up hope that it would survive. She noted how well it was doing now.

"Kaydee called him 'Victor' because he overcame such trials those terrible first two weeks. Kaydee had names for each animal born at home before we put the herd out here to pasture."

Joey laughed. "That's funny. I had a steer that I called 'Victor' too. Originally he was a runt but he suckled two cows. One cow had lost her calf and she adopted him. There was no way I could keep them separated. But the real mother wouldn't surrender her calf so he just fed off both of them. Boy, you should have seen that sucker grow!"

Helen laughed too. "Good for Victor! And good for the cows too, I guess."

"Yea, cattle can be interesting." Joey went serious again. "I hated it when I had to sell off my cattle and move off the farm after Vince came back and claimed the land. It was his land but I added the cattle when he went into the military. I loved every single one of those animals. And I had names for each one of them too – all sixty-three of them! I never penned them for inoculations. I'd just come up to them at home or in the pasture, say 'Whoa old boy' or 'old girl,' jab the needle in the rump, and send them away happy."

"I had one cow, named Polly, who used to follow me around like a puppy until she got a carrot or an apple as a treat. I started her on that from when she was a calf and she never outgrew it. Polly loved her treats! Cattle all have personalities, just like people. Some are loveable, others are funny and others are a bit of a pill, but they are never dull."

Helen considered that for a moment then reflected regretfully, "We never got close to our cattle that way. Michael never liked them. He called them 'dumb animals.' To him, cattle were strictly a 'cash crop'. He never allowed Kaydee to take Alvin anywhere near them because he feared for his safety, I guess."

Joey was shocked but he tried his level best to sound unaffected. "That's really too bad. Animals can be your best friends and they will protect you if they feel you are in danger. Alvin would never have been harmed by the cattle but he might have got a lot of pleasure from their friendship."

"I guess we missed out on a lot of things," Helen said pensively.

"No problem," said Joey. "Life isn't over yet. It's never too late to build relationships, even with animals. Just give them a chance and you'll see how much pleasure they bring to your life."

"I don't think our cattle will trust us like your cattle did. Michael was never really kind to them so they are rather skittish when people get close."

"Not to worry," Joey countered. "I'd be willing to bet that by next spring I'll have them licking my hand. You just wait and see." Helen looked at him doubtfully.

He winked. "Mark my words. I'll remind you next spring."

As they walked along the fence Helen remembered pounding in the posts and wondered who the witness was that related the story that day at the fair causing Michael's ballistic mood that had culminated in that ultimate tragedy.

"Penny for your thoughts," Joey interjected. "You have been quiet for so long, I wondered if I had upset you somehow."

"Oh no, Joey. I could not be upset with you. I was just remembering something, but it's not worth even thinking about. Some things are best forgotten."

"That's good Helen, because you know I would never do anything to upset you."

When they got home, Kaydee had supper ready to go on the table and Helen insisted Joey stay and eat with the family. Joey was glad to be included in the family meal.

Later that evening Helen told Kaydee about Joey's experiences on his farm, how he loved animals, and his interaction with his cattle. Kaydee listened with interest and wonder.

"Joey's farm must have been a wonderful place. I wish I could have heard his stories. I could write about them." Kaydee said enthusiastically.

"Perhaps you can get him to tell you those stories some day. He probably has tons of them," Helen offered. Kaydee's eyes lit up with anticipation as she considered the interesting opportunities associated with the prospect of such a venture.

School had been so pleasant for Kaydee this month that she could not believe her good fortune. The kids were actually nice to her now that she had shed her own inhibitions and allowed them to get close to her. Some of the girls were even including her in their circles. It was a new experience for Kaydee and she liked it. She now found school work much easier and even enjoyable. Everyone seemed to be bending over backwards to offer her assistance. It was as if they were competing against each other which one could be most helpful, all of them trying to help her catch up because they wanted her in their class! Why had she ever thought that they disliked her? Was it possible that she had been the one that had shunned them instead of the other way around? How very different this school year was from the one she finished in June!

Kaydee worked hard at her studies and utilized all the assistance that the other kids offered her. No one mentioned her father, but it seemed obvious that they were all aware of her story and were trying to be understanding and supportive. Ed and Sandy Norchak continued giving her regular tutoring after school and Joey would pick Kaydee up in the evenings to take her home. Kaydee's hard work and her diligence were paying off. An avid reader before, she now exploited every bit of knowledge that she gleaned from textbooks, reports, essays or articles offered by anyone as guidelines or examples. Deeply humbled by their support, Kaydee never failed to give credit to her advocates which further endeared her to her classmates.

Thanks to Ed and Sandy Norchak's clarification that Kaydee's problem was not her lack of intelligence but a situational issue which had now been resolved, even the teachers all banded together to help her catch up. It looked as if she had a good chance of closing the gap of grades that had branded her as a retard in the previous years. She was happy, well liked and quickly becoming a popular teenager. The transformation in Kaydee was beyond belief. Ed and Sandy Norchak revelled in the validation of their original conviction that Kaydee possessed tremendous potential for learning if she were given the opportunity.

At the farm, Joey wanted to finish cultivating the last of the stubble fields, but Helen worried that the constant jarring on the tractor would put a strain on his stitches so she added an extra cushion for him to sit on. He started to toss it away but her pained expression made him put it back on the seat.

Joey laughed at her. "It's okay, Boss!" then added more seriously, "Don't worry, Helen. I won't throw it away when I leave the yard. I promise to use the cushion until you take it away from me. That okay with you?"

"Thank you, Joey. Just promise me you won't do anything to strain yourself, please." Joey looked at her. She was genuinely concerned about him. He knew that. Biting back his pride, he crooked his finger until Helen came close.

"I wasn't going to tell you this because it is downright embarrassing but since you are so worried about me, I think it's just as well that you know the truth. Dr. Walley gave me a girdle to wear to protect my stitches and my insides against any strain. I have been wearing it all this time and I am wearing it right now. Besides, I don't intend to do anything to endanger my health. You need me and I want to be here until you kick me out. I'm not going to do anything to jeopardize that, so stop worrying, okay?" He repeated, "OKAY?"

Helen was choked up with emotion but she nodded. Joey started the tractor and turned his attention to the cultivator behind him. Helen was grateful she could walk away without having to talk to Joey anymore. She could not understand it. Lately, she was always so close to tears whenever Joey talked gently to her, or teased her, or even laughed at her as he did just now. She was happy and yet sad at the same time. Her emotions were all over the place. What was the matter with her?

The wedding was coming up in two days and she was looking forward to it with great anticipation. The idea of going to that wedding with Joey as an escort promised to be a thrilling evening. It was true he was only her escort by virtue of being her partner as a groomsman and she a maid of honour in a wedding party. Still, they would be together and she could not even be faulted for it by the most malicious gossip mongers if such there should be.

Helen made arrangements with Angie Gohlane to take the baby and keep her over the weekend. Alvin and Jaynee would attend the wedding as ring bearer and flower girl. Both kids were absolutely thrilled at the idea, though both Helen and Kaydee worried somewhat about Jaynee getting through the performance because she was so shy. Katreena, however, had every faith in Jaynee and was positive about her ability to do it.

For the umpteenth time, Helen and Kaydee checked everybody's wardrobe and all the other essentials for the gala weekend but they kept finding more things to pack that they deemed were "important." Joey had no idea how many more bags would accumulate.

"We're only going to be staying there for one night, girls," Joey reminded them.

"I know, Joey but I don't want to be caught unprepared. This wedding has to be perfect."

"It will be, so stop worrying," Joey chided. In spite of his nonchalant tone, Joey felt himself drawn along into the excitement, though he tried hard to cover it up.

"Granny and I will be at your house by seven," Joey promised. "We'll pack our suitcases in your car, drop Dayna off at the Gohlanes and we should be at Katreena's before nine."

Helen was now counting the hours until they could be on their way. Kaydee was probably doing the same but Joey appeared calm. He smiled indulgently at their excitement and enjoyed their energized behaviour. He found it appealing to see them so animated. Ever since he had met the family, he had waited to see such smiles and hear such enthusiasm in their voices. That he could now witness it brought him much pleasure and gratification.

Yet he felt bereft and alone. Why? He had always been content to be a loner. Now, for some odd reason, being a loner had lost its allure. His empty life stretched out desolately before him. He longed for the completeness of belonging to someone. He envied men who had families to take care of, someone special to whom they mattered above all else in the world. He wanted to belong to somebody, to be needed, valued, appreciated, and to have somebody belong to him. Wistfully he watched Helen and her family...

Katreena had made hair appointments for them all for Saturday morning. Neither Kaydee nor Helen had ever had their hair done by a professional and they were both excited and nervous.

Saturday morning finally arrived and Helen and Kaydee were up well before the sun even considered breaking through the bonds of darkness. They showered and stuffed their essentials into the suitcases, and packed the suitcases in the trunk of the car. They zipped the wedding attire into the long garment bags that would keep them fresh and free from dust and creases, then hung the bag near the door to be put in after Joey and Annie's bags were loaded into the trunk.

By the time Joey and Annie arrived at seven, the kids were washed and fed, the kitchen was clean, and everything was ready to go. With Annie and Joey's suitcases and the garment bags loaded, Helen locked up the house and they left for the Gohlane place, where they dropped off Dayna and all the supplies Angie would need for the weekend. They were on their way!

Helen sat in front with Joey and Alvin sat proudly between them on the wide seat. He had become an ardent admirer of Joey, emulating him at every opportunity. It was actually quite cute to watch and Joey considered it quite an honour to have Alvin hero worship him that way. Jaynee, being shy, was more reserved. She sat primly between Kaydee and Annie trying her best to look the part of the princess that they had told her she would look like at the wedding. She was excited and nervous but with Kaydee at her side she felt comfortable and safe.

Because Helen was so uneasy about Jaynee's performance, Dusty and Katreena had arranged to take Alvin, Jaynee, Joey, Kaydee and Jessie to the church for a practice run while Helen and Annie were at the hairdressers. That would familiarize them with what they were expected to do. With Jessie and Kaydee walking ahead of them, the two small kids might feel confident enough to follow through with their roles. Their performance was not crucial to the ceremony but it would certainly add that magic touch and Katreena sincerely hoped that the kids would be alright. She wanted them to be able to look back on the wedding with fond memories just as she knew she would.

The rising sun shone straight into Joey's eyes and even bringing the visor down did not help. It was just a bad time of the day to be driving east! Helen always had a pair of sunglasses in the side pocket of the door and she took them out, cleaned them and handed them to Joey.

"Thanks Helen. I usually carry mine along with me but they are in my truck on your yard. I just plain forgot them," he confessed.

Helen laughed. "Don't feel bad. If this were your vehicle I'd probably be in the same position. I don't need them. I can just move my head and avoid the glare."

"Yea, you just turn my way. I won't mind in the least. It may even help." He teased softly and Helen blushed.

"Okay, you two. Stop whispering over there," Annie scolded from the back. "I hear you."

"My. My. What big ears you got Granny," Joey laughed.

Annie grabbed at Jaynee's coloring book and swatted the back of Joey's head. "And don't you ever forget it, you hear?"

Joey ducked. "Boy, I thought grandmothers were supposed to spoil you, not swat you over the head." They all laughed.

"You don't let that fellow get away with no smart remarks there, Helen. You know what they say: 'Give them an inch and they take a mile.' He'll tease you mercilessly if you let him get away with it."

"I promise I'll keep him in line," Helen bantered back.

"Oh no! Now it's two against one. No fair. Alvin, I need help!" Joey complained.

"You got it, Joey. Put up your dukes, you guys," and Alvin brought up both his little fists in front of his face swinging his body from side to side boxer-style, as if to fend off enemies.

Everybody roared with laughter. Even Jaynee giggled though she could not see Alvin since they were both sitting low in their seats.

"I think I'm gonna have to give you some boxing lessons, little man, if you're going to be my bodyguard. I may need some serious protection." Joey drawled, John Wayne style, as he looked down at Alvin's tight little fists. "There may be trouble in them dar hills, pardner."

"Don't worry, pardner. I'll protect you," Alvin replied, trying to match Joey's drawl, still holding his fists in front of him.

"Oh, for heaven's sake Joey! Now look what you've done! You've got him doing it." Annie groaned from behind.

"You stop pickin' on my partner there, Lady," Joey remonstrated with mock sternness. "Silence, woman!"

Kaydee and Helen were roaring with laughter, Jaynee giggled shyly but Joey and his grandmother maintained their austere poses, playing their parts with obvious relish. Alvin puffed out his chest, put on a scowl and tried to imitate Joey.

They continued teasing, joking, laughing and eventually settled down to serious discussions about the upcoming wedding just before they hit Lanavale. Kaydee marvelled at how pleasant this trip had been and how short it had seemed. Going to Lanavale with Father had always been such a morbid experience... Kaydee snapped herself back and resolved to never look back again, determined she would not let anything spoil her happiness today. Joey had personally and deliberately enlisted Alvin's participation in the fun and encouraged everyone to contribute to the light-hearted mood. She was going to revel in that.

They arrived at Katreena's house just after eight, unpacked the car and settled into their rooms. Dusty was not there. In deference to the superstition that the groom should not see the bride before the ceremony on the day of the wedding, he, Wayne, Della and Jessie had rented rooms at the Holiday Inn last night and left Vance and Janine to help Katreena with any last minute details. Janine took her role seriously and herded all the women into her car to go to the hairdressers. Vance, Joey and Alvin were left to decorate Helen's car with the flowers and streamers prepared for that purpose. Katreena's car was already decked out.

As soon as the hairdressers were done with Katreena, Kaydee, Jaynee and Janine, Janine drove them to the church for rehearsal where Joey, Jessie and Alvin were already waiting.

Helen had to have her hair dyed, permed and set, so that would take much longer. Vance would pick up Helen and Annie later. It was a mad rush but it worked like clockwork. By one o'clock, everyone was back at the house ready for a light lunch, before dressing for the wedding ceremony. They had to be there by quarter after two.

Vance took Joey and Alvin to his place to dress up and "give the girls privacy to prance around in their bras and panties without having to hide from the men," as he put it. The girls laughed nervously but they did appreciate the gesture. Helen confidently handed Alvin's clothes to Joey as they left. When all the ladies were ready, Janine scooted home to get her gala dress on and sent the men back across the street to Katreena's to wait for the rest of the group. Della drove up then and joined them. All the women were primped and looking like they just stepped out of a Fashion Magazine. Katreena, once more expressed her gratitude to Janine and Vance for their assistance and support.

"I just could not have done all this without you two," she acknowledged.

Janine gave her an impetuous hug. "Honey, we are honoured to be of service. What are friends for if they can't help you marry your hunk?" They all laughed. "Seriously, you know we'd have been terribly insulted if you had not asked."

Joey's breath caught when he saw Helen. He had never seen her all dolled up this way, with her makeup and her hair professionally done and wearing that beautiful gown that showed off her new curvy figure since she had put on those few pounds this summer. When Joey had first seen Helen, she was a lanky boney figure with hardly any shape at all. Her straight grey hair and pale complexion had done nothing to make her attractive either. Now her hair was a shimmering golden brown, softly waved and piled high off her neck and face to emphasize her delicate features. There was a radiant glow in her eyes and in her cheeks that did not come from makeup alone. Helen was happy and it gave her that special glow. Joey could see it. This woman in front of him was nothing short of gorgeous and Joey was completely captivated. Kaydee and Jaynee too, had come alive. Joey suddenly felt very proud to be associated with the family.

"Phew," he whistled. "Am I the lucky guy that is supposed to be escorting these beautiful ladies to the ball? What have I ever done to deserve such an honour?"

Jessie and Kaydee giggled, Jaynee smiled shyly and Helen blushed profusely. Annie, Katreena, Della and Janine watched with amused approval but Alvin was perturbed. "Don't I look nice too, Joey?" he queried.

Everyone laughed and Joey whisked him up in his arms. "You, my little man look like a very handsome fine gentleman who is in charge of leading your little sister up the aisle. You are the most important of all, because without you they cannot get married. You will be carrying their rings. Everyone will be watching for you and waiting for you. Do you think you can handle all that important responsibility? I'm counting on you to do your part, you know."

Alvin's face lit up with wonder, then his head bobbed up and down eagerly. "You bet, Joey. Just like we practiced. I won't let you down, I promise."

"All right then, what are we waiting for? We can't have the groom waiting alone at the altar! Let's get this show on the road!" That was Vance, in charge of operations again.

Chapter 46

The church was packed with guests and Dusty and Wayne were already waiting at the altar. Joey took his grandmother's arm and led her to one of the front pews then hurried to take his place with Dusty and Wayne. Vance and Janine sat down next to Annie in the pew just as Father Rory Caddish stepped forward to the altar. The organist started the wedding march and all eyes turned to watch the entrance at the back of the church. The photographer was ready with his camera to capture the memorable event on film. Katreena had arranged for Jessie and Kaydee to walk up the aisle together first and they would be followed by Alvin and Jaynee.

Approving glances followed the girls as they slowly made their way to the front of the church. Alvin and Jaynee followed behind them. The two kids were greeted with gasps of awe and admiration from the crowd. Jaynee was like a princess, the frilly skirt of her dress rustling softly as she turned side to side deliberately dropping the petals across the full width of the aisle. She smiled demurely at the camera and the admiring crowd, carefully picking the flower petals from her little lace basket as she walked beside her proud big brother. Alvin was obviously taking his role seriously, concentrating on carrying out his "important responsibility" like he promised. He stopped next to Joey and waited for his nod of approval that he had done well. Only after he got it, did his face break into a smile. Jaynee stood next to Jessie and Kaydee at the end of the line, her pale blue dress a complimentary contrast to the girls' deep sapphire long slim gowns. Flashing cameras lit up the church.

Della walked in next, followed by Helen, stepping slowly in time to the music, their light blue gowns whispering softly as they walked. Finally, Katreena came walking proudly up the aisle, her head high, her radiant smile reflecting Dusty's eager one. Wayne was taking all this performance in stride but Dusty and Joey were enthralled with wonder, just as were Kaydee, Alvin and Jaynee. To Dusty and Joey, it was basically Katreena and Helen that had them so spellbound but Kaydee and the kids were fascinated by the whole scene. They had never been to a wedding, much less one where they were among the honorary participants. And because this was Granny's wedding, it was so much more special. They were absolutely mesmerized.

Dusty was euphoric. All this last summer he had dreamed of this day. In fact, he had dreamed about it since that first day way back in May when he was first introduced to Katreena. There was something appealing and attractive about this captivating woman and Dusty had felt smitten from the beginning, though he had to work hard at gaining her trust. Even when they had established a comfortable relationship after their return home, there had been some tense and anxious days when problems at KD Acres had seemed so insurmountable that he wondered if he could ever compete for Katreena's attention and love. Today was the zenith of all the hopes and dreams of his whole life. He had never felt this way about any woman in his life and he could not believe that this, his wedding day, was really happening at this point of his life.

A hush fell over the assembled guests as Father Caddish intoned the words of the service. Kaydee's heart swelled with pride and happiness. How life had changed since last spring! Even in her wildest dreams, she could not have envisioned this. Last spring she had not considered a life that could be anything but that endless desolation and despair that had been her lot since she was old enough to understand.

Silent images coursed through her mind and hovered like morbid phantoms of gloom. Was this really happening or was it simply another melancholy illusion that her anguished mind had conjured up in an effort to escape the stark reality of her tormented years? Kaydee desperately fought her way past the demons that haunted her. No, her father was gone, his anger and his venom silenced forever, buried for eternity, never to inflict his poison on her again. Kaydee skimmed over the last three months and reflected on the changes in their lives. She had just begun living her life that long ago day back in July. It was a lifetime ago. This could not be a dream. She had never dreamed it. This was real!

"And now you may kiss the bride," Father Caddish said and a cacophony of voices broke into Kaydee's reverie. The service was over, Kaydee realized. Granny was married and everyone was cheering and

Dusty was kissing Granny and everyone was smiling happily. This was real. It was true. This was not an illusion, not a dream, not a figment of an overactive imagination! Kaydee felt blessed and humbled as she followed the entourage outside.

Katreena was also feeling humbled and blessed. Never in all these years, had she even considered that this moment might come to pass. Ever since Daniel had died, Katreena had never contemplated remarriage to another man. Until Dusty came along, she had never met anyone worthy of such a thought. Then this witty and passionate man entered her life and all her perspectives had changed. Like the proverbial puppy, Dusty had uncomplainingly waited for her scraps of time. Then, when he was needed most, he simply stepped in and took on those critical responsibilities as required. How could she be so lucky twice in one lifetime? She turned her eyes heavenward and mutely whispered, “Thank you, Lord!”

As they left the church, they were inundated with congratulations and good wishes from everyone. Helen had tears in her eyes when she hugged her mother then Dusty. “I am so happy for you,” she choked. “You two were meant for each other.”

“Thanks Helen,” Dusty hugged her back. “I must admit, there were times when I thought I could not compete with you. But now I feel very fortunate – and completely confident. Life will be great for all of us, you’ll see. I promise you I will take good care of your mother.”

“I know you will. You’re that kind of man,” Helen smiled through her tears.

Kaydee found it difficult to get anywhere near Granny and Dusty so she patiently waited her turn. This had to be a dream – a dream she never wanted to wake up from. Here she was, on the steps of this big church, holding on to Jaynee and Alvin, her grandmother had just got married, her mother was looking like a queen, and everyone in her family was happy! Who would have ever believed this scene was possible?

Jessie was waiting next to her and the kids and Kaydee looked over at her new friend.

“Hey Jessie. You know what?”

"No. What?" Jessie asked eagerly.

"We're related now." Kaydee and Jessie both laughed and hugged.

"Me too. Me too." Jaynee piped up as usual and the girls picked her up between the two of them for a triple hug.

Not to be outdone, Alvin poked at Kaydee. "Does that mean I am related too?"

Jessie laughed as she pumped his outstretched hand. "You just bet you are Alvin. We're all related now!"

"I'm so glad to have you as part of our family," Kaydee told Dusty when she finally got near enough to congratulate him and Granny. Jaynee hung back slightly but in typical "Jaynee fashion" she shyly offered her own "Me too." They all laughed and Jaynee, embarrassed, hid her face into the folds of Kaydee's dress.

Careful not to alarm her, Dusty knelt down beside her and gently turned her towards him.

"You know what, Jaynee? I am very happy to be part of your family too. Now can you give me a hug just like you give your Granny? I really need one so badly."

Jaynee hesitated, looked to Kaydee for approval and when Kaydee nodded, Jaynee wrapped her little arms around Dusty's neck in a tight embrace. Dusty swooped her up in a tight hug and whirled her around as Jaynee giggled in ecstasy. "Now, that is my girl. Thank you very much Jaynee. Now I know I belong to the family!" Jaynee's smile could have lit up the whole world and from that moment Jaynee became Dusty's most avid fan.

Katreena and Helen's eyes filled with tears. They suddenly realized that Jaynee had never had a hug from a man before. She had always shied away and retreated whenever Joey or Dusty had come near her so both had given her that free space she had seemed to require. Now they realized that it was her fear of Michael that had made her cringe from men in general. She simply did not feel safe in a man's presence. Joey realized what was happening as well and it tugged profoundly at his heartstrings. Right from the beginning, Joey had noticed that Jaynee had a special attachment to Kaydee but he had never thought much about the reason behind it. Now it all became clear to him. Michael was a tyrant, Helen had been unresponsive, Alvin was Daddy's boy and poor Jaynee had no one other than Kaydee and, only occasionally, Granny. Joey made a silent vow to give Jaynee special attention; to wipe away that fear and mistrust and to make her feel cherished and loved. Dusty's innocent action had awakened a sleeping Jaynee that no one had even known existed and all of them felt moved to tears by this insight.

Alvin stood aside, not quite knowing what was expected of him at the moment but seeing Jaynee so enraptured with Dusty made Alvin feel left out. He had attached himself quite solidly to Joey in the last couple of months, so he looked to him for direction. Joey was quick to notice Alvin's discomfiture and surreptitiously tapped Dusty's shoulder. Dusty noted the direction of Joey's gaze and realized that Alvin was waiting. By now, both men understood the desperate need these kids had for affection and Dusty scooped Alvin up with his other hand.

"And how about you, my little man? Is there a hug for me somewhere?"

Alvin gave Dusty a quick hug and then wiggled his way down from Dusty's arm. Once on the ground, he extended his hand up to Dusty for a handshake and stated very formally. "Welcome to the family, sir."

Dusty's eyebrows rose but he suppressed the urge to laugh. He took Alvin's hand and shook it vigorously. "I thank you, kind sir. I shall do my best to live up to all my responsibilities." Then bowing low, he put Jaynee down and stood up straight. Clicking his heels together he saluted Alvin. "Thank you again sir."

"You're welcome, sir, but you can call me Alvin." Alvin returned the salute and stepped back to take his place beside Joey as the crowd broke into an uproarious applause.

The cavalcade of about twenty cars finally left the church heading for the Caribbean Club, led by the three streamer-bedecked cars of the bridal party. Alvin insisted on riding with Joey, obviously looking to him for guidance and support and Joey was secretly proud to be considered his role model. Jaynee stuck to Kaydee but her adoring eyes followed Dusty's every move. It was obvious that she was smitten. Kaydee and

Jessie both noted it with interest.

"Someone's in love," Kaydee told Jessie with a wink. Jessie nodded giggling.

Jaynee rode with Kaydee and Jessie in the back of Wayne and Della's car, sitting primly like a princess, trying hard to act grown up, aware that she was a significant member of the principal party on a special occasion. When they arrived at the Club, Jaynee clung to Kaydee's hand, afraid to let go lest she lose sight of her. Her shyness was an integral part of her nature, and she found it difficult to relax amid so many strangers. Everyone she knew seemed to be busy somewhere else or with someone else and Jaynee felt forgotten in the melee.

The photographer was waiting for the group as they disembarked from the vehicles, snapping away at every opportunity. Outside of the bride and groom, of course, Jaynee was the one who captured a good deal of the spotlight. Even Alvin noticed that and, not to be outshone, a few times came of his own accord to stand beside his little celebrity sister for the photo ops.

They posed for group pictures in front of the rose bower that stood in one corner of the banquet room and then everyone went to their pre-assigned tables for the banquet.

Kaydee looked at her mother. She was talking with Joey, laughing at something he had said. She looked happy and at ease. Joey was looking at her with that tender look of admiration. Watching the two of them always made Kaydee feel all warm inside. Kaydee could not help hoping that eventually the happiness that Granny had found with Dusty would rub off on her mother and that someday, Joey and her mother would find that same happiness together. Mother looked good. She was alert, vibrant, enthusiastic, happy, ALIVE! Joey was already Alvin's hero. There was a dream in Kaydee's heart and Joey could make that dream come true.

The meal was barely finished when the band started playing in the other room. People left the dining room and moved to the hall part with tables and chairs along the walls which left the centre of the floor clear. Jessie, Kaydee, and Jaynee sat at a round table with Annie while Vance and Janine joined the wedding party at their table. Dusty and Katreena started off the dancing. They were joined by Wayne and Della and Joey and Helen. Joey apologized to Alvin and explained that he had to go dance so Alvin came to sit with the girls. Vance and Janine joined the dancers as the photographer ran around the floor taking pictures of all the couples. When other people crowded onto the floor, the photographer retreated into a safe corner.

Jessie giggled. "I think he is afraid he's going to get trampled."

"If not him, then his equipment." Kaydee agreed. "Though I think that equipment means more to him than his life by the way he's always guarding it."

Annie sat quietly watching the dancers but Kaydee thought that she had her eyes on Joey and her mother most of the time. Though she said nothing, Kaydee was certain there was a satisfied smile on Annie's face as she watched Joey's admiring gaze on Helen. Jessie watched Kaydee, whose eyes kept straying from Helen and Joey to Annie and back again. Jessie knew Kaydee quite well by now and she was astute enough to guess what was on Kaydee's mind.

"Make a nice couple, don't they?" Jessie remarked.

Kaydee awoke from her daydream, slightly embarrassed to have been observed. She blushed with guilt. "Guess my fantasies are pretty obvious, eh?"

"Only as the light of day," Jessie smiled back. "But don't worry. I'm not passing judgment. As a matter of fact, I approve wholeheartedly. Besides," and Jessie dropped her voice to barely a whisper, "I think you have very strong allies in those daydreams." Her eyes indicated Annie whose eyes were still following Helen and Joey as they danced around the floor.

"I know. We already have the rainbow. All we need is that pot of gold." Kaydee smiled.

When the music stopped, somebody brought a chair and placed it in the middle of the room. They led Dusty to it and made him sit down, then took off his shoes and put them in front of him. Next, they brought Katreena to him and made her sit on his knee. Only some of the crowd knew what this was about, the others stood watching intently to see what was going to happen. The guests were told to form a circle and dance around the couple as the music started to play. As the men passed in front of the bride, they put money into Dusty's shoe as payment for a chance to dance with the bride. Once the crowd realized how the game was played, they all joined in the fun and started playing tricks on Dusty, dancing with Katreena longer than the allotted minute and Dusty had to go "rescue" his wife from these cheaters. Some guys came back more than once, disguising themselves by stealing another man's hat or a woman's scarf which they tied babushka-style over their head so that Dusty would not know it was the same fellow. Everybody got into the act and they really hammed it up. In the end, they made Dusty empty all the money from his shoes and give it to Katreena. Since she had nothing to put it in, she had to borrow a sock from Wayne to put the money in. They would not let her use Dusty's socks. It was hilarious. Everyone was holding their stomachs, from laughing so hard.

They went back to more dancing, some fancy Ukrainian dance that only a few of the crowd were familiar with but many got on the floor to try to learn the new steps. That, too was comical to watch because some were able to pick up the sequences quickly but others kept getting so mixed up that they just provided a comedy show for those that sat and watched their clumsy efforts.

After the midnight lunch, everybody lined up in twos to make an arch from the front of the hall to the doorway. Dusty and Katreena had to pass through that arch before they could leave the hall. If the people were short, their arch was low and Dusty and Katreena had to duck low to get under it. Jessie and Kaydee held Alvin and Jaynee on their shoulders to make the arch high enough for them to go through. The kids were tickled pink to be able to be part of the arch for Granny and Dusty. Jaynee squealed with delight and Alvin was all smiles. Once the bride and groom left the hall, everybody started going home. Katreena and Dusty had gone to a hotel for the night so Helen, Annie, and the kids had the house to themselves. When Joey said he was going to Vance and Janine's house for the night, Alvin reluctantly bid him goodnight. It had been a wonderful evening and everyone was totally exhausted.

Next morning, everyone was up early at Katreena's house and Helen prepared a light breakfast of toast and coffee or milk or juice for the kids then looked through the window at Janine's house. Sure enough, Joey was outside removing the streamers from the car, so she tapped on the window and beckoned him in to have breakfast with the family.

"I don't know about the others but I thought it would be nice to go to church," Helen told Joey. "Then we'll have brunch and head for home, unless we run into Wayne and Della or maybe by some fluke into Mother and Dusty. I doubt if they left for the honeymoon yet."

"Well, Janine and Vance are coming to church and I'm sure they'll join us for brunch. As for the others, who knows? It's anybody's guess. I would not be too surprised to see them all there though. Anyway, we'll play it by ear." Joey supposed.

Just then the phone rang. It was Katreena. "Everybody up there?" she asked. "Good. We'll see you all in church. We have reserved Chemille's for brunch for fourteen. We've asked Father Rory to join us. We'll see you there then," and she hung up.

"Okay," Helen announced. "It's Chemille's, for brunch. We have reservations and Father Rory will be joining us. Joey, could you let Vance and Janine know while we clean up here?"

Joey walked across the street and was back in a few minutes. They packed their baggage in the trunk in preparation for the trip home then piled into the car and followed Vance and Janine's car to the church. Alvin was still preoccupied by the wedding and, seated between Helen and Joey, he kept chattering about all the exciting things that he had seen and done last night. His head kept turning like a corkscrew as he addressed himself to Joey, to Helen then to Kaydee and Annie and back again to Joey. Since no one else had an opportunity to stick a word in edgewise, they just listened and smiled indulgently at his enthusiasm. Joey parked the car and they walked into the church together – "as a family" – Kaydee thought to herself. It made her feel proud and important. Once inside, Kaydee immediately spotted Jessie and leaving the others behind, she and Jaynee went to sit with Jessie. Alvin stuck with

Joey and sat between him and Mother which made Kaydee happy. They were already looking like a family!

Always well behaved in church, even in his hyper state, Alvin remained perfectly still throughout the service. Once out the door he was again a rotating spitball, full of ideas, memories and stories all tumbling out helter-skelter in total abandon following no sequence or rhythm. They piled into the cars and left for Chemille's for brunch where they were met by the maître d' and escorted to a long white linen covered table with flowers and candles. The room was large with several other tables throughout the room. As they sat perusing the menus, Helen had to shush Alvin several times, reminding him that someone else was talking. Alvin would pipe down – until he forgot again. He was just too excited to observe good manners at this point. But then, they were all pretty animated this morning.

It was after the waiter had served everyone and they had started eating that the maître d' entered, escorting two men to a table at the other end of the room. Alvin saw the men and immediately jumped off his chair and darted after one of the men yelling "Daddy, Daddy!" Shocked and surprised, Helen turned to look and seeing the man Alvin was running to, her face went ashen and she folded over in a dead faint, her knife slipping from her limp hand and clattering to the floor. The man turned in surprise to look at the little boy tugging at his pant leg and Kaydee froze as she stared, openmouthed, at her father's unmistakable image and his shocked expression. Katreena and Annie jumped up to help Helen but froze at the sight of the man who had created this uproar. They stared in utter disbelief at the man they knew they had buried just a couple of weeks ago. In their astonishment, they almost forgot about Helen, then regaining their sanity they turned to help her. Everyone was now crowding around Helen. The maître d' jumped into action calling for the staff to get an ambulance.

Realizing that the stranger did not know or acknowledge him, Alvin slunk back to the table and Joey picked him up, holding the bewildered child tightly in his arms. It was utter mayhem in the room now. Even total strangers, other patrons of the restaurant, were getting involved, trying to help. Someone waved some smelling salts in front of Hèlen's nose and she started coming around, moaning incoherently. The two new guests stood at the other end of the room staring, aghast at this melodrama, and wondering what had caused it.

Dusty regained his composure first. He approached the men, his hand extended to the man who was such a dead ringer for Michael Boyer.

"I beg your pardon, sir. My name is Dusty Duganyk. I apologize for this commotion but you look exactly like someone we used to know and our group is in a total state of shock."

The man eyed Dusty rather suspiciously but his curiosity got the best of him. He accepted Dusty's handshake. "Hello. My name is Maxwell Cartrite and this is Judd Sherman. I was wondering what that was all about. I have never made an entrance into a room with quite this kind of impact before. I don't know if I should be pleased, flattered, insulted or frightened. Who WAS this look-alike of mine, and why did everyone freeze up when they thought I was him?"

Dusty pondered over that question. Should he tell this stranger the whole sordid story or should he sugar coat it? Maxwell was looking at him with genuine and sincere interest. He deserved to hear the real story – perhaps not all the gory details, but certainly the parts that gave validity to the reaction his appearance on the scene had generated. Besides, Dusty wanted to know something about this stranger too. How could two people look that much alike that even those closest to them could not tell them apart? This was bizarre!

"Let's sit down," he told the men and motioned them to a table near the far wall. "You are the exact image of Michael Boyer, the dead husband of the woman who fainted and the father of the kid who called you Daddy. Michael also had three other children. There was a tragic accident and Michael was burned very badly back in July. He died as a result of those injuries a couple of weeks ago. When you walked in, it was like Michael had risen from the grave. That is the reason you made such an impact. I am sorry if we disturbed your Sunday dinner. May I ask if you have siblings?"

Maxwell was fascinated by the story but surprised by the question.

"Actually I have no siblings that I know of. I was adopted as a baby but my mother DID tell me that I had a twin brother but that my folks could not take care of two kids so they gave me up. She never told me anymore about my folks or even if she knew who they were. My parents could not have their own children and they were very good to me. I never pursued the issue of my real parents because I didn't want to know a family that could give their kid away like that. Who was this Michael Boyer?"

Dust suddenly felt uneasy. He did not wish to malign Michael to this stranger. It wasn't his place to do that. But should he introduce Maxwell to the family now? He wondered about that.

"Perhaps another time. Could I have your number or a place where we could contact you? Today is an unusual day for all of us. I just got married yesterday and we're leaving for our honeymoon in a couple of hours but our family would definitely like to get to know you. Could we perhaps arrange another more convenient day for that meeting?"

Maxwell looked over toward the group. The ambulance had arrived, but Helen was sitting up under her own power, still grey as a sheet but obviously not willing to go with the ambulance people. She was trying to send them away.

"Perhaps that would be best," Maxwell said. "I think we have all had our excitement for the day. Let's leave it for after your honeymoon."

"Good plan. See you then, and sorry for all the drama."

"No problem," answered Maxwell. "Congratulations and have a nice honeymoon." They exchanged addresses and phone numbers and Dusty rejoined the family to finish his breakfast.

"Who was that?" Katreena asked the minute Dusty rejoined them.

"Oh, just some fellow passing through," Dusty lied. He didn't want to create any upheaval in Helen's life now when he had no time to deal with the fallout and he certainly had no time to brief Joey about such complications. Better to leave that problem for when they got back home and resumed some normality in their lives again.

Chapter 47

Vance shook Joey's hand. "You take good care of yourself there, man. I want to see you here often from now on." The two men had established a close bond over the weekend.

"If I don't, man, it certainly won't be for lack of trying," Joey assured him with a wink.

Vance understood and smiled. Joey's interest in Helen had not gone unnoticed.

Dusty and Katreena were leaving for the honeymoon and they hugged everyone as they bade their farewells to the group.

"You two take care of each other," Dusty told Joey and Helen. "We will be expecting a good progress report when we come back, you know." Joey nodded and squeezed Dusty's hand tight.

"Keep writing Kaydee," Wayne and Jessie called to Kaydee as she got into the car.

"I promise," yelled Kaydee as they drove off.

It had been a wonderful weekend albeit a bit of a strain, physically and emotionally, for everyone involved. They were all ready for some peace and quiet – and a sense of routine.

As Joey drove onto the main highway, the vitality went out of every body and exhaustion claimed its due. Soon everyone was fast asleep. Kaydee, however, was too agitated to sleep. She wondered who that man was that had almost made her heart stop beating. Mother had almost lost it there and just when she and Joey were looking so happy together. Dusty said he was just a stranger passing through but Kaydee could not forget that face. It was absolutely incredible how much the man looked like Father. She forced herself not to think about that anymore. The stranger was just that, a stranger! He happened to look like Father, that was all. Father was dead. He was buried. Mother was happy. Kaydee did not want to get ahead of herself but oh, how she wanted to see Mother and Joey together. It would be just the most wonderful dream in the world. She could ask for absolutely nothing more.

Mother had been riding in silence for a while and Kaydee thought that perhaps she, too, had dozed off. Kaydee saw Joey glancing at her and at Alvin every now and then but he remained silent. It was Mother who first broke the silence.

"Are you tired, Joey?" she whispered, careful not to wake anyone up.

"No, are you?" Joey whispered back.

"I don't know what I feel," she sighed, "but I know I should feel exhausted."

"Me too." Joey snickered. "I know. That's Jaynee's line."

They both chuckled quietly but to Kaydee the marvel was in watching them silently sharing a common joke together. Kaydee continued to keep her eyes closed but her mind was racing in all directions, good things, bad things, funny things, mysterious things and bizarre things. The miles rolled by and soon they were pulling into the Gohlane driveway. Joey stopped the car and Helen went inside. Alvin and Annie woke up. Annie groggily looked around in surprise to find that they were almost home. Jaynee just slept on peacefully.

"My goodness, I must have been tired. I slept all the way." Annie yawned.

Helen came out of the house, followed closely by Angie Gohlane carrying a bag with Dayna's supplies. Joey jumped out to open the trunk and helped Helen load the bag and its contents into the limited free space left beside their other baggage.

"Angie tells me that Fred Archer passed away last night," Helen announced and both Joey and Annie gasped in shock.

"I thought he was doing so well. I saw him there at the hospital a few times but I thought he was on the mend." Joey seemed sincerely shaken.

"He had another stroke and this one did it," Angie explained.

"Poor Josie, she'll be so lost." Annie, the community's guardian angel was all compassion. "Joey, do you mind if we take a drive over there this evening? I know you're tired. I've rested and you haven't but I'd like to go at least for a little while. Perhaps there is something I can do."

"No problem, Granny. I'm fine. We'll go whenever you want."

They said goodbye and thank you to Angie and left for KD Acres. There Joey helped Helen carry the luggage into the house then stowed his and his grandmother's suitcases into his truck. "Take care of yourself Helen. I'll be by tomorrow. In the meantime have a good night – and get a good rest. This Archer funeral is going to be another tough couple of days so you'll need all the rest you can store up." Joey turned back and added in a low voice so the others wouldn't catch it. "Thanks for the great weekend, Helen. I really enjoyed it." Then louder to the others, a cheery, "Bye for now. See you tomorrow," and he was gone.

Helen watched them drive away. Joey turned and waved. Helen, Kaydee and the kids all waved back. Helen carried the sleeping Dayna to the crib, laid her down and with Kaydee's help, they unpacked the suitcases. They worked in silence, emotionally spent by the events of the day. Neither one wanted to bring up that mysterious stranger that had shocked them almost into insanity. Six-thirty was way too early for bed but they were all ready for it. Helen put some sandwiches together and they didn't even sit down to eat. Each one grabbed a sandwich and munched on it lethargically. Even the hyperactive Alvin was spent and listless.

After clearing off the remains of the makeshift supper, Kaydee retired upstairs to write about the wedding but found that mysterious stranger intruding into her memory. She found it difficult to formulate a logical thought. Finally she just gave up and went to bed.

The sun was shining brightly through the window when Helen awoke the next morning. She glanced at the clock. Half past seven! Joey would probably be in the yard by now. And Kaydee had to be ready for school in forty minutes. Helen jumped out of bed, grabbed the dressing gown and went racing up the stairs to wake Kaydee. She could not believe everyone was still asleep considering they had gone to bed so early the night before. But Kaydee was already up, her bed was made, her clothes all laid out and her school books were ready to go.

"I didn't want to wake you so I didn't want to go downstairs until I absolutely had to," Kaydee explained. "Did you sleep well Mom?"

"I was dead to the world. I can't believe I slept so long. And the kids! I even checked to make sure Dayna was breathing! Joey is probably at the shed by now."

"Nope, he's not here yet. I checked. No truck. Don't worry. Annie probably had him run her over to the Archers. Remember, she was concerned about Josie? Anyway, I gotta run, or I'll never be ready for that school bus."

Kaydee grabbed her clothes and her books and ran downstairs for her shower. Helen checked on Alvin and Jaynee and seeing them still asleep went down to the kitchen, got Kaydee's school lunch ready and started preparing a casserole to take over to the Archers. As she mixed the ingredients for the casserole, she thought of that strange man from yesterday. It was eerie how much he resembled Michael. Oh well, they say we all have a double somewhere. It was just that it was such a shock seeing that man like that. She decided to put it out of her mind. It was just a coincidence, not worth thinking about.

It was after ten when Joey's truck pulled into the yard. He came running into the house, full of apologies but enthusiastic and excited, because Darrel Cochrane was coming to prepare the groundwork for the new shed. Smiling patiently, Helen waited for him to finish babbling.

"I'm sorry," Joey apologized. "I just get so carried away. Whack me across the face when I do that again, okay?"

Helen laughed. "Wouldn't you be sorry – and shocked – if I took you up on that one? And may I remind you that you are not on a time clock. So there is no need for you to apologize."

Joey looked relieved albeit still somewhat embarrassed. "Well I just got so excited. Freeze-up is anywhere around the corner these days and I can start organizing things inside, maybe even before we bring the cattle home."

"All right, Joey. I only have one stipulation and that is that you promise me that you will not do any heavy work on that shed until the doctor says you can."

"Helen, I promise you I will take proper care of myself. I want to stick around so I won't jeopardize my position here."

"Thank you Joey, I needed to hear that." Helen spoke calmly but she looked rattled.

Joey noted Helen's chagrin. He was touched by it. Knowing she was concerned about him was enough for now. Deliberately he changed the subject back to the business at hand.

Darryl arrived soon after and the men set to work taking only a short break for lunch and a ten minute tea break at three on Helen's insistence.

Helen got supper ready but waited until they finished and came in of their own accord. They were exhausted but had broad smiles on their faces, pleased with a job well done.

Joey was excited as a kid. Kaydee half expected him to grab Helen in a triumphant hug or something as he exclaimed, "Wow, I never thought we'd make it, but man that feels good! First thing tomorrow morning I'll see if the Daciuk boys can come and get that foundation poured this week. With any luck, we can start framing next week. Thanks so much Darryl."

Right after Darryl left, Helen apologized to Joey, left Kaydee to stay with the kids and drove the casserole to the Archers.

"I know this is late, and I'm so sorry." Helen explained about Darryl's tight schedule with the dozer and explained how the boys had worked all day so she could not leave sooner.

Josie's sister was in charge. Josie barely seemed functional with grief and shock. "Thank you so much, Mrs. Boyer. As a matter of fact, we haven't had supper yet. We've been snacking all day but this will be just what the doctor ordered. We all need a decent meal."

"Good," Helen said and went to offer her sympathies to Josie who was sitting in the living room talking with a couple of women who had come to offer their condolences.

"I honestly thought he would make it," Josie said tearfully "but then he got that other stroke and he just couldn't fight anymore. I don't know what I'm going to do now."

"We will all be here to help with whatever you need," Helen told her gently. "Right now the hardest thing will be the funeral. After that, we'll see what needs to be done. Don't worry."

They chatted for a while and then Helen left. She knew from recent experience that constant crowds can be tiring at a time when emotions are drained. That family needed peace now.

The funeral was on Wednesday and both Joey and Helen attended. Helen brought Angie Gohlane to KD Acres to stay with all three kids because Annie wanted to attend the funeral too, and Kaydee was in school.

Joey had made the arrangements for the foundation to be poured for the shed on Thursday. In the following weeks, the shed started taking shape. Helen was happy, Joey was whistling all the time, the kids seemed contented and even Jaynee was warming up to Joey. She didn't shy away from him anymore but was still somewhat reserved.

Kaydee juggled her hours between regular classes and the special tutoring she was taking at the hands of the Norchaks. Over and above that she was spewing out poetry and prose at every opportunity. Life was a dream. Kaydee was almost afraid she might wake up and find that it was simply that impossible illusion she had never dared hope for an eternity ago.

On the third of November, Joey received an early morning call to go back to work at the plant in Toronto.

"Sorry Mr. Prichard, but I have found something much better." Joey told his old boss and hung up the phone. He ran around the table and hugged his grandmother jubilantly.

"I'm not going back!" he crowed. Pleased with his decision, Annie smiled.

Joey settled back into his "job" as if nothing had changed. He didn't even tell Helen about the call. Together with Helen, he filled the self-feeders while Annie stayed in the house with the kids. Then they drove to the pasture and brought the cattle home for the winter. In his spare time Joey continued to work on the shed.

Dusty and Katreena came back from their honeymoon cruise and settled in Portmont.

"Portmont is a good place to locate just in case Kaydee ever ended up at the Academy," Katreena told Helen when they came to visit. "Dusty's house is much bigger and he has such a beautiful garden there. I hate to give up the mobile in Lanavale. It is closer to Zelena and it has that gorgeous deck and that skylight that both Dusty and I love. But Portmont is more practical for us."

Helen laughed. "What big problems you two have! Choosing which of your two beautiful homes you are going to live in!"

Katreena laughed too. Then on a serious note "You know, Helen, what I am most grateful for, is how your life has changed. I thank God every day for what He has done for us – all of us! But it is the changes in your life that make me feel free and happy now! I could never feel this way when Michael was here."

Helen cut her off. "Don't Mom! Don't even bring his name up. Let's bury those memories."

"I'm sorry sweetheart." Katreena apologized. "I agree." Then switching subjects, she asked, "How is Kaydee doing by the way?"

"You know Mom, I'm sure Kaydee will be able to make up her grades and catch up to the rest of the kids her age. She is working so hard. I can never repay the Norchaks for everything they are doing for her though. Kaydee spends so much time there and they are so patient with her. They work so hard to help her. I feel I owe them something but they won't accept any payment for anything. Joey usually picks Kaydee up about half past eight most evenings, so she even has supper there but Sandy won't accept grocery money and with no garden I can't even help with vegetables! They have transformed Kaydee into a happy, healthy teenager. She has absolutely blossomed under their tutorship. I can't begin to imagine how I can ever make it up to them."

Helen actually seemed troubled about it and Katreena empathized with her. She too, felt a mountain of gratitude for this altruistic couple who had opened their hearts to Kaydee, who put her needs so clearly ahead of their own. But if they refuse payment for their time and efforts, was there anything anyone can do to show gratitude?

"You know, I think there is some kind of award that the government gives to people who do exceptional work in the community. I don't know what it's called but I'll try and get some information about it. Wouldn't it be a pleasant surprise for them if we nominated them and they got it? It carries a lot of prestige with it, along with a monetary remuneration, I think. If they won't take money from us, they cannot refuse the monetary award."

"That would be just wonderful!" Helen exclaimed excitedly. "That would give them recognition, prestige, honour and a financial reward. Wouldn't it be fantastic if they got it?"

"I'll investigate and let you know. If anyone ever deserved that award, those two are it."

Dusty came back from the shed where he had been visiting with Joey.

"Joey has done wonders in that shop," he said. Dusty was impressed. No doubt about it.

"Isn't he amazing?" Helen said proudly. "He's so organized and he's always thinking of something else he can make or do to improve things. He's always among the cattle. He can pet any of them anytime and they don't walk away from him. It's like a totally different herd."

Dusty raised his eyebrows at Katreena as they exchanged meaningful glances.

Dusty winked at Katreena. "Methinks Joey has won more hearts than just the cattle."

Helen swatted at Dusty with her towel but she was blushing. Katreena laughed at them both. She was impressed too – and pleased!

Chapter 48

Katreena and Dusty didn't visit as often now, confident that Helen's family was under the competent care of Joey. Dusty told Katreena about Maxwell but together they decided not to introduce Maxwell to Helen yet. They did, however, meet him several times for dinner and told him all about Michael and his sordid past. Shocked to hear how brutal his brother had been, Maxwell was eager to meet the only real family he had in this world. Still, he agreed that they might find it traumatic. He would wait till Dusty and Katreena felt that it was the right time to come.

"Maybe by Christmas," Katreena promised.

Back at KD Acres, memories of Michael's reign of terror were forgotten as pleasant new memories displaced them. Joey came everyday to check the cattle, pump water and when the feed got low in the feeders, he brought his grandmother to stay with the kids while Helen came out to help hammermill feed to refill them.

Things were going along well at KD Acres so Dusty and Katreena decided that this might be a good time to introduce the issue of Maxwell's existence to Helen and Kaydee, and to gauge their reaction to the issue of the stranger that looked so much like Michael.

They drove out to the farm late in the evening so as to have quiet time with Kaydee, Helen and Joey while the smaller children were already asleep. Dusty specifically asked Joey to bring his grandmother along because there was something they wished all of them to hear.

They had some problems getting Alvin to go to bed so it was almost nine-thirty when the adults were finally alone and free to talk.

Dusty cleared his throat and looked at the curious faces waiting so patiently for the announcement that he had promised would be so important and interesting for them.

"You remember that stranger that walked into Chemille's that day after our wedding?"

Startled gasps resounded from the group and four stunned faces stared openmouthed at Dusty as if ready to devour him.

"Go ahead," Joey prompted hoarsely. "Who was he?"

Helen and Kaydee were at the edge of their seats, their faces pale but their attention now totally primed.

"Well Katreena and I have been in touch with him. In fact, we've been working with him to check up on hospital records and we are now pretty certain that he is Michael's twin brother. Michael's parents had twins but they gave one of the boys up for adoption right after birth. The Cartrites could not have any children and they gladly adopted the newborn baby boy. They lived in a small town called Asperton, in southeastern Manitoba near the Ontario border. That is where Maxwell, as they called him, grew up. He says he had a very loving and happy home. His adoptive parents died in a boating accident seven years ago. Maxwell was married but his wife died in an automobile accident two years ago. They had no children so he is all alone now. He works as a heavy equipment operator for the highways department. He is very eager to meet you. He seems like a very decent fellow, very friendly and sincere. Not at all like Michael." Dusty added. A dead silence hung in the room as the group processed this information.

It was Annie that gained her composure first. "They just gave away their child like that? That's barbaric! What kind of people do that?" Annie asked incredulously.

"From the little I heard about Michael's father," Helen said, "he was a pretty rough fellow. Michael never had anything good thing to say about him. Mind you, Michael didn't really talk much about his family."

"Perhaps they did Maxwell a big favour by giving him away in the first place. Otherwise he might have grown up to be like Michael," observed Annie.

"Oh God help and deliver us," shuddered Katreena.

"Amen to that," said Helen vehemently.

"We checked the hospital records and there is no doubt that this man is really Michael's twin brother but from talking to him he is as different from Michael as different could be."

"It would be nice to meet him. You say he is a nice fellow?" Helen was hesitant, still uneasy about meeting Michael's double face-to-face.

Kaydee shared her mother's misgivings, but she trusted Granny's and

Dusty's judgment. If they thought meeting Maxwell Cartrite was good for the family, then it must be alright.

"Perhaps we can have him here for Christmas," Katreena suggested. "Would it be alright to bring him then? He is so eager to meet all of you."

Helen thought it over. "That would be great. We'd love to meet him," she looked to Kaydee for approval and Kaydee nodded. "But I think I should extend an official invitation to him to come. He might feel uncomfortable coming on his own but it would be nice to meet even sooner," said Helen. "Would that be possible?"

"Well, he's a working man, remember, and it is a bit of a distance." Dusty said. "How about just inviting him down for Christmas? I'm sure he would appreciate that since he is alone now."

"That's an excellent idea," said Helen and Kaydee echoed her agreement. Dusty handed Maxwell's address and phone number to Helen and she promised to get the invitation out the next day.

They talked till almost eleven o'clock finalizing plans for the best Christmas they had ever had and then Annie and Joey left for home. Dusty and Katreena stayed over till the morning.

The following Friday, while Helen was putting Dayna to bed, Joey asked Kaydee to see if she could put Jaynee down too. "I want to talk to the rest of you so come down as soon as the girls are asleep."

When Helen and Kaydee joined them Joey put Alvin on his knee and made his proposal.

"Since this is a free weekend for Kaydee, I have a special idea. What if Granny babysits the girls tomorrow and the four of us go out and find us a nice Christmas tree?"

The room fell silent as three mouths gaped open in surprise. "You'll have to dress well. The snow will be deep but it will be fun." Joey looked hopefully from one face to the other.

Kaydee was the first to give an enthusiastic assent followed immediately by Alvin. Mother was sceptical but interested.

"Come on, Mom," Kaydee encouraged. "It would be so much fun."

Mother looked at Joey. He winked at her and smiled with that twinkle in his eye.

Helen thought it over. "Why not?" she said brightly.

"Yes!" Alvin whooped and gave Joey a hi-five

"Shhhhhh," Kaydee whispered with her finger to her lips. "You don't want to wake Jaynee. She'll want to come too but she won't be able to walk in the deep snow and we can't carry her and the tree also."

"Oh, yea," whispered Alvin. "We can't tell her where we're going."

"No, it has to be a secret for now," Joey whispered back. "Can you keep a secret?"

Alvin nodded and put his finger to his puckered lips.

"Okay," said Joey. "Now off to bed with you and I'll see you in the morning."

The next day Joey brought Annie to KD Acres to stay with the girls. While she distracted Jaynee, the others dressed and sneaked out to Joey's truck. Joey gave them elasticised wristbands with jingle bells sewn onto them.

Kaydee waved her hands above her head and started to sing. "Jingle bells, Jingle bells, Jingle all the way..." the others joined in the merriment as they drove out about five miles to a forested area which contained a variety of trees, among them pine and spruce.

They trudged through the deep snow singing and panting, inspecting the evergreens from every angle noting the shape, height, and width of each until they spotted a beautifully shaped Scots pine that was thick and verdant and just the right size.

"This one looks good," Helen sang out. They all agreed it was perfect. Joey cleared the snow from around the trunk and used a saw to cut the tree as close to the ground as possible. Handing the saw to Kaydee, he picked up its trunk and told Helen how to hold the top so as not to damage the delicate small branches. With Joey in front, and Mother behind him, carrying the other end, followed by Alvin, then Kaydee, they sang and panted and laughed their way back to the truck. Dropping Kaydee and the tree in the yard, Joey, Helen and Alvin drove to town for decorations. They were back in an hour. Annie had lunch ready but everybody was too excited to eat. Joey set up the tree in the living room and the decorating frenzy was on. Jaynee ran around handing the colored bells and balls to Kaydee to hang "right here" and "right there."

There was an awed hush as Joey plugged the lights in. The tree came to life with color and twinkling lights and tears flooded Helen and Kaydee's eyes. They had never had a Christmas tree in the house before, much less any decorations because Father had never allowed it. Now Alvin and Jaynee stared, fascinated beyond words, their eyes wide, their mouths open. Even Annie came to admire it, standing behind Helen and Kaydee with her arms around each. They hugged each other, all three wiping tears that just would not stop flowing.

Helen watched the delight in her children's eyes with an ache in her heart. Turning to Joey, she choked out a tearful "Thank you."

"You're more than welcome, Helen," Joey whispered back with a wink, happy that he was able to provide them all with this simple little bit of pleasure.

Helen looked at her family so aglow with happiness and awe. Choking back tears and the golfball-sized lump in her throat, she announced, "We are going to make this the best Christmas we have ever had. We'll have carols and laughter and candles and Christmas cake and twinkling lights and streamers and a great big turkey with all the trimmings. We'll just have ourselves a great big party! Who's with me?"

"I am, Mom, I am," Kaydee and Alvin whooped in unison.

Jaynee looked at them and feeling that something was expected from her as well, she added her eager "Me too." Alvin did a little jig in the middle of the floor, then ran to Joey and raised his hand for a hi-five.

Kaydee beamed and gave Helen a big hug. "Thanks, Mom." She choked through her tears.

Over the next few days Helen set out to prepare the Christmas feast. Because Kaydee still spent most of her time in school or at the Norchaks with classes, Annie eagerly offered her assistance to Helen and together they filled the house with the delectable aromas of holiday cooking.

On Christmas Eve, Mother picked up Joey and Annie and they all went to midnight Mass together. In church, Alvin sat proudly between Joey and Mother, who was holding Dayna in her arms. On Mother's other side was Jaynee sitting next to Kaydee, her constant protector. Annie sat at the end. Together they took up the whole pew. Contentedly, Kaydee eyed "her family" and dreamed her dream.

Chapter 49

On Christmas day, Dusty drove Katreena, Della and Jessie up in one car and Maxwell Cartrite drove in behind them.

Maxwell had come to Portmont and Wayne had driven with him to show him the way. They arrived at KD Acres just after eleven. Joey, Annie and the Norchaks were already there.

"This is Maxwell Cartrite, folks. He is Michael's twin brother that we never knew about till now. He is the newest member of this family." Dusty introduced the guests to Maxwell explaining who they were and their connections to the family.

Helen, Kaydee, Alvin and Jaynee were mesmerized by his resemblance to Michael as were Annie and the Norchaks.

"Wow," said Maxwell. "Yesterday, I was all alone in the world, and today I have all this family. I feel so blessed. And at Christmas yet! Thank you all for accepting me into the family."

"We are the ones blessed," Helen told him fervently. Everyone echoed her sentiments and soon the room was abuzz with cheery voices all excitedly welcoming Maxwell into the family circle. Everyone was eager to know Maxwell's story. Alvin and Jaynee hung back, too overcome by the noise of the big crowd of people and their unusually boisterous behaviour.

"Just one more couple," Helen announced, and we can start serving. Katreena and Dusty exchanged glances, wondering who else Helen had invited. Just then Vance and Janine drove up and Katreena squealed with joy at seeing her old friends. With the welcome hugs over, Helen heralded the women to the kitchen, loading each one with dishes full of food to take to the huge festive table set with the new candelabra and poinsettias she had purchased for the occasion.

"And thank you Lord for all your blessings on this home and all who dwell in it." Dusty finished a solemn grace and everyone responded with a heartfelt "Amen."

Kaydee heaved a sigh of contentment as she watched and listened to the gay chatter of this big extended family of which she was now such an important part. They ate, told jokes, laughed and enjoyed the camaraderie of the group. At an unexpected lull in the conversation, Dusty broke into a carol, Joy to the World, and the rest joined in, adding their voices to the loud chorus till Rusko set up such a mournful howl that they ran outside to see what the noise was.

"He thinks he's in the wrong yard," Kaydee told Jessie, laughing. "He never heard carol singing and laughing at Christmas before."

As Joey walked by he heard Kaydee's comment. "Get used to this, Rusko," Joey called to the dog, "you're gonna hear lots of this from now on!"

"Amen to that," said Katreena. Whereupon the revellers picked up the old negro spiritual and started singing again. "Amen, Amen, Amen..."

"This is such a wonderful day!" Kaydee sighed. "I am so afraid that I will wake up and..." she could not bring herself to finish the thought.

Sandy Norchak hugged her.

"This is no dream, Kaydee. Your life is as it should have been all along. You were forced onto a very bad detour. But you're on the right track now. That's all that matters."

Sandy had developed a fondness for the girl far beyond a teacher-student relationship and she wanted to erase all of Kaydee's bad memories. "Enjoy your life Kaydee. You earned it."

The party finally ended with a thunderous rendition of "We wish you a Merry Christmas." They bid their farewells with heartfelt thanks and promises of getting together again soon."

That Christmas was the forbearer of the life to come at KD Acres. The relaxed atmosphere continued into the new year. Kaydee continued with her extra classes, determined to close the gap between her classmates and herself. Everyone, her family, her teachers, and even her classmates at school went out of their way to help her to achieve her goal any way they could. Winter was too busy for Kaydee to notice the cold, the inconvenience or adversity.

Granny and Dusty visited at least monthly. A couple of times they brought Maxwell with them. Alvin called him "Uncle Max" and became great buddies with him, much to Maxwell's delight, but Alvin's hero was still Joey. Jaynee shied away from him though Maxwell tried hard to win her over. Perhaps his resemblance to Michael was just too much for her to ignore. They were now a normal happy family.

Summer was almost upon them and with it, the approach of the end of the school term. It would be the culmination of Kaydee's scholastic achievements. She had finally caught up to the rest of the kids her age and she was confident that she would be promoted at the end of the school year. She would be in Grade eight next fall, right along with all the other kids her age. She would be going to regular classes. Their school always held graduation exercises at year end. Back in May, the kids had asked her to be valedictorian for the Junior High graduating class. She had withheld her acceptance for the position until she was certain that she had successfully completed all her grade seven exams. With her graduation assured, she now happily agreed to deliver the valedictory address.

Chapter 50

"And this next award has been given out only on very special occasions to students who showed extreme diligence in their studies. This year, the decision to give this award to this recipient was wholly unanimous. I doubt if we have ever had a student more deserving of this award than this year's winner. Overcoming incalculable hardships that set her back far behind in the previous years, she has, nonetheless, been able to advance at an incredible rate and has proven her acumen in numerous examinations and assessment reviews. I have to confess to a degree of scepticism myself when the recommendations for her nomination came across my desk. I simply could not believe such strides were possible. But I conducted personal interviews with her myself and we did full faculty reviews as well. I am pleased to say I am now a believer. So it is with greatest pleasure that I present the Bedson Faculty Award for 'Student Showing Most Improvement' to Katherine Danielle Boyer, known to all as Kaydee Boyer."

The crowd rose to their feet and exploded into deafening applause as Principal James Neilson held out the award towards a shocked and bewildered Kaydee. Sandy Norchak helped Kaydee get up and ascend the stairs. Sandy left her then and went back to sit down, leaving Kaydee to make her own way forward. Mr. Neilson waited patiently as Kaydee came tremulously towards him. The applause continued on and on as Kaydee stood shaking before Mr. Neilson. They stood waiting for the noise to subside.

Finally, by holding up his hands for silence, the crowd became quiet and Mr. Neilson extended both hands to her, the left passing her the scroll, his right clasping hers in congratulations. "I am sure my late grandfather never dreamed this award would ever be this justified. Everyone is rooting for you. Congratulations and best of luck in the future, Kaydee."

Kaydee's quivering "Thank you" was totally lost in the boisterous cheering that once more erupted from the zealous crowd.

Kaydee's feet felt like jelly as she descended from the podium. The

Norchaks and her family met her at the foot of the stairs hugging her, laughing and crying all at once, congratulating her amidst rounds of resounding applause that just refused to abate. Family and friends were all beaming with pride and happiness for her and everyone stood in line for a congratulatory hug.

"We are all so proud of you!"

"Good luck!"

"Congratulations!"

"Atta girl!"

Kaydee was overwhelmed by the enthusiasm of the crowd. She had had no idea that this was coming. These assemblies had never seemed like that big a deal to her. Because she used to be in Special Education class, none of her family ever attended the event. Often parents or family chose not to even attend unless there was some specific reason for them to do so. But today the auditorium was packed to capacity. It was as if the crowd had come expecting something special. Even Mom, Granny, Dusty and Joey had come. She had been rather surprised when they all said they were coming. Granny and Dusty had arrived the day before and when Granny heard that Helen and Edna Gally were planning to attend, she offered to join them. Amy Gally was getting the Neilson Mathematics Award for Outstanding Achievement in a course on accounting, so Edna was going to watch the presentation. Helen was going along with Edna for support.

Dusty looked dejected. "You girls are all going and you plan to leave us here behind? Well, what if we refuse? Joey, how about you and I crash that party as well?"

Joey was quick on the draw. "I think that sounds like an interesting way to spend an afternoon. Count me in." And so Kaydee's family was all there in the audience for her award presentation. Jaynee, Dayna and Alvin were home with Annie.

Kaydee sank down into her chair, too overcome with emotion, her body refusing to hold her up anymore. The shock was just too much. The whole school, the teachers, the students and her family were all cheering for her, supporting her and encouraging her. It was more than she had ever dreamed of. She, Kaydee, who less than a year ago, had been considered – and actually called – a moron, a retard! Uncontrollable tears clouded her vision and spilled onto her flushed cheeks. She found it impossible to speak or even swallow, past that lump that obstructed her throat and restricted her air supply.

Eventually, and thankfully, the continuation of the program on the podium had recaptured the attention of everyone so that she was no longer the centre of attention. She was able to retreat to relative obscurity. Helen and Katreena both noted her discomfort but understanding her need for a timeout, turned their attention to the activity proceedings on stage.

At the end of the student presentations, Mr. Neilson once more stepped up to the microphone and held his hands up for silence.

"This next announcement is only indirectly connected to this school, but because it includes members of our faculty, I thought that you would be interested to hear that Ed and Sandy Norchak have been awarded the Governor General's Award for Humanitarian Services to the Community. This is a huge honour for the Norchaks and carries with it a monetary award as well. So next week, Ed and Sandy Norchak are off on an all expense paid trip to Ottawa to receive their award from the Governor General of Canada. Congratulations, Mr. and Mrs. Norchak. You have done us proud! Have a wonderful trip. Could you come up please and take a bow?" He waited until they mounted the podium. "Ladies and Gentlemen, Ed and Sandy Norchak!" Mr. Neilson extended his hand out toward the Norchaks and the crowd roared.

Ed and Sandy were stunned as they stood up to receive the applause and congratulations. They had had no inkling that this was coming. Kaydee looked at Sandy and understood her chagrin. The crowd had somebody else to focus their attention on. Ed and Sandy Norchak were in the spotlight now. Though Kaydee did not know it, Katreena, Helen, Dusty, Joey, Dwayne, Della and Jessie were all in on this one. They had pooled their resources to fill out the nomination papers and succeeded in rewarding her benefactors with some well-deserved compensation for their sacrifices.

With the assembly concluded, everyone made their way out to the hall for coffee, donuts and fellowship. Kaydee's knees were shaky, her head was spinning and she could not detect a single coherent idea in her head. She was totally drained, her unsteady legs just would not hold her up. She sank into the nearest chair with the grace of a rag doll. She appreciated all the attention. It was sincere and well meaning. She knew that, but she could not take any more excitement today.

Mustering every ounce of energy she could draw together, Kaydee accepted congratulations, graciously thanking everyone for their good wishes. She declined the refreshments, knowing full well that her stomach could not accept even a tiny crumb at this point.

It seemed like an eternity before the crowds started to dissipate and Kaydee's knees regained their stamina to hold her up again. Surreptitiously Kaydee manoeuvred her way ever closer to the exit, hoping her family would follow and not make her hang around longer than absolutely necessary. Helen noted Kaydee's pallid countenance and realized how traumatic this afternoon had been for her unsuspecting daughter. These last ten months, she had had little time for anything but study and write and she had applied herself diligently to those tasks, aiming for that ultimate goal of one day catching up to her classmates in scholastic development. But it had been a rocky road, a difficult climb and an intense grid. It had taken its toll on Kaydee and this shock was the coup de gras that had kicked the ground out from under her feet.

They had all gone through major life-altering experiences last summer but Kaydee had not taken a reprieve. She continued to work in that pressurized environment barely taking a breather because school started and the funeral followed before she even had chance to get to know her classmates. Kaydee's resolve to close the gap between herself and her peers had almost exhausted her but this final surprise had thrown her totally off balance.

With the countless goodbyes and thank you's over, they left for home. Dusty gave Kaydee a quick hug and Joey patted her arm before they entered the car. Respecting Kaydee's need for peace, they drove home in silence.

At home, Kaydee told them she was tired and went upstairs to lie down. Katreena checked on her but she was already fast asleep so she gently covered her with a blanket and tiptoed out.

Annie was ecstatic when she heard of Kaydee's award.

"Perhaps we should have forewarned her," Katreena reflected thoughtfully. "It was such a shock. She never suspected anything even when we all offered to go."

"I thought she might wonder when Joey and I decided to come along," Dusty said.

"You slipped it in so casually, I would never have suspected it myself," Helen countered.

"Well it was a draining experience but a rewarding one. She's definitely earned this rest." Joey commented.

They sat there talking in low tones marvelling at the miracle that they had witnessed just a few hours ago. Kaydee had been so down beaten for so long that short of the family, almost everyone had accepted her as mentally deficient. Then the removal of the oppressive burden had transformed her into this intellectual sponge that absorbed knowledge and tenaciously retained every fragment she ingested. It made everyone sit up, take note, and re-evaluate her acumen.

The Norchaks, in particular felt vindicated. They had been the first to recognize the potential concealed beneath that quivering protective cocoon that Kaydee had withdrawn into. The Norchaks had utilized every conventional and unconventional method at their disposal to coax Kaydee out of her shell but it had taken an act of God to liberate her from her bondage. Michael's passing was the only key that opened the security lock to the prison wherein Kaydee's acuity was entrapped. However, once those parameters had been removed, her potential to excel became boundless. There were times when the Norchaks had to prod the establishment to pave uncharted avenues for Kaydee's persistent progress and advancement. The Norchaks had a vested interest in Kaydee's accomplishments. She had become like family to them these last ten months. They had spent every possible moment they could spare to coach Kaydee, expecting no other return than to see her attain her potential. So

Kaydee's success was a tribute and an accolade for them as well. They revelled in her progress – and now, her reward.

It had been Katreena's idea to keep the award a secret from Kaydee. When Sandy Norchak had called Helen that afternoon two weeks ago with the news that Kaydee was being considered, in fact, was a shoo-in for the award, Helen had immediately informed Katreena. Together they had contrived the scheme to withhold the information from Kaydee. Dusty and Joey were in on the conspiracy. They all connived to attend the ceremonies but make it sound like a casual coincidence. The school never publicized the award recipients prior to presentation so Kaydee had been unaware she was even being considered.

Chapter 51

Kaydee woke with a start. Completely immersed in darkness and silence, she tried to orientate herself to her surroundings. Awareness seemed illusive however, just beyond her grasp. She was still lying on her stomach so she turned over on her side and peered into the shadows for some clue about her whereabouts but neither the silence nor the darkness yielded any suggestions. This was creepy! Feeling constricted by the blanket, she tossed it off and sat up. The sudden movement made her feel dizzy and she reeled against the darkness trying to regain her balance. Steadying herself with her hand, she felt the softness of the pillow and realized she was on a bed, her bed, her bedroom. She was home!

She reached over and felt for the light switch of her bedside lamp. The room lit up and she realized she was fully clothed. Memories flooded back. She remembered receiving the award, the accolades from the teachers, the friends, the family... The family! Where was everyone? She heard no talking, no TV, not even a whisper! Bewildered, Kaydee went into the hallway, flicking the lights on as she advanced. What time was it anyway? She glanced at the hall clock. Quarter to eleven. They might all have gone to bed. She made her way downstairs, stepping softly, listening for any sound that would indicate someone's presence. The light was on in the living room so she headed for that.

"Well hello, sweetheart, how are you feeling?" Mother looked up from the book she was reading. No one else was in sight.

"I'm fine. Where is everybody? This place is like a morgue. Did Dusty and Granny and Joey leave? And where are the kids?" Kaydee seemed disorientated and confused.

"Relax honey. It's okay. You looked so played out that we thought we'd give you a chance to rest in peace. The girls are asleep. Joey and his grandmother went home and Granny and Dusty took Alvin to a show. Are you alright? You look dazed. Did you sleep well?"

"Yes, I did, but it was so weird waking up in total silence and darkness." She shuddered. "I must have been pretty wiped." She could not believe that she had slept away part of the afternoon and evening.

"We checked on you a few times but you were sleeping so soundly, we didn't want to disturb you. Are you hungry? We saved some of the roast beef and gravy for you. I can make you a hot beef sandwich."

"Thanks, Mom but no. I'll be alright. I don't really feel hungry."

"That was nice of the school to offer you that award, honey. You cannot imagine just how proud and happy we all are for you. Congratulations again, sweetheart."

"Thanks Mom, but it would have been easier if I had known it was coming."

She recalled the shock rippling through her body and the energy draining out of her when she was called up to receive the award. Would it have been easier had she known it was coming?

"I'm going upstairs. I have some ideas I'd like to record," Kaydee said. She was just starting up the stairs when the phone rang. Mother went to answer it and Kaydee listened.

"Oh hello Joey," she heard her mother say. "Yes, she's fine, she just got up."

Kaydee continued up the stairs.

Shortly after eleven, she heard Dusty's car drive up. Kaydee sighed. She put down her journal and went downstairs. They would want to talk to her. She should look happy. Heavens, she **was** happy!

"Honey, you're awake!" Katreena rushed to wrap Kaydee in a warm embrace, gazing into her eyes with genuine concern. "Are you feeling alright? You looked so distressed, we were worried about you." Dusty stood back watching anxiously.

"I'm fine, thank you all. It was just such a shock and I guess it just took all the wind out of my sails. I'm sorry I worried you all."

"No honey, it's I who should be apologizing. It was my idea to keep it a surprise. I didn't realize how traumatic it would be for you. I'm so sorry." Katreena's confessed contritely.

"You knew? You all knew about it?" Kaydee was flabbergasted. Suddenly, all the events of the previous day fell into place like a jigsaw puzzle when all the pieces fit right. "That was why you and Dusty came out and that was why you all came to the assembly, even Joey!"

"Honey I'm sorry," Katreena pleaded. "I just thought it would be a beautiful surprise. It was such an honour and we're all so proud of you. Please forgive me for deceiving you." Kaydee stood there processing all this new information in her mind.

"I know you meant well, Granny, but walking up to that podium today, in front of everybody that way, it was torture for me. The shock had me reeling to the point of mental incompetence. I don't even remember thanking them for the award. I must have looked like the moron they had all considered me to be not so long ago. I never did thank them, did I?"

They all laughed but it was Dusty's affectionate voice that assured her, "Yes, honey. You did say 'thank you' though I doubt if many people heard you. They were so busy cheering for you, no one cared if you thanked them or not. You know something, young lady? You have a lot more friends out there than you ever imagined. They are all very, very happy for you."

"Joey was really worried about you." Helen told Kaydee. "He called a few times to see how you were doing. He's had a stake in this too, you know. His pick-ups of you at the Norchaks were very important. Without his help, you may not have had that opportunity."

"I know, Mom and I am going to thank him myself tomorrow."

"Wasn't it nice for the Norchaks to get that big award from the Governor General? And they are going to Ottawa! Sandy looked every bit as shocked as I was when my award was announced. I'm so happy for them. They deserve it. They are so nice."

"That was what we thought," Helen said. "I tried to offer them payment for all their help but neither Sandy nor Ed would accept anything. Then your grandmother told me about this award and we thought this would be the perfect way to repay them for their kindness."

Kaydee was dumbfounded. "Do you mean you had something to do with that award?"

"Well you have to nominate people for it. There are a lot of papers to fill out but we all pitched in while Jessie, Della and Wayne helped with some of the wording so it was a combined effort. We thought this would be a way to thank them and to recognize them for all the good things that they do for the community," Helen explained.

"I'll have to thank Jessie and her parents. It was very nice of them to help. And thank you Granny and Dusty. I'm glad the Norchaks got that award. They really do deserve it but I don't know if I should tell Sandy that it was my family that set those wheels in motion." Kaydee laughed. "Such surprises can really knock the wind out of you. I should know!"

Chapter 52

Kaydee could hardly contain her excitement. Jessie was coming down for the weekend and she said she was bringing good news. But that was not all that was making Kaydee bubble like an effervescent drink. There were several reasons for her elation. Last night after the kids were all in bed, Mother and Joey had shared a secret with her. Joey had asked her if she would mind it if he married her mother. Kaydee had been so overjoyed she had squealed in delight, almost waking the kids up. She kept reliving that wonderful moment again and again.

"Are you kidding me?" she shrieked, hugging each of them in turn. "Of course I don't mind! I've only been waiting for this for, like, forever! This is just too wonderful to be true. Who else knows about this?"

"Nobody, so far. We wanted to get your opinion first. Your approval is the most important of all. We wanted to know what your response would be before we went any further."

"My response! Surely you can't have doubted my approval. I have been afraid to hope." she exclaimed as she hugged them again. Joey was obviously pleased but he pressed on.

"Thank you, Kaydee. That means an awful lot to both of us, but now we have to ask you a great favour. We want you to keep this a secret for a few days. Just until Sunday," he added quickly seeing Kaydee's face fall in disappointment. "You see, I have planned a big dinner at Zelena House for the whole family and that is when we are going to announce it but we need you to act as if you know absolutely nothing about this till then. Can you do it, Kaydee?"

"Even if it kills me!" she promised and crossed her heart. "And it probably will," she warned, "because right now I'm so happy, I want to shout it from the rooftops."

The other wonderful things were not secrets so she could express all her enthusiasm without having to hide her euphoria.

Her book of poetry was being published and should be coming out soon. She had signed the contract in February. It was going to be a hard cover and Kaydee had seen the preliminary proofs of it. A very nice young lady by the name of Alveta Rose had designed the cover and she also did some illustrations for the poetry. It wasn't a big book, but it was her first and Kaydee was thrilled about it.

Kaydee mused about that meeting with Wayne and Della. What had really taken Kaydee off guard was the fact that the "blue section" of her poems was the one that Wayne and Della considered the most powerful. She had written those when she was most angry and hurt. In those poems, she had poured her heart out. At the time – in fact, even now – she still thought of them as gloomy and mediocre. All they had been was a purging of emotions, a venting of pain, anger and frustration. Yet those were the poems that attracted Jessie's attention that first time when she read them last August. Kaydee thought back about the pathos that had inspired those poems. One of those poems even alluded to the weight of responsibility she felt about watching over her little brother: "How unlike a thorn you bear the fluted rose" she had written.

Alvin had done a lot of growing up in this past year but it seemed like he had a severe case of verbal overflow, jabbering all the time. He was constantly asking questions. Kaydee marvelled at Joey's patience with him. The two spent a lot of time together. Joey had become such an integral part of their lives now that she could not imagine a life without him in the family. Joey was easygoing and cheerful and Kaydee was just thrilled that soon he would be part of their lives permanently. The hardest thing for her now was pretending she knew nothing about their forthcoming marriage. Her whole being was screaming with exultation and triumph.

Kaydee had just finished weeding the petunia beds on the south side of the house when Dusty and Granny pulled into the yard. Jessie came flying out from the back seat squealing with excitement and waving a large white envelope in her hand.

"Kaydee! You did it! You did it. Your book of poems is coming out next month and Dad wants you to do some promotional appearances. Do you think you can make it? You can stay at my place. Oh, it would be so great. Please say you can, Kaydee." Jessie was babbling and hopping up and down like a marionette, her eyes like large sparkling pools of shimmering water.

"Promotional appearances?" Kaydee queried in awe. Wide-eyed, she stared at Jessie in alarm. The thought of public appearances terrified her. "Do I have to do that?"

"Well no, you don't really have to, but it would certainly help sales if the public could meet you. People always want an autographed copy of a book, you know."

Kaydee thought about it. Granny and Dusty stood by, listening to the conversation. Granny picked up on Kaydee's apprehension and volunteered a helping hand.

"You don't have to make up your mind yet, sweetheart. It is still a month away and promotions like that don't necessarily have to be scheduled that far ahead. Think about it and then decide if you want to do it."

Helen was already preparing supper and soon Joey pulled into the yard with the tractor. Supper was a noisy affair with enthusiastic reports about Kaydee's book which Dusty was probably deliberately embellishing.

Promptly after dessert was served, Joey made his apologies and left for the field again. "I want to finish that summerfallow before the rain that they are predicting for Sunday. When that is finished, the rest can wait if necessary." Helen walked out with him and they talked for a couple of minutes before he left.

On Saturday, Joey finished the summerfallow just as the first raindrops hit the ground. Joey was jubilant. Actually, Katreena thought unusually so but she attributed that to his beating the weatherman at his game. Joey went to the washroom, had a shower and changed into clean clothes which he had obviously brought for the purpose. They sat and visited casually till supper. Kaydee and Jessie came downstairs to set the table and help put the food on. Helen brought out a bottle of ginger ale and poured a glass for everyone to go with supper.

"And what are we celebrating, might I ask?" Dusty teased jokingly.

Joey raised his glass and piped up quickly, "To the success of the season," he crowed. After supper, before leaving for home, Joey turned to everyone and announced, “Tomorrow, after church, we are going to Zelena House for dinner and it’s on me. Now goodnight all.” Then he turned and walked out the door. Dusty and Katreena looked at Helen but she merely shrugged her shoulders “I don’t know” fashion and went to put Dayna to bed. Kaydee and Jessie went upstairs while Dusty and Katreena were left to entertain Alvin and Jaynee.

Chapter 53

Joey and his grandmother arrived at the church after the family and quietly slipped into the pew behind Helen and her family, whispering "Good morning" as they did so. Helen was engrossed in the service and Kaydee was oblivious to anything other than her own countless blessings, which at this time were paramount in her mind. She was feeling humbly grateful.

After the service, they headed for Zelena House where a table was preset and waiting for them in a little alcove just off the main dining room. Obviously, Joey had made reservations. They sat down and the waiter was beside them immediately to take their order. Not long after, the appetizers arrived. Just before they started eating, the waiter returned carrying a tray with a bottle of champagne and a smaller bottle of ginger ale, both of which he turned over to Joey. With great flair and calculated flourish, Joey opened the bottles, aware of their eyes on him. Deliberately keeping them in suspense, he went around the table pouring the bubbly fizz into each adult glass and ginger ale into the children's glasses.

Everyone sat silently, waiting for Joey to finish with his peculiar ritual and proceed to something more conventional, like eating, for instance. But Joey had the floor and after pouring the last glass, he slowly walked back to his chair and sat down. Taking his glass in his hand he slowly raised it, then turned to Kaydee and gave her a wink. Kaydee beamed and nodded. That completely confused everyone which was exactly what Joey intended to do. Joey was playing them to the hilt and Dusty was almost ready to get up and strangle him, he was so exasperated.

Finally, Joey spoke. "I have an important announcement to make."

Dusty whispered to Katreena, "About damned time too!"

Joey heard that and in mock seriousness, admonished Dusty, "No prompting from the peanut gallery, please!" Dusty made a face and everybody laughed.

Joey started again, deliberately dragging it out for effect. "I have an important announcement to make." Then turning to Kaydee, "Kaydee, come on over and help me out here, okay?" With a giggle, Kaydee ran over and stood behind her mother and Joey. Raising her glass high, she squealed with delight, "They're going to get married!"

The room reverberated with a thunderous roar as cheers and applause erupted from everyone. Congratulations and good wishes swelled, accompanied by hugs and kisses and questions about dates and details and everything else associated with marriage announcements.

"Sorry, Mother. I wasn't trying to keep you in the dark but we wanted to get Kaydee's approval first. I knew you and Dusty would approve and Joey was just as certain his grandmother would be pleased so we just decided to tell everybody together. Alvin is already so attached to Joey that trying to separate the two would take more than a couple of diesel engines and Jaynee has also accepted Joey as a member of the family. We really didn't expect opposition."

Annie spoke up and reiterated her delight with the union. "Welcome to the family, all of you. Joey has been so happy lately that I knew something was in the works. He's a good man, Helen. He'll be good to you, I can promise you that. You have my most sincere blessing. It's like you have been my family all along anyway. This will just make it official."

Dusty shook Joey's hand. "When's the big day? And don't drag out the answer like you did the announcement or so help me I'll clobber you, son-in-law or no!" They all roared.

"Actually, we have not really set a date yet." Joey spoke to Dusty but swept his gaze over the whole group. "There are lots of details that have to be worked out yet, financially being uppermost, of course. I will not be a kept man and I don't want to benefit from my wife's fortune. I want this to be my place – our place actually. We have to make the joint ownership official. I have the money to buy the place and that has to be settled before marriage. There are other issues as well, as you are all probably aware of – like moral ones for instance. Propriety dictates that Helen should wait a year after the death of her husband before remarrying again. So the earliest possible time will likely be somewhere in the fall. We have just not thought of definite dates yet. But thanks for your support man. I promise you, you will not regret it."

"I know we won't Joey." Dusty's voice turned husky. "You have become a pillar of strength for this whole family."

Jessie had been aghast when Joey called Kaydee to "help." Kaydee had not given her any clue about Joey and her mom. Jessie had no inkling about what to expect today. When the announcement came, it was not a complete surprise to Jessie, though she had not been aware that it had progressed to that stage. Kaydee's happiness and delight were so genuine that the euphoria was contagious. She pumped Kaydee for details.

"Honest, I didn't know until last Friday myself," Kaydee defended herself. "I've been so busy with my studies, I haven't had a chance to monitor their activities. Besides, I was seldom even home half the time. I was either at school or at the Norchaks or upstairs writing so I honestly didn't really see it coming either. I have to admit though that I have been **hoping and dreaming** for it to happen. I cannot be happier about it. Now we can be a real family."

Everybody was now talking loudly and excitedly about Joey and Helen's future plans so Kaydee turned to talk to Jessie, speaking in a lower voice so only Jessie could hear her.

"Jessie, you cannot imagine wanting to be part of a normal family because you have always had one, but I never had a family before. Joey makes us a family. It's that impossible dream that people are always talking about and now it's coming true for us. My life is so wonderful now that I'm petrified I will wake up and find it is only a dream. Can you understand what I'm saying? I seem to have won some kind of lottery in the game of life. School is wonderful, I even got awards for it; my poetry is published, I have many wonderful friends and supporters in my life – like you, for instance, and now, I also have a family! Life is a dream, a wonderful dream!"

Kaydee suddenly realized everyone was listening to her. They all had tears in their eyes.

"I'm sorry," she apologized. "I should shut up."

Jessie leaned over and gave Kaydee a big hug. "Sweetie, don't apologize. You deserve every bit of it."

"Amen to that," they all agreed in unison.

Kaydee hugged her back. "Thanks Jessie. By the way, thanks for your help in getting that award for the Norchaks. They really do deserve it. And thank your folks."

Alvin and Jaynee had been sitting quietly taking in all these momentous events. For once Alvin was quiet. The fervour of the adults seemed to exclude him but now Alvin suddenly got an idea. He walked up to Joey, tugged at his sleeve and asked simply, "Does this mean you will be my new Daddy?"

Joey picked Alvin up in his arms, held him close and told him tenderly, "I guess that means I will be your new daddy. Would you like that?"

"Yea," Alvin breathed smiled directly into Joey's eyes. "So can I call you Daddy now?"

"You sure can, son." Joey answered, his voice husky with emotion.

Jaynee, not to be outdone, ran up to Joey and in typical Jaynee fashion, piped up, "Me too. Me too." Everybody laughed, even Joey could not control a chuckle as he answered, "Yes sweetheart, you, too. You may call me Daddy anytime." Joey picked her up for a hug.

Kaydee had been watching and listening to all this and her mind flashed back to her own father for whom the word "Daddy" coming from her had been such an insult. She recalled the day she had tried to call him "Daddy." He had been so furious with her. Tremulously, she walked up to Joey and with tears streaming down her face, she said "I never called my father 'Daddy'. He hated it, though he liked it from Alvin, so I never had a 'Daddy' before. Would I be asking too much if I wanted you to be my 'Daddy' too?"

Joey put Alvin and Jaynee down gently, held out his arms to Kaydee. Swallowing the huge lump in his throat, Joey choked out a husky "I'd be honoured to be your 'Daddy' Kaydee, for as long as we both shall live."

With Dayna in her arms, Helen tearfully joined the embrace between Joey and Kaydee.

Kaydee beamed, rejoicing about this new secret in her heart, the one she would be proud to tell, not just to people, but one she could even reveal to God Himself!

Other books by this author:

Roots ~ A Life In Review

Small Beginnings

Sally Snowflake's Christmas (children's book)

December 2012

Cassie's blog: http://cassiesroom.blogspot.ca/

Cassie's Bookstore: www.lulu.com/spotlight/cmerko